Alison

By Pamela Hill

Published by Juliana Publishing

Book cover design and print by
Hillside Printing Services

Published by Juliana Publishing

Juliana Publishing
Highview Lodge
Oulder Hill Drive
Rochdale
OL11 5LB

Printed and bound in Great Britain by Hillside
Printing Services, Rochdale Tel: 01706 711872
www.hillsidegroup.co.uk

IBSN 978-0-9559047-1-4

Several brilliant streaks of lightning illuminated the bedroom, instantly followed by a deafening clap of thunder. Alison Haythorne leaped from her bed and peered between the curtains at the depressing sky. It was her first day at a new job and she had hoped to arrive at the Agency looking at her best, rather than windswept and bedraggled, although the latter was looking the more likely as a thick blanket of black menacing clouds hovered overhead.

From childhood, Alison had been taught that first impressions were of paramount importance and she smiled, transferring her thoughts to her late mother, while questioning how she could possibly make her way in life, devoid of her mother's support. She had not merely been Alison's mentor; she had been her close friend too, that was until their respective roles had been reversed six months ago, when Margaret Haythorne's terminal illness had been detected, that unforgettable and heartbreaking day when Alison's world had fallen apart.

Alison had no recollection of her father, Michael, who had met his death in a freak accident when she was only a few months old and thereafter, Margaret had raised her daughter single-handedly.

Widow's Benefit, a mere pittance, barely put food on their table and had it not been for the generosity of Margaret's parents, the two of them would never have survived during the first few years.

Additionally they had been forced to downsize to a much smaller house.

Two years prior to Michael's untimely death, his parents had objected vehemently to their only son's imminent marriage to a *common working class girl* they considered to be totally unsuitable but Michael flatly refused to be influenced by their unwarranted and disrespectful remarks, though he was distressed when the formal wedding invitation sent to them by Margaret's parents, brought no response.

After Michael and Margaret's wedding had taken place, his parents never contacted him again.

When Alison was born a year later, Margaret sent several photographs and a friendly letter, informing them of the birth of their new granddaughter, at the same time suggesting it might be fitting to bury the past but once again they failed to reply.

Following their son's fatal accident, she wrote to advise them of Michael's tragic death. They neither sent flowers nor did they travel to his funeral but a few days later, Margaret was the recipient of an evil letter, penned by her mother-in-law, informing her that their son would still be alive had he listened to them instead of moving to the north of England to marry her.

Alison could still recall the disgust she felt when, at the age of thirteen, her mother communicated the malevolent actions of her paternal grandparents.

She questioned why there was such hostility and rancour in the world. Wasn't there enough without deliberately generating more? Her father had been tragically killed at the age of thirty and her mother

2

had lost her life when she was only forty-six; their combined total was barely a lifetime.

As an only child, Alison was now entirely alone. Following their retirement fourteen years ago, her maternal grandparents, Joyce and Alfred Appleby, had moved south to Brighton. They offered Alison a home with them following her mother's death but after careful consideration, she declined their offer, assuring them she would be fine on her own.

Alison had grown up quickly during the past few months. Her recently acquired attitude of mind and stoicism belied her mere seventeen years. She had been very close to her mother and had been allowed to make her own decisions and had learned valuable lessons from her mistakes. Adverse discourse that had passed between them had been too insignificant to be worthy of mention.

She had respected her freedom and independence and had never abused her mother's trust. Compared to other young teenagers, she felt privileged to have had such a selfless and compassionate mother and confidante whose love more than compensated for the lack of material things accessible to her friends. Her mother was never demanding, even towards the end of her life and was distressed when Alison was forced to leave her job to provide her with the care she needed during her final few months.

When Alison left school at the age of sixteen with eleven GCSE passes, she registered for work with a local Employment Agency where Jenny Joyce, the Manager referred her for a secretarial job to cover a year's maternity leave and it was during that period of time that her mother's cancer was diagnosed and she was obliged to leave after only six months.

It was now three weeks since her mother's death and time for her to evaluate her life. She felt a need to spend time in the presence of other people, notwithstanding a greater need to earn a living.

During her mother's illness, Alison had remained in regular contact with Jenny who was very supportive and willing to lend a sympathetic ear. She was therefore thrilled to be offered work at the Agency when Jenny telephoned her a week ago to say that *she* had a vacancy to fill. It was nothing demanding, she explained but at least it would be remunerative employment till something more challenging arose. The salary was adequate and it would certainly help with the mounting pile of bills and in particular the Funeral Director's account; in fact anything would be preferable to living hand-to-mouth on handouts from the State as she and her mother had had to do for the past six months. Moreover, she would have a close friend as opposed to a stranger to help ease her into employment once more. For that fact alone she was grateful.

She checked the time. It was almost eight o'clock and Jenny had asked her to arrive about nine-thirty the first morning.

As she showered, she was excited although a little concerned at what might lay ahead.

After towelling her hair, she stared for a moment at her reflection in the mirror, believing she looked a little peaky but then what did she expect? Her life had been in turmoil during recent months. Perhaps

4

now, things might start to improve, she anticipated as she hurried to dress.

She fixed her make-up, applying enough to hide the unsightly dark circles around her green almond-shaped eyes and slipped into her smart casual outfit. She brushed her dark curly hair, collected her bag and umbrella and as she was about to close the door behind her, she hesitated briefly before stepping out into the beginning of a new life....a life she prayed would be happier than the one she had suffered of late.

'Wow, you look a sight better than you did the last time I saw you!' Jenny exclaimed as Alison walked into the office. 'How are you feeling?'

She placed her soaking wet umbrella in the stand by the door. 'I'm still all at sixes and sevens but it takes time to re-adjust. I'm feeling alright I guess. You'd do better to ask me again at the end of today, that's if you're still employing me then.'

Jenny laughed. 'I've already told you....there's no pressure; ease yourself in gently at your own pace. I've been here on my own for ten days so any help will be a bonus. I'll give you simple tasks until you find your feet but let's determine the priorities first. I'll show you the back office where we brew up.'

Purposely, Jenny made no reference to the death of Alison's mother, aware she needed time to settle in. She would be a willing listener later.

Jenny, aged twenty-two, was Manager of the busy Employment Agency owned by her father who also owned many other branches around the North-West area. She had joined the family business when she left school at sixteen as a fun-loving, high-spirited gregarious young woman who lived life to the full. Though Jenny had few academic qualifications, her vibrant personality more than compensated for her lack of educational diplomas and she definitely had the requisite skills to manage the Agency and do so efficiently. It was indisputably Jenny's total lack of application, rather than her lack of ability that was her downfall, her head-of-year re-iterated at annual parents' evenings.

Jenny's father used to despair at her lack of self-discipline and repeatedly warned her that she would never make anything of her life if she failed to alter her immature ways but his remarks fell on deaf ears as she never doubted there would be work for her in one of her father's Agencies.

John Joyce was an affluent and innovative entrepreneur with diverse business interests and throughout her youth, Jenny had wanted for nothing. John laid the blame at his own door for having allowed Jenny too much freedom in her youth but on a more positive note, she had a dynamic presence and felt comfortable with everyone she met. Although self-assured she was respectful and everyone loved her.

Her physical appearance was dazzling. Standing five feet ten inches tall and of perfect form her wide right-angled shoulders guaranteed that her attire, no matter how casual or spectacular, hung beautifully. Her perfectly straight teeth were as white as freshly fallen snow-flakes and when she laughed, her blue expressive eyes were her most beautiful assets.

Within an hour or two, Alison felt at ease and the front office was looking tidy again. As Jenny spent a large proportion of her time on the telephone, the mundane tasks had been forced to take second place while she had been alone for the past two weeks.

Alison was in awe of Jenny's natural aptitude to multi-task. As Jenny answered a telephone enquiry, she dealt with customers simultaneously yet everyone was afforded the most professional attention.

'How do you keep focused when you're speaking to several people at once?' Alison questioned.

'I've been doing this job for six years,' she stated. 'You'll be just as competent in a week or two.'

Alison paid very close attention to the procedures Jenny explained. As the week progressed, she had taken several telephone calls from employers with vacancies to fill and although she hadn't dealt with personal customers, she felt she was ready to try.

On Friday around midday, Jenny announced that she needed to go to the bank and she offered to call for the sandwiches for their lunch on her way back, thus leaving Alison in charge during her absence.

Following several telephone enquiries that Alison handled competently, the door suddenly opened and a young man appeared.

With a beaming smile, he approached and asked, 'Are you new? I haven't seen you before.'

'Yes, I started here Monday,' she informed him.

'So, do you think you'll like working here?'

'I'm sure I will. May I help you with something?'

The young man continued to smile at her. 'Yes, I registered for work a month ago and I haven't heard anything yet so I was wondering if there was anything in my file.'

'I'd be happy to check Sir if you'd give me your name please.'

'I'd prefer to provide you with my phone number and then maybe you could give me a quick call and tell me when you'd be available for dinner.'

She felt the colour rising in her cheeks and hastily replied, 'I'm sorry, we're not allowed to date clients but I'd be happy to check your file if I could have your name please.'

He laughed audibly but it was a congenial chortle and Alison believed that had they met in different circumstances, she might well have been inclined to accept his invitation. 'Apologies....I've embarrassed you. Do forgive me. Were you to find me a suitable job, I wouldn't be your client anymore and maybe I could ask you again. I might succeed in persuading you next time. My name's Richard Anderton.'

Without responding, she opened the filing cabinet and flicked through the folders but after completing her search twice she could find nothing under that name. 'I'm sorry Sir. I can't find your file,' she told him apologetically.

'And I believed this to be a well-run Agency,' he retorted huffily.

'I really am sorry. Let me check on Jenny's desk. What kind of employment are you registered for?'

'I'm an airline pilot. I don't expect you've many of those on your books,' he stated pretentiously.

'I'm sure you're right,' she said, trawling through the mountain of files on the desk. 'No, it's not here either. Perhaps you could call back in about fifteen minutes when Jenny will be here, or if you prefer, leave me your number and I'll ask Jenny to call you this afternoon if that would be convenient.'

He beamed at her again. 'I knew you wanted my number when I first offered it but you had to keep me in suspense didn't you? Tell me I'm wrong.'

Before there was time for a suitable response, the door opened as Jenny returned.

'Richard, what are you doing here?' she shrieked, rushing towards him and throwing her arms around his neck. 'It's ages since I've seen you.'

'I've just been winding-up your young assistant. I must say she's terrific. Where did you find her?'

They glanced at Alison, who, rather bewildered, was trying to make sense of the situation.

'Tell me you haven't been spinning her the airline pilot nonsense with the phony name. Alison this is my brother, Richard. He's an awful tease. He runs another of our Agencies in Cheshire. Since I moved into my own flat I've hardly seen him.'

'I'm delighted to meet you Alison and I apologise profusely,' he said ashamedly. 'I wasn't teasing you all the time. I meant every word about dinner.'

'Well, we'll have to see about that,' she laughed.

'What are you whispering about?' Jenny asked.

'Nothing that need concern you,' he advised her. 'Right, I'll be on my way. Don't forget what I said Alison. I'll be in touch. I'll talk to you soon Jenny,' he called to her as he was leaving.

'He's a terrific guy and I love him to bits,' Jenny told her. 'He's my twin but as he's an hour younger

9

than I am, I have a tendency to treat him like a little brother. He's still living at home with mum and dad but they don't get involved in his daily life. Richard was involved with a girl and it ended disastrously a few months ago. Sadly, since then he seems to have lost confidence in the fairer sex. He still dates very occasionally but he's afraid of showing his feelings anymore. He was upset when his girlfriend dumped him for a guy at work but he'll get over her in time. We all lose someone close one way or another but we just have to stop moping about and move on.'

No sooner had Jenny uttered those words than she realised her faux-pas. 'I'm so sorry Alison. My big gob ought to carry a Government Health Warning. I just didn't think.'

'Don't worry about it. We live in a society where unspeakable tragedies occur all the time and you're right; we have to learn how to cope with our losses. I'll always love and miss my mother but she taught me how to be strong in the face of adversity so you don't have to avoid speaking her name. Thanks to you, I've managed to get through my first week that I see as the first week of the rest of my life and I'm happy to say I've enjoyed every moment, even your brother's good-humoured hoax. He comes across as a genuine, respectful young man. I hope you appreciate how fortunate you are to have a family, Jenny. I have nobody now.'

'Yes you do....you have *me* and don't forget that. We'll be here for each other, right?'

'Right,' she replied, feeling happier. Things were starting to look better already.

'Answer the phone will you?' Jenny called out to her. 'I'm half way through a column of figures.'

Alison scurried from the back office and grabbed the telephone. 'Fresh Start Agency, good afternoon, Alison speaking.... How may I help you?'

'I was wondering whether you had any vacancies yet for an airline pilot,' the caller asked on a laugh.

'Hello Richard. I'm sorry but Jenny can't come to the phone. Can she call you back shortly?'

'What makes you think I want Jenny when I have you on the end of the line?'

'You're teasing again. Are you at the office?'

'In answer to your first remark, no I'm not and in answer to your second, yes I am and I was thinking about you. I have the strangest feeling I'm going to be hungry tonight and I was hoping you might have dinner with me because I don't like eating alone.'

'I see. So have I to assume that's the only reason you're asking? Now if you'd said something to the effect that you'd have really enjoyed my company, I might have been tempted.'

'Now who's teasing? Please Alison; I'd like you to join me, if only to give me a chance to apologise for my behaviour last week and to show you I can be exceptionally charming if I try very hard.'

She laughed. 'Let me check my social diary first and I'll call you back.'

'Don't forget. I'll be waiting.'

'I won't. Bye Richard.'

'Who was that?' Jenny asked.

'Richard. He wants to take me to dinner tonight.'

'So did you accept?'

'Er....not exactly. Do you think I should?'

'Yes....go for it. He treats his girlfriends very well and you'll have a great time.'

'I'm not his girlfriend. I've only met him once.'

'Well, you never will be if you keep refusing. To be perfectly honest, he's been pestering me for days about what *I* thought your reaction might be, but as I told him, we work together and I wasn't prepared to become entangled in his romantic relationships.'

'You just have. You told me to go for it.'

'Well that's different when it's you who's asking. Call him back. You'll enjoy it and you need something nice to look forward to. Tell him you'll go.'

'You're right. Why shouldn't I have an enjoyable evening out?'

It was a half-hour's drive to the country restaurant that looked very expensive as they approached the brightly illuminated imposing building. Alison had rarely visited restaurants and so doing in the company of a young man was a novel yet exhilarating experience. Her mother's gold neck chain provided a decorative adornment to her smart black dress and she was pleased she had chosen something to wear in keeping with the exclusive establishment.

Richard held the door as she entered and instantly they were greeted and escorted to their table by the Maitre D' who appeared to know Richard well.

It was a lovely restaurant and the roaring log fire in the lounge bar was most welcoming on that cold and wintry early December evening.

'What would you like to drink?' he enquired.

12

'I'd like a glass of orange juice please.'

He seemed surprised. 'Are you sure you wouldn't prefer anything stronger, perhaps a glass of wine?'

Mindful that the bar waiter was hovering, Alison leaned over to Richard and whispered, 'I can't. I'm not old enough. Please....orange juice will be fine.'

He quickly ordered the two drinks and apologised for his persistence. 'I'm sorry. I didn't mean to....'

'Don't worry. It's alright, really,' she interrupted. 'I'm almost eighteen but some people regard me as quite a bit older. I've had a difficult life where I've had to grow up very quickly. Age is just a number and I definitely don't feel as if I'm only seventeen, in fact some days I feel more like seventy!'

At that they laughed which broke the ice.

Throughout the evening their conversation flowed naturally. Richard made no reference to his former relationship and their total dialogue covered everything *but* previous partners which pleased Alison as her love-life had been virtually non-existent but for a few schoolgirl infatuations as a young teenager.

As they were preparing to leave the restaurant at the end of a lovely evening, he remarked, 'I haven't told you how charming you look tonight. You look very sophisticated in black.'

Feeling a swift and burning flush of colour in her cheeks, she stammered, 'Th....thank you,' and shot ahead of him to the door.

When Richard turned off his engine at her house and walked her to the door, she was unsure whether to invite him inside for coffee but the decision was made for her when he stated that he had thoroughly enjoyed their evening. He leaned towards her gently kissing her cheek and then he left.

As Alison locked her front door, she reflected on the evening that had been a pleasurable experience. Richard had been very attentive. His manners had been nothing less than impeccable and he certainly knew how to entertain a young lady.

For the first time since her mother's death, Alison didn't feel as lonely as she had felt for the past few weeks and when she closed her weary eyes, she had Richard in her thoughts as she fell into a deep sleep.

The next day at the office, Jenny couldn't wait to hear about the evening and she bombarded Alison with questions the very second she opened the door. 'Did you enjoy your evening? Was that restaurant nice? So, what happened after? Are you seeing him again? Hurry up Alison....dish the dirt....don't keep me in suspense. I want to know everything.'

'Alright....don't burst a blood vessel. Everything was great. We enjoyed interesting conversation and the food was excellent,' she answered guardedly.

'And?'

'And what?'

'*You know*! What happened afterwards when you got back to your place? Did he….did you….?'

'Stop it,' she laughed. 'Mind your own business.'

'*You did*!' Jenny squealed.

'*No we didn't*. He didn't come in so stop prying.'

She was pleased when the telephone rang because she wasn't enjoying the embarrassing interrogation. She wasn't worldly like Jenny. Jenny was fantastic. She was so lively and Alison had no doubts that she had experienced a fair few sexual relationships but Alison was different; even the mention of sex made her feel uncomfortable and embarrassed.

She could recall when, as a schoolgirl, her friends would describe their intimate experiences in detail but Alison had no such incidents to relate and could often be appalled by friends' disclosures. She didn't feel she was mistaken in her belief that she should save herself for the man she truly loved when that day arrived and she was very relieved that Richard had made no sexual advances towards her. After all, he might not ask to see her again and since she had nothing of material value to offer, she wasn't ready to lose the one precious thing she had saved for the right man. If that meant she was different, she could live with that. It was her body and her decision.

When Jenny had finished on the telephone, there was no further discussion of the matter. It had been merely girl talk.

Alison had been working at the Agency for three weeks when Jenny asked, 'What have you planned for the Christmas break? Are you going to spend it with your grandparents?'

'No, they generally stay at a hotel over the Christmas period. There's plenty of entertainment laid on and they've gone to the same place for years.'

'So where are you going then?'

'I haven't given it much thought. It'll be my first Christmas alone and frankly I'm dreading it, in fact I'll be glad when it's over.'

The discussion ended there but a day or two later, Jenny bounced into the office in her usual excitable fashion and announced she had arranged for Alison to spend Christmas with her family. 'I know you'll love it and my parents insist. We've plenty of room for you to stay as long as you want.'

Alison was taken aback. 'It was very kind of your parents to invite me but I couldn't possibly think of imposing on your family; they don't know me.'

'Rubbish! Richard knows you,' she argued.

'Jenny, I haven't heard a word from Richard since the night we went to the restaurant. I wouldn't want to embarrass either of us by being at your place, so I'm sorry, I couldn't possibly accept.'

'Now you're being ridiculous. I've told you what he's like. He's afraid of making another mistake. I know he'd want you there and I won't accept your refusal. In any event, I always get my own way, so there's no point in arguing, besides which, I'd have a rotten time thinking of you alone. You wouldn't want to spoil *my* Christmas would you?'

'Well....I suppose if you put it like that, how can I refuse? I'd be delighted to come. Please thank your parents very much and tell them I'm really looking forward to meeting them.'

She was delighted to be seeing Richard again but she would need to keep her distance and above all avoid transmitting any unwanted messages, though that could be quite a challenge, she felt.

When Jenny arrived at her door laden with parcels, Alison was wrapping her Christmas presents.

'Do you know, I love Christmas but the shopping really is horrendous! All morning I've been hustled,

16

bustled, pushed and shoved. I've had to queue for ages everywhere and I'm exhausted. Can I put the kettle on? I'm gagging for a drink,' she grumbled. 'My poor legs are ready to fall off.'

'Sit down and I'll do it. I'm just wrapping mine. I did most of my shopping last night after work so I know exactly how you feel.'

'Do you mind if I wrap these and leave them here until Christmas Eve? Richard is such a big kid that he'll search the flat until he finds them all if I leave them there. You'd think he'd have grown out of his childish ways at his age.'

'No problem....leave them here, though I'm quite surprised to hear that. I would never have believed him to be so excitable; he seems so level-headed.'

'Believe it. He's the same when it's his birthday.'

Timidly she asked, 'Does he know *I'm* coming?'

'He does and he's looking forward to seeing you. Just don't rush things. I know he likes you but he's still getting over his earlier involvement. Richard is extremely sensitive and it takes time to rebuild your confidence when you've been badly hurt.'

'I guess so. He obviously thought a lot about her.'

'Yes he did but then better for him to have found out what a cow she was sooner rather than later.'

As they wrapped their parcels, Alison was in deep thought, trying to imagine his frantic efforts to find his presents. She was very envious that she had no family with whom she could have shared Christmas but Jenny was compassionate and Alison knew that her family would make her welcome in their home. Moreover, she would spend time with Richard.

'*Merry Christmas everyone*!' Jenny yelled as they stepped into the most magnificent house Alison had ever seen. 'This is Alison.'

Jenny's mother hurried towards Alison and kissed her warmly on both cheeks. 'I'm delighted to meet you at last. I hear you're a real asset to the Agency.'

'I don't know about that,' she laughed. 'I've a lot more to learn but I have an excellent teacher. Jenny makes everything appear so easy, Mrs. Joyce.'

'Call me Elizabeth. We don't entertain formality here. This is my husband. John, this is Alison.'

John shook her hand heartily. 'I'm always pleased to meet a conscientious employee who makes me a hefty profit,' he laughed, taking the girls' coats.

'Take no notice,' Elizabeth interjected. 'All John thinks about is profit. I keep telling him....he should get a life. After all, you never know what's around the corner do you?'

Jenny and Alison exchanged glances. How easy it was to make an innocent faux pas but she was right.

The ensuing silence was rapidly brought to an end by Jenny who asked, 'Where's Richard?'

'Doing his last minute Christmas shopping,' her mother replied. 'Why don't you put your Christmas presents under the tree with the others and I'll pour you both a drink.'

Alison gazed around the room while waiting for Elizabeth to return with the drinks. It was tastefully decorated and a magnificent Christmas tree towered majestically by the French window. As they placed their presents around it, Jenny informed her that her parents had acquired the majority of the decorations and baubles during their foreign travels. Compared to the poverty Alison had known, the riches in this room alone were incalculable.

'This is the most beautiful house I've ever seen,' Alison told Elizabeth when she returned.

'Thank you my dear, though it's really far too big for us now.'

They heard the front door closing. 'That has to be Richard....late as usual,' Elizabeth remarked.

He entered, displaying the infectious broad smile Alison had seen so often. Her heart skipped several beats as they made eye contact. 'Merry Christmas,' he said, striding over to greet her. She felt a sudden rush of colour, wishing she could maintain control over such reactions to his presence. 'It's great to see you again,' he added and kissed her tenderly on the lips. 'Er....I hope that's not alcohol in your glass.'

'But it's Christmas,' she told him light-heartedly. 'I'm allowed to make *some* exceptions to the rules.'

'How's work going?' he asked, sitting beside her.

'Great thanks. I'm feeling much more settled now and I'm steadily coming to terms with living alone. I've enrolled at night school for cookery. I wanted to experiment with modern-day recipes.'

'In that case, perhaps I should be your first guinea pig when you're ready to test your newly acquired culinary skills on someone. I'm pretty liberal where food's concerned, so what do you say?'

Alison's head was spinning. Was Richard putting the ball in her court for her to make the next move or was he just being polite? She had never invited a young man to dinner and the fear of his refusal sent a shiver down her spine. She paused before saying bashfully, 'When I feel a bit more confident, maybe you and Jenny could be my first dinner guests?'

'Who mentioned Jenny? I'm shocked! Surely you wouldn't want to poison *two* members of the same family would you?'

Alison nudged him good-humouredly. 'When you pluck up the courage, let me know and I'll be happy to oblige but remember you'll be putting your life in my hands.'

Richard was quick off the mark. 'And what pretty hands they are too,' he declared, taking hold of one which she quickly withdrew.

She slanted her eyes at Jenny who was listening avidly to every word and when Elizabeth appeared stating lunch would be ready in fifteen minutes, she was grateful for the intervention at that very fitting moment.

Alison stood in silence by the open bedroom door, overwhelmed by the splendour of her bedroom that was furnished in Louis XV style, before confessing, 'I feel totally out of my comfort zone in your home Jenny. I'm not accustomed to being in the company of such wealthy people and I don't know how to....'

'*Stop right there*!' she interrupted heatedly. 'Most of my so-called friends came from affluent families and they were some of the rudest people on earth. Wealth doesn't buy breeding. It's family values that are important. You are the first genuine person I've met in a long time and it's pretty obvious that your mother had breeding as it shows clearly in you. The fact you were poor was due to tragic circumstances but the reality is, you have risen above that, clearly signifying your upbringing and your mother's love. What you have, money couldn't buy. You would fit in anywhere, with anyone and someday, you'll have everything you want in life. You're only seventeen, yet you have qualities of self-confidence, decorum and impeccable manners that could never be bought with any amount of wealth. I really envy you.'

'You envy me?' she asked in disbelief.

'Yes! I wouldn't have had enough courage to face what you've faced. I've never struggled to survive. I'm not as clever as you. You have the wherewithal to adapt to any situation whereas I merely take from my family since I've known nothing else. Meeting you really opened my eyes. I've always associated with arrogant little rich girls, striving to outdo each other with their designer clothes, fancy cars and big houses, none of which is important. It's what's on the inside that matters, so never put yourself down. You could do anything but I can only ever work for dad. I've taken handouts by choice not by necessity like you, so that makes you the better person.'

'I'm sorry. I was only....'

'Listen, it's Christmas Eve. Let's enjoy ourselves. Yes, you do have a superb room, so make the most of it. Come and see the view over the garden. I was hoping it might snow; I love it when it snows.'

Downstairs, a similar tête-à-tête was taking place between Elizabeth and her close friend Maud, who had just arrived with her family.

'So, who's this friend of Jenny's?' Maud asked.

'Alison....the new girl who works with Jenny and whose mother died recently.'

'Yes, I remember. She's quite young isn't she?'

'In years perhaps but not in life experience. She's had a hard time of late but she appears to be coping remarkably well. She and Jenny hit it off from the outset. She's not the usual type of girl Jenny would associate with, I'm pleased to say, so once I knew she'd be on her own over Christmas, I insisted she come here. I'm hopeful Alison will have a positive influence on Jenny. She's very self-disciplined and has such an endearing disposition considering what she's been through.'

'Poor child! Let's hope that everything soon starts to improve for her,' Maud replied.

'I hope so too,' Elizabeth sighed. 'Nothing can be worse than losing both parents by the tender age of seventeen. I'm pleased she accepted our invitation.'

Elizabeth gestured to Alison as she returned to the living room. 'Alison, allow me to introduce you to our close friends, Harold and Maud Taylor. Harold is John's business partner and this is Mark their son who manages one of the branches in Stockport. We have been friends for years and they generally join us for lunch on Christmas Eve. Mark won't be here long as he's meeting his friends later, so we'll have a quick drink first and then I expect you'll be ready to eat. Is it white wine for you Alison?'

'That would be lovely, thank you.'

As she sat down on the sofa, Mark made a point of sitting beside her. 'Do you enjoy the work at the Agency?' he enquired.

'I love every minute. I meet some real characters in a day's time. I like meeting people.'

'Have you always done that type of work?'

'No, my last job was secretarial so I didn't meet anyone there.'

'Is that why you left? I'm sorry....this is like the Spanish Inquisition isn't it?'

'Not at all. My mother was ill so I had to give up my job to look after her. Sadly, she died at the end of October and then, three weeks later, it turned out that Jenny had a vacancy that I was happy to fill.'

'I'm so sorry. I keep asking the wrong questions. Shall I disappear, come back and begin once more? I'm starting to feel like a complete fool.'

She laughed, assuring him he was nothing of the kind. 'So, have you always done Agency work?'

'Yes, when I left University, I went straight into the office at Stockport. We have seven members of staff, which makes it the largest office in the group. I started at the bottom, learning the ropes and now I'm the Manager but I might be starting a different type of work if our new business venture takes off. We're branching out into Property Management as there are so many advantages to owning a string of properties. Everyone requires housing and there's a growing need for both reliable landlords and decent properties to rent. Should we decide to press ahead, things should start happening in the New Year.'

Alison became aware of Richard's presence when with a hint of annoyance in his voice, he remarked, 'What are you whispering about? I hope you aren't monopolising my favourite girl, Mark.'

23

'You shouldn't have left her alone with the better man,' Mark said with biting wit. 'She's charming.'

'Will the two of you stop that? I'm enjoying some intelligent conversation and learning new business skills,' she stated assertively and they howled with laughter. Secretly, she was delighted that Richard's feathers appeared ruffled, hoping he was jealous of the attention shown by Mark.

'Another drink, Alison?' Mark asked.

Before she had time to answer, Richard butted in, 'She's fine. She doesn't drink much alcohol.'

She strove to contain her laughter. Had there been any doubt in her mind a moment ago, there wasn't now. Richard *was* jealous which showed he cared.

When Mark was ready to leave, Alison didn't fail to notice that Richard's eyes stared intently as Mark kissed her goodbye.

It was a thoroughly enjoyable evening with Maud and Harold stealing the show with their boundless repertoire of highly amusing anecdotes and Alison was sorry when it had to end. Everybody had made her most welcome and she ached with laughter.

When Harold and Maud's taxi arrived, Maud embraced her. 'You must come to dinner with *us* soon. Mark would like that. Take care darling. Goodnight and I hope you have a truly lovely Christmas.'

Alison was awakened Christmas morning by a rap on her bedroom door. 'Are you awake yet? It's nine o'clock. Can I come in?' Jenny shouted impatiently and without awaiting a response, she burst into the room, dragging her from her bed. 'Quick! Look!'

Jenny hurried to the window and pulled back the curtains to reveal a thick white blanket of snow as far as the eye could see. 'Doesn't it look beautiful? Don't you just love a white Christmas?' she sighed pensively. 'By the way, how did you sleep?'

'Great thanks. I slept like a log.'

'A Christmas log?' she smiled. 'Get ready. I don't want to miss a single moment of Christmas Day.'

'Merry Christmas,' Elizabeth called as Jenny and Alison appeared in the kitchen.

Hot on their heels, John and Richard made their entrance. 'Brrr! It's nippy out there. Good morning Alison. Did you sleep well?' John asked as Richard nodded in acquiescence as if his own question had been pre-empted.

'I slept very well, thanks, in fact I'd still be asleep now had Jenny not called me to look at the snow.'

'Doesn't it look lovely? It's so Christmassy when it snows,' Elizabeth stated. 'Right everyone, breakfast is ready. Please take your places and would you see to the Champagne John?'

They laughed as the cork made a huge explosion.

When John had filled all the glasses, he raised his and proposed a seasonal toast to everybody before they savoured a hearty breakfast of smoked salmon and scrambled eggs, after which they retired to the sitting room to open their presents.

Jenny went first to retrieve hers as had been customary from her being a small child, while Richard on the other hand, always went last.

Jenny was thrilled with the furnishing items she received for her recently acquired flat.

'Have you seen her flat?' Elizabeth asked Alison.

'No, not yet though I've seen lots of photographs. It looks lovely and very modern.'

'They've not been built long. There's a tendency nowadays to build apartments rather than houses.'

'That's because the developer makes more money from flats,' John cut in. 'Building vertically, rather than horizontally, reduces land costs. If a developer provides parking space instead of a garage for each unit, that saves on building costs too. It's surprising what fits on a small piece of land and....'

'*Excuse me*!' Elizabeth quipped. 'Are we opening our presents or forming a construction business?'

Everyone laughed, including John who promptly held up his hand in submission. 'Apologies. I soon get carried away. Who's next for their presents?'

'You, unless Alison wants to go,' Elizabeth said.

'No, I prefer to wait if that's okay with everyone. I'm like Richard,' Alison said.

When Richard caught her eye, there appeared to be a hidden message in his smile.

'Right, it must be your turn next Elizabeth,' John stated after opening his, slanting a sideways glance in Richard's direction.

Elizabeth collected hers from the ever-decreasing pile. She opened Alison's first and gave a squeal of delight to see the designer silk scarf she omitted to buy three weeks earlier when shopping with Jenny and which she bitterly regretted afterwards. 'Thank you very much, Alison. It's beautiful, isn't it John?'

'If you say so. I don't profess to be *au fait* about silk scarves. I don't wear many myself,' he quipped and when they laughed at his witticism, he added, 'Yes it is and the colours are perfect for Elizabeth.'

Elizabeth removed the paper to find a selection of body products from Jenny. 'Thank you. It's exactly what I wanted,' and turning to Alison she said, 'At my age, you need gallons of these products, not that *you* would know with your flawless complexion.'

Alison smiled, thinking that were she to appear as radiant as Elizabeth at her age, she'd be delighted. Elizabeth was an elegant and sophisticated woman whose glossy, titian-coloured, shoulder-length hair curled naturally and her symmetrical facial features accentuated her large hazel eyes which persistently smiled. She had to be in her mid-forties but looked a good ten years younger.

Elizabeth's final gift was in a shallow rectangular box....a Christmas card that read, 'Elizabeth, thank you for twenty-five years of sublime contentment. Enjoy your gift. What does one buy for the woman who has everything? With love, John.'

Graciously she said, 'How kind John.'

'Well, aren't you opening the gift?' he asked.

'I've opened them all,' she said, looking round.

'Well, that's something of a mystery. I was sure it was under the tree with the others. Richard, did you bring everything from the garage?'

'I think so Dad. Was it a small package?'

'Come along. Let's go and find it. Richard must have dropped it,' John said, taking her by the hand.

Elizabeth knew it was a ruse but she nevertheless played along. She would repeatedly find small gifts hidden away where he knew she'd eventually find

27

them. Often a gift would lay undetected for several weeks, or she might discover something hidden in her linen basket or in the cutlery drawer. It was his way of showing just how much he valued her. On this occasion however, nothing could have prepared her for what greeted her as John opened the garage door, for standing there in all its glory was a silver Mercedes sports car. 'Merry Christmas darling,' he said with a loving smile as he kissed her.

'Oh….is that really mine?' she cried in disbelief.

Excitedly, she summoned everyone to the garage, before opening a door and releasing the unrivalled smell of new leather.

'It's fantastic! I can't believe you had it delivered without my knowing. How long has it been here?' she asked.

'Three days,' he laughed. 'You like it then?'

'Like it? I absolutely adore it. Thank you so much John,' she said and gave him an affectionate kiss.

As they made their way to the sitting room, John, straight-faced, advised the others that with the new business venture, he would need Elizabeth to work for him and a fast car would get her around quickly. It was simply a question of economics, he said.

'Don't kid yourself,' she cried. 'You'll not see me once the snow's gone.'

John poured everyone another drink, and with all the euphoria about the car, Elizabeth inadvertently handed Alison a pint of beer instead of her glass of white wine. Everyone found that hilarious, with the exception of Alison who believed that in order to be courteous, she might have to drink it.

'It's the little baby's turn now,' John proclaimed. 'Richard always has to save his until last.'

'What about Alison? She hasn't opened hers yet,' he rejoined touchily. 'You know I *always* go last.'

As Alison stood up, he stopped her. 'I'm teasing. You're our guest so you may have the final place of honour,' he said as he went to collect his parcels.

From his parents, he received an annual subscription for the Golf Club and Jenny had bought him a personal CD player to replace the one he'd recently broken. Alison bought him a CD and a book about American Football, the latter being one of his main interests.

When he made the rounds, thanking everyone, his lips lingered affectionately on Alison's, causing yet again the colour to rise vividly in her cheeks.

At last it was Alison's turn and she collected her presents swiftly. One remained which bore a simple message, 'To Mr. and Mrs. Joyce with my sincerest thanks for your kindness. Have a lovely Christmas, Alison.'

She gave it to Elizabeth and John. It was a boxed bottle of Dom Perignon Champagne for which they thanked her most graciously.

She saved Richard's gift until the end, her fingers trembling nervously as she removed the wrapping paper and everyone's eyes were upon her when she lifted the lid of the velvet covered box.

She was close to tears to discover a delicate gold bracelet, almost identical in design to her mother's gold necklace. 'Oh Richard....it's lovely. Thank you so much,' she cried.

29

Earlier, she had tried to envisage how she would feel when the time came to embrace Richard for his gift but the moment provided the means when she leapt at him, throwing her arms around his neck and hugging him tightly.

'So tell me, are you enjoying Christmas with our family?' Jenny queried while fastening the bracelet around Alison's wrist.

'More than you'll ever know,' she replied, though with a hint of melancholy. 'You're so lucky to have a family Jenny. Don't ever take them for granted.'

When Elizabeth invited them to take their places at the table, everyone laughed when Richard asked for more time for Alison to finish her pint of ale.

On entering the dining room, a vibrant picture of Aladdin's cave sprang into Alison's mind.

The grandiose circular walnut table was magnificently decorated and laid with exquisite bone china and lead crystal glassware and the embellished gold cutlery complemented the ornamental centre-piece, consisting of gold and crimson fruits, surrounding varying heights of gold candles, tied together with lavish bunches of gold and red ribbons.

John lit the candles as they were taking their seats and Alison studied the place settings, recalling the etiquette she had learned to use the cutlery from the outside first.

Each person had a small gift to open and Alison was overjoyed with her pretty pearl earrings.

The Christmas meal was nothing less than a feast fit for a king and afterwards, when Elizabeth began to clear the dishes, Alison jumped up to help.

'Leave those. I'll see to them,' she told Elizabeth.

'You're a guest my dear, I wouldn't hear of it.'

John expelled a roaring guffaw when indignantly, Alison countered, 'If I am a guest, then I think you have to respect my wishes and allow me to help or I shall be embarrassed.'

'There's no point in arguing. Sit down,' John told Elizabeth at which point Richard and Jenny jumped up too and started to help clear away.

'Good God!' John cried to see Richard collecting the dessert plates. 'Hang on a minute while I write out directions to the kitchen.'

Richard glared pointedly at his father but allowed the remark to pass unchallenged.

'Many hands make light work,' Jenny quoted as she flopped down on the sofa when they'd finished.

'I've found some party games for later,' Richard made known with a beaming smile and the family members groaned.

When Alison reacted with a quizzical expression, Jenny whispered, 'You'd have more enjoyment on a sinking ship in the frozen Antarctic....believe me.'

Resentfully, Richard retorted, 'I heard that.'

'I'll make a nice pot of coffee,' Elizabeth said and when Alison followed her to the kitchen, she added, 'I'm so pleased that you and Jenny are friends. I've missed her very much since she moved into her flat and I've been worried about her too but she seems settled now she's met you. Until a few months ago, she was rather wild and I was becoming concerned about the company she was keeping....especially as one hears so much about drugs these days and....'

'Jenny doesn't do drugs,' Alison interrupted. 'She hates the very thought of them.'

'Well, that's such a relief to know, if you're sure.'

'I'm positive. I'd be the first to know as I spend every day with her. She's detached herself from her old friends now, in fact, we were only talking about that last night.'

'Please don't think I'm prying. I'm not expecting you to divulge any secrets. I've always allowed my children their independence and privacy but of late it's become a dangerous world and as a mother, I'm naturally concerned for both of them.'

'I understand. It was mum's main concern when she knew she wouldn't be here for me much longer but she needn't have worried for I would never mar her memory by conducting myself inappropriately.'

'Come here,' she said, taking Alison in her arms, surprised at her worldliness. She was so young, yet spoke with the wisdom of an adult. 'It's quite clear that your mother was a *very* special person.'

'Yes, she was and I miss her terribly,' she sighed.

'Right, take any card from the pack but don't show it to me. Let the others see it,' Richard announced.

Alison selected one from the pack and held it up for everyone to see. It was the five of diamonds.

'Right, put it back in the pack. Don't let me see it. I'll shuffle the cards now and find it....Ready?'

Following a resounding '*Yes*,' from everyone, he deftly shuffled them and displaying the top card he announced assertively, 'The King of Spades.'

'*No*!' everyone howled.

As he continued to mishandle and drop the cards, while revealing more that were also incorrect, John was the first to control himself sufficiently to speak. 'Promise me you'll never give up your day job,' he told Richard who joined in the laughter too.

Alison studied him, at a loss to imagine why his former girlfriend had hurt him in such an uncaring way when he had such a kind disposition and it was then she realised she had more than just a feeling of friendship for him.

Alison was waiting by the door with her holdall as John appeared with Elizabeth.

'Are you sure we can't persuade you to stay until the New Year?' Elizabeth asked.

'No thank you. I've a lot to do at home and once I'm back at work, I won't have time,' she said with a watery smile. 'Besides which, I'd hate to overstay my welcome or you won't ever invite me again.'

'Nonsense, you're welcome anytime you want to come,' Elizabeth remarked.

'You're too kind. I don't know how I would have survived over Christmas without your hospitality. It's been tremendous....really.'

Elizabeth hugged her. 'Take care and *do* keep in touch....and if you need anything at all, don't forget we're only at the end of a telephone.'

Richard and Jenny walked downstairs together. 'I think you've packed everything. I really wish you'd stay longer,' Jenny said.

'Well, I did say when you invited me that I would only impose for a couple of days and I've been here for three. Besides, it'll take me at least two days to write up my diary of events.'

John picked up Alison's bag. 'Ready?' he asked and she nodded.

Richard kissed her on both cheeks. 'Are you sure you wouldn't like to see another magic trick before you leave?'

'*Definitely not*! There's only so much punishment a girl can take,' she grinned before following John through the doorway.

Alison remained quiet and preoccupied during the journey home, hoping that nobody had sensed anything untoward about her hasty departure. She had barely slept the previous night, unable to obliterate Richard from her thoughts. She was crazy to think there could ever be anything between them. She'd mistaken his friendship for affection and she must now do her utmost to eradicate all thoughts of him from her mind.

She was abruptly jolted back to reality when John declared, 'Here we are. Would you like me to come in with you?'

'Thanks but I'll be fine now. Enjoy the remainder of your Christmas and a Happy New Year.'

'Same to you, Alison. Take care my dear.'

When Alison unlocked the door, she was greeted by a cold demoralizing atmosphere in the silent empty house. Apart from a few Christmas cards, there was no evidence of festive cheer there.

She shuddered, turned on the gas fire and flopped down on the settee where she began to sob. She was unable to attribute her melancholy to any particular cause. It was a number of things and predominantly disgust and repentance at having enjoyed a splendid Christmas when she should have been grieving for her mother. She felt envious that the loving family with whom she had spent the past few days were so complete when she was so lonely and furthermore, she was at a loss to understand the feelings she had developed for Richard.

She cried herself to sleep and remained asleep for several hours. When she awoke, although the room was now warm, her fingers were quivering; she was trembling and for the first time in her life she was afraid. Recalling how her mother had told her that a cup of tea cured most ills, she decided she'd test the theory and as she sipped the freshly brewed tea, she brought to mind all the promises she had made but how could she be strong when she felt so wretched?

She was sobbing so hard that for several seconds, she didn't hear the telephone ringing and when she eventually answered, it was Jenny.

'Hi, I was starting to worry. Where were you?'
'Er....sorry, I couldn't er....get to the phone.'
'Are you ill? You sound awful. What's wrong?'

'I feel terrible. I don't know what's wrong. I can't stop crying,' she sobbed uncontrollably.

'Right that settles it. I'm fetching you back to our house. I'll come and get you now.'

'*No*,' she shrieked. 'No....I'll be fine. Please....just leave me to sort myself out.'

'It's too late. I'm already on my way.'

Before Alison had time to argue, Jenny hung up.

Within ten minutes, Jenny and Elizabeth arrived.

'I'm not coming with you. I don't have any clean clothes so I'll have nothing to wear. Besides, I've a million things I need to do here,' she protested.

'Whatever you need, we can provide between us,' Elizabeth informed her demonstratively. 'Don't be argumentative. You'll feel better in a day or two. If you stay here on your own, you won't be able to do the things you need to do, so it's for the best. I'd be failing in my duty as a parent if I left you alone. I'll bring you home when you feel better. I promise.'

Without another word, Alison accompanied them to the car, too dispirited to quarrel. She didn't want any company; she just wanted to sleep to obliterate the confusing thoughts invading her mind.

Immediately they arrived home, Elizabeth helped Alison upstairs and put her to bed. 'You're possibly coming down with a cold,' she suggested, although it was apparent to Elizabeth that Alison's symptoms were much deeper-rooted than that.

When Elizabeth went into the kitchen, Jenny was pacing the floor anxiously. 'How is she now? I was frantic when I saw the state of her. Do you suppose she'll be alright?' she gabbled with concern.

'Yes, she'll recover but it might take a little time. Do you happen to know who her doctor is?'

'Yes, she's with Dr. Martin like we are.'

Elizabeth called John to the kitchen. 'Would you find me Alan Martin's phone number please? He's Alison's GP. I'm sure he wouldn't mind if I were to call him at home.'

'Of course he wouldn't mind. I'll get his number.'

John had known Alan Martin socially for several years and his wife, Emma, had been at school with Elizabeth. It was Emma who answered the call.

'*Elizabeth*,' Emma squealed enthusiastically. 'Oh, how nice. Merry Christmas. How's the family?'

'Everyone's fine thanks but I have Jenny's friend here who's a patient of Alan's. She's rather poorly and we don't know what to do. Would Alan mind if I had a quick word with him?'

'Of course he wouldn't. I'll just call him. Listen, are you doing anything later? We're having a small cocktail party at eight if you fancy a change. I know it's difficult at Christmas but you're very welcome if you'd like to pop round for an hour or so. There's enough food for fifty and we'd love to see you.'

'Well, I won't promise but if we can get away we will. I've been tied to the kitchen for days so it'd be a most welcome escape, thank you Emma.'

'Alan's here now. I'll put him on.'

'Hi! Merry Christmas. What's wrong?' he asked.

She outlined Alison's symptoms while he listened carefully. 'I'll be round in fifteen minutes. I think I know what's wrong with her. To be honest, it was only a matter of time before this happened.'

Elizabeth felt very guilty about the inconvenience to Alan over the Christmas holiday period and she apologised when he arrived.

'Listen, I should be thanking you. You've got me away from the house for half an hour or so. Do you have any idea what it's like when Emma's cooking for guests? Every time I turn to face her, she shoves something else in my mouth for me to taste, another new creation. I'm absolutely stuffed. Really, you've done me a favour,' he said with a broad grin. 'Right now, where's this young lady I came to see?'

They went up to Alison's bedroom and Alan took hold of her hand to check her pulse. She murmured, opened her eyes and tried to sit up.

'You lay back and rest and tell me how you feel,' he said softly as Elizabeth left the room and Alison sobbed bitterly while pouring out her heart to him.

Alan returned to the kitchen about fifteen minutes later. 'I take it you know that Alison lost her mother recently?' he asked and without awaiting a reply he went on, 'That's the cause of her illness. Until now, she's been unable to come to terms with her grief. Everybody grieves in a different way. Her way was to soldier on and by keeping herself occupied, she believed she was doing okay. Conversely, she was merely deferring the inevitable, so we've just had a lengthy discussion and she's finally agreed to allow me to help her. I'm starting her on medication right away so would you get this prescription tomorrow and ensure she takes the prescribed dosage? If you could allow her to stay with you for a few days, I'm sure it would be beneficial to have friends around.'

'She'll recover fully, won't she?' Elizabeth asked anxiously.

'Quicker than you think. Alison's a tough nut but even the toughest nut cracks with enough strain and she's borne more than her fair share of stress lately but don't worry. She's a very determined girl.'

Elizabeth expelled a huge sigh of relief. 'Are you having a drink, Alan?'

'No, I'm alright, thanks. I ought to get back. I'm the chief taster, remember? By the way, Emma said to remind you about the party. She hopes you'll be able to make it....in fact we both do.'

'Well, I don't know....what with Alison....'

'She's fine. I doubt she'll awake before morning. Anyway, see how things progress. Emma would be over the moon if you were to put in an appearance. Say cheerio to John for me. We'll organize a game of golf as soon as the weather permits.'

When Alan had left, Elizabeth crept upstairs and was relieved to find Alison sleeping.

'You must go to the cocktail party,' Jenny stated. 'If there are any concerns, I promise I'll call you.'

'You're right. I don't suppose we'll be missed for an hour or so. I'll see what your dad says.'

When Alison awoke the next day and recalled the previous day's events, she felt very embarrassed at the imposition on Jenny's family. Initially, she felt unsteady but once the light-headedness had passed, she brushed her hair and went downstairs.

Elizabeth, who was cooking the breakfast, turned round when she heard movement behind her. 'Good morning,' she said. 'How are you feeling?'

'Embarrassed! I don't know what happened to me yesterday. I'm *so* sorry for the trouble I've caused.'

'You've been no trouble whatsoever. I'm relieved that Jenny phoned you. Do you feel any better?'

'I'm a bit tearful but I slept okay. I can't believe what time it is.'

'Sleep is the best healer. You need plenty of rest and I intend to make sure that's what you get. Have you any recollection of Dr. Martin calling?'

'Yes. Thanks for that. He was really kind and he spent some time explaining what was wrong. Now, with the benefit of hindsight, I realise I was foolish. Apart from Jenny, I had nobody close to rely on for support. I've no family to speak of so I tried to go it alone and I did a lousy job didn't I?'

'I don't agree. For a girl of your age, I'd say you have managed admirably. Have you no relatives?'

'I just have my maternal grandparents who live in the South of England.'

'So you've no relatives any closer?'

'No. I've no aunts or uncles. My paternal grand-parents could still be alive but I've neither seen nor heard from them since the day I was born.'

'Why is that?' Elizabeth queried and when Alison revealed the details, she was shocked. 'They're evi-dently a strange couple to behave in such a callous manner. I can't believe they didn't turn up for their only son's funeral and then for them to blame your mother for his death....why, it's abominable.'

'Well, we haven't met so, as the old saying goes, "What you've never had you never miss,". I haven't a clue whether they're dead or alive or where they lived for that matter and I wouldn't associate with such people even if I did know. My mother was the sweetest person ever and we lived our lives in total unison. I felt I'd lost a part of my own being when she died. There's such a huge void in my life now.'

Elizabeth was choking back tears as she listened to the worldly expressions flowing from this young girl's lips.

'We'll always be here for you and you must never imagine you're imposing. John and I had a lengthy discussion and you can stay here until you're well.'

'Thank you but I insist on earning my keep and I promise I won't do anything to retard my recovery nor will I abuse your very kind hospitality.'

Elizabeth took her in her arms. Although she was hardly more than a child, she carried the weight of the world on her shoulders yet displayed a rational approach to life. Her mother must have been proud.

'There must be an epidemic of some kind,' Jenny announced as she bounded into the kitchen. 'People were queuing to the door at the pharmacy counter. I thought I'd never get away.'

'They must be buying antacids, due to their over-indulgence at Christmas,' Elizabeth laughed.

'Hello you,' Jenny said, looking surprised to see Alison sitting at the table. 'How's tricks?'

'I'm feeling a bit better today thanks.'

'Good. I've just picked up your prescription,' she said, throwing the package on the table.

'Thanks. What would I do without you?'

'Hey Mum, you'll never guess who I saw near the pharmacy counter.'

'I've no idea. Go on....who?'

'Tracy.'

'*Richard's* Tracy?'

'The very one and she was with a guy who looked old enough to be her father.'

'Well, perhaps he was then.'

'No, we've met. *He* definitely wasn't her father, unless he was her *sugar* daddy,' she chuckled.

Elizabeth expelled a shrill laugh. 'Good luck and good riddance too. I found her very temperamental. I wasn't sorry it was over. Richard's disposition is better suited to a more thoughtful girl, in fact a girl like you Alison.'

She was horrified. 'Oh Elizabeth, I can't imagine Richard would ever be interested in a girl like me. I'm far too unsophisticated. I originate from a very humble background,' she said, feeling embarrassed.

'*Manners maketh man,* Alison, not sophistication, wealth, property or power. Believe me, some of the most offensive and vulgar individuals I've ever met are from the aristocracy,' Elizabeth replied.

'I'm sure you're right, when compared to the less familiar quotation by Evelyn Waugh, "Manners are especially the need of the plain. The pretty can get away with anything."'

'That's the point I was trying to make, although it was more eloquently expressed by you. You have all the requisite qualities of good breeding, so you can feel at ease in anyone's presence. I noticed that the moment we met and returning to what I said, I feel sure that Richard finds you as enchanting as the rest of us do. What do you say Jenny?'

42

'I agree. You only have to watch him when she's around. He never takes his eyes off her.'

Alison felt uncomfortable and decided it was time to make an exit. 'Is it alright if I go to my room for an hour or so? I feel a little shaky.'

'*Mi casa es su casa*,' Jenny said. 'Feel free to do as you please. I'll pop up when lunch is ready.'

When Richard returned, he was concerned to hear of Alison's illness. 'Is she really bad?' he asked.

'She has to rest but that doesn't necessarily mean bed-rest,' Elizabeth explained. 'She came down this morning though she didn't stay long. She's pale but I'm sure she'll feel a little better in a day or two.'

'But she will recover won't she?'

'Yes, in fact there was a noticeable improvement today. Dr. Martin prescribed tablets to help her.'

Changing topic Jenny asked, 'How was the party at Emma's? Were there lots of people there?'

'About twenty I'd say and it was lovely. As usual, she excelled with the canapés. I don't know where she finds her inspiration.'

Flippantly Jenny announced 'I saw Tracy today.'

'*Jenny*! You really are insensitive and tactless at times,' Elizabeth admonished her angrily.

'It's okay mum,' Richard cut in. 'I don't give two hoots about Tracy now. It was a liaison I'd prefer to forget but that doesn't mean I fall apart at the mere mention of her name and it wasn't all bad. We had some good times but looking back, it wouldn't have worked. My sights are set elsewhere now but I have to wait for the right time and place before making my move.'

'And who might that be?' Jenny questioned with a glint of merriment in her eye.

'You'll be the *last* person to find out, dear sister,' he stated on a laugh and then went upstairs, leaving the two most influential women in his life to speculate about his surprise announcement.

During the next few days, Alison started to show signs of improvement. Initially, she remained in her room where she had time to reflect. Her attitude of mind steadily became all the more positive and her distressing and negative thoughts were beginning to fade. Despite her infirmity, she continued to update her diary and when, one morning, she opened it at the current page, she realised that the next day was New Year's Eve. It was then she made her decision, that from the start of the New Year, she would put her troubles behind her. 'There'll be no further self-pity,' she scribbled hastily. As she closed her diary, Richard knocked on her door.

'Are you decent? May I come in?' he called out.

'Yes, please do.'

He crossed the room and sat down on the edge of her bed beside her. 'Do you feel better? I've hardly seen you since you came back.'

'I'm a lot better thanks. I've no doubt the magic pills from Dr. Martin helped, although he did insist they were quite mild.'

She felt guilty. What she omitted to say was that she had deliberately kept herself hidden away when Richard was home. It was bad enough that she had feelings for him but when Elizabeth had suggested *she* was the right type of girl for Richard, she was worried that a similar suggestion might be made in his presence and were Elizabeth to embarrass him, then she would simply succeed in driving a wedge between them, which was the last thing she wanted. Despite her strong belief that her feelings were not reciprocated, he was a valued friend and her close bond with the family could be jeopardised if an ill-conceived remark were to be made.

Fortunately, Richard had spent much of his time away from the house over the Christmas period and Alison, from her bedroom, could see his car leaving when he went out, so she had carefully planned her visits downstairs to coincide with his absences. As luck would have it, her furtive behaviour had raised no suspicion for which she was relieved. She didn't want him to know she was purposely avoiding him.

'So are you?' he questioned.

With a quizzical look she asked, 'Am I what?'

'You seem very preoccupied, Alison. I just asked if you were coming downstairs.'

'Sorry, I was miles away. Yes, I am.'

As she arose, Richard quickened his pace to open the door. 'You can't imagine how relieved I am that you're feeling better. I've been so worried.'

'Thank you. It's been a trying time and I'm not a person who succumbs to defeat without a battle but this has been a battle I had little chance of winning. Now I've had time to put things in perspective, I've turned the corner, thanks to everyone's support.'

'We've all been invited to a New Year's Eve dinner party at Maud's house,' Elizabeth informed Alison.

'It's very kind of her to include me but I wouldn't want to impose. I appear to have been doing that all Christmas but it *would* be lovely to see them and it might help to have a change of environment.'

'Excellent, that's settled then. I'll give her a call, unless you'd prefer to talk to her yourself.'

'I would prefer to call her myself. I think it would be more appropriate so I may thank her properly for her kind invitation.'

Elizabeth smiled to herself. Although Alison was so child-like and reticent on the one hand, she never failed in political correctness.

Alison chatted to Maud for fifteen minutes. Maud was happy-go-lucky and loquacious and Alison was sure there would be more anecdotal accounts at her dinner party. She thanked her and stated how much she was looking forward to seeing the family again.

The next morning, she asked Jenny if she knew of a florist where she could buy flowers for Maud.

'There's one next door to my hairdresser. I have an appointment there at ten. Why don't you book in too and have a re-style? It might just give you a bit of a boost. She's an excellent hairdresser.'

'It sounds like a good idea, though at the moment, I'm more concerned about what I shall wear. I don't have any decent evening wear. It's mainly everyday stuff in my wardrobe.'

'Try some of mine. I've loads of evening outfits.'

She was amazed at the vast quantity of clothes in Jenny's wardrobe. Most still had the labels attached and had never been worn. Those were additional to the clothes kept at her flat.

'I'm wearing this, so you choose whatever takes your fancy,' Jenny said. 'Try a few on and I'll tell you how you look. What about shoes?'

'I have my black shoes that I wore Christmas Eve and my small black evening bag too, so I'm alright for accessories. I also have my gold chain with me.'

'And your matching gold bracelet from Richard,' Jenny reminded her with an impish smile.

'Indeed,' she agreed without rising to the bait.

Everything in the wardrobe bore a designer label and she felt like a catwalk model in each of the half dozen outfits she selected but she relied on Jenny's expertise to make the ultimate decision. Alison had never worn designer clothes; she had never been in shops that sold such clothes and felt self-conscious when she tried on an elegant red dress that showed off her figure to perfection. 'Promise you won't tell anyone it's yours,' she begged.

'Of course I will. I'll shout it over a loud speaker. I'm not stupid, though I might just tell Richard that you're wearing a sexy figure-hugging red dress to catch his eye.'

'*I'll kill you if you do*!' she screeched indignantly before they fell onto the bed laughing.

'I don't believe my eyes,' John spluttered when the three women emerged. 'How can I focus on driving with such a bevy of beauty in my car?'

They laughed at his complimentary remark.

Jenny was wearing a silvery-blue silk trouser suit and silver high-heeled shoes and she carried a small silver evening purse.

Elizabeth had chosen to wear a full-length black dress with a most revealing bodice that accentuated her curvaceous breasts. Her plain black accessories complemented her attire and she looked stunning.

Alison looked elegant and much taller in her long red dress. Her hair, that had been re-styled, tumbled across her shoulders in soft curls, framing her pretty face. Jenny had persuaded her to wear red lipstick, identical in colour to her dress. No one would have guessed she was only seventeen.

'Where on earth is Richard?' John said, becoming agitated when he still hadn't appeared five minutes later. 'He's always late for everything.'

Within seconds, he hurried downstairs, wearing a smart grey suit, a white shirt and a bright red tie.

'Dressed to match his girl,' Jenny proclaimed.

Richard couldn't take his eyes off Alison and as they made their way outside, he whispered, 'You're sensational this evening. That's a gorgeous dress.'

'Thank you. I love your suit,' she replied softly.

Alison felt more at ease with Richard, her having accepted the fact that they would probably never be anything more than good friends. She was looking forward to the dinner party and pleased to be seeing Maud and Harold again.

She stared ahead in total disbelief as John swept up the long impressive drive and parked outside the main entrance to the imposing house, the very sight of which took her breath away.

'How's that for a house then?' Jenny said.

Harold opened the large oak double doors, hailing them heartily. 'A Happy New Year,' he called out.

Together they chanted, 'Happy New Year to you,' as they stepped into the grand hall with a very high ceiling, from which hung three crystal chandeliers, glistening and sparkling like a host of brilliant stars. Elaborately carved items of antique furniture were strategically sited around the oak-panelled hall and Alison's eyes were instantly drawn towards a life-size marble figure of a nubile Greek maiden.

Maud hurried towards them in her usual buoyant fashion with arms outstretched, followed by Mark who halted as his eyes came to rest on Alison.

'Wow! You look stunning! Red is definitely your colour,' he remarked, kissing her on both cheeks.

'Thank you Mark and you look rather dapper too. That's a snazzy shirt and I like the haircut. It suits you,' she said with a beam that lit up her face.

'How are you dear?' Maud asked with concern.

'I'm much better thank you and I'm delighted to be here in your beautiful home. It was very kind of you to invite me and I hope to do your food justice. I'm told you are a very talented cook.'

'Oh I don't know about that,' she answered with a chortle. 'See what you think when you've sampled the goods. I enjoy cooking, though I don't make too many fancy dishes. Harold prefers wholesome, old-fashioned food but I'm more ambitious when I have dinner guests. I definitely don't possess Elizabeth's flair for presentation though.'

'What absolute balderdash,' Elizabeth interjected. 'You've always been a creative cook and you're the only person I know who can produce an entire meal without her kitchen resembling a bomb site.'

Harold cautiously interrupted to question whether they intended to spend the evening in the hallway, admiring each other's culinary abilities, or whether instead they might like to follow him to the drawing room for cocktails. He had a skilful way with words and the ability to diffuse any situation instantly *and* raise a laugh at the same time.

Harold and John had been in partnership for more years than they cared to commit to memory. When they first started the business, they were young and able-bodied and they devoted the requisite time and effort to make it succeed and when they diversified later, they provided an employment field for scores of people, most of whom were still in their employ.

When Harold's widowed mother died he inherited a more than moderate estate and it was then that the family moved to Ryefields.

Maud fell in love with the house the moment she saw it. She once related to Elizabeth that it felt like the perfect family home when they walked through the door. She never tired of entertaining friends and the superb landscaped gardens provided her with an interest best described as a labour of love.

Maud had recruited a live-in housekeeper Dinah, when Mark was young, although Dinah was treated more like a family member than an employee.

Though responsible for the daily chores, she was given a free hand in the organisation of her duties. She had been invaluable to Maud, having played an active role in the care of Mark when he was young.

When the family moved to Ryefields, Dinah was given a sunny south-facing en-suite bedroom, overlooking the rear garden. It was bright and spacious and had a lower-level seating area. A bay window across one corner of the room overlooked woodland and during the long summer evenings, Dinah would position her chair by the window and sit for hours enjoying the scenery.

Dinah greatly valued her position with this caring family who paid her very well and provided private medical care but of late, she had become concerned that her duties were becoming very demanding. The problem was her age. Though in good health, Dinah was in her sixties and Ryefields was a large house.

The Christmas preparations had been particularly tiring for Dinah, only too aware of Maud's exacting standards but age creeps up on everyone, she had to admit finally, although she had no idea what would happen to her were she to leave these caring people to whom she had grown so attached.

She entered the drawing room with the silver tray and proceeded with John's help to serve the drinks. She dressed formally for special occasions to avoid her being mistaken for a guest, but after seventeen years' service, the regular guests knew her well and were envious of Maud's *special acquisition,* as they called her kindly. She was one in a million; always professional in the way she conducted herself.

Alison sipped her orange juice that was cool and refreshing. As she was still on medication, alcohol, however limited, was not permitted.

Mark was like the proverbial bee round the honey pot. Where Alison moved, he was there by her side and she was conscious of Richard's piercing gaze.

Maud returned and called the guests to order. 'We can start dinner if you're ready,' she announced.

As everyone left the room, Mark turned to Alison and whispered, 'I'd like us to get together after the holiday and go for a meal, just the two of us.'

He regarded her optimistically awaiting her reply.

She smiled. 'That sounds lovely but please let me recover first. This is my first social evening since I became er….poorly. I don't want to overdo things.'

'Let's leave it for a week then and I'll call you.'

Suddenly Harold yelled, '*Get your skates on you two. Everyone's waiting. There'll be plenty of time later for your canoodling. We're starving in here*!'

Everyone laughed except Alison who thought she would die of embarrassment. Her face matched the colour of her dress and when she slanted her gaze in Richard's direction, his face was like thunder.

Jenny leaned over and whispered, 'Mark's honing in on your patch. "*He who hesitates is lost.*" Don't lose sight of that, little brother. "*Procrastination is the thief of time,*" and other things....'

'Just shut your rip and mind your own business,' he snarled irritably.

Alison was pleased she had been seated between Harold and John, away from the two young men.

'A rose between two thorns,' John commented as she took her seat.

Following a lengthy uncomfortable silence, Maud and Dinah appeared and proceeded to serve the first course. Harold proposed what was to be the first of many toasts that evening to the New Year and they raised their glasses in accord.

52

It was a delightful meal. Elizabeth remarked that Maud had excelled once more and everyone agreed.

Jenny and Alison helped clear the dishes, despite protestations from Maud although she was secretly appreciative of their help after such an arduous day in the kitchen. Dinah had asked to be excused after serving the entrée and Maud made a mental note to discuss the matter with her the next morning. It was so unlike Dinah to disappear when there was work to be done and she was most concerned.

When everyone had settled down after the meal, Harold made the rounds, topping up glasses while Maud fussed around her guests with a gigantic box of assorted chocolates that no one could face.

'For Christ's sake, shift the bloody things away!' Harold chastised her in no uncertain terms. 'Can't you see everyone's stuffed?'

Mark had taken his usual place beside Alison and Harold had already begun to relate incidents from his never-ending repertoire of hilarious anecdotes, still insistent every single one was true.

There was uncontrollable mirth at his mannerisms as he not only narrated but acted out the events with meticulous precision.

He was such a witty man, Alison thought and to watch him fool around so good-humouredly belied his true status as a man of such great standing and self-discipline in his professional life. She tried to imagine what her father would have been like, had he lived. She had little knowledge of him, although was aware there had been much unhappiness in his life when his parents had renounced him. His father had been a strict disciplinarian, she'd been advised, whereas his mother had been a compassionate and meek woman, kind towards everyone she met and it had distressed Michael when she, in particular, had reacted in such a callous manner.

She suddenly became aware Richard was asking a question. 'I'm sorry. I was on another planet.'

'I asked if you'd like to see another card trick.'

'*Oh Lord*!' John exclaimed. 'Do you have to keep punishing the poor girl? The last time you showed her a card trick, you had her in bed for a week.'

Everyone laughed at John who could be dry when he had a mind to be. Mark however, didn't miss the opportunity of the moment and with a broad smirk, he leaned towards Alison, whispering loud enough for Richard to hear, 'I'd run out now and get a pack of cards if I thought that would work for me.'

The innuendo infuriated her. She was angry with Mark, not so much for the inference of his remark, but because she wasn't aware whether anybody else had overheard. Embarrassed, she looked round and realised, with the exception of Richard, the others remained oblivious of Mark's foolish comment.

'Do you have a moment Mark?' Richard growled abruptly and stood up. He strode from the room and Mark followed. No one appeared to notice anything was amiss but she was concerned as she didn't want to be the cause of any friction between Richard and Mark. Although furious with Mark, she would have been quite capable of dealing with the issue herself without being offensive but it had now been taken out of her hands.

She hurried from the room unobtrusively and on hearing dialogue from the direction of the kitchen, she approached and heard Richard's raised voice. 'I can't imagine what on earth possessed you to make such a vulgar offensive quip. Alison was noticeably embarrassed and humiliated. In spite of her mature appearance, try to remember she's little more than a child,' he yelled. 'She's very naïve.'

Before Mark had chance to respond she stormed into the kitchen. 'How dare you speak of me in that way? I am neither a child nor am I naïve and I don't need *you* to fight my battles. I'm more than capable of fighting my own, thank you. There was no need for this unpleasantness. As for you Mark, it was an ill-conceived and foolish comment to make in front of the others but I'd have found it easy to retaliate had we been alone. The fact that others were there caused the embarrassment, not your stupid remark. You are the ones behaving like children and *never* assume I am naïve because I'm not. I don't want to drive a wedge between two friends. I'm content for all three of us to be friends and I'm demanding you end such juvenile behaviour. Life isn't about trying to score points at another person's expense. *Is that clear*?' she said acidly and strode from the kitchen, leaving them both speechless.

On her way back, Maud appeared in view. 'I was just wondering where you'd gone Alison. Are you alright dear?' she enquired.

'Yes thanks, I was taking my tablet and I needed water,' she lied convincingly and quickly changing topic she added, 'May I ask a favour Maud?'

'Of course dear, what is it?'

'Please don't think it rude of me to ask but would you show me round your beautiful home?'

Enthusiastically she gushed, 'I'd be delighted to. Nothing would give me greater pleasure.'

Alison was given the grand tour and was amazed at the vast number of rooms she entered.

'I used to get lost when we first moved in,' Maud confessed when Alison remarked that she had never seen such an enormous house.

Every spacious room had its own colour scheme and theme and the innovative use of pastel shades accentuated the size of each one further. At the rear end of the house was the boys' playroom, as Maud described it. That housed a full-sized snooker table with a well-stocked bar, and it wasn't difficult for Alison to envisage how many hours Mark, Harold and their friends spent there. The library and master study were located side by side and a further study, for Mark's use, was situated at the other side of the house beside a pleasant sun lounge where a passage led to a locked door. She gasped as Maud opened it to reveal an indoor swimming pool, surrounded by tropical plants, where blue and white sun-loungers were grouped alongside high stained-glass windows overlooking the garden.

'It's like Hollywood. It's beautiful. I've only seen houses like this in films,' she gasped.

Alison lost count of the number of bedrooms she entered, the majority with en-suite facilities, and the sweeping circular oak staircase was a true work of art with ornamentally crafted finials adorning huge decorative balusters. Each antique item of furniture had its own story to tell.

'I would need to make this tour a hundred times to absorb everything. It's unbelievable Maud.'

'Come, I haven't shown you my favourite room yet. It's the music room,' she advised, opening the door into the most resplendent room where the soft furnishings were truly exquisite. '*Grandeur*' sprang to her mind as Alison stared in admiration and awe. Two cream sofas, upholstered in embossed brocade coordinated with the flowing window drapes, which adorned floor to ceiling windows and situated in the centre of the room was a superb ebony grand piano, occupying little space in the titanic room.

'This was my mother's piano,' Maud said quietly. 'I hadn't the heart to dispose of it when she passed away. She was a professional pianist and my father bought it as a wedding anniversary gift when I was a child. She used to sit for hours playing music. She adored it. I still have it tuned six-monthly, although sadly, no-one plays it anymore....Mark would never learn,' she continued with sorrow in her voice.

'May I?' Alison asked as she stroked the lid.

'Do you play my dear?' Maud questioned.

'Just a little. I had lessons when I was young. We had a small second-hand upright piano but I had to dispose of it when mum became ill. She needed her bed downstairs and we had to make room for it.'

'I'd love to hear it played again,' Maud sighed.

Without a word, Alison nervously took her seat at the piano and opened the lid, conscious by looking at the aged discoloured ivory keys and the German

57

manufacturer's brass plaque, that it was indeed an instrument of excellence. To loosen her fingers, she ran them up and down the keys and she familiarised herself with the tone before progressing to a piece by Mozart. Maud wept quietly, recalling how often she had listened to her dear mother's performances.

Alison had slipped spiritually to another universe, oblivious of time and place as she gloried in these special moments, swiftly moving from one piece of music to another.

Neither of them heard a sound as the door opened and the others listened silently, reverently and with deep admiration to this gifted young woman whose accomplishments knew no bounds.

Only when closing the lid did she become aware of the presence of everybody when they applauded. It was an emotional moment for all present.

'It's a minute to twelve. Have you all got a drink?' Harold asked and everyone replied with a nod.

They started their countdown ten seconds before midnight and on the initial stroke of twelve, Harold proposed yet another toast when they each drank to the New Year by which time, the heated exchange of dialogue between Richard, Mark and Alison had long been laid to rest.

As they grouped by the bay window, the sky was ablaze with fireworks in a myriad of colour.

It had been a wonderful party, Alison reflected as she watched the spectacle outside.

The food had been excellent and it was the dawn of another year that she hoped would be special for all present. They were fine people and Alison loved each and every one of them.

Within an hour their taxi had arrived and as they were taking their leave, Mark smiled apologetically at Alison though no words were spoken.

Along with the others, she thanked her hosts for a wonderful evening she would never forget. Maud in return thanked Alison for the music which had been such a delight, she said, and for her lovely flowers.

It was early morning New Year's Day and Alison was sitting at her window looking across the garden where a scattering of evergreen shrubs added a spot of colour to the otherwise bare wintry borders.

She put on her robe and made her way downstairs but there was no sign of life.

After filling the kettle, she scoured the headlines of the papers while waiting for it to boil. Each story related to the war in Iraq and she sighed, wondering if it would ever end. Each fatality of the horror was a member of a family and loved by someone. It was all so futile.

Her thoughts were interrupted as Jenny appeared.

'Hi there. What time did you get up?'

'Just a few minutes ago. The kettle's on.'

Jenny covered her mouth and yawned noisily. 'It was a good night at Maud's wasn't it?'

'It certainly was and as a bonus, Maud gave me a conducted tour of the house.'

'Isn't it fabulous? She adores that house.'

'That's no surprise. Who wouldn't adore it? Tell me something. Is er....Mark involved with anyone?'

'Not as far as I know. Why, are you interested?'

'No, I just wondered as he's good-looking and he dresses well. I'd have thought he'd be attached.'

'Mark likes to play the field. We had something going about a year ago but then we drifted apart. I'd rather be with someone from further afield. I don't want to bring our families and the businesses closer together than they are now.'

'Are *you* seeing anyone at the moment?'

'No, I'm not moving in the right circles. Some of my friends went off to University while others, like me, moved into their own places, away from their parents' roving eyes but with the expense it entails, there's no money left for socialising. I went through all the motions of having wild parties, when everyone turned up with piles of booze but I had to spend the next day cleaning up vomit and tidying up after they left the flat an absolute tip, so the novelty soon wore off....and then you never knew who you were going to wake up with,' she laughed.

'Oh Jenny, how awful!' she gasped.

'I didn't mean *wake up* having had *sex*. We were all so drunk that everyone bedded down where they could but I quickly became stalled with the drunken parties. Once I stopped them crashing at my place, they found somewhere else to trash, I'm pleased to say. Besides, who needs friends like that?'

'Who indeed. So are you lonely on your own?'

'It would be nice to have someone to talk to, have a laugh and share a meal with. I've often thought of advertising for a flat-mate but there's no guarantee of what you'll end up with. Do you get lonely?'

'Now there's a joke if ever I heard one. As soon as I went home to an empty house after Christmas, I went to pieces immediately. Ask me again when I go home in a day or two.'

'You're going back so soon?'

'The longer I stay, the harder it'll be to go home. I can't keep delaying the inevitable. I'm better now and I've imposed on your family too long already.'

'I'm sure mum will have plenty to say about that when she knows. Listen, I don't want to put you on the spot, but why not move in with me at the flat? You'd have your own room, your own space and it would work out much cheaper for both of us if we shared all the expenses. I'm not suggesting you sell your house. You could keep it on as an investment property and rent it out. I daresay it would bring a few hundred quid a month in for little outlay and it would be there to return to if things didn't work out at the flat. What do you say? We get along well.'

'You're right, we do get along well but you're my boss. I'd hate to land you in a position where, if you needed to sack me, you felt bad. It's an interesting proposition though because I have plenty of debts I could pay off with a second income.'

'If you don't mind my asking, what are they?'

'The Funeral Director for one. I owe him nearly a thousand pounds and there's a few utility bills I've not paid. I've applied to the Social Security Office for help but I've heard nothing yet. Since I started at the Agency, I've only received one month's pay and I've spent most of that on Christmas presents. Mum took out an Insurance Policy when dad died, but the premiums were very low so I don't expect it to be worth much but every little helps. I've written to the Company but as you'll be aware, the wheels of bureaucracy grind very very slowly. They rarely process your claim with the urgency and efficiency they practise when selling you the Policy.'

'In that case I think you should seriously consider my offer. It'd solve all your financial problems and leave you with money over for yourself. After what you've suffered lately, you deserve that. If you like, I'll have a talk to dad. He and Harold are exploring the advantages of Property Management. Asking a few questions doesn't commit you to anything.'

'You might as well. What harm can it do?'

'Do you feel up to looking round the shops for an hour or so? The January sales start today. I'll treat you to lunch if you'll come with me.'

She smiled. 'How can I refuse an offer like that?'

'Right, be ready in an hour then....no longer.'

'Have you learned to drive yet?' Jenny enquired as they made their way towards town.

'No, there was never any point. I couldn't afford a car and lessons are expensive I believe. I'm hoping to learn when I've sorted everything else out.'

'I took my driving test when I turned eighteen but only because dad paid for it and he also bought me a run-around car when I passed. I thought I was the bee's knees. It was an old banger so I called it *Eve*.'

'Why *Eve*?' she asked, looking puzzled.

'Surely you've heard of *Adam and Eve* of olden times? Old car? *Eve*? Come on, wake up Alison.'

'Sorry, I'm a bit slow. It must be the orange juice I drank last night. It's discombobulated my brain.'

Jenny chuckled. 'I had plenty to drink last night,' she confessed. 'I was rather squiffy towards the end of the night but not too much so to appreciate your expertise on the old ivory keys. I was sure everyone would burst into tears when we crept in. How long did it take you to learn to play like that?'

'I was seven or eight when I first started to learn. My piano teacher lived a few doors away. He was a lovely man who found me an old upright piano that one of his pupils was disposing of and I learned and practised on that for many years until he died, not long after his wife died. Mum said he'd lost the will to live when he lost his wife. It's sad isn't it?'

'It is but it's a fact of life. We ought to make the most of the time we have and I intend to do just that when I've parked up. A few hours' retail therapy is exactly what you need.'

It wasn't busy in town and Jenny concluded, as it was New Year's Day, many would-be shoppers had stayed at home in the belief that the shops would be closed.

'I much prefer it like this,' Alison stated. 'I hate it when everyone's pushing and shoving and then you have to queue to pay....and there's always someone at the till who has a problem with a credit card.'

'Tell me about it. It happens to me all the time.'

'I didn't see your parents today. Did they go out?'

'Yes, they went to Maud's for dad's car. He likes to be master of his own destiny. He'll never leave anything to chance, so he wouldn't have considered calling a taxi to take us there on New Year's Eve as they can be very unreliable at the best of times. He would have hated to arrive late for the meal.'

'And what a meal *that* was,' Alison said. 'Maud's very capable and Harold is such a scream. I'd have listened to his stories all night. They're an amazing couple and so well suited aren't they?'

'Yes and Mark's a really nice guy when you get to know him. Do you like him?'

She hadn't intended mentioning the contretemps of the previous evening but since Jenny had raised the subject, she acquainted her with the details.

Jenny found it hilarious that Alison had barged in the kitchen at that inopportune moment, especially when she explained how she had given them a good dressing down.

'Oh Alison....to have two dashing young suitors almost duelling at dawn. How gratifying is that?'

'In different circumstances, maybe, but not when the one you fancy thinks he's your baby-sitter,' she remarked gloomily.

No sooner had Alison uttered the words than she realised her mistake and would have given anything to retract them but it was too late.

'So you *do* fancy Richard. I *knew* it!'

'Jenny....please forget what I said. The words just slipped out. I'll never speak to you again if you tell him so promise me you won't say anything.'

'What's it worth then for me to keep my great big gob shut? I know....you can move into the flat and I'll promise not to breathe a word. Cross my heart and hope to die.'

64

'That's blackmail. If I'm honest though, I haven't thought of much else since you asked me. Alright, let's give it a go.'

'*Fantastic*! Let's grab some lunch and we'll talk it through, I'm starving.'

'Me too and promise, not a word to Richard?'

'My lips are sealed and I hope it works out for the two of you. I really do.'

Alison didn't reply but secretly she hoped so too.

The planned two-hour shopping spree had already lasted for three hours, despite Alison's protestations as Jenny continued to drag her from store to store.

'There'll be time to rest when we're home,' Jenny told her. 'You're not going back till you've bought a nice outfit. You never buy yourself anything.'

'Well, I never any money,' she complained.

'Then use your credit card. A few quid isn't going to bankrupt you.'

Alison knew she would have to submit but Jenny was right. Everything she possessed was dated. She couldn't remember the last time she'd bought a new outfit. She was overloaded with bags and every one was Jenny's. It did seem a shame to miss out on a sale bargain and once she moved in with Jenny, her financial status would improve so she shouldn't feel guilty about having a treat, she convinced herself.

'I saw a lovely trouser suit in the shop where you bought the faux-fur coat. It'd been reduced to half-price. I'd love that if I could squeeze into it.'

'I didn't see it. I must have missed it,' Jenny said.

'Looking at this lot, I doubt you missed anything. Will there be room for my stuff when I move in?'

'Didn't I say? I'm getting you a cardboard box,' she joked. 'Actually, I was about to suggest that we call at the flat later and you can have a look round.'

'I'd like that. It looks terrific on the photos.'

'First things first. Let's retrace our steps and find that trouser suit and if it fits, you buy it. Right?'

'Alright, you win.'

Back at the shop, Alison systematically fingered through the rails. 'Here it is. What do you think?'

'It's lovely and it's *Oui*,' Jenny told her, looking at the label.

'What does that mean?'

'*Oui* is the label and that's one of the best *and* it's cashmere too. Go and try it. It's a superb cut which means it'll hang nicely. That's a bargain if it fits.'

When she reappeared, Jenny remarked, 'You look great. You need higher heel shoes, then you'll look like a cool fashion model on the glossy front cover of *Vogue* and don't even ask what *Vogue* is.'

'I know what *Vogue* is. I'm not stupid. I can play the piano,' she rejoined and both girls laughed.

As they lumbered their way back to the car with all the bags Alison was delighted with her purchase. It was New Year's Day 2003….and with or without Richard she intended to enjoy the year ahead.

'The building's security gated which gives me more peace of mind when living there alone,' Jenny told her as she unlocked the door to her flat. 'I chose the end flat because the view is so much better.'

When they entered, Alison could smell new paint and remarked that a home felt clean and fresh when newly decorated. It was spacious and modern, yet it felt cosy and at once she knew she could live there.

It had been a good start to the New Year, a day of surprises *and* she had treated herself to a beautiful designer cashmere suit.

A further surprise awaited her when she returned with Jenny to the family home. A huge bouquet of white lilies was on the hall table together with a gift card noted, 'Alison, I hope all is well. Mark.'

'He obviously regrets his silly remark. You have to forgive him,' Jenny said.

'I already have,' she responded, gathering up the flowers. 'I'll put these in water. I adore lilies....'

When Elizabeth and John arrived home, Elizabeth heaved a sigh and flopped on the sofa beside Jenny. 'Did you think we'd got lost?' she asked.

'We went to the January sales so we haven't been back long. Where have you been?'

'At Maud's.'

'*Until now*? I thought you'd just gone for the car.'

'We had but there was a crisis when we got there. Perhaps you didn't notice last night but Dinah went up to bed before we left, which was unusual. Maud was concerned and said she would speak to her this morning about her hasty departure.'

'Well, maybe she was drained,' Jenny exclaimed. 'When all said and done, Dinah must be well over sixty and she works really hard for Maud. Perhaps Maud shouldn't expect so much from her.'

'*Out of the mouths of babes and sucklings....*' she recited. 'It appears everybody apart from Maud had realised that Dinah was finding it difficult to cope. She's not as agile as she was so it takes longer these days to do her chores. Anyway, it was brought to a head this morning, for when Maud raised it, Dinah burst into tears, gave her notice and rushed upstairs. She was locked in her room when we arrived.'

'You're joking.... Poor Dinah! What happened?'

'Well, as you can imagine, Maud was in a terrible state when we got there so I did my best to console her. Harold asked me if *I* could try to get to the root of the problem and so I went upstairs and knocked on Dinah's door repeatedly until she let me in. The poor soul was beside herself and her speech almost incomprehensible but when she calmed down I was then in a position to ascertain just what was wrong. She's absolutely worn out and has been so for some time but still she soldiered on regardless. She told me that she came over from Ireland as a young girl and landed a job in service and has known no other life. She always lived on the premises wherever she worked, so she has no home of her own and though Maud pays her well, what she's saved wouldn't buy her a house, so if she left there, she'd have nowhere to go. Every time Maud enquired if she could still manage her duties, she mistook Maud's concern as adverse criticism of her work. Afraid of losing her job, she worked harder, so it was a vicious circle.'

'Carry on,' Jenny stated edgily.

'I explained that if Maud had known the situation, she would have provided additional help but Dinah didn't accept that. She believed Maud would have simply terminated her employment and taken on a younger and more able housekeeper to replace her.'

Jenny was shocked. 'That's ridiculous! Dinah's a grafter and Maud wouldn't find *anybody* to match her exacting standards. So what happened then?'

'I told her she had simply let things get on top of her and that she should have mentioned it to Maud months ago....that Maud would *never* have turned her out on the street and that they regarded her as a family member. I said I would go and clear up this unpleasant misunderstanding immediately and that she shouldn't worry about a thing....that everything would turn out right when....'

'And did it?' Jenny interrupted anxiously.

'Yes, between us we managed to resolve matters. Maud was upset when I explained her concerns and couldn't imagine why Dinah would believe that she would cold-heartedly fire her but I had to explain to Maud that Dinah wasn't like us. She's always been in service and although she was treated well, to use her own words, she knew her place. Still, the issue has been resolved now, I'm pleased to say. Dinah is to remain as senior housekeeper and Maud will take on a junior assistant. Dinah will be responsible for training and overseeing the work of the new recruit. She'll still have various duties to perform but on a much lesser scale and Maud will be sure to keep a close eye on her in future....so everything ended on a happy note,' Elizabeth sighed.

3

'The amount of rubbish in this room would overfill a ten-ton truck,' Alison grumbled. 'No joking, I bet I've flattened twenty cardboard boxes already.'

'Save some. It's surprising how many you'll need when you empty your cupboards,' Jenny advised.

'Well, I can only bring what will fit in my room. My kitchen cupboards are full of pots and pans and you've more than enough. I was talking to your dad who suggested I leave the furniture in the house, as that would bring in more rent. All I need here is my bed and my dressing table. The rest is personal stuff and paperwork. I've an ottoman that'll fit at the end of the bed for my spare bedding and towels.'

'Right, the hall cupboard is finally empty,' Jenny announced as she moved the last two rubbish bags. 'If I could get my dad to fix two shelves and a few hooks, we could use this as a cloaks' cupboard and there'd still be room to stash your suitcases.'

'Suitcases?' Alison laughed. 'I don't have any.'

'So what do you use when you go on holiday?'

'You haven't an inkling of what it was like trying to make ends meet on state benefits. We barely had money for food. We never had holidays.'

'So, you're saying you've never been abroad?'

'*Abroad*? I've never even stepped out of Greater Manchester. I've never been *anywhere*.'

Jenny was shocked. 'I'm sorry. It's hard for me to imagine what it was like for you and your mother. I didn't realise you were *that* poor. I've taken things for granted, so I know nothing of the real world.'

'You don't have to feel sorry for me. Mum and I were fine. A holiday would have been lovely but it wasn't possible so I never gave it a second thought. If you put it in perspective, a holiday lasts a couple of weeks and then it's over. What my mother and I had lasted for seventeen years. Someday, when I'm free of debt, I might book something in a moment's madness.'

As Jenny continued with her chores, her thoughts were on another matter. An idea was stirring in her mind but she would keep it to herself for now.

When Alison had boxed up what she was taking, John and Richard brought a van to take it to the flat.

Elizabeth brought Alison a pair of cream curtains and a pretty silk flower arrangement for her room. They were amazed at the transformation when they took a step back to view the finished result.

Elizabeth expressed her delight to Alison that she and Jenny were to be flat-mates. 'When Jenny told me she might advertise for someone, I was frantic. I had visions of her taking in a *bunny-boiler*!'

'Well you don't have to worry about me. I'm not a psychopath,' Alison replied reassuringly.

'I know that my dear. That's why I'm pleased you agreed. It'll be good for both of you.'

'And think how much I'll save in bus fares with a lift to work every day.'

Within a week, Alison had found a suitable tenant for her house. A young couple from the south were relocating and needed a place to rent until their own house was sold. They were delighted with Alison's small, neat house which met all their requirements.

The same week, Alison received a letter from the Social Security Office, advising they would pay her late mother's funeral account, and arrears of benefit owing to her easily met her other outstanding debts.

The week after she'd moved into the flat, Alison received a call from Mark inviting her to dinner at a new restaurant in the city. She accepted graciously, thankful there was no animosity between them.

It was the first time she had been alone with Mark and she found him to be witty and charismatic. Like his father, he had a wealth of humorous anecdotes, mainly about his university days and although she doubted the validity of many of them, he made her laugh and she felt at ease in his company.

Their conversation covered an extensive range of subjects and she howled with laughter at his vivid portrayal of the interviewees for the post of house-keeping assistant to Dinah, who had insisted on her presence during the interviews conducted by Maud.

'Following receipt of many written applications, it was decided to interview six candidates from the information supplied,' he informed Alison.

'The first candidate was dressed in a very low cut cropped top and equally revealing *micro* skirt, dad told me who was also quick to advise that what she lacked in clothing was more than compensated for by exposed flesh, with her large boobs hoisted up to her chin,' he laughed. 'Dad was in the library when she walked past, heading for the study, and as mum glanced in, she was disgusted to see dad giving the thumbs up sign, so *her* interview ended abruptly.'

'I can well imagine,' Alison howled.

'The next candidate's beautifully manicured nails cost her the job. Dinah suspected *she'd* never done any housework in her life. Mum told me that Dinah was merciless, skilfully revealing their weaknesses by asking questions they should have been able to answer but couldn't and when they had interviewed four, Dinah was adamant that not one of them was suitable, not that mum needed any persuasion.'

Mark took a sip of his wine before continuing.

'The fifth and penultimate candidate was a single woman in her early forties but appeared older. She was plain and shabbily dressed and her big, clumsy laced shoes emphasised her enormous feet. She was quick to inform mum that everyone called her Tilly, though her given name was *Hilda* Trotter. Despite looking downtrodden, she was clean but had a thick mop of unkempt straggly hair. Though she failed to present herself looking at her best, characteristics of diplomacy and responsibility to duties were clearly demonstrated in her answers. She hadn't worked in service formerly, though was well acquainted with domestic duties, having cared for her invalid father who had recently died, she stated, and as they had been renting Council property, she would now have to leave. When they made a tour of the house, Tilly asked practical questions, at the same time showing a keen interest in the duties she would be required to perform. Then she asked whether the post would be residential but mum, not having anticipated that particular question, agreed to give consideration to that possibility, were Tilly to be successful after all the other candidates had been seen,' he told Alison.

73

'As Tilly was leaving, she grabbed mum's hand and shook it vigorously while thanking her for the opportunity to attend for interview and then gushed, "Thank you again Ma'am," and curtsied. Mum was absolutely gobsmacked and pretended to cough and clear her throat in an attempt to stifle a laugh.'

'Oh that I'd been a fly on the wall,' she smirked.

'Ditto, but I've still to tell you about the final one yet,' he guffawed coarsely, bringing her to mind.

'She was a young woman....I'd say about twenty years old and her face was plastered with make-up. She was wearing the highest wedge-soled shoes I'd ever seen. When I came home from golf, she was in the hall waiting to be seen and she called out to me, "Ee, it's a grand 'ouse i'n't it? D'yer live 'ere?" and when I stated that I did, she said, "I thought it were you in that picture. I were sayin' to mesel' afore yer walked in, 'E's a bit of alright.' Answer me summat will yer....are yer married luv?" I cleared my throat and replied that I wasn't married and then she said, "Ee, fancy. I were only thinkin' it'd be just my luck if yer were wed."'

Tears of laughter streamed down Alison's face.

'At that moment, Dinah appeared in the hall as if by magic, to my great relief I have to say, and she called to the young woman but as she stood up, she twisted her foot and almost fell over. I rushed to her aid to steady her and she said, "Ee, I ne'er thought I'd be in yer arms that quick but we don't 'ave time for a quick bit of *'ow's yer father* now, 'cos I 'ave to look sharp for me job interview....but 'appen I'll catch up wi' yer later."'

74

Alison felt close to a convulsion as she listened to his graphic revelation. 'So, when are you seeing her again?' she asked with tears of laughter in her eyes.

He screwed up his face and gurned, causing her to howl so vociferously that other diners turned round.

'Based on *your* lack of recommendation, do I take it she didn't get the job?'

'Of course she did but sadly, by the time mum got around to contacting her, she'd been snapped up by someone else,' he said glumly. 'It's such a shame.'

'So, to be serious, did you employ Tilly?'

'Yes, there was never any contest. She's settled in really well and she's so efficient. She meets mum's high standards and she looks quite presentable now. Mum handed Dinah a hundred and fifty quid to take Tilly out for a couple of black skirts, white blouses and a pair of more becoming though sensible shoes and while they were out, Dinah marched her into a hairdressing salon for a haircut, maintaining that a smart appearance was most essential when working in service. Tilly was happy and anxious to comply and Dinah reported that Tilly was tickled pink with her new tidy hairstyle *and* it's taken years off her.'

'Is she living in now?'

'Yes, she's next to Dinah and they spend a lot of time together in the evenings. Tilly understands that Dinah's in charge but it doesn't interfere with their friendship. She's a good worker, so it works well.'

'It's exactly the same with Jenny and me and now I've got money in my purse, which is a novelty.'

'Right....so *you* can pay for the meal,' he laughed then quickly added, 'I'm joking. This is *my* treat for your excusing my reprehensible behaviour on New Year's Eve.'

'In that case, I accept but I insist on paying next time,' she answered with an agreeable smile.

To that, Mark made no comment, content with the thought of a further evening with her. She was fun; there was nothing artificial about her *and* she was stunning. He had seen many heads turn as they took their seats and was proud to be her escort. She was different from girls he had previously dated, some of whom were lewd and brash after consuming two or three drinks and her easy manner had contributed to a very pleasant evening.

Back at the flat, she invited him in for coffee.

Jenny was watching television when they walked in but she turned it off to hear about the new restaurant before making her excuses to go to bed.

When Alison returned from the kitchen with two mugs of coffee, Mark tapped on the cushion beside him to indicate where he wanted her to sit. Initially she was hesitant but then thought it better were she not to appear ill-at-ease at such close proximity.

'I've had a lovely evening, thank you,' she said.

'So have I but it's not over yet,' he stated, causing her concern. She felt a sudden rush of adrenalin and wondered what hidden meaning lay in his remark. Although his inopportune comment on New Year's Eve had been excused, it remained in her mind and she hoped he wouldn't treat her invitation for coffee as something more meaningful or suggestive.

She was uncomfortable with her awareness of the way dating progressed in modern times and for her age, she had little experience of men. A romantic at heart, she likened herself to a Jane Austin heroine, worshipped from afar and culminating in her hero on bended knee, requesting her hand in marriage.

She was angry with herself for her stupidity and didn't know what to do next but she wasn't alone in her thoughts. Mark had observed the sudden change in mood and as he recalled his words, he wondered if he might have sent out the wrong message but to try to clarify his words would only result in further embarrassment. Moving swiftly to a different topic he asked, 'Did you like the décor in the restaurant?'

'I loved it. They obviously spared no expense on the furnishings as well as the reproduction French décor and the background music was very pleasant and tasteful without being overbearing.'

'Do you like all kinds of music or just classical?'

'There isn't much I don't like though I do prefer a tune of some sort that I don't always find in present day hits but in the main, I enjoy most music.'

'Have you ever been to the Bridgewater Hall?'

'No, it's on my list of things to do. Have you?'

'A few times. You'd love it and the acoustics are remarkable. I could pick up a programme of forth-coming events and if there's something you fancy, I could take you. It doesn't matter if it's mid-week as the concerts are over quite early.'

Gratefully, she said, 'Thank you, I'd enjoy that.'

'So, how are things now you're back in full swing again?'

'Never better. Everyone's been so thoughtful and I could never repay them for what they've done.'

'Nobody expects repayment. Everyone was happy to help but if you really want to do something, may I suggest you call to play the piano for mum again? She's never stopped talking about your recital.'

'It was hardly a recital. It was nothing more than a few rusty excerpts but if that's what your mother wants, I'd be happy to play for her, in fact nothing would give me greater pleasure.'

'She didn't ask in case you thought her impolite.'

'*Impolite*? What, after all *she*'s done for me? I'd do anything for her Mark and if my music gives her pleasure, then I'll willingly play for her.'

'Good, that's settled. Gosh, look at the time,' he said, jumping up and heading for the door. 'I'll call you when I have a programme for the Bridgewater.'

As she leaned to his side to turn the key, he took hold of her and kissed her tenderly on the lips. 'I'll look forward to the next time,' he said with a smile.

'I can't believe it's so quiet. It's ten o'clock and the phone's only rung twice today. It's *never* like this on a Monday, Alison,' Jenny said.

'Well, it's pouring down, so maybe the would-be clients are hanging on until it stops. It's bad enough being out of work without getting soaked as well.'

Jenny emitted a huge sigh. 'Wouldn't you love to be sitting on a hot beach sipping a cool drink?'

'Mmm....sounds lovely.'

'I'll tell you what we'll do....let's lock up, hurry home, get our passports and clear off. Do you think anyone would miss us for a fortnight? I could just manage a couple of weeks in hot sunny climes.'

'Me too but there's a small problem. I don't have a passport.'

'Right, so we'll have to stay here then. Seriously though, you *should* get a passport. If you wanted a last minute bargain, you'd need one and they take ages to arrive sometimes.'

'But I'm not planning anything just yet so there's little point my having a passport that could expire before I've even used it.'

'They last ten years. Surely, you'll be going away in the next ten years. I'll get an application form the next time I'm in the Post Office. Besides, everyone needs photographic ID nowadays. Listen, we have a client,' Jenny squealed when the telephone rang.

She grabbed the handset but it was her old friend, Antonia who she hadn't seen for ages. 'Happy New Year to you as well,' Alison overheard Jenny say as she sidled into the back office to make a drink.

Alison stared at the grey cloudy sky as she waited for the kettle to boil and reflected on her enjoyable evening with Mark.

She smiled as she recalled his account of the girl wearing the high wedge-soled shoes. When she had related that amusing tale to Jenny, she had howled with laughter at her vision of the rough-looking girl who'd had Mark half-way up the aisle.

When she returned to the office with two mugs of coffee, Jenny was still chatting to her friend.

After the call ended, Jenny told her they had been invited to a party at Antonia's new apartment on the following Friday. 'Stick an entry in the desk diary will you? Just write *Antonia's party.*'

Until a year ago, the two had been inseparable but then they had drifted apart except for the occasional telephone call or luncheon after Antonia had moved in with a guy she'd met at the hospital.

'She's a physiotherapist and she's recently moved into an upmarket apartment nearby so she can avoid the rush hour travelling to work,' Jenny explained.

'So, isn't she with the new boyfriend anymore?'

'Oh no, she never stays long with anybody. There are too many distractions. She enjoys the good life.'

Jenny omitted to tell her Richard had been invited too. That was better kept quiet now that Alison was seeing Mark, she decided. Jenny hadn't the slightest intention of getting involved in their love triangle.

'What's the occasion?' Alison asked.

'It's a house-warming party. She wants everyone to see her flashy new apartment. *Daddy* bought it. He's loaded, so it will be something really special.'

'I'm not used to house parties. What do we take?'

'Booze. That's always welcome at a party. She's invited a few from the hospital too so that should be a welcome change from the usual raucous rabble.'

'Will we be coming home when it's over?' Alison asked anxiously, recalling Jenny's explicit account of some of the parties she'd hosted.

She laughed. 'We'll definitely be coming home. Don't worry; I'll take good care you.'

'In that case, I'll look forward to it,' she replied.

Antonia's party was to be held on the thirty-first of January. How the time had flown since New Year's Day, Alison reflected.

She was writing her diary and flicked back a few pages to see some previous entries. She had neither seen nor heard from Richard since the beginning of January when he had removed the rubbish from her house and he had behaved indifferently towards her then despite her efforts to make conversation. Still, if he was hell-bent on ignoring her, there was little she could do about it. She had no intention of doing the running, she wrote in her diary before slamming it closed.

'You ought to get that published,' Jenny told her as she walked in with her neatly ironed clothes.

'Yeah right!' Alison remarked. 'I can just see the jostling crowds rushing to queue for a first edition of my ramblings about daily mundane matters. It's a pile of rubbish. I first began to write a diary when mum was ill. Every day was very precious then and I recorded things as a keepsake, so I've habitually continued to write it since she died. Rest assured it would be of no interest at all to anyone but me.'

'Wait till after the party!' she chuckled and before Alison had time to even open her mouth, she asked, 'What are you wearing on Friday?'

'That dress I wore when I went out with Mark.'

'Great choice,' she said, still omitting to disclose that Richard might be there.

It was after nine when they arrived at the exclusive apartment building situated beside the waterfront.

'I told you it would be something special,' Jenny said as they admired the impressive reception area. 'Apartments cost an absolute fortune in here.'

Jenny rang the doorbell twice before the door was thrust open and the noise inside was deafening.

'Darling!' Antonia gushed, 'How nice to see you and you must be Alison. Some have arrived already but there's plenty to come yet. Give me your coats. Go in, grab a drink and I'll catch up with you later.'

Jenny passed her the bottles while complimenting her on her short chic new hairstyle.

'Thank you darling. I fancied a complete change but then you know me....always on the lookout for something or someone different.'

The doorbell rang again and Antonia disappeared as Jenny and Alison made their way to the lounge where dozens of guests were chatting in groups.

'*Jenny*!' someone called, '*Over here*!'

When she turned round, she recognised one of her old school friends and hurried over to her, leaving Alison alone, though not for long.

As she made her way to the drinks' table and was about to pour herself a glass of wine, someone said, 'Please, allow me. Do you prefer white or red?' and Alison looked up into the most piercing blue eyes she had ever seen.

'Er....white, thank you,' she answered.

'My name's Simon....Simon Ward and you are?' he enquired in an educated voice.

'I'm Alison....Alison Haythorne.'

'And are you employed at the hospital too, Alison Haythorne?' he asked, staring deeply into her eyes.

'No, I work with Jenny, Antonia's friend.'

'I thought I hadn't seen you before. I would have remembered *you*. Would you like to sit down?'

82

Without awaiting a reply, he ushered her to a sofa and held out his hand for her to be seated. 'So, tell me Alison, have you known Antonia long?'

'No, we've only just met but Jenny's known her for quite a while.'

Two people joined them on the sofa, encouraging Simon to move closer. He curled his arm round the back of the sofa, his fingers coming to rest upon her bare shoulder. 'Do you live nearby?' he questioned with a penetrating gaze that unnerved her.

'No, I live a few miles away,' she said, frantically looking round the room for Jenny.

He moved even closer and Alison felt extremely uncomfortable. Hurriedly, she finished her drink as an excuse to escape but he had no desire to let her go. 'I'll get you a drink in a moment but first I want to know *everything* about you. Just try to relax,' he said, stroking her shoulder and causing her shoulder strap to slip down her arm. 'Are you here with anyone else, apart from Jenny I mean?'

She felt sick and wished she could attract Jenny's attention but Jenny was nowhere in sight.

'Here you are. I've been looking all over for you,' a voice interrupted and she looked up into the eyes of Richard, relieved to see a familiar face. 'There's someone here who's longing to meet you. Will you excuse her?' he asked, looking pointedly at Simon.

'Certainly,' he acknowledged, rising from his seat courteously as she arose. 'It was a great pleasure to meet you. I'll see you later perhaps.'

Alison didn't linger long enough to respond and swiftly moving forward with Richard, she thanked him for his intervention. 'I wasn't aware you'd be here tonight,' she said.

'I didn't expect you here either but it seems it was fortunate I *was* here, assuming I didn't overstep the mark for a second time,' he stated frostily.

Irately Alison retorted, 'What's your problem and why have you suddenly developed *attitude* whenever you see me? I'm extremely grateful to you for rescuing me from that er... moron but why did you bother when you obviously dislike me so intensely? I thought we'd moved beyond New Year's Eve. I'm not going to apologise for the way I spoke to you. If you can't accept you were out of order, that's *your* problem, not *mine*. What Mark said didn't deserve such an outburst from you and the way you referred to me was totally uncalled for.'

'Ah yes, *Mark*,' he stated sarcastically. 'Incidentally, how was the little tête-à-tête at your exclusive restaurant? I imagine *Mark* treated you very well,' he continued with special emphasis on the name.

'For God's sake Richard, grow up! We went for a meal. Must I run my social life by you every time I go anywhere? Are you suddenly my keeper?'

He didn't answer but instead glared icily at her.

'I can't figure you out but thanks for rescuing me and now, if you'll excuse me, I'm here to enjoy the party.' With a toss of the head she walked away to find Jenny, halting en route to pour herself another much needed drink.

'Where've you been hiding? I've been looking for you,' Jenny stated. 'This is Tom Garfield. Tom, this is Alison, my flat-mate. We work together too.'

'I'm pleased to meet you Tom.'

'Likewise,' he replied. 'It's a good party isn't it?'

She choked inwardly. Based on the last half hour, she would be relieved when it was time to go home but she smiled sweetly and agreed with him.

'Have you met anyone nice?' Jenny asked.

'Not yet, though I've spoken to a few people,' she answered without further elaboration of her answer.

'Tom works at the hospital with Antonia and he's a Surgical Registrar. Our paths have crossed when I've visited Antonia at work but we've never had a lengthy discussion before. He's from South Africa.'

'Why would anyone come to rainy England from a temperate country like yours?' Alison asked him.

'We have rain too contrary to popular belief but I came here to study medicine and opted to stay here. Someday I might go back. My family are in South Africa so who knows what the future holds?'

'Who indeed?' she replied, with meaning known only to her. 'Where's the bathroom Jenny?'

'I'll come with you. Excuse me a minute Tom.'

Out of earshot Alison remarked, 'He seems nice.'

'He's a dish *and* he's available!' she told her with a glint in her eye. 'Is there nobody here you fancy?'

'Not yet but I did get caught up with a nauseating slob who was all over me like a rash but I escaped.'

'Oh? Did you manage to get his name?'

'Simon.'

'*Not* Simon the gynaecologist?'

'Simon Ward,' she replied.

'That's the one. He works on ENT....ear, nose and throat.'

'I thought you just said he was a gynaecologist?'

'That's what everyone calls him but I'm sure you can work it out for yourself. You were lucky to get away. Many have failed. "*No,*" doesn't exist in *his* vocabulary. He was in the lift one morning when I called to meet Antonia for lunch. That brief episode was more than enough. I bet he wasn't invited here. He'll gatecrash any party. He's just a creep.'

'You can say that again.'

Alison said nothing of Richard's intervention, nor did she mention she was aware of his presence.

'Are you *really* enjoying yourself?' Jenny asked.

'Yes, there appears to be a decent crowd here. It's just a shame I don't know anyone.'

'You do, you know Simon,' she laughed. 'When we go back, I'll introduce you to some of my many friends of bygone times. They're a friendly bunch.'

As the evening progressed, Alison met several of Jenny's friends. Staff-nurse Heather Jones, who had attended to her mother, recognised her and made a point of going to chat to her. 'It's good to see you. How are things at home?' she asked diplomatically.

'Mum died in October. It was very sad but she'd suffered long enough. It was time to let her go.'

'That's a sensible attitude. I just wish all relatives could see it that way. Are you enjoying the party? I would have come across earlier but you were busy with Simon so I thought it better not to intrude.'

'I wish you had,' she grimaced.

'Poor Simon. He's totally clueless where women are concerned. He really thinks he's God's Gift and he comes on to all the girls but he never manages to find a regular girlfriend so he'll be single forever if he doesn't mend his ways which is a shame because he's a well-respected doctor. He's also an excellent conversationalist and he's well connected too. He'd make some woman a good husband if he could just restrain his overzealous sexual appetite but I'm not going to tell him. I have to work with him. I take it you've heard his nickname?' she laughed.

'Yes but not until after I'd escaped,' she smirked.

When two young men approached and introduced themselves to Alison, Heather took her leave. Then within seconds, the two men became four and soon, the previously unknown young woman had become the major attraction, completely encircled by a host of young men, all vying for her attention.

As she continued to laugh and joke with the ever increasing crowd, she caught a glimpse of Richard, standing stony-faced in the background, far enough away to be distant from the group, yet close enough to eavesdrop on the interactive exchanges that were taking place.

As she finished her remaining drop of wine, her empty glass didn't go unnoticed as numerous offers were made to replenish it. In fact all the young men were attentive to her needs and when ultimately she took her leave, one or two pursued her, handing her a business card, complete with telephone number.

'You're very popular,' Jenny remarked as Alison sat down. 'I went for a drink and could hardly fight my way past all your admirers.'

'I can't imagine why. One minute I was alone and the next, I was completely surrounded.'

'If you'd seen yourself in that dress, you'd know.'

In a tone of utter panic she screeched, 'Don't tell me it's caught up in my knickers. I'd die!'

'No, you fool. It's a fabulous and very sexy dress. That's why they're all falling over you *and* you're a new kid on the block. They know the others. If you play your cards right tonight, you could be running off into the sunset with a wealthy doctor.'

'I'm quite happy as I am thank you,' she retorted indignantly. 'I'm having a great time and that's all I came to do. I didn't come to find a husband.'

'I did,' Jenny laughed. 'It's time I found a regular bloke. What do you think of Tom? Don't you think he's great? He wants to see me again so he's going to give me a call to arrange something.'

'He's charming and handsome too. Yes, I thought he had an endearing manner. Where is he now?'

'Talking to Richard. Did you know he was here?'

'Yes, I saw him earlier. He was a bit grumpy and we ended up having a few words. I wasn't going to mention it until later, but since you….'

'Alison,' she cut in. 'He's jealous if anyone pays you attention, like that doctor you were mauling.'

'*I wasn't*!' she protested angrily. '*He* was all over *me*! I was trying to get away when Richard rescued me and I told him I was grateful. What did he say?'

'Nothing at all. I'm more perceptive than you are. He's crazy about you. You must know that.'

'Well I know what I see and hear, and what I see is a petulant young man and what I clearly hear are sarcastic comments I wouldn't make to somebody I liked and he was very rude about Mark.'

'That's my point. He knows Mark took you out a few days ago because he called me at the office the next day. It's obvious Mark's trying to score points and remove Richard from the running as Mark told Richard he was taking you out.'

'Richard hasn't contacted me once since we went to dinner weeks ago. Mark however *did* invite me out so am I to turn down all other invitations I get? You're wrong. He has *no* feelings for me and while we're on the subject of Richard, you knew he'd be here tonight but you didn't tell me did you?'

'Alright, I knew he was invited because Antonia told me but I didn't know if he'd come and I wasn't prepared to get entangled in your love triangle.'

'You're at it again! I'm not *in* a love triangle and I just wish everyone would leave me be. I'm sick of the lot of you.'

She was on the verge of moving away as Antonia appeared with a bottle of Champagne.

'It's a fab party, isn't it? Where are your glasses? It's fizz time. You'll definitely have to come again Alison. You stole the show tonight. Everyone wants to know who you are,' she disclosed while pouring Champagne into each of their glasses.

'I guess it's because I'm new and I'd like to thank you for inviting me. It's a great apartment.'

'Thanks. Have you had a good look round?'

'Oh no, I wouldn't presume....'

'Codswallop! Clare, be a darling and show Alison the apartment while I finish pouring the Champers.'

With a broad smile that lit up her face, a stunning blonde approached. '*You're* Alison? I've heard a lot about you. Come with me and we'll have a chat as I show you round. Are you coming too Jenny?'

She jumped up instantly. 'You bet I am!'

Compared to the flat shared by Jenny and Alison, Antonia's was huge with three spacious bedrooms, two of which had en-suite facilities, in addition to a further guest bathroom. The grand open plan dining hall, flanking an ultra-modern kitchenette and fully equipped study, led to the lounge where the French windows opened to a patio, overlooking the water.

It was superbly furnished and Alison admired the unusual paintings, some of which had been painted by Antonia, Clare advised her.

'I'd forgotten she used to paint,' Jenny said.

'She still attends classes but I believe it's become more of a social gathering than an art lesson. Quite a few of her artistic friends are here tonight. I don't know if you've ever met Paul but he's here. He's a brilliant artist. He's one who's succeeded in making a very lucrative living in painting. He gets loads of commissions, often from abroad, so he travels a lot. He's worth a fortune, he's well respected in the art world and he's such an unassuming guy.'

'Paul?' Jenny said pricking up her ears in interest.

'Paul Trantor. Don't you know him?'

'No, I don't. Introduce me; I like a talented guy.'

'Jenny....you like *all* guys,' Clare reminded her in a dry laconic manner and the three of them laughed.

When they returned, Paul was nowhere in sight.

'I'll bring him over if or when he surfaces,' Clare promised. 'I'm sure he was still here a few minutes ago,' she added as she left to join Antonia.

'Do Clare and Antonia both work at the hospital?' Alison asked.

'Heavens, no! Clare couldn't work in a hospital. She's a solicitor in the city.'

Their discussion was interrupted by a young man leaning towards them. 'Alison, please excuse me. I didn't want to leave without saying how enjoyable it was to have met you. You have my card with my number and I hope you'll give me a call. Mine's the blue one,' he laughed, alluding to his awareness she had received others. 'I'd very much like to see you again. Perhaps we could have dinner one evening?'

On a smile she replied, 'I might just do that.'

He smiled back at her. 'I hope you do. Goodnight then, and please don't leave it too long to call me.'

'Wow, what a dish! Who's that?' Jenny probed.

'I haven't a clue.'

'What do you mean, you haven't a clue? You've let him go without knowing who he is?'

Impassively she answered, 'He's the *blue* card.'

'What blue card?'

'Well, when I was the centre of attention earlier, three young men gave me their business cards and asked me to call them. He gave me the blue one.'

'Where are they then? Find them and let's have a gander who he is. Hurry up, I'm dying to know.'

Alison opened her bag and deliberately took her time in removing the cards from her purse.

Jenny couldn't wait any longer and snatched the cards from her hand. Wide-eyed, she stared intently at the blue card. 'I do *not* believe what I'm seeing!' she gasped. 'Tell me….how do you do it?'

'Do what? Why, who is he?'

'Only the well-heeled and talented artist, Mr. Paul Trantor and he wants to take you out to dinner. You really do have all the luck.'

Alison was propped up in bed, writing in her diary about the action-packed evening when Jenny tapped on her door. 'Are you awake? Can I come in? I've brought you a coffee.'

'Yes,' she called, grateful for the welcome drink.

Jenny groaned, 'I think I had one too many at the party. I feel like something the cat's dragged in.'

'Well, I don't feel terrific either, in fact I was just writing about how unpopular I must be with all the other girls last night. I managed to commandeer all the eligible men to the exclusion of everyone else. I had words with both you and Richard and on top of all that, the evening culminated in my stealing the attention of the very man you wanted to meet.'

'Don't talk daft. It's not your fault that you're the most popular girl in the world. I probably hate you just a little bit but you're still my best friend. He is gorgeous though. Are you going to call him today?'

'Which one?' she asked with a supercilious laugh, prompting Jenny to throw a cushion at her.

'He seemed keen for you to call but then if you'd rather not, I could. He might turn his affections to me then,' she joked with a jaunty shake of the head.

'I don't mind. I'm not interested *really*. I was just being polite. I didn't want to embarrass him.'

'Don't lie to me. I bet you've made some cryptic comment about him in your diary. Show me.'

'No,' she laughed, her cheeks turning pink.

'*I knew it*! You fancy him don't you?'

'Well, I suppose I wouldn't refuse an evening out. It could be fun.'

'*Especially when he takes you back to his flat to show you his proverbial etchings*!' Jenny screeched as she rolled on the bed, laughing at her own joke. 'Seriously, you should go. Leave it a couple of days before calling and then you don't appear too eager.'

'I'm sure you're right but if I leave it too long, he might think I'm not interested. I don't know what I should do. I'm not used to making the first move.'

'He won't think that at all and absence makes the heart grow fonder. I bet he's lying on his bed now, clutching a pillow and calling, "Oh Alison, Alison, wherefore art thou Alison?"' she yelled theatrically before bursting into uncontrollable laughter.

'Just zip it! You can't be serious about anything,' Alison snapped but as Jenny was mopping the tears from her eyes, Alison joined in till they both ached.

It was Sunday and they had nothing planned for the day. 'Let's drive to Cheshire,' Jenny proposed. 'It's lovely countryside and lots of places serve lunch.'

'Good idea,' Alison replied enthusiastically.

After enjoying a leisurely drive, by accident, they happened upon an eighteenth century country pub with a roaring log fire, where a multitude of highly polished items of brassware hung from the original hand-crafted beams. The simple hand-written menu offered an extensive selection of wholesome locally produced food that was to exceed expectations.

After lunch, they relaxed peacefully, mesmerised by the flickering flames in the black iron fire grate oblivious of everything and everyone around them.

It had been an enjoyable afternoon, Alison stated as they returned home.

They spent the remainder of the day playing CDs and dozing on the sofa and would have remained so but for the telephone ringing which aroused them.

As Jenny went to take the call, Alison went into the kitchen and quickly returned with two coffees. Jenny was still on the telephone. She gesticulated to Alison to hand one of the mugs to her, suggesting it was to be a lengthy conversation.

'You'll never guess who that was,' Jenny said. 'It was Tom. He's taking me out on Friday.'

'That's great. Where to?'

'He wouldn't say. It's a surprise but he told me to get dressed up and be hungry. I'm so excited now. He's picking me up at seven-thirty.'

'Well, for once, try to be ready on time and don't forget I won't be about to be reaching and fetching for you. All being well, I'll be on the train by then.'

'Of course. I'd forgotten you were going to your grandparents' house for the weekend.'

'It also means I won't be under your feet when he brings you home.'

'He seems keen. He's been trying to get through all day. I forgot to check the answerphone so I'll do it now in case we've missed any more calls.'

There had been six missed calls. No message had been left on the first two. The third was a message from Tom, stating he would call back later, as was the fourth and on the penultimate call, again there was no message. The final call however brought a shiver to Alison's spine as she listened intently.

'Hi Alison. Paul Trantor here. I called Antonia for your number. I wanted to say it was great to meet you on Friday and confirm what I mentioned about getting together. I didn't want you to believe it was the drink doing the talking, in fact I only had a few. I'd really like to see you. I've thought of little else since Friday so please, give me a call. Bye.'

For several moments, she didn't speak and it was Jenny who broke the silence. 'Right lady, call him. He's made a move so you've no excuse now.'

Jenny plumped up the cushions on the settee and promptly sat down, making herself comfortable and eager to listen to every word.

'*You can get lost*! No *way* am I making that call with you in the room, you....'

'Alison....I do believe you were about to utter an expletive,' Jenny interposed with a piercing laugh.

'Yes. I'm not phoning Paul with you here. I don't eavesdrop when you talk to your boyfriend.'

Jenny screeched with laughter. 'So he's suddenly your boyfriend now?'

'*Get out*!' she yelled, throwing a cushion at her.

Alison sat quietly after Jenny left the room. With her eyes closed and breathing deeply, she aimed to compose herself and disperse her butterflies.

She dialled his number. 'Hello, is that you Paul?' she asked nervously as he answered. 'It's Alison.'

'Hi there! Thanks for returning my call. I do hope you didn't mind me calling Antonia. How are you?'

'Fine thanks. Listen, I'm sorry I didn't call sooner but we've been out most of the afternoon and I've only just picked up your message. I did intend to.'

'Have you been anywhere nice?'

'We went for a drive into Cheshire and stopped at an old pub for lunch. It was lovely.'

'Well, I'm happy to hear you've been making the most of your weekend. I've just been idling around, mainly thinking of you and hoping you'd call me.'

She felt a rush of adrenaline. 'Er....I'll take that as a compliment. Thank you Paul,' she stuttered.

He laughed boyishly before saying, 'The reason I called was to ask if you'd anything arranged for the weekend. I'm going to London on Saturday to meet an agent about an exhibition planned for spring and I wondered if you'd care to join me? The meeting shouldn't last for more than two hours and then I'd be free for the rest of the day. Before you refuse, I promise it would be totally above-board. We could travel back late on Saturday and see a show first.'

'I'm sorry Paul. I've made plans for the weekend. I'm visiting my grandparents who live in Brighton. It was arranged two weeks ago and as I've already refused their invitation twice, I can't change it now. I'm going down on Friday evening.'

She didn't state whether she would have accepted had it been possible, therefore Paul didn't know if that was a polite way of refusing his invitation.

Feeling dejected he said, 'Don't worry. It was just an idea. Maybe we can get together at a later date.'

'That would be nice,' she responded, immediately regretting her answer. Why couldn't she have given a more appeasing or convincing reply, she chastised herself instead of coming out with the stock answer for, 'Thanks but no thanks!'?

'Right then, you enjoy your weekend and I'll look forward to talking to you soon. Bye Alison.'

When Jenny reappeared she said unhappily, 'I've just blown it with Paul. I can be such a buffoon at times. I doubt he believed a single word I said,' and she went on to relate the entire conversation to her.

'Well, *you* know it's true. It's just a pity that Paul enquired about the weekend you're going away. It's like waiting for a bus. You wait an hour, then three arrive. It's Sod's Law but I'm sure he'll call again.'

'I can't imagine there's *anything* more exasperating than trying to sort out train times and ticket prices!' Alison shrieked, banging down the telephone. 'I've made loads of calls already. There's no direct train and on *one* route quoted, I'd have to change *three times*. Can you believe that? Furthermore, the price varies by fifty pounds depending on the provider.'

'It'll sort itself out,' Jenny said sympathetically.

'But it won't. *I* need to do it and some people are very rude. They keep you on hold while they talk to another caller and when they deign to come back to you, they've got it all wrong. I could scream!'

'I'll put the kettle on and make some calls for you later. Between us, we'll get a good deal, you'll see.'

'I won't hold my breath. So, have you heard from Tom about where he's taking you on Friday?'

'No, he still won't tell me and he's adamant that I won't prise it out of him.'

'It's nice to have a surprise. It's all part and parcel of the intrigue especially when you have a new guy. I wish I had. I seem to have problems with all mine. Richard nearly chokes if he has to speak to me and Mark is doubtless goading him, hence *his* attention towards me and lastly, I've managed to offend Paul Trantor. I don't know what's wrong with me.'

'When we get home tonight, we'll talk. Perhaps I can help boost your confidence but you must agree to accept criticism in the way it's meant and not get annoyed, otherwise I won't say a word.'

'I will, I promise.'

'Right, forget it. That's an order from the boss.'

Following a slow start, it developed into a chaotic morning but by midday, the callers had eased off.

Alison took advantage of the lull and went for the sandwiches for lunch. Moments later, Paul Trantor sauntered in, much to Jenny's surprise.

'Hello Paul,' she said. 'Alison's just nipped to the sandwich shop. She'll be back in a minute.'

'Er....have we met?' he queried, looking surprised that she knew who he was and why he was there.

'At Antonia's party. Alison and I are flat-mates.'

'Of course....how stupid of me. You're Jenny.'

'I am.'

He hesitated a moment. 'So then you're probably aware I spoke to Alison yesterday?'

'Yes, she was delighted to receive your call and to be honest, she was gutted that she'll be away this weekend at her grandparents' house in Brighton.'

'Well, if we're being honest, I didn't know if that was an excuse because she didn't want to see me.'

'On the contrary, Alison really *is* going, *if* she can get a train. It's a bit of a sore point at the moment. She's been on the phone for hours. It's an absolute nightmare trying to sort out train timetables.'

'Isn't she driving down?'

'She doesn't drive. She hasn't taken her test yet.'

'Right. So when is she going?'

'Friday, after work. She needs to get an early start because it takes hours with all the changes. It'll be midnight when she arrives if she leaves at six.'

'Listen, don't mention that I've been here Jenny. I need to make a few calls and I'll be back within the hour. Promise me you'll forget this conversation.'

'What conversation?' she grinned. 'Go on! She'll be back any second.'

Jenny felt pleased with herself. All she had to do was keep a straight face when Alison returned.

'What a queue!' Alison griped when she returned. 'I thought I'd *never* get served. You'll never guess who I saw, looking like the cat that got the cream.'

'Who?' Jenny asked, hoping it wasn't Paul.

She grimaced. 'The irresistible womaniser, Simon Ward. When I think how he made my flesh crawl.'

'Ah, but remember he's a doctor. That alone gets him women. Be honest, you found him attractive at first before you knew what he was like. Correct?'

'I suppose....'

'So that's what he relies on, his charisma. Some girls will do a turn for anyone.'

'They must be desperate to sleep with him, that's all I can say! I prefer a well-mannered guy who will wine and dine me and show me some respect.'

'Like Paul Trantor?' she asked, winking over her shoulder at Paul who had just walked in quietly.

'I know nothing about Paul Trantor. I only spoke to him for a few minutes but he seemed nice and as you were very quick to point out, he *is* rather dishy. I'd have liked to get to know him better.'

'There's no time like the present. Paul's standing right behind you. I'll clear off and leave you to it.'

'Right....and pigs might fly,' she laughed.

'Hi Alison,' Paul interrupted before she could say anything she might later regret. 'I hope it's okay to call in at your work place.'

Alison whipped round on her chair but before she had chance to reply, Jenny whispered, 'I'm off out. See you later,' and she gave Paul a knowing wink.

'It's not a problem, me being here?' he asked.

'Not at all but I'm surprised. How did you know where I worked?' Answering her own question she nodded and said, '*Antonia*' and they both laughed.

'Do you mind that she told me? I had to beg. She refused at first but then when I asked where Jenny worked, that amused her, as it was obvious I knew you worked together.'

'I'm glad she told you and I'm pleased to see you because I do need to explain something. I really *am* visiting my grandparents. That wasn't an excuse.'

'Such a thought never crossed my mind, though if you believe that, you'll believe anything,' he stated. 'I wondered whether you were trying to protect my feelings so I needed to see you to be sure. I'd rather have my feelings dented a little now than continue making a fool of myself, so here I am, in the flesh.'

100

'But I still can't see you. I won't be here.'

'Are you driving there?' he asked, not wishing to betray Jenny's confidence.

'I don't drive yet so I'm travelling by train.'

Paul scowled. 'Oh, surely not. It's an *awfully* long journey by train. It takes forever. You have to keep changing. You did say Brighton didn't you?'

'Yes, why?'

'Because Brighton is the worst place in the whole world to travel to by train. Listen, why don't I drive you there?' he said, and as she opened her mouth to protest he continued, 'I have to be in London by ten o'clock Saturday morning so I must leave early but if I travelled down Friday night, I could drop you at your grandparents' house, stay at a Bed and Breakfast and then I wouldn't have to set off as early on Saturday to get into London. I could also drive you home Sunday. I hate driving long distances alone so you'd be doing me a big favour if you accepted.'

'But you told me you were coming back Saturday so that's two night's accommodation to pay for. I'm sorry; I couldn't possibly take advantage like that.'

'I said I'd be returning Saturday because I didn't want you to feel uneasy when I invited you. I never do the return trip in the day. It's too tiring. I always stay there overnight but I was prepared to make an exception had you been willing to join me. So, is it to be a comfy car, door to door with good company, or a miserable train with strangers, sitting about on platforms waiting for connections?'

'Thank you. It's a very kind offer and I accept but only if you're sure and I'll pay half to the petrol.'

101

'You'll do no such thing.'

'Then I shall travel be train.'

'Alright, you win. We'll sort it out. I'm delighted we're travelling together because I'm really looking forward to finding out everything about you.'

'You might be sorry about that. Mine isn't such a happy story but you're welcome to hear it.'

They continued to discuss his work, his interests and his aspirations for the future.

'I was always led to believe that art was a volatile occupation,' she remarked.

'You're right, it is. Many fail and make nothing.'

'If that's the case, what's your secret of success?'

'I believe you need a lot of luck and talent too of course but above all you need somebody to believe in you enough to back you and market your work. I've been fortunate. When you look back at the Old Masters, very few made a decent living, if anything, yet after they died, their paintings became priceless collectables once the critics began to appreciate the incredible talent. It's all about recognition and keen marketing. That's it in nutshell,' he said and staring intently into her eyes added, 'Please join me tonight for a drink and we can talk about you instead.'

Alison was rarely impulsive but there was something about him that intrigued her. 'Okay,' she said. 'I can be ready by eight but I mustn't be late home.'

She jotted down her address and gave it to him.

'Scout's honour, you'll be home by ten-thirty.'

When Jenny returned she carped, 'Well, that took a while and a half. I've tramped past that door more than a dozen times. I almost died of hypothermia!'

'Sorry. We started talking....you know how it is.'

'Never mind that. I've been dying to get in to find out what's going on. Are you two an item now?'

Alison giggled. Jenny liked to know every minute detail. 'Paul's driving me to Brighton on Friday.'

'Is he? So does that mean what I think it means? Are you spending the weekend with him?'

'*No*! I'll be staying at my grandparents' house but Paul will bring me home on Sunday.'

'Brilliant. How did you manage to swing that?'

'He offered. He's going to London on Friday now so he'll drive me to Brighton and stay in a Bed and Breakfast, travel to London on Saturday and collect me on Sunday *and* he's taking me out tonight.'

'Oh, be careful! Put a foot wrong tonight and you might end up wrecking the weekend.'

'I won't wreck anything. Do you think he's cute?'

'I think he's wealthy. That's better than cute.'

'I can't decide what to wear tonight Jenny. I don't want to appear overdressed when we're only going for a drink. What about the cashmere suit?'

'That would be perfect. You'll look very elegant and sophisticated and even if Paul's in casual gear, you won't look out of place.'

When she reappeared with five minutes to spare, she looked stunning. 'That looks better with higher heel shoes and your hair looks lovely too. He'll be impressed and very proud to be your escort.'

'I feel nervous,' she confessed. 'This feels like a proper date. Somehow it was different with Richard and Mark because they're more like family.'

When the bell rang, Alison jumped up anxiously.

'Stay where you are and calm down,' Jenny said reassuringly. 'You'll be fine. I'll let him in.'

When Paul caught sight of Alison, his eyes lit up. 'Wow, you look terrific!' he exclaimed. 'I wish I'd had a wash and shave now.'

She smiled at his remark, without failing to notice he was dressed in expensive casual yet smart attire.

'The perfect couple,' Jenny stated. 'Go and enjoy yourselves while I stay here alone for my sins.'

'Where would you like to go?' he asked her as he started the car.

'I don't know. I'm not familiar with the area. I've only lived here a few weeks.'

'We'll go to the Red Lion then. It's quiet there.'

'This is a very nice car Paul. Is it a BMW?'

He laughed. 'No, it happens to be a Porsche. Do I take it you're not very knowledgeable about cars?'

'The word you're looking for is *clueless*. I know *nothing* about cars. You see what happens if I try to act intelligent?'

'Everyone must learn about the various types and there are so many on the market nowadays....'

'Don't patronise me Paul,' she remarked, feeling embarrassed. 'There's no excuse whatsoever for my failure to recognise a Porsche. I feel really stupid!'

'Don't worry,' Paul laughed. When you go to buy your first *Roller*, I'll come along with you to make sure the dealer doesn't palm you off with a *Mini*!'

He drove into the car park of a modern stone-built pub. 'You'll love the interior. The view through the rear windows is incredible. Assuming we can find a suitable table, you'll see thousands of lights. I had a superb meal on my first visit and they have quite an extensive menu.'

'And I believed artists never ate.'

'Many don't because they can't afford to and the more fortunate simply eat junk food. I've had more than my fair share of rubbish over the years.'

'Over the years? You sound as old as Methuselah when you put it like that.'

'I'm twenty-eight and never been kissed. Look, a table by the window....let's claim it before it goes.'

She was shocked to learn of his age. Paul neither looked nor acted like a man of twenty-eight. Alison wondered how he would react when he discovered she was only seventeen, eleven years his junior.

Paul, of rugged though distinguished appearance was around six feet tall and characteristic of many males in his profession, his straight blonde hair was shoulder length. A slight quiff fell over his forehead and deep laughter lines edged his blue eyes.

'Isn't that striking?' he said, referring to the view.

'Yes, it is. You can see for miles. I've never seen as many lights and just look at all those stars.'

'There's a clear sky so we have a perfect evening to appreciate the view. Right, what would you like to drink?' he asked, pulling out her chair.

'Orange juice please.'

'Orange juice? Are you sure about that? Are you alright?' he asked with concern.

'Yes of course I am. I hardly ever touch alcohol.'

'Well, please correct me if I'm wrong but I seem to recall you putting a few away at Antonia's party.

I was the one to re-fill your empty glass *and* I saw you with other drinks, as well as Champagne!'

Indignantly she asked, 'Were you watching me?'

'In one way I was. I was beguiled by your beauty, intrigued by your innocence and fascinated by your feminine charm,' he teased. 'Have a proper drink.'

'*No*!' she exclaimed, 'I won't....I can't. Ask me again in a few weeks' time and then I will.'

'Do tell me what's wrong....please. Are you afraid I'll take advantage if you have an alcoholic drink?'

Alison was digging herself deeper and deeper into a hole and causing him to become more concerned. 'Alright, I'll tell you. If I have an alcoholic drink I might get arrested. I'm under age. Satisfied now?'

His mouth fell open in disbelief, then he laughed.

Humiliated and embarrassed, she retorted, 'I fail to see why you find *that* so entertaining.'

'Oh, Alison, I'm so relieved. I thought there was something wrong, the way you reacted. I'm sorry.' He leaned towards her and brushed his lips against her forehead affectionately. 'Please don't be angry. I didn't mean to laugh. So, you're eighteen soon?'

'Yes and will I be glad. Each time I go out, I face the same humiliation. I might look eighteen but that doesn't change the date on my birth certificate.'

'Well, I'd have put you in your early twenties and the likelihood of being asked for ID must be slim.'

'Maybe but imagine the disgrace were I asked. I'd be breaking the law. It's easier to refuse a drink.'

'Unless you're with someone as persistent as me. I didn't mean to upset you. It never occurred to me that you were under age,' he said, taking her hand.

'Well, it could be said I've had a tough time with adult responsibilities from an early age. I feel older but in a few weeks' time it won't matter anymore.'

'Am I forgiven? Pretty please?' he pleaded.

'Yes, so may I have an orange juice now please?'

He leaped to his feet and hurried to the bar. When he returned with the drinks he whispered, 'Perhaps you're not eighteen but you can definitely teach the women here a thing or two about fashion. You look amazing and that's a fabulous suit you're wearing.'

Paul placed the drinks on the table and pulling his chair closer to hers he said, 'I want to hear all about you because you're a very intriguing young lady.'

He listened to her disclosure without interruption, disturbed by her story yet impressed at her ability to have coped so well in the face of such adversity.

She found him to be an excellent listener. Though she didn't habitually discuss her personal life with strangers, she found herself pouring out her history to this man, with whom until today, she had barely exchanged more than a dozen words but she didn't regard him as a stranger as he showed true concern.

'Are you close to you grandparents in Brighton?'

'Not very. I rarely see them. I talk to them on the phone but distance is the great divide. They weren't around when I was little as they moved to Brighton and we couldn't afford to visit. Mum missed them. They'd visit us every so often but as granddad grew older, he didn't like driving such long distances.'

'Your other grandparents? Are they still alive?'

Although she had deliberately omitted to mention them, since the question had been posed, she felt no requirement to defend them and when she revealed how shoddily they had behaved Paul was disgusted. 'Listen, I don't think about them because I've never known them,' she stated. 'They'll answer at the day of reckoning if they haven't already done so. For all I know, they could have been dead for years.'

'And you never felt like finding them to tell them what you thought of their behaviour?'

'You can't be serious. I wouldn't dream of giving them the satisfaction. Besides, I never knew where they lived so I couldn't even if I wanted to.'

Changing the subject he asked, 'So what are you planning for your eighteenth birthday?'

'Nothing. I haven't told anyone. I've only just got a job so I can't afford much. Jenny and I might go out for a meal if I decide to tell her.'

'Am I not invited too?' he asked optimistically.

'We'll see. You might have moved on by then.'

'Not a chance,' he said with an affectionate smile, kissing her cheek tenderly. 'I'm going nowhere.'

Alison was comfortable with Paul's easy manner and didn't feel embarrassed when he kissed her as it was simply a spontaneous act at certain opportune moments, displaying amity as opposed to passion.

Suddenly he exclaimed, 'Have you seen the time? It's almost eleven o'clock. I'm so sorry!'

'It's okay, I have a key but we should leave now.'

When they arrived, Paul walked her to her door. 'I'd like to call you tomorrow,' he whispered.

Shyly she said, 'Yes, I'd like that,' and before she could speak another word, Paul engulfed her in his arms and kissed her with deep passion. The strength of his body and the warmth of his breath electrified her and she responded with equal ardour.

Their embrace lasted several moments and when they finally moved apart he gazed tenderly into her eyes. 'Thank you for a wonderful evening,' he said and gave her a shorter kiss on the lips. 'Goodnight.'

Alison unlocked the door and went inside and for some moments, she leaned quietly against the door, panting breathlessly before removing her shoes and tiptoeing to the lounge, only to be met by Jenny.

'What time do you call this? You'll be in trouble with the boss if you're late for work tomorrow.'

She grinned. 'In that case, I'd best be off to bed.'

'Oh no you don't. You're not going anywhere till I've heard every last detail after I've waited up.'

'Well if I'm not going to bed, I'm having a mug of coffee so are you having one too?'

As she made her way into the kitchen, Jenny was hot on her heels. 'Hurry up Alison, don't keep me in suspense, how was he? Was he terrific or what?'

'He's fantastic and he made me realise I've never had a proper date before. We had an amazing time.'

'Oh God, what are you telling me? Paul didn't try anything did he?'

'*Jenny*!'

'Well, someone has to look out for you Alison.'

'I'm more than capable of taking care of myself. I don't need any advice from you thanks very much.'

'So, what did you talk about?'

'Mainly me. He wanted to know everything about me and so I told him everything.'

'*Everything*? You told him you're a *virgin*?'

Alison gave her a threatening glare. 'I'm going to my room if you don't stop! You've got sex on the brain. Of course we didn't discuss things like that.'

'I bet you thought about it though,' she grinned.

'I might have but *thinking* and *doing* are two very different things, not that *you'd* know.'

'That may be so but you're the one missing out.'

'I beg to differ,' Alison countered snootily. 'Until tonight, I hadn't met the right person.'

'*Oh. Until tonight*! So *he's* going to be the one?'

'I'm not having this conversation. I'm off to bed.'

'I only wanted to know if he'll be your first. Your first is the one you remember.'

'Well, I certainly won't be telling *you* if he is and I doubt *you* can remember far enough back in time to *your* first, so get off my case!'

'I've touched a nerve.... You're crazy about him,' she squealed and Alison attempted to stifle a laugh. 'That's it. You *are* crazy about him. I knew it. Are the feelings mutual do you think?'

'Early indications would suggest so. We really hit it off. Seriously, he's a great guy. I like him a lot.'

'Did you snog?'

'That's a horrible word. He kissed me goodnight.'

'Peck or passion?'

Bashfully she replied, 'Passion.'

'And did you reciprocate passionately?'

'Goodnight, Jenny. I'll see you in the morning.'

'Is that all I get when I've waited up all night?'

'No one forced you. *Goodnight*!' she repeated in raised voice and left the room, clutching her mug of coffee and with a self-righteous smile on her face.

110

4

'That must be the busiest morning we've had since I started work here. There's been a bus load through already!' Alison exclaimed breathlessly as the door closed behind the last person. 'Talk about bedlam! I'll stick the kettle on. I'm gagging for a drink.'

'Me too. Maybe people are popping in to find out what happened last night between you and Paul.'

'Shut up and give it a rest will you. You've heard all you're going to hear.'

'That's not fair. I tell you all *my* intimate details.'

'Don't you mean you ram them down my throat? I *never* ask *any* personal questions about whether or not you've slept with them,' she retorted.

'Well, according to you, I sleep with everyone on the planet and it's not true. There were at least *two* guys at Antonia's party I haven't slept with….yet,' she made known and they both laughed.

'That has to be Mark and Tom,' Alison replied.

'I was discounting Tom, and Mark wasn't there. I was referring to that slime-bag Simon Ward and to Paul if you must know. I *have* slept with Mark but it was a long time ago.'

'A long time ago? You're only twenty-two.'

'Well, I started early, so there's not much point in stopping now.'

'You might have to soon if there's nobody left.'

Jenny shrugged her shoulders arrogantly. 'When I run out of options, you'll be the first to know.'

It was affable banter. They did it most of the time but there was never any ill-feeling. Each knew the other's boundaries and if one tried to cross too far, the other would call a halt.

'Have you heard from Tom again?' asked Alison.

'Not yet. Are you seeing Paul again this week?'

'I doubt it but he's supposed to be calling me later today. We haven't made plans for the weekend yet.'

'Do you think you'll see him over the weekend?'

'It's unlikely. He'll be in London and I doubt my grandparents would be happy if I met up with Paul when they haven't seen me for ages.'

'Has Paul any family?'

'I didn't ask but there'll be time to find out about him on our long journey.'

'I hope there are no skeletons in his closet. By the way, I forgot to give you this,' she said, removing a brown envelope from her bag. 'I picked it up when I was trailing up and down the pavement yesterday, while you and Paul were whispering sweet nothings as I almost froze to death outside.'

She let the remark pass unchecked. 'What is it?'

'A passport application. Fill it in now and you can get your photos from the booth two doors away.'

'I don't see why I must do it now,' she grumbled.

'*Everyone* has a passport. If you wait till you need one, you probably won't get it in time. The Passport Office is busy during the summer. One of the guys at Antonia's party does a booze cruise every month to Calais and he said he'd take us one weekend but you won't be able to go without a passport.'

'Alright, if it shuts you up, I'll fill it in tonight.'

'Fill it in now and then it's done.'

'I can't really afford the fee,' she protested.

'You can pay it with the train fare you've saved.'

'But I've promised to pay half to the petrol.'

'That's a mere fraction of what you'd have to fork out for a rail ticket. Whip out and get your photos. I could do with a damn good belly laugh.'

'Why, what do you mean?'

She sniggered. 'It's obvious you've never seen a passport photograph. They're always vile.'

As she went out she snarled, 'You won't leave me alone till I do but it's an absolute waste of money.'

When she returned, she looked harassed. 'Do they knowingly make those contraptions complicated so nobody can understand them? Three women tried to help and still we couldn't follow the instructions, so I enquired in the café where the owner said he was fed up of people asking for help. After all that, just look at them,' she said, hurling the photographs on Jenny's desk. 'I look like Frankenstein's Bride!'

Jenny scrutinised them and howled with laughter, collapsing on her desk in hysterics, while stamping her feet alternately as she guffawed.

'Alright, *enough*!' Alison bellowed, snatching the photographs from her hand. 'They're not *that* bad.'

'I don't know. If I were on border control, no one looking like that would enter *my* country,' she said.

'Well, you wanted a good laugh so you got what you wanted at my expense,' she snarled.

Ignoring her petulance Jenny said, 'You could get Dr. Martin to sign that they're a true likeness. It has to be someone of standing who knows you well.'

'Well, if he's prepared to sign that I look like that, then he's a liar. Nobody looks like *that*,' she yelled.

'You do. The camera doesn't lie,' she guffawed. 'I thought they were quite good actually.'

'Just shut it. I'm going for my lunch break,' she snapped, ramming the photographs in her shoulder bag. She rushed through the door with the sound of Jenny's continuing laughter ringing in her ears.

She returned an hour later with a pile of shopping bags. 'Look what I've found for grandma,' she said, removing a brushed-cotton nightdress and matching négligée from one of the bags. 'Aren't they pretty?'

Jenny agreed. 'Yes and they'll keep her warm.'

'When they came for mum's funeral, there was a nightdress on the bed that had seen better days and granddad wears cotton pyjamas so I got him a fresh pair. I don't suppose Paul phoned while I was out?'

'Yes, so he's calling again at one o'clock. I was going to enquire whether he'd had you between the sheets yet but I thought better of it.'

'I could kill you Jenny! Don't *dare* say anything like that to Paul.'

'I wouldn't have to if you told me.'

'*There's nothing more to tell.* Why do you get a kick out of winding me up every few minutes?'

'Because you're daft enough to let me. For God's sake, lighten up Alison.'

Alison sat down at her desk without another word and when Paul telephoned, Jenny answered his call. She leaned back in her chair as if the conversation were to be lengthy.

'Yes, she's been back a while Paul. I believe you enjoyed your evening.... Have you....? No, I've not been there.... Brilliant! I'll have to try that then....'

114

Though furious, Alison was quick to grasp it was another wind-up and knew if she reacted, she would simply be playing right into Jenny's hands.

She picked up a file and disappeared into the rear office, where, within seconds, Jenny appeared.

'Paul's on the phone,' she said, embarrassed that her attempted wind-up had failed on that occasion.

'Thanks. I'll take it here,' she replied frostily.

'Right. I'll er....transfer him.'

Alison felt smug in her handling of the situation. Though she knew it was merely a game of winners and losers, Jenny was always the winner so she had reached a decision that there'd now be two competing players. Without any stipulation in Alison's job description that she must be the butt of all the jokes, she would retaliate likewise when provoked instead of allowing her emotions to get the better of her.

'Hi Paul. How are you today?' she asked.

'Missing you,' he sighed. 'I wanted to thank you again for a lovely evening. I really enjoyed myself.'

'Me too. So, what are you up to? Painting?'

'No, paperwork and I hate it but I haven't called to talk about work. Were you tired this morning?'

'No, I was fine. Why, were you tired?'

'Yes, I didn't get to sleep for ages. I kept tossing and turning and thinking about you.'

'I was thinking about you too.'

'I can't wait until Friday to see you again Alison. It's almost a week away.'

'No, it's only three days away,' she laughed.

'That's an eternity. What are you doing tonight or tomorrow night? Are you free?'

'Well, there's nothing of any consequence in my social diary but I've loads to do before Friday.'

'Do it tonight and Thursday and see me tomorrow please. We could go back to the Red Lion and have something to eat. What do you say?'

She needed no persuasion. 'Yes, I'd like that.'

'I'll pick you up earlier if we're eating, say seven-thirty. How does that sound?'

'Fine. I'll see you tomorrow then. Bye Paul.'

Alison closed her eyes and in her mind she could see Paul sitting at his cluttered desk, poring over a hotchpotch of overdue paperwork and she smiled to herself. She found him to be such an unpretentious and uncomplicated guy who had made no attempt whatsoever to conceal his feelings for her and she hoped that her inexperience of men wouldn't drive him away, especially after her brief encounters with Mark and Richard had proved somewhat disastrous. She had made it obvious to each of them when they kissed her, that she would go no further, but being unlike other girls, how would she react when Paul made a move, which he would do sooner or later?

Her thoughts were dispersed by Jenny who came into the room and asked, 'Are you alright?'

'Yes, sorry. I was miles away,' she said but Jenny wasn't convinced and she became more concerned by Alison's behaviour as the afternoon progressed, in the belief *she* was the cause of the stony silence. She was in a quandary. Were she to raise the matter again, she might cause further hostility yet were she to say nothing, the disagreeable atmosphere might well continue to the end the day.

116

Barely a dozen words had escaped Alison's lips when she put on her coat. 'I've some errands to do. I shouldn't be long,' she told her abruptly.

'Take your time. We're not busy,' Jenny said but there was no amicable response.

Jenny was troubled. It was so out of character for Alison to take matters this far. She was accustomed to Jenny's outrageous behaviour and took it in her stride but this was different. If things were no better when she returned, Jenny would have no option but to bring matters to a head as this misunderstanding could continue no longer. It had to be resolved.

As Jenny awaited her return she became worried when, almost an hour later, Alison still hadn't reappeared. Never before had she taken time out during working hours and though entitled by her Contract of Employment, she rarely took her permitted hour for lunch. She would eat her lunch whilst typing if there were urgent letters to post. She was a reliable and conscientious employee.

Suddenly, the door opened and Alison walked in. Jenny kept her head down to avoid eye contact but watched her stacking her shopping behind her desk.

Alison removed an envelope from her bag. 'Will you or your dad ask Dr. Martin if he would sign my passport form please? Everything's in there and it's ready to post. I've had two more photos taken. The others were a joke. You can take a look if you like.'

Jenny opened the flap, peered inside and removed them. 'Those are a vast improvement. They're a lot better than mine. Did you go to a different booth?'

'No, I used the same one but I understand it now.'

Jenny took a deep breath. 'Listen, I know you're annoyed but I didn't mean to upset you. I was just having a laugh about the photos and I'm sorry.'

'What *are* you going on about? Those others were diabolical! That's why I've got some new ones. I'm not angry at you. We both had a laugh about them.'

'But I thought….'

'Forget what you thought. I've things on my mind that are nothing to do with anything you've done.'

'What's wrong then? Is it to do with Paul? Have you two had an argument?'

'No, we're fine, at least at the moment we are.'

'What's that supposed to mean? Come on Alison, spill the beans. Whatever it is, it can't be that bad.'

'It's worse than bad. It's terrible.'

'Are you seeing him again before Friday?'

'Yes, we're going out tomorrow.'

'So what's making you so miserable then?'

'I don't want to talk about it. Leave me be. I'm a waste of space where men are concerned. None of them ever want to see me again after the first date.'

'Well, I don't hold any records for stability where men are concerned. I've had more one-night stands than the London Philharmonic. I'm guessing this is about sex. You're afraid you'll lose Paul if you turn him down. Am I right?'

Although Alison didn't speak out, Jenny noticed a slight nod of the head.

'Oh Alison,' she said, closing her arms round her. 'You've such a lot to learn about men. I intended to speak to you last night but you went out with Paul. Tonight, we'll relax with a drink and discuss every-

118

thing. You're just confused because your hormones are all over the place. You'll laugh at all this later.'

'I enjoyed that Pizza,' Jenny said, licking her lips.

'Yes it was delicious,' Alison concurred, pouring herself another glass of wine.

'Are you ready to talk? You know I won't repeat anything, especially to Paul. I was joking before.'

She sighed. 'I don't even know where to start.'

'Well, try the beginning. That's generally the best place to start and I won't interrupt. Here, let me top up your glass. You might find it easier if the wine loosens you tongue. Take your time. I've turned the answerphone on so we won't be disturbed.'

Alison spoke about her evening with Richard and opened her heart to Jenny about what she believed her feelings had been for both Richard and Mark at the time. She told her how utterly demoralised she had felt when both seemed to have rejected her but she knew now that her feelings for them paled into insignificance when compared to what she felt for Paul and it terrified her. Though unable to bear the thought of losing him, she wasn't ready or willing to pay the high price she believed necessary to hold onto him. 'Previously, I was in love with the notion of being in love, if that makes sense to you. It was a new experience and I was flattered. I hadn't had a boyfriend before and I guess I enjoyed the attention but it's totally different with Paul,' she explained.

Jenny listened caringly, allowing her to continue uninterrupted. At times there were tears and at other times she was composed though it was apparent she was totally confused. Jenny allowed her to continue at her own pace until finally she said, 'That's about the measure of it and I don't know what to do.'

'Well, first of all, if you don't know what to do, you do nothing. That's rule number one. You and I are very different people. I've always regarded myself as a good time girl. I like a laugh and yes, I've had my share of blokes but as a teenager, I hung out with a gang of yobs who smoked cannabis, stayed out most nights and slept around. There was a huge amount of peer pressure to experiment with drink, drugs and sex. I never took drugs despite the temptation but I did have the odd drink, I stayed out late, often all night and because most of the girls had sex at an early age, I did too,' she confessed.

'In retrospect, many of my so-called friends were very shallow and now I can't imagine what I saw in them....but with you it's a different story.'

'How?'

'Because you kept to a lifestyle of moral values.'

'But I had plenty of freedom.'

'Listen, we're from different backgrounds. I don't want to appear patronising but you didn't have the same peer pressure because you had no money.'

'But you don't need money to get your kit off!'

'No, but it helps if you've had a few drinks first and you've a nice place to go to get it off. It helps to have the ambience. I didn't stand about screwing on street corners. I'm not a whore!'

'I never said you were. I can't understand this.'

'Right....why didn't you have sex when you were fourteen?' she asked with an exasperated sigh.

Angrily she remonstrated, 'I didn't want to.'

'Why not? Your friends were at it, weren't they?'

'*No* they were *not*!' she said heatedly.

'I rest my case. Mine were. That's the difference between us. Peer pressure.'

'You didn't have to follow suit. Don't you have a mind of your own?'

'*Right*!' Jenny yelled. 'We're getting somewhere now. Haven't *you* got a mind of your own? You say *no*! It's that easy....and you should know better than me. You've been saying it for seventeen years.'

'So what if Paul walks away like the others did?'

'They didn't. That's just your paranoia. Mark and Richard aren't ruthless and I very much doubt Paul is but if I'm proved wrong and if he won't respect your values, he's not worthy of you, so it's preferable that he walks away now rather than later when he's taken what you're not yet willing to give. My advice is to keep the relationship casual and should things start to get out of hand, let him know he'd be your first and you're not ready. He'll respect that.'

Horrified she said, 'I couldn't tell him *that*!'

'Why, because you'd be too embarrassed?' Jenny asked and when Alison nodded, she stated, 'Well, if it's too soon to talk about it, then it's definitely too soon to hit the sack with him.'

'You do have a way with words but you're right.'

'Then make it clear to him. I don't have all those complications in my life. I simply enjoy myself and move on.'

'But you can't do that forever. Surely there has to come a point when you need to settle down?'

'I agree, in fact I might just decide to play hard to get with Tom. You've heard the saying, "treat 'em mean, keep 'em keen." Come on, let's have another drink and I'll hammer you at Scrabble. We need a change of topic. Trust me, everything will be fine.'

Paul arrived at precisely seven-thirty the following evening and Jenny went to let him in.

'You're very punctilious,' she remarked.

'I'll take that as a compliment as I haven't a clue what it means,' he said on a burst of laughter.

'It means you're meticulous about conventions of correct behaviour and etiquette or, to put it in plain English, you turn up when you say you will.'

'Thanks, now I understand. You must remember, I'm just a simple artist, not a scholar.'

'There's nothing simple about you. Come on in.'

No wonder Alison was in such a frenzy about the fear of losing such a gorgeous hunk, Jenny thought, directing him to the sofa.

As he sat down, Alison appeared and he instantly stood up again, grinning from ear to ear. 'You look amazing,' he said, kissing her gently on the lips.

'Thank you and you look smart too. Nice jacket.'

'Well, I have to make an effort when I'm taking an extra special lady to dinner,' he declared with a broad smile, giving her another affectionate kiss.

'Don't mind me,' Jenny interrupted. 'In fact, I'll go out of the room if you like.'

He laughed heartily. 'No, we're off now.'

'Enjoy your evening and remember to spare some thought for me having beans on toast,' Jenny said.

En route to the car he remarked, 'I like Jenny. She always has some witty comment to make.'

'You're right. I was saying earlier how she has a way with words,' she answered without expounding on her remark. 'Are we going to the Red Lion?'

'Is that where you'd like to go?'

'I don't mind. I'm just happy to be seeing you.'

'That's a sweet thing to say. In that case, there's a good *chippy* in town.'

'Nothing beats a good *chippy*,' she giggled.

'Actually, I've taken a bit of a chance and booked at a new Chinese. I hope you like Chinese.'

'A Chinese *chippy*? Great! Is it a takeaway?'

'I'd love to take you away.'

'You are doing....to Brighton on Friday.'

'You know exactly what I mean....just the two of us. Would you like that?' he queried but when she avoided his eye, he apologised. 'Sorry, I shouldn't have said that. I simply meant I like spending time alone with you. An evening passes very quickly and then I have to wait for days to see you again.'

'It's alright. I understand because I feel the same.'

Paul turned into the car park and switched off his engine. 'Here we are, so how's this for an authentic Chinese Restaurant? It's only been open six months but you won't get a table without a reservation. It's very well patronised but we can easily find another place if you don't fancy it.'

'Not likely, it's fantastic,' she replied chirpily.

'Great, let's go in. I'm ravenous,' he said, leaning towards her to give her another kiss.

As they stepped into the reception area, she was

instantly impressed by the brightly coloured décor, predominantly red and gold, but the bright Oriental artwork was amazing and unlike anything she had ever seen before.

'It's unbelievable,' she gasped, catching sight of the ornamental lanterns that illuminated the ceiling with reflected colours from the stained glass.

'It's nothing like as garish inside. It's rather traditionalist in fact. The entrance is bold to impress the client but you'll find a more conventional mood in the restaurant where you would expect more peace and tranquillity to appreciate the delectable food. I do believe they've struck the right balance.'

'Good evening Mr. Trantor and to you Madam,' the Manager said, walking hurriedly towards them. 'Your table is ready if you would follow me Sir.'

He escorted them to an intimate corner table, out of view of the other diners.

Once they were seated Paul confessed that he had been unwilling to share her with anyone and he had specifically requested that particular table.

As she studied the menu, she wondered how often Paul had dined there and with whom. Immediately acknowledged by the Manager, he had managed to secure the most intimate table in the restaurant and yet he could only have reserved it the previous day. She studied him as he perused the menu. What exactly did she know about him? He'd divulged little or nothing of himself yet she had been persuaded to reveal her personal thoughts and the most intimate aspects of her life that she had never disclosed to a living soul. Maybe she'd been too hasty in her trust

124

of him? What if he were a Gigolo? What had Jenny said? Yes, that she was simply trying to protect her but from what? What did Jenny know about him? A hundred thoughts raced through her mind. She felt a little woozy and in need of some air.

As Paul glanced up, he perceived a worried look. 'Is everything alright?' he asked with concern.

'I....I need some air that's all. I feel light-headed.'

Paul threw his napkin down and helped her to her feet. 'Let's go outside. It's quite warm in here,' he stated, escorting her to the door where he spotted a seat. 'Sit down. Put you head between your knees.'

He sat beside her and held her hand. 'Would you like me to take you home?'

'No, give me a couple of minutes and I'll be fine.'

'Has anything like this happened before?'

'No, I just felt faint. Let's walk. I feel okay now.'

He put his arm around her as they walked through the gardens of the forecourt. 'You really scared me in the restaurant,' he told her.

'I'm sorry but it was scary for me too....a kind of panic attack but I'm fine now. Let's go back in.'

As they retraced their steps, Paul stated, 'Do you recall we talked the other day and I said that taste in art varied from one individual to another? Well, this restaurant illustrates my point. Maybe your subconscious found the décor in reception so objectionable it made you nauseous. It had to be something quite distasteful to react so quickly.'

'That's absolute codswallop Paul. Besides, I like the artwork. It's in keeping with the establishment and makes a bold statement. I believe the Chinese

125

artist responsible for those wild and glitzy paintings captured the spirit he wanted to achieve.'

'But don't you find them rather vulgar?'

'No. Outrageous perhaps but certainly not vulgar. It's a gallant use of colour and thought and I would imagine the artist was delighted with his results.'

'You're merely surmising. You couldn't possibly know that.'

'On the contrary, I believe I do. Somebody of his calibre and sophistication wouldn't have sanctioned his paintings being hung had he not been satisfied with his work. It's quite obvious from his attention to detail that he loves his work.'

When they re-entered the reception she continued, 'Look at this one for instance. The dragon is a mere fraction of the whole canvas, so he has paid special attention to the head for dramatic effect and painted it disproportional to the body.'

'So, what does that tell you about the artist?'

'He's powerful, resolute and strong-minded, also unafraid to display his feelings, yet he's tender and caring in his recognition of beauty, noticeable from the delicate brush strokes on those flower petals.'

He threw back his head and howled with laughter. 'You're very astute. I'm impressed Alison.'

The Manager approached and enquired, 'Do you like the paintings Madam?'

'Oh yes, very much. They're beautiful.'

'I'm so pleased but not surprised. Everyone likes Mr. Trantor's work. He's a most talented artist.'

As she reeled from the shock of that unexpected disclosure, the Manager ambled away with another two guests while Paul continued to derive pleasure from Alison's obvious embarrassment.

'So that's how you managed to acquire the most intimate table?' she asked red-faced.

'Of course!' he exclaimed. 'Why else?'

One day but certainly not then, she would answer Paul's question. Jenny was right. She *was* paranoid.

Jenny was waiting up for the detailed résumé of the evening's events and she howled at Alison's vivid report of the panic attack and the ensuing conversation about the celebrated artist who turned out to be Paul.

'I suppose it could have been worse. I could have been really offensive about his work and ruined the entire evening and how would he have felt then?'

'Well luckily you weren't but more to the point, how *does* Paul feel about you?'

'He doesn't say very much but he shows genuine affection. He's very spontaneous and tactile.'

'Actions speak louder than words. I noticed Paul was very caring. The moment you appeared in the room, his face lit up. So what's happening Friday?'

'If I could be away from work by four, hopefully we could be on the road by five.'

'As I'm seeing Tom, if it's quiet, I'll finish at four too. Did you find out anything else about Paul?'

'No, by the time I'd finished running round like a headless chicken, the evening passed quickly. It's a terrific place and the food was superb. You should get Tom to take you there next time. You won't be disappointed I can assure you.'

5

It was a good six hour drive to Brighton and when they eventually arrived at her grandparents' house, close to eleven o'clock, Alison was exhausted. Paul had telephoned ahead to reserve a room in a private hotel within half a mile of the house.

He carried Alison's bag into the cosy living room and she introduced him to her grandparents, Alfred and Joyce. Following the usual pleasantries, he left to book into his hotel right away.

'I'll call you tomorrow. I'm going to miss you so much,' he sighed, and after checking that Joyce and Alfred were well out of sight, he gave Alison a long lingering kiss before saying goodnight.

She returned to the living room where Joyce had appeared with a tray of tea and biscuits.

'Get stuck into them. Yer've 'ad a tirin' journey. It's a right pity yer young man 'ad to rush off like 'e did. I'll bet 'e could've murdered a drink o' tea,' Joyce remarked in her broad Lancashire dialect. 'E seems a pleasant enough young feller from the little I saw of 'im. What's 'e do for a livin'?'

'He's an artist.'

'An artist,' Joyce repeated in a manner that spoke volumes.

'He's very successful. He's very talented.'

'D'y'ear that, Alfred? 'E's a talented artist.'

'Who is?' he asked.

'Our Alison's intended. 'E's an artist.'

''E's what?'

'*An artist*!' she shouted.

'What does 'e paint?'

'Pictures yer damn fool! What d'yer think artists paint?'

Alison was finding it hard to control her laughter at the humorous repartee between her grandparents but she felt however that she should clarify matters before the moment of opportunity was lost forever. 'Grandma, Paul's a good friend, that's all. He isn't my *intended*. He simply offered me a lift to save me from a terrible train journey.'

'Oh, so yer not courtin' then?'

'No, Grandma, like I said, he's just a friend.'

'So, who are yer courtin' wi' then?'

Before she could answer, Alfred shouted, '*Who's courtin*'?'

'*Nobody*,' Joyce yelled.

'So why d'yer keep goin' on about it woman?'

'Why don't yer get to bed out o't' road an' I can 'ave a bit o' peace?' she grumbled.

'If *you* buggered off to bed, we'd all of us 'ave a bit o' bloody peace,' he answered grumpily.

Alison's concentration lapsed as she directed her thoughts to Paul, hoping he was settled in his hotel following his gruelling journey.

As she carried the tray to the kitchen and stacked the pots on the sink, Joyce appeared. 'Yer can leave them pots an' get yersel' up to bed 'cos I know yer must be tired. There'll be plenty o' time to catch up wi' all yer news in t'mornin'. Get yer bags.'

Joyce took her to her room and kissed her good-night. 'I'm right glad yer 'ere. Sleep tight lass,' she said, closing the door behind her.

Her eyelids were drooping and she welcomed the thought of sleep. She didn't envy Paul who needed to make an early start for London the next morning. She had given him her mobile phone number to call following his meeting and she was looking forward to that when it rang and she answered it quickly.

'Hi, you weren't asleep were you?' Paul asked.

'No, I've just come upstairs. How's your hotel?'

'It's fine and I have a nice room on the front.'

'What are you doing?'

'I've just had shower and now I'm lying between crisp white sheets, wishing you were here with me.'

'Stop it Paul.'

He laughed. 'Then you shouldn't have asked me. You can't stop me wishing. I really want you.'

'Go to sleep.'

'I can't. I can't stop thinking about you.'

'Then close your eyes and start counting sheep.'

'I've already tried that and it doesn't work.'

'Then keep trying. I'm going now. I'm tired.'

'No, don't go yet. Sing me a lullaby first.'

'*Get lost*!' she shrieked on hearing Paul's muffled laughter in the background.

'Tell me the truth. Are you missing me too sweetheart?'

'Yes, very much,' she sighed.

'I'll call you after the meeting finishes tomorrow and say hello to your grandparents from me. Goodnight Alison.'

'Goodnight,' she whispered.

She was thinking about Paul and his crisp white sheets as she fell into a deep and welcome sleep.

She hurried downstairs the next morning. 'I'm so sorry Grandma. I'd no idea it was so late.'

'It doesn't matter lass. Yer needed yer sleep. Are yer feelin' a bit more refreshed now?'

'I'm on top of the world. Where's Granddad?'

''E's just 'ad 'is breakfast an' 'e's gone out for a paper. What would yer like for yer breakfast?'

'Could I have a slice of toast please?'

'Why don't yer try a nice bacon butty?'

'Oh, no thank you. I never eat much breakfast.'

'That's what's wrong wi' young lasses nowadays. Yer all skin an' bone. Now in my day, we alus 'ad a proper breakfast inside us an' we ne'er ailed nowt. Young men then liked a lass wi' a bit o' fat on 'em. Yer like twigs now. Are yer sure? It's no bother.'

'Toast will be fine, really.'

'By the way, yer young feller called in on 'is way to London. I told 'im yer were fast asleep, so 'e said 'e'd ring yer later. 'E wanted to take us all out for a meal tonight an' 'e did argue when I refused 'im. 'E kept insistin' but like I told 'im, we don't eat nowt fancy, an' yer granddad, well it'd just be wasted on 'im. I didn't want 'im spendin' all that 'ard-earned money on meals for us, so now 'e's just takin' you.'

Alison was ecstatic but felt she must display some show of disappointment. 'But Grandma, I'm here to see *you*. I don't want to go out and leave you.'

'Listen. We've got all day to clack, so a couple of hours'll make no matter. Anyroad, yer granddad'll be fast asleep as soon as 'e's 'ad 'is tea, so 'e won't miss yer an' I don't wanna miss all my programmes on t'telly on Sat'day night. Go an' enjoy yersel' an'

131

mark my words, 'e fancies yer. I can sense when a feller fancies a lass an' 'e's such a courteous young feller. Yer should stick tight to 'im.'

'I'll remember that,' she laughed.

It was strange, she reflected, how dialects altered throughout the generations. Her grandparents had a very strong dialect yet her mother's had been much less pronounced and while unable to judge her own, she felt hers was a little more refined though it was always apparent to others that she was, as grandma would say, a proper Lancashire lass.

Paul had an educated speaking voice without any identifiable dialect but as he had moved around the country, perhaps he had picked up some of each on his travels, she speculated. It was impossible to determine his place of origin from his speech.

Still with only limited knowledge of Paul, she had learned that he was born and raised in Staffordshire and that his parents and his older married sister still lived there. During the journey, Alison had quietly enjoyed the ever-changing scenery, allowing him to concentrate on his driving. Tonight, she might learn more, she thought.

When Alfred returned with his newspaper tucked under his arm, he commented, 'It's a bit nippy out theere lass. There's a proper chill wind.'

'Sit here by the fire. I've hardly seen you yet,' she said, moving to the far end of the settee. 'It's lovely and warm here.'

''Ave yer 'ad yer breakfast yet?'

'Yes thank you Granddad, I've had some toast.'

'Beans on toast?'

'No, just toast.'

'I'm not struck on beans. They gimmee wind.'

'Yer'll 'ave to speak up a bit,' Joyce interrupted. ''E's a bit mutton jeff but 'e won't 'ave an 'earin' aid. 'E reckons there's nowt wrong wi' 'is ears.'

'What's she sayin'?'

'Nothing Granddad. Do you still play bowls?'

'Do I what?'

'Play bowls?'

'Speak up lass.'

Joyce intervened once more and yelled, 'She were askin' if yer still played bowls?'

'There's no need for yer to shout, yer daft bugger! I'm not deaf.'

Alison couldn't control her laughter any longer. It must be like this all day long, she thought.

Clearing her throat, she asked, 'Do you like living in Brighton, Granddad?'

'Aye I do lass. It's champion.'

'Do you and Grandma go for walks?'

'Yer right lass, she can talk. She ne'er shuts up.'

By now, Alison was suffering from exhaustion of effort and went to find out what Joyce was doing.

'I'm makin' a sweetloaf an' after, I'm makin' a few sandwiches for our dinner, 'cos I don't want to overfill yer when yer goin' out. I've a bit o' boiled 'am in t'fridge an' we can 'ave some pickles an' all. We're 'avin' roast beef tomorrow wi' proper York-shire puddin', not that muck they sell ready made.'

'That sounds lovely Grandma. Can I help?'

'No lass. It's all in 'and but yer can stop and talk to me if yer want. Yer'll get more sense out o' me

133

than yer granddad. 'E's a stubborn old fool. I 'ave to say everythin' twice. 'E just doesn't listen. 'E's proper aggravatin'!'

'But you think the world of him, don't you?'

'Aye, 'e's better than nowt I expect. I'll miss 'im when 'e's gone. 'E's a lot worse lately. I think 'e's losin' 'is marbles. 'E talks right daft sometimes an' other times, 'e talks proper. It's a queer do.'

'Yes it is,' Alison sighed. She'd certainly noticed a marked deterioration in Alfred's health since her mother's funeral.

'So, 'ow are yer doin' at 'ome dear? 'Ow are yer managin' wi'out yer mum? Yer must miss 'er such a lot. I ne'er thought I'd outlive my own daughter.'

'I do miss her but it was a blessed relief when she died. She was very bad towards the end but I try to think of the good times. She was a fantastic mum.'

'Aye, an' a good daughter too. Me an' yer grand-dad ne'er 'ad a minute's trouble with 'er an' as for yer dad, 'e were a nice feller....thought the world o' yer mum 'e did. It were a right pity that 'e died like that an' you only a baby but yer mum 'eld 'er 'ead 'igh an' owed nobody nowt. She were a very proud woman, an' did 'er best to raise yer proper in spite of all 'er troubles. She were right 'appy wi' 'ow yer turned out. She wrote me 'ow yer were 'avin' piano lessons an' 'ow well yer were doin' at school. Yer were alus 'er pride an' joy.'

Alison could see she was close to tears and inter-rupted, 'Mum used to make sweetloaf. She said you taught her to cook and I never once missed sitting down to a hot meal when I got home from school.'

134

'Yer can't beat 'ome cooked grub, as yer grand-dad alus says. 'E reckons it puts 'air on yer chest.'

'I don't think I fancy that,' she giggled and Joyce joined in the laughter too.

'Yer granddad'll be asleep now. Go an' wake 'im up an' tell 'im 'is dinner's nearly ready.'

She felt privileged to sit with her grandparents as they ate lunch, though there was sadness in her eyes as she glanced from one to the other, knowing she would only see them again, were she to visit them. From this visit, she would take away evocative and nostalgic thoughts of these caring people who lived a simple yet happy and rewarding life together....

After helping herself to a tempting slice of sweet-loaf, she told Joyce it tasted just like her mother's.

'I'll write down the recipe if yer like lass an' then someday, when yer've a family o' yer own, yer can tell 'em all yer grandma taught yer 'ow to make it.'

'Yes please,' she said, drying a tear from her eye.

It was just after one o'clock when Paul telephoned.

'How's my precious girl?' he asked.

Alison disguised her voice and replied, 'Will you hold on please, I'll try to find Alison,' leaving Paul feeling utterly confused and embarrassed.

Moments later, she said, 'Hello, is that you Paul?'

'Who was that?' he asked. 'I feel really stupid.'

'Why, what did you say to her?'

'Er....I can't remember,' he edged, eager to avoid further embarrassment by repeating the remark.

'Was it something about your precious girl?' she queried, continuing with the pretence.

He paused momentarily. 'That was *you* wasn't it? Just wait till I get my hands on you.'

'Mmm....I'll look forward to that,' she chuckled.

Paul sighed. 'Me too. I can't wait to get back.'

'How was the meeting?'

'We were just tying up loose ends and I had a few papers to sign. I'll be back in a couple of hours.'

'Have you eaten?'

'No, I'm going to eat you when I get back, totally devour you in fact.'

'You're doing it again Paul. Behave!'

'Where's the fun in behaving? Before I forget, did your gran tell you we're going out tonight?'

'She did. You don't miss an opportunity do you?'

'You sound a bit annoyed. Are you?'

'No and it was kind of you to invite my grandparents too. I've managed to persuade them to join us.'

There was silence lasting several moments before she asked, 'Are you still there Paul?'

'Er....yes. So why did they change their minds?'

'They didn't. I'm just winding you up. I told you I'd get my own back for the embarrassment I felt at the Chinese restaurant. Two can play at that game.'

'I love you, Alison Haythorne. There, I've said it now. I love you so much,' he repeated sensually.

Alison was shocked. Things were moving quickly and her head was spinning.

'Let me give you time to think about that and I'll call you later. I'd best hit the road now. Bye.'

'Bye Paul,' she murmured quietly.

As she closed her mobile, it rang again and it was Jenny.

'Just a quickie. How was the journey?' she asked.

'Exhausting. It took six hours. There was a lot of traffic. We arrived here around eleven o'clock.'

'Were your grandparents pleased to see you?'

'Oh yes and I them. They're so sweet. You'd love them and nothing's too much trouble.'

'And is Paul sweet and keeping out of trouble?'

'Yes but *I'm* struggling to keep out of trouble.'

'Are you on the verge of conceding defeat?'

'I'm sure Paul hopes so. He called me just before you did and he told me he loves me.'

'So how do you feel about that?'

'I have mixed feelings about everything. I'm very confused. I pine when we're apart and freeze when we're together. What's wrong with me?'

'You're in love I guess but what would I know?'

'Oh, Jenny, I'm sorry. How was the evening with Tom? Did it not work out as well as expected?'

'It was amazing. We had a fabulous time until we came back here and then it went pear-shaped.'

'Why, what do you mean?'

'He never came on to me. I played soft, seductive music and we had a few brandies and we talked and talked some more....and that was it. He went home.'

'Was he annoyed about something?'

'No, he was fine. We got on well and he asked to see me again tonight. I just don't understand.'

'So are you seeing him tonight?'

'I might as well. I've nothing better to do.'

'But you parted on friendly terms?'

'Yes, we had a cuddle for a minute or two before he shot away.'

'Maybe he was trying to show you some respect. It was your first date and all blokes aren't alike.'

'All mine are!'

'Anyway, you said you might play hard to get.'

'Well, yes I did but I don't see what that's got to do with the price of fish. Tom stole my thunder. He was the one who buggered off playing hard to get. I was absolutely ripping.'

'Oh Jenny,' Alison howled with laughter. 'You're such a scream. Maybe he's a virgin and he's shy.'

'I think that's rather unlikely in this day and age. Where would you *ever* find a virgin? Why, they're as rare as rocking horse muck.'

'Er....you're talking to one.'

'Yes dear but not for much longer I'll guarantee.'

'You are so wrong.'

'I am so right. Incidentally, have you come across your present? I think I dropped it in your bag.'

'No, I haven't unpacked much, nor have I given the gifts to my grandparents yet. I'll find it when I go up to my room. Thanks. Paul's on his way back from London. He's taking me to dinner tonight.'

'Nice one. Have a fantastic time and I'll see you tomorrow. Don't do anything I wouldn't.'

Alison removed the few remaining items from her bag and put them away. How differently she would have packed had she known she would be spending time with Paul. She had only brought a blouse and skirt and a jumper to go with her jeans. She would look so drab compared to everybody else in the res-taurant who would be stylishly dressed. Apart from her make-up bag, she had nothing more to unpack.

138

Typical Jenny, she thought. Wherever the gift was, it definitely wasn't in her bag. Maybe it had slipped off the bed as she was hurrying to pack.

When she took the gifts downstairs for her grandparents, Alfred was snoring and Joyce was dozing in front of the gas fire. They looked so peaceful that she hadn't the heart to arouse them and she left the bags with them and went back to take a shower.

Afterwards, wrapped in her bathrobe, she picked up her diary from the bedside table and wrote, 'It's lovely to be with my grandparents. Granddad seems to be fading fast and grandma does well to keep up. Paul will be back soon. He phoned and told me he loves me. I'm sure I love him too though I couldn't bring myself to tell him. He's taking me for a meal tonight and I can hardly wait to see him again.'

She closed her diary and returned it to the bedside table. Her hair, still damp, had fallen in gentle curls around her shoulders. She lay down on the bed and inhaled the sea air, so clean and invigorating. When her eyelids drooped, she allowed them to close and her thoughts returned to Paul and then she dreamed he was there, calling her name....'Alison, it's Paul.' In her dream she responded with a loving smile that showed her feelings for him, though no words were spoken. 'Wake up darling,' he said tenderly and she felt his lips touch hers. She reciprocated with avid passion and only when his arms closed around her did she awake with a start to find him in her room.

'Oh Paul, I'm so pleased you're here. I've missed you so much,' she cried as she hugged him.

'I'll wait for you downstairs,' he said. 'Hurry up.'

'Give me two minutes.'

'Make it one. I've already waited far too long,' he said, closing the door.

'Why don't yer go a walk on t'sea front?' Joyce suggested to Paul. 'Wrap up an' yer'll enjoy it.'

'That sounds a great idea. I'm sure Alison would like that. I'll nip back up and ask her.'

Alison dressed in jeans and a jumper. She slipped her make-up purse in her bag and shot downstairs, sold on the idea of a walk by the sea.

'There's no need to 'urry back,' Joyce called out.

Paul drove to the sea front and managed to find a parking space. Hand in hand, they strolled the full length of the promenade and there were serious and tender moments when Paul kissed her sensually.

'Did you give any more thought to what I said?' he asked.

'To be honest I've thought of nothing else, Paul.'

'Oh….so does that mean you were shocked?'

'I guess I was. I certainly wasn't expecting that.'

He raised his eyebrows apologetically. 'I couldn't help myself. It just came out but it's true.'

'But we hardly know each other Paul.'

He turned to face her. 'Try putting me out of my misery and tell me how you feel about me. You are such a private person that I find it hard to read your emotions.'

'I'm scared. I'm not used to having such feelings. Please give me a little time.'

They walked in silence, each in deep thought till Paul asked, 'Do you fancy an ice-cream? Come on, move yourself; I'll race you to the van.'

Suddenly their anxiety was forgotten as they ran hand in hand, shrieking like children.

'I've nothing appropriate to wear tonight,' Alison said. 'Are there any shops nearby do you think?'

'We'll ask someone. What are you looking for?'

'Something dressier than jeans and a sweater.'

'Look, a couple with a dog. They must be locals,' he surmised and before long, Alison was fingering through racks of dresses in a stylish boutique.

'That's very classy,' Paul said, pointing to a black dress on a window model. 'You look nice in black.'

'It's a classy price too. I could buy *three* dresses for that amount of money back home,' she told him.

'Do you like it?'

'It's gorgeous but I'm not spending that much!'

'What size are you?'

'Size ten or maybe twelve. It depends on the cut.'

Paul called out to the assistant. 'Do you happen to have a size ten or twelve in this please?'

'Paul, I can't afford *that*!' she protested.

'I can, so don't argue,' he cautioned her.

The assistant returned with the dress. 'This is size ten but I'm sure it will fit you. The fitting room is over here if you'd like to try it on.'

'Go on. Go and try it on,' Paul insisted and when Alison protested once more, he repeated, '*Just try it on for heaven's sake*!'

She returned with the dress over her arm. 'It's too tight,' she told him.

'No it's not. I know you're not speaking the truth. Does it fit?'

'Yes and it's lovely but it's far too expensive.'

'We'll take it,' Paul informed the assistant.

'But Paul….' she whispered.

'What have I told you about arguing?' he said.

'Thank you. It's the most beautiful dress I've ever had,' she said appreciatively and gave him a kiss.

'Where's the hotel in relation to my grandparents' house?' she asked as they were driving back.

'Just down the road. You can see it on your right, there with the white pillars. If you like, I'll give you a quick tour before I take you home,' he said, turning into the car park. 'Don't leave your dress in the car. Someone might break in to steal it.'

She followed Paul inside where he was welcomed cordially by the receptionist. 'Good afternoon Sir. How was London today?'

'Tiresome as always and the traffic is worse each time I visit.'

'Sorry to hear that. Your key Mr. Trantor….enjoy the rest of your day, Sir.'

'I fully intend to,' he replied as he directed Alison upstairs to the first floor.

Entering a man's hotel room was a novel experience but she didn't feel threatened by Paul. It was a pleasant room and through the bay window was an uninterrupted view of the sea. The room was nicely furnished and had an en-suite shower room.

'Show me your dress,' Paul said quietly and when she turned to face him, he was sitting on the double bed with his back to the wall. He had a solemn and disconcerting air about him and his penetrating eyes unsettled her.

'You've already seen it,' she replied nervously.

'I'd like to see it again,' he said as his eyes stared even more deeply into hers.

In silence, she lifted the dress from bag and held it up in front of her.

'Will you put it on....please?'

'I don't think so Paul. You'll see it later,' she said with her heart racing.

'Please Alison. I'd like to see you wearing it, just for me. The bathroom's over there,' he told her in a persuasive yet resolute manner.

Without another word, she went to the bathroom and removed her clothes. After she stepped into her dress, her hands were trembling and the zipper end repeatedly slipped through her clammy fingers. She paused, attempting to regain her composure before opening the door. Nervously she called out, 'I can't manage the zip. Will you help me please?'

Paul slid from the bed and walked behind her and when he touched her, he was deeply aroused by the feel of her silky skin and the sight of the tantalizing lacy straps of her black underwear. He fastened the zip and turned her towards him, eyeing her up and down. 'You are so beautiful,' he sighed seductively before kissing her forcefully.

She remained unresponsive, uncertain of how to react. After Paul had unzipped her dress, she felt his hands around her waist, fondling her bare flesh as he kissed her neck. Panting breathlessly, he ran his fingers over her body. Her heart was pounding and though she wanted him as much as he wanted her, she was afraid and felt vulnerable, knowing where this would lead were she not to stop him now.

Following a natural impulse she grabbed both his hands and cried, '*No Paul.... Please don't*!'

Instantly, he obeyed, withdrawing his hands and she hurried to the bathroom to remove her dress.

She hesitated before re-entering the room, where he was sitting on the edge of the bed, his head held in his hands. Knowing he was distraught her heart went out to him.

'I'm so sorry Paul,' she said but he didn't answer. 'Speak to me, please. Say something....anything.'

'What would you like me to say? One minute you lead me on and the next you reject me. I genuinely believed you loved me the way I love you.'

'I do love you Paul but....'

He wasn't paying attention. 'Do you play all men like this?' he interrupted. 'Do you drive all of them crazy and then walk off leaving them in pieces?' he added almost tearfully. 'I love you and I want you. Can't you see how I feel or is it that you just don't give a damn about my feelings?'

She closed her arms round him, her face touching his. 'Please don't be angry. The thing is, I've never *been* with other men, ever, well not er....that way,' she stammered.

Instantly, Paul grasped what Alison was painfully trying to explain and when he looked up at her, she nodded. 'I have nothing of material value to give to any man Paul but I have something I've saved for one very special man and now I've found him.'

His tearful eyes spoke a thousand words and contritely, he took hold of her hand. 'Darling, I could never describe how I despise myself at this moment and I'm truly sorry. It never even crossed my mind. I've been so self-centred and selfish.'

'You're not selfish. How could you have known?'

'The signs were there but I failed to see what was staring me in the face. I feel so bloody stupid. How could I have been so inconsiderate? You must have been terrified. Can you ever forgive me?'

'There's nothing to forgive. Kiss me Paul.'

He kissed her gently and pulled away.

'I meant properly,' she murmured softly, pulling him towards her.

He kissed her again but so forcefully that he took her breath away. As they moved apart, she stroked his hair and smiled. 'I know what Jenny would say if she were here now.'

'Tell me,' he said, kissing her lips repeatedly.

'Are you really sure you want to hear?'

'You're going to tell me anyway so carry on.'

'She'd say, "Go for it kid. Get his kit off!"'

He laughed. 'That's definitely what *she'd* say but what would *you* say in reply to that?'

'Nothing as I'd be otherwise engaged. I've waited eighteen years for this,' she whispered seductively, sliding her hand inside his shirt. 'Get your kit off!'

Earnestly he asked, 'Are you really sure darling?'

'Never more so in all my life,' she declared with a loving and meaningful smile. 'I love you so much.'

'Alison, it's almost five o'clock. Wake up.'

'Leave me alone. I want to stay here forever.'

'So do I but unfortunately we can't. We should be at your grandparents' now. I'm going for a shower.'

When he reappeared, his hair wet and dishevelled, he kissed her lovingly. 'Take a shower. You'll feel so much better. I'm only concerned for you. What would your grandparents say? Come on, wake up.'

She didn't care what anyone said or thought. She was deliriously happy. She loved Paul; he loved her and nothing else mattered.

As she dried her hair, she was reflecting on those past few hours, remembering how tender and caring he had been. Jenny was right when she had said that you never forgot the first time. Alison would never forget hers as long as she lived.

She opened the door and called, 'There's a hair-brush in my make-up purse. Will you get it please?'

As he removed the brush, two other items fell to the floor....a lipstick and a small package that Paul instantly recognised.

He stooped to retrieve the items and was laughing as she reappeared. 'What....? What's that?' she said, staring at the content of his outstretched hand.

'You're asking *me* when it was in *your* make-up purse?'

'*I'll kill Jenny*!' she screeched when she read the front of the packet. 'I hate her. I do. I could kill her. Banana flavoured indeed! Whatever next!'

To escape from his unequivocal enjoyment of her embarrassment, she shot straight into the bathroom, banging the door behind her.

'Sorry we're late Grandma,' Alison said. 'I needed to buy a new dress for tonight. I just brought casual clothes with me.'

146

'No need to apologise. Did you enjoy yersels?'

'Very much so,' Paul stated, directing a sideways glance at Alison.

'I'll have to get changed now. Why don't you talk to granddad? You'll have to speak loud as he's hard of hearing,' she warned him before running upstairs with the bag containing her new dress.

He was soon to discover that a conversation with Alfred was anything but simple. It was more likely that Alfred didn't pay attention, he deduced. Alfred might be slightly hard of hearing but he could hear well enough when it suited him.

'Yer a tall lad,' Alfred said. ''Ow tall are yer?'

'Almost six feet, Alfred,' Paul answered clearly.

'I thought yer were. Still that'll be 'andy I expect, like when yer doin' a ceilin'.'

'A ceiling?' Paul asked quizzically.

'When yer paperin' a ceilin'. That's yer job i'n't it, paintin' an' decoratin'?'

He laughed. 'No, I'm an artist. I paint pictures.'

'Nay lad, I 'aven't been to t'pictures for donkey's years. I can't remember t'last time we went. *Joyce, this young feller wants to know when we last went to t' pictures*,' he called out and Joyce walked from the kitchen drying her hands.

'It's fine. I didn't ask that. Alfred misunderstood.'

''E's good at that. Don't let Alfred wear yer down lad. 'E's 'ard work,' Joyce said before returning to the kitchen.

'I imagine it *is* 'ard work. I were a bricky an' that were 'ard work too.'

'When did you retire, Alfred?'

147

'It'd be fifteen year' ago. It were gettin' right cut-throat if yer know what I mean.'

'Yes I do. Do you like football?'

'Not now. I've a job on walkin', wi'out tryin' to kick a ball as well. I used to play a bit when I were a young feller. I like it though when it's on t'telly.'

Alfred's eyelids flickered then closed and Paul sat quietly beside him, enjoying the tranquillity.

Meanwhile, a different conversation was about to take place in Alison's bedroom after Joyce had ventured upstairs to have a talk with her granddaughter.

'Ee yer look a proper picture, lass. Is that yer new frock?'

'Yes, Paul bought it me. It's beautiful isn't it?'

'It is that. I've ne'er seen owt like it. Yer a lucky lass to 'ave a smart young feller like 'im. 'E thinks the world o' yer. 'E can't take 'is eyes off yer.'

Alison avoided eye contact as she reflected on her feelings for Paul, not wishing to reveal, nor indeed raise suspicion about what had occurred earlier.

'Yer've reached an age now lass where yer 'avin' to make difficult decisions. I wanna mention a few things that I'm sure yer mother would 'ave told yer, 'ad she been here, God rest 'er soul. I weren't born old you know. I used to be a young lass too, an' we 'ad all them same feelin's then as young 'uns 'ave now. Just 'cos we didn't run around an' shout it off t'rooftops, it didn't mean nowt never 'appened. I'd 'ave spent every wakin' hour wi' Alfred if I'd 'ave 'ad 'alf a chance but everythin' were different then. What young folks do now is the same as what we'd 'ave done then. We 'ad feelin's as well so sex isn't

148

somethin' *your* generation dreamed up. It's gone on for many a long year, right back to Adam and Eve an' long afore that too. I'm not daft, Alison. I know yer've been back to yer young feller's 'otel. All I'm sayin' is that yer should take what yer can from life while yer able. Look at yer poor mother, 'ow young she were when she died an' yer dad, 'e 'ad no life at all....cut off in 'is prime, 'e were.'

Alison was feeling very uncomfortable but Joyce continued, 'An' there's little point in tryin' to pull t'wool over *my* eyes. If yer didn't want me to know, then yer should 'ave covered your tracks instead of makin' it so obvious.'

'I don't know what you mean,' she spluttered.

'Listen, when a young feller leaves 'ere in one set o' clothes an' comes back 'ere in another, it's clear to me, 'specially as 'is 'otel's at th'end o't'street. I might be old but I'm not simple. Stick tight to 'im. 'E's a gradely lad that one. Ee, I feel tired now,' she said with a huge yawn. 'I expect it'll be a late night waitin' up for yer an' I could 'ave done wi' an early night as I've a roast dinner to attend to tomorrow. I take it yer young feller'll be 'ere for 'is dinner too?'

'Yes, thank you Grandma. He'll be delighted and I promise we'll be back early tonight.'

'Good God lass! Do I 'ave to spell it out t'yer?' I meant a *very* early night, so if yer comin' 'ome I'll 'ave to wait up! 'Aven't yer got an overnight bag?'

She leapt off the bed and threw her arms around Joyce's neck. 'Oh thank you Grandma and we'll be here straight after breakfast,' she cried excitedly.

'I doubt that somehow,' she grinned.

As Joyce left the room, she said, 'Don't say nowt to your granddad. Remember yer still 'is little lass.'

Alison hurriedly stuffed a few clothes in her overnight bag and ran downstairs.

Paul smiled. 'You look radiant. Are we ready?'

'Well, *I'm* certainly ready *and* willing,' she stated with a challenging smile, passing him her overnight bag. 'We'll have to see whether you are *able*!' and in reply to his quizzical expression, whispered, 'I'll tell you all about it in the car....'

'I still can't believe this is real,' Paul commented as he held Alison close. 'I keep imagining I'll wake up and you won't be here. I couldn't wait to get out of that restaurant. I thought we'd never get the bill.'

'So tell me Paul, did you have everything planned from the start?'

'Not exactly, although I did book a double room. The more I thought of it, the more I hoped it might be a possibility but I almost ruined things, owing to my excessive enthusiasm. When I brought you here earlier, I was going mad. I'd never wanted anything in my life like I wanted you at that moment.'

'I could tell. I could see it in your eyes. You were like a wild animal and for a while, I was afraid but I wanted you just as much. I'm sorry I was so silly.'

'No, I should apologise for forcing the issue.'

She smiled. 'Maybe *that* finally brought me to my senses. You knew, Jenny knew and grandma didn't take two seconds to work it out. She surprised me with some of the things she said earlier. She's very broad-minded for her age. I was quite shocked.'

'They're both great. I enjoyed chatting to Alfred, though most of the time, we were at cross-purposes. Do you think they'll make it to the wedding?'

She looked at him quizzically. '*Whose* wedding?'

'*Ours* of course!'

'Er....are you proposing to me Mr. Trantor?'

'I most certainly am Miss Haythorne.'

'Well, you might have done it properly on bended knee,' she teased light-heartedly.

Paul leaped out of bed and dropped on one knee. 'Miss Haythorne,' he said in solemn voice, 'Would you do me the great honour of becoming my wife?'

'Get back in bed before anyone comes in and sees you like that,' she screeched with laughter.

'So will you marry me if I do?'

'Well, I've known you for a week and a day so I think that's long enough to know my own mind. Of course I will. I thought you'd never ask.'

'I'm so happy,' he said giving her a hug. 'I meant to buy Champagne and oysters tonight but I forgot.'

'Why oysters?'

'Because they're supposed to be an aphrodisiac.'

'You are joking! That's the last thing you need.'

He laughed, happy to accept her remark as a compliment. 'Incidentally, don't strut around in front of me in that sexy red underwear if we're going out or we won't be going anywhere.'

Primly she asked, 'Why....do you disapprove?'

'Not at all, it's superb but I'd have expected your choice of lingerie to be much more conservative.'

'It usually is. I only bought it a few days ago.'

'So *you* were planning ahead too?' he smirked.

'I guess I must have been,' she admitted.

He kissed her gently. 'You make me so happy.'

Paul collected a magnum of Champagne, together with a beautiful bouquet of flowers on their way to Joyce and Alfred's. 'I'm looking forward to Joyce's roast beef lunch,' he said. 'I do miss home-cooked food. It never tastes the same in a pub somehow.'

'Grandma's an excellent cook, so you'll enjoy it. I can't help feeling guilty though. I've hardly spent any time with my grandparents over the weekend.'

'Are you complaining?' he said with a wide grin.

'Certainly not. This has been the most memorable weekend of my life, Paul.'

'And mine too,' he answered affectionately. 'I'll be sorry when it's over. I don't want it to end.'

'I wonder how grandma explained my absence to granddad. He'd be very upset if he knew I'd spent the night with you. I'm still the little granddaughter in his eyes.'

'Play it by ear. Joyce will have the answers. She's a wily old bird. I'm going to feel awkward walking in there, knowing I seduced their granddaughter.'

'Excuse *me* Paul! According to my recollection, was it not *I* who seduced *you*? You had given up on the idea if my memory serves me right.'

'Don't you believe it. I was just perfecting plan B when you butted in and took over.'

'What a lie. There was no plan B, was there?'

'I refuse to answer that on the grounds it might be incriminating. I have my reputation to consider as a great lover who can capture any female in the land.'

'My Gigolo!' she giggled.

152

'I'm no Gigolo,' he guffawed. 'Right, we're here and I feel as if I'm about to face a firing squad.'

'Then you can imagine how I felt when I looked into your wild eyes yesterday. That was a whole lot worse. Anyway, it's not even twelve o'clock yet so we're early.'

'Give me a kiss. I might not live to get another.'

She leaned over and planted a long lingering kiss on his lips. 'Thank you for everything. I love you.'

When Alison knocked on the door, it was Alfred who answered it. ''Ello lass. Why didn't yer use yer key?' he questioned.

She was about to fall at the first hurdle until Paul prodded her and Joyce shot to her rescue. 'Yer forgot yer key when yer went out this mornin'. I saw it on t'sideboard where yer left it last night,' she said.

'Oh, right.... I wondered where it was.'

Paul was close on her heels with the Champagne and flowers. 'These are for you and Alfred. Alison and I would like to thank you for all you've done,' he said, giving Joyce a meaningful look.

Joyce thanked them, gave them a hug and walked away to attend to the flowers.

'Did yer both 'ave a good night?' Alfred asked.

'Excellent! It couldn't have been better, could it?' Paul replied, winking at Alison.

She glowered at him and whispered, 'Just pack it in. You're going to make me laugh.'

'Where did yer get to after yer meal 'cos yer were late gettin' back?'

'Help me out here Alison? Where *did* we go? For the life of me I can't remember.'

153

'I'm going to kill you!' she mumbled.

Turning to Alfred she answered, 'We went a walk Granddad....along the sea front.'

'Weren't it too cold? It's little wonder yer didn't catch yer death. Yer were 'ardly wearing owt.'

'I couldn't agree more, Alfred,' Paul smirked.

Furiously she told Paul, 'I won't warn you again! You're starting to embarrass me now.'

'Get over 'ere an' sit yersel' down near t'fire. Are yer feelin' 'ungry lad?' Alfred asked.

'I'm starving. I'll certainly enjoy my lunch.'

'It'll be all that walkin' last night. It gives yer an appetite.'

'Indeed it does,' he grinned.

'Yer don't really notice at t'time but yer do t'day after when yer've overdone things. Still, a young fit feller like you should be able to manage.'

'I managed *very* well,' he replied with a sardonic smile, winking at Alison.

'I'm going upstairs now and you, young man, are skating on very thin ice,' she snarled threateningly. 'I'll deal with you later.'

As she stormed off, she overheard the end of their conversation. 'What's up wi' Alison? Is she mad at yer? She looked mad.'

'She's a woman Alfred. They're all mad.'

'Aye, yer not wrong theere lad,' he agreed.

'This beef is absolutely superb and your Yorkshire puddings are the best I've ever had. You're a good cook. I hope it's rubbed off on Alison,' Paul said.

'It's a pleasure t'cook for someone who enjoys it.

154

'Ave another puddin' an' there's plenty more beef.'

'No thank you. I've had sufficient,' he replied.

'I 'ope yer've left room for apple pie an' custard.'

'I'll certainly try that when everybody's finished. Have you made that too?'

'Yes. I don't much care for ready-made stuff.'

Alison's lack of input to the discussion had gone unnoticed by everyone except Paul. He had tried to involve her earlier but she wouldn't answer him. By ignoring him, she sent out a strong message that he had gone too far earlier. She was annoyed because he had made her feel uncomfortable.

'Shall we open t'Champagne?' Joyce asked Paul. 'Me an' Alfred'll never drink all that. Anyway, if 'e 'as too much, it might give 'im ideas,' she chortled.

'Good thinking. I'll attend to it Joyce if you find some glasses. You'll have some darling?' he asked, glancing in Alison's direction. 'I'd like to propose a toast and tell your grandparents our exciting news.'

Without looking up she nodded her head.

'Yer quiet lass. Are yer tired?' Alfred enquired.

Without pausing for thought, she said, 'Yes I am.'

'It'll be all that walkin'. Did yer not sleep well?'

'Yes, I slept *very* well,' she stated sharply, hoping Joyce would return shortly with the glasses and that someone would change the subject.

Paul was grinning from ear to ear when she cast her eyes in his direction and she was livid.

As Paul filled the glasses, he passed them round but when he took Alison hers, he quietly remarked, 'You wound me up *twice* yesterday but I didn't take umbrage, so now it's payback time. Trust me, I can beat you hands down at this game....so if you can't stand the heat, I suggest you get out of the kitchen.' Then he raised his glass and called, 'Good Health!'

He waited for the dust to settle before he stood up again. 'Joyce and Alfred, I'd like to wish you many more years of happiness. I know I speak for both of us when I tell you how much we have enjoyed your very kind hospitality,' and then, addressing Joyce, he continued, 'Alison and I have a lot to thank you for. It's been a most memorable weekend and last night, I asked the loveliest girl in the world, Alison, to be my wife and I'm delighted to say she accepted my proposal of marriage. I would therefore like you to raise your glasses and share in my good fortune.'

He smiled warmly at Alison. 'Thank you so much for making my life complete. I love you darling. A long and happy marriage,' he toasted.

Paul raised his glass and as Joyce dried her tearful eyes, Alfred stated dryly, 'Yer could do a lot worse. 'E's a gradely lad. All the best to both o' yer!'

It was almost time for them to leave and Alison was distraught.

She clung to Paul who supported her as she wept openly, for each time she had to say goodbye to her grandparents, she wondered if she would see either one of them again.

Alfred shook Paul's hand vigorously. 'Take good care of 'er lad,' he said, his eyes welling with tears. 'She's all we've got now. Don't ever let 'er down.'

'Don't worry Alfred. I'll always take good care of her. You look after each other and I hope to see you again soon. Goodbye Joyce and thanks again for all your kindness,' he said, kissing her goodbye.

He took the bags to the car and waited for Alison, feeling a strong affection for the caring couple who had taken him into their home as one of the family.

Red-eyed and heartbroken, Alison climbed in the car and waved until they were out of sight.

Later, when opening her bag, she found an envelope and on the outside was written, 'To our dearest Alison'. Inside, there were two sheets of paper. The first was a recipe for sweetloaf and the second was a note saying, 'We won't be able to see you on your special birthday but we hope you have a truly wonderful time. I'll post your card. With love from both of us.' With the note was a cheque for two hundred pounds and Paul remained silent as she wept.

The journey home was uneventful with very little traffic. Alison slept for the most part, awaking only when Paul stopped in a service area for petrol.

'I must have dropped off. Have we far to go?' she asked, rubbing her eyes.

'We'll be home in an hour. We're near Stafford.'

'Didn't you say your family lived round here?'

'Yes, fifteen minutes away. Let me fill the tank, then we can park up and grab a coffee. My mouth's dry and I need to stretch my legs.'

As they relaxed with their coffee, Paul asked, 'Do you feel better after your sleep?'

'Yes, I'm alright now thanks. I was so tired.'

'It'd be all that walking last night,' he laughed.

'Don't dare start on that again. I can't recall when I was ever as embarrassed in my life!'

'Blame Alfred then. He asked the questions. I just answered them. You must admit, it was hilarious.'

'Did you see me laughing?'

'You're always winding *me* up so it was my turn. Are you angry with me?'

'Very much so,' she said but the glint in her eye said otherwise.

Hand in hand, they made their way back to the car stopping momentarily when Paul took Alison in his arms to embrace her. 'Thank you for a weekend I'll never forget as long as I live,' he said softly.

'Nor will I and we have the rest of our lives ahead of us.'

'Did you call Jenny to tell her our news?'

'No but I'll tell her everything when I'm home.'

'*Everything*?'

'Well....not everything. There are certain things I would never share with anyone.'

When they arrived at the flat, Jenny wasn't there. 'She'll be out with Tom,' Alison surmised. 'Do you fancy a coffee?'

'A quick one please and then I must be off, much as I don't want to but I've loads to do tomorrow.'

Alison hugged him. 'I'm going to miss you,' she said, then whispered something in his ear.

'Stop it. Behave,' he replied, grinning from ear to ear. 'I think I'd better pass on that coffee.'

Their small-talk was interrupted by Jenny's voice. 'Is that you? I didn't think you'd be back yet.'

She turned to find Jenny in her housecoat and in her shadow, another figure appeared, buttoning his shirt. It was Tom.

'Did you have a good time?' Jenny enquired.

'Amazing,' Alison answered with an informative expression that Jenny immediately understood.

'Paul, have you met Tom?' Jenny asked.

'Briefly at Antonia's,' he replied, shaking Tom's hand. 'Nice to see you again Tom.'

'Likewise,' Tom said. 'Hi, Alison,' he added with a guilty expression.

With disparaging derision, Alison mumbled softly to Jenny, 'Huh! So much for playing hard to get.'

'You know me! I'll tell you all about it later,' she answered out of earshot of the men.

'What are you whispering about?' Paul asked.

Jenny quipped, 'If we had wanted you to hear, we wouldn't have been whispering, so keep it out. It's girl talk. It's private.'

'I doubt *that* word exists in *your* vocabulary,' he replied cynically and turning his attention to Alison he added, 'I'm off. Come on, walk me to the door.'

'Me too,' Tom said. 'I've come to recognise that I'm no longer welcome when women have things to discuss. I'll call a taxi and I'll be on my way too.'

'Can I drop you somewhere Tom?'

'Thanks Paul. That'd be great.'

Alison followed Paul to the door while Tom went to find his shoes.

'I'm going to miss you so much,' Paul said.

'Same here.... Oh Paul, I forgot to tell Jenny our news. Come back and we'll tell her together now.'

'You tell her all about it when I've gone. I can't stand hysterical females,' he said on a laugh as he kissed her goodnight. 'I'll call you tomorrow.'

'See you soon Alison,' Tom added with a wave.

No sooner had she closed the door than she was accosted by Jenny, bombarding her with questions.

'Hang on, first things first. I need a hot drink.'

'I think *I* need a brandy,' Jenny told her.

'Better idea. I'll have one too; in fact I may need two or three.'

'So come on, spit it out. Did you sleep with him?'

'Well, if I'm perfectly honest, I don't remember sleeping much at all,' she replied light-heartedly.

'I knew it. I should have put money on it. So how did that come about? Where were you?'

Alison divulged everything but the most intimate details and Jenny chuckled when she described the preamble to her telling him to get his kit off.

'Fancy thinking about me at a time like that.'

'It was your fault I was in that situation. You're a bad influence on me. I'm not complaining though. Anyway, I haven't told you the best bit yet.'

'There's *more*?'

'There is. Paul's asked me to marry him.'

'*Fantastic*!' she cried. 'I take it you accepted.'

'I did. I'm crazy about him.'

'I'm not surprised at that. He's a great guy. I'm so pleased for you Alison and I hope everything works out right for you. Fancy your grandma getting in on the act too. She's as bad as me, which reminds me, did you find my surprise gift?'

'Actually, Paul did and I've been meaning to reprimand you for that. I could have died when it fell out of my make-up bag and Paul picked it up. How could you do such a rotten thing to me? I had some

160

explaining to do. I was so embarrassed and more so because all he did was laugh *and* he accused me of deliberately planning everything beforehand.'

'I wish I'd been there to see your face.'

'I'd have killed you there and then!'

'I was looking out for you. You can never be too careful these days with STDs.'

Alison looked stunned. 'What's up?' Jenny asked. 'Come on, tell me what's wrong?'

'I never gave any thought to STDs. All weekend, not once did it cross my mind....not even when Paul found your....'

'Alright, calm down. I'm sure everything's fine. I can understand *you* not thinking of protection but I can't believe *he* could be so irresponsible. Paul's a man of the world and should know better. Are you absolutely sure he didn't use protection?'

'I might be stupid but I'm not *that* stupid Jenny!'

'When are you seeing him again?'

'I don't know. We've nothing arranged yet.'

'My advice is to forget about it until you see him. There might be a simple explanation.'

'Like what?'

'I don't know. Maybe he's been tested, or maybe it was his first time too. Alright, it wasn't then,' she acknowledged as Alison flashed a withering glance. 'You'd know more about that than me but tormenting yourself won't alter anything. Speak to him face to face. Here, give me your glass. I'll fill it again.'

'To the top,' she said. 'I feel like getting drunk.'

'Er, not till you've heard about *my* weekend. 'I've been dying to see you to tell you all about Tom.'

During Jenny's account, Alison suffered lapses of concentration but finally she convinced herself that Paul loved her too much to have placed her in any danger. There had to be a satisfactory explanation.

'Are you listening properly now?' Jenny asked.

'Sorry, go on. You have my undivided attention.'

Two brandies later, the two inebriated girls were approaching the end of their revelations. 'Has Tom been here all weekend then?' Alison asked.

'He stayed last night but went home after breakfast and came back about five o'clock today. You'd have missed him had you been a little later. He was hoping to be gone before you got back.'

She looked surprised. 'Why....am I such an ogre?'

'No, he's quite shy and he was worried you might not feel at ease if he was here.'

'It doesn't bother me. Has he not got a car?'

'Yes but I brought him so we could have a drink.'

'And do you really like him? Is he the one?'

'It's early days. I've only known him for a week.'

'Well I met Paul the same night and we're getting married. I know I'd never want anyone else.'

'Yes, but you said that about Richard.'

'No, I said I fancied him but I never said I'd like to spend the rest of my life with him. I still like him and Mark too but it's a completely different feeling. I love Paul. I can't bear to be apart from him.'

'Well, if you want him to stay over any night, it's your home too. I don't mind at all.'

'Thanks but Paul's got a place of his own so we'd probably stay there.'

'So where's his pad then?'

'I don't know. I haven't been there yet.'

'You've promised to marry the guy and you don't even know where he lives? I don't believe you. For all you know, he could have a wife and ten kids.'

'No he couldn't! He's not old enough, though he *could* have five or six,' she laughed. 'I never asked him to take me after your smutty remarks about him showing me his etchings.'

'Well, you've seen his etchings now so it's about time you checked him out. Has he told his parents?'

'Give him chance for heaven's sake. It was only yesterday he asked me to marry him.'

'I'm not saying there's anything wrong. Everyone who knows Paul Trantor says he's a good catch but he's managed to escape every girl's clutches so far. Just be careful, that's all I'm saying.'

'I *am* being careful. I know exactly how he feels,' she said, though she still had the nagging thought in her mind about what they had discussed earlier.

The telephone interrupted her thoughts and Jenny said, 'It's for you. It's Mark.'

She took the receiver. 'Hi Mark, how's things?'

'Fine and how are things with you?'

'Never better. So what do you know?'

'I've made enquiries about forthcoming events at the Bridgewater that might be of interest to you. On Wednesday there's one you might fancy, the Halle Orchestra.'

'That sounds terrific. How much are the tickets?'

'Nothing....it's my treat.'

'No, I fully intended paying for them, so I insist, otherwise I won't come.'

163

'I'm not arguing. We'll sort it out. Shall I book?'

'Oh yes please! I'm assuming you'll pick me up.'

'I'll be there by seven but be ready. I have to park and they don't like you going in once it's started.'

'I will. I'm really looking forward to that. Thanks Mark. It should be a great evening.'

'That was Mark,' Alison said as she hung up.

'I know it was Mark. I answered the call. What do you think you're playing at?'

'Why, what do you mean?'

'I just heard you arranging to go out with him.'

'He's taking me to a concert, that's all.'

'Is that so, and does he know about Paul?'

'Well er....no but I'm not interested in Mark that way. We're friends who just have a laugh together.'

'What do you think Paul would say if he knew?'

'I intend telling him. He won't mind at all.'

'Well if I were a guy marrying a girl like you and she told me she was going to a concert with another guy, I'd have plenty to say and Paul will go mad.'

'But I'm doing nothing wrong. It's just a concert.'

'Well I think you should call him back and cancel or at least, tell him about you and Paul.'

Irately she said, 'Right, I'll call him back but I'm not cancelling the concert. I'll tell him about Paul.'

Jenny sighed. 'Answer me this. How do you think you'd feel if Paul took another girl out?'

'He meets girls all the time in his line of work. He probably has nude models posing in his studio but it doesn't mean anything to him. We love each other.'

'You're very naïve, Alison. This is going to cause trouble and I mean *big time*! You mark my words.'

6

'It feels such a long time since I was here,' Alison remarked, unlocking the office door. 'It was only a normal weekend yet it seemed so much longer.'

'From the tasty bits I was privy to, I would hardly define it as a normal weekend,' Jenny remarked.

'You know what I mean. It was only two days.'

'What did Mark say when you called him back?'

'I told him Paul and I had got engaged and Mark said he was a great bloke. He was happy for us.'

'So you're still going to the concert then?'

'Yes, I love music. I'm not losing my identity just because I've met someone.'

'So does that mean you'll continue to go out with Mark once you're married?'

'No of course not. That's different.'

'You're virtually married *now*. You're engaged to him, you've slept with him, so how's it different? If you want my opinion you're asking for trouble.'

'Well I don't want your opinion so let it drop.'

'There's another thing too,' she said, unwilling to lay the matter to rest. 'Richard phoned on Saturday after hearing you'd gone away with Paul. He wasn't a happy chappy. He wanted to know if it was true.'

'Oh *did* he?' she cried. 'And what did you say?'

'I told him you'd gone to visit your grandparents and that Paul had offered to drive you. That's all.'

'Thanks a bunch! I'm accountable to Paul, to you, to Richard, to Mark; is there anybody else that I've forgotten? What about the window cleaner? What's he had to say about it?'

'Look, I'm just telling you so you'll be prepared.'

'Prepared? Prepared for what? I don't believe we are having this conversation. It's nothing to do with Richard. Where was he when I wanted him? What gives *him* the right to question *you* about *my* social life? I suppose you also gobbed to Richard that you had slipped a pack of banana-flavoured condoms in my bag. Well, you'll be able to gob again now that I was too dim-witted to use them won't you?'

'I'm sorry Alison. It was Antonia who mentioned to Richard that you were away, not me.'

'At the time Paul called Antonia, no arrangements had been made. I hadn't met Paul properly then, so if Paul told Antonia, he would have had to call her for a second time. I find that hard to believe.'

'Well, what if he did? He was only giving you a lift. Maybe he called to thank her and it could have been mentioned then.'

'Well, I'm off to the loo now, so if you want, you can stick an announcement in the paper and shove a notice in the window as well for all I care.'

By the time she returned she was calm and lost no time in apologising. 'I'm edgy today. I suppose I'm worrying about what I'll say to Paul.'

'Have you called him yet?'

'No, I'll call him from the back office. I just came in to see if you were busy but as it's quiet, I'll call him right away. I'm not discussing it on the phone so I'll only be a couple of minutes.'

'Don't worry. You'll sort it out. The only reason I mentioned Richard was to put you on your guard in case he mentioned it. I agree with you, it's nobody

166

else's business but Richard *is* my brother and when he asks, I have to answer. I'm piggy in the middle.'

'I know. I was annoyed at Richard, not you.'

Paul was out when Alison called him so she left a message but he still hadn't returned her call by the time she went out at lunchtime for the sandwiches.

Jenny was on the telephone when Alison returned and when Jenny saw her, she lowered her head and spoke quietly as if it were a private call.

When Alison brought her a mug of coffee, Jenny was still talking but she quickly terminated the call.

'That was Tom,' Jenny announced but Alison was unconvinced and her doubts were confirmed later in the day when Tom *did* call, saying he'd been trying to call earlier but that the line had been engaged.

Shortly afterwards, Paul called. 'Hi Babe, are you missing me a much as I'm missing you?' he asked.

'Probably more so. I'm having a really lousy day. I've been trying to reach you. Where've you been?'

'Out on business,' he replied.

'What sort of business?'

'Just business.'

'Forget it. Just tell me to keep my nose out. I was only trying to show a bit of interest.'

'What's wrong sweetheart? You sound rattled.'

'Let's just say it isn't the happiest day of my life.'

'So when *was* the happiest day of your life?'

'There's two actually. Saturday and Sunday were my happiest days ever.'

'That's sweet darling. Surprisingly enough, mine just happen to be the same two days.'

'Paul I need to talk to you. Are you free tonight?'

167

'Tonight's not the best. Why, what's wrong?'

'I just need to talk to you about something.'

'You're not having second thoughts are you?'

'Don't be silly. Of course I'm not. Please, I don't want to wait another day.'

'Let me see what I can reschedule and if possible I'll see you later then. I'll come over to yours.'

'No. Can I come to your place Paul?'

'Er....I don't think that's such a good idea.'

She had an uneasy feeling, unable to understand why Paul was being evasive. Was Jenny right? Was he married or living with someone? He wasn't, she told herself. He'd given her his telephone number. He wouldn't have done that had someone else lived there too. She was being paranoid again.

'Are you still there Alison?'

'Yes, I'm still here. Listen, it doesn't matter. Just forget it. I'll talk to you whenever. Bye Paul.'

She felt anxious and confused and lingered in the back office, reflecting on their brief discussion. The telephone rang and when she answered it, the caller hung up instantly. When it happened on two further occasions, Alison became very concerned. 'There's something peculiar going on,' she told Jenny. 'I've answered three calls now and nobody spoke.'

'I'll get the next one and if it's a heavy breather, I'll give him such a bollocking!' she stated angrily.

Alison chuckled and returned to the rear office to type a letter. She disregarded the next call but could hear Jenny's muffled voice so that wasn't the heavy breather. When Alison opened the door, Jenny said sharply, 'Try Directory Enquiries,' and hung up.

'Who was that?'

Unconvincingly she said. 'A wrong number.'

It had been a peculiar day with numerous strange telephone calls, none more so than that purportedly from Tom that hadn't been from Tom at all. So why had Jenny lied? It made no sense. She was her best friend, yet she had definitely lied to her.

After typing her last letter, Alison gathered all her mail together. As Paul hadn't called her back, she assumed he'd been unable to rearrange his evening and she decided she'd have an early night, hoping a decent night's sleep might eradicate the embryonic paranoia. She didn't want to be ill again.

'I'm off to the Post Office. Some need weighing for the postage. I won't be long,' she told Jenny.

When she returned, Jenny was sitting by her desk, her back to the door with the telephone to her ear. Alison heard her say, 'What a good idea Paul,' and when Alison closed the door, Jenny spun round and looked embarrassed.

Offhandedly Alison questioned, 'Is that Paul?'

'Er....yes, he wanted to speak to you, so we were chatting until you returned. Alison's here now Paul. Hang on,' she said, handing Alison the receiver.

'Hi Paul. Is everything alright for later?'

'Yes. I'll pick you up at seven-thirty but I'll have to leave at nine. Okay?'

'Are we going back to your place?'

'I thought we could go for a drink.'

'No, I've told you.... I want to see you alone.'

She heard him sigh. 'What's going on Alison?'

'I'll tell you later when I see you.'

When Paul arrived ten minutes early, Alison was ready and waiting. As soon as he rang the doorbell, she went out and followed him to the car in silence.

Paul looked anxious. 'When are you going to put me out of my misery Alison?' he asked.

'It's my misery not yours, plus I've had an absolute stinker of a day. I'm worried to death and there have been a few strange phone calls at work.'

When Paul attempted to embrace her, she showed no response. 'Am I in your bad books?' he queried.

'You might be but we'll discuss it later.'

'Fine. Where shall we go then?' he asked frostily.

'I've already told you....back to your place.'

'I'd rather not Alison.'

'Why not Paul? Have you something to hide?'

'Whatever gave you that idea?' he said earnestly.

'Just try to see things from my viewpoint because I find it rather strange. I've known you for less than two weeks and during that time, I've slept with you, agreed to marry you and I still don't know the first thing about you. You allegedly come from Stafford and you claim to have a sister. That's your CV. I've no idea where you live. I don't suppose you've told your parents we're getting married and most importantly, I can't talk about what's bothering me while we're driving around. How's that for starters?'

Paul was fuming. He stamped his foot to the floor and the car screeched away at high speed. He drove like a madman before stopping abruptly on an unlit car park.

'Get out!' he demanded.

She looked round and felt afraid. 'Where are we?'

'Wait and see. If I told you, you wouldn't believe me,' he replied brusquely as he took her by the arm and hoisted her from the car.

Surrounded by empty cans and beer bottles, a pair of drunken vagrants were sleeping rough alongside the wall of the car park and she shuddered as Paul pulled her past them before leading her to an almost derelict building, across a flagged floor to a lift that he pushed her inside. He dragged the heavy open-lathed door across, pressed the button and it started to rise slowly and noisily.

It was a sinister and terrifying building. It smelled musty and she was afraid for her life. Many of the light bulbs were broken or missing and rubbish was strewn everywhere. When the lift stopped abruptly, he dragged back the door and pushed her forward. Taking a key from his pocket he unlocked a sturdy door and slanting his eyes in her direction advised, 'You're in no danger but I need you to imagine this is our very first date; you know nothing whatsoever about me and this is where I've brought you.'

When he opened the door, everything was in total darkness. 'Voila Mademoiselle,' he said, gesturing with his hand for her to lead the way. He edged her forward into the darkness and she heard the heavy door clang shut behind her. 'Welcome to the world, or perhaps I ought to say to the *underworld*, of the humble artist,' he added, turning on a dim light.

It took her some time to focus through the shady obscurity that lay before her and she stared fearfully into a vast and open space that appeared infinite. As Paul continued to ease her ahead, they walked away

171

from light back into darkness. 'Keep straight ahead as I direct you and you'll come to no harm but you have to remember we're still on our first date.'

She took dozens of minute steps yet the vast room still seemed endless. Leading her to the right he put on another light and the draught from an ill-fitting window caused it to swing eerily from side to side, casting shadows on the old crumbling brick walls. Ahead of her was a neatly made bed. He pushed her down on the bed and as she tried to stand, he held her there, while leaning across to light a table lamp, standing on a wooden box on the floor.

'Welcome to my home, Alison,' he said bitterly. 'I trust you'll enjoy our first date and that you'll be comfortable here.' He positioned himself alongside her and wrapping his arms around her body, asked, 'How would you like to kiss me and make love to me? Do you want to see me again? Remember this is still our first date. Do you enjoy humiliating me?'

Rising from the bed, he knocked down antiquated light switches until the entire room was illuminated. 'This is where I live and this is how I live. Now do you understand? How could I ever invite a beautiful creature like you to a hovel like this?'

Alison began to walk round. Apart from the poky sleeping area, Paul had no home in the true sense of the word. This was his studio....his life. Everywhere she moved there were art materials; easels holding partly completed works, finished paintings standing majestically against the contrasting backdrop of the crumbling walls, portraits, sketches, piles of prints, brushes and paints. She was truly amazed by what

172

she saw as she continued her painful journey round the room. She felt regret for her earlier mistrust and unable to bear her shame she started to cry.

He took her in his arms. 'Have you had enough? I can take you away from here or get you a drink.'

'I....I'd like drink please Paul.'

'Good, so would I. I would have brought you here in time but you pre-empted my invitation. Sit down. I may not have the finest accommodation but I do have the finest wines. Try this one,' he said handing her a glass of red wine. 'You're honoured because I rarely bring anyone to my studio. I generally eat out and this is where I sleep. My makeshift shower and loo are behind that door. I suppose you could say I live like a hermit and as for my CV, my parents *do* live in Stafford and I *do* have a sister. In spite of my humble lifestyle, I am a successful and many would say, talented artist. I make tons of money from my commissions; I enjoy the finest wines and most of all I adore a beautiful girl named Alison who finds me hard to understand. Is there anything else you'd like to know? Ask whatever you like and I promise not to be cross again. Artists can be temperamental. I'm afraid it goes with the territory but believe me, I have nothing but love, respect and admiration for you and so I want you to talk to me about anything that bothers you. I want to spend the rest of my life with you, without secrets or misunderstandings.'

She stretched out her hand and took Paul's hand in hers, her eyes red from the tears she had shed.

'Today when you asked to talk to me urgently, I moved heaven and earth to alter my plans. I had an important visit arranged this evening and tomorrow, I was fully booked too so I had to go cap in hand to three clients to change tomorrow's appointments to a later date. Do you know where I should have been now? I should have been with my parents. I wanted to tell them about our engagement, so you see, they would have known by now had you trusted me but then we haven't yet reached the *real* point at issue have we? If there's another matter about which you have reservations regarding my integrity, you might like to tell me now. I could answer before you ask the question or quite simply refuse to dignify your question with an answer but whether or not you ask is your decision. I would prefer that you trusted me well enough to know I would cause you no harm.'

'I've nothing further to ask and I'm sorry. I love you Paul and I *do* trust you.'

'Thank you,' he said, brushing his lips across her forehead. I don't aim to sound patronising but you are very young and innocent in lots of ways. That's part of your charm and a quality I fell in love with. Just remember I'll always be around to protect you. I'm going to take you home now. This fleapit isn't a suitable place for a genteel young lady like you. Tomorrow, my parents will be given our news and I know they'll be delighted for both of us.'

He led her back through the studio, turning off the lights one by one and within minutes, she was back in Paul's car feeling safe again.

'Where will we live when we're married Paul?'

'I haven't given it any thought yet but it definitely won't be here. We'll choose somewhere together.'

'Will you keep the studio?'

'I haven't thought about that either. I need lots of room. That's why I rented that depressing hell-hole. It wasn't the location that attracted me but the space I needed to do my work. However, there's been talk that this entire district might be redeveloped, so any decision might well be taken out of my hands.'

When they arrived at the flat, he switched off the ignition and asked. 'Are you alright now darling?'

'Yes I am,' she replied with a warm smile.

'I'm sorry I was angry. You had every right to be concerned. We've come a long way in such a short time and I should have shown more understanding. I've lived alone for many years with nobody else to consider. I very rarely socialise due to the demands of my work. I hardly ever visit my parents and I'm absorbed in my work to the exclusion of everything and everyone else but meeting you has changed my life. My behaviour tonight was uncalled for but I'll try harder in future, I promise. I'd *never* harm a hair on your head. Please believe me darling.'

'We need to get to know each other Paul. That's all I wanted.'

'I know and we'll work things out,' he promised, kissing her gently.

'Good luck tomorrow with your parents.'

'They'll be fine. They're forever asking when I'm going to settle down with a nice girl. I'll give you a call Wednesday morning and maybe we can snatch an hour or so on Wednesday evening.'

'I can't on Wednesday. I'm going to a concert at the Bridgewater Hall.'

'Oh? Who are you going there with?'

'Mark's taking me.'

'*Mark Taylor*? Huh, I don't think so Alison!'

'I'm sorry Paul. What did you say?'

'I said you're not going with Mark to a concert.'

'I most certainly am. He's been trying to arrange this for weeks.'

'I don't give a damn. You're not going and that's final. Mark Taylor indeed. Have you any idea what people call him?' Without awaiting her response he said, '*Testosterone Terrorist* because of the way *he* puts it about. He's had more....let's leave it at that.'

She laughed at that remark and said calmly, 'Paul, Mark's just a friend. He's never been my boyfriend. He knows we're engaged. I told him yesterday.'

'You saw him yesterday when we got back from Brighton? I don't believe this,' he retorted angrily.

'Calm down. You promised you wouldn't do this again. I didn't see him. He phoned about the tickets and he's pleased for us Paul. I've been out with him before and he's a perfect gentleman. I couldn't hurt his feelings when he's gone to all that trouble.'

'So *my* feelings aren't important? Does that mean I can date other women?'

'I'm not doing anything wrong Paul and I won't be spoken to like that and I *am* going to the concert. You were lecturing me earlier about trust but that's one-sided apparently. If you don't trust me now you never will so perhaps we're not as ideally suited as we believed. I'm not going to tell Mark I can't go. I owe a great deal to him and his family and I intend to remain a close friend to all of them so maybe you

176

should cancel the visit to your parents. Goodnight,' she said acrimoniously and hurried from the car.

As she unlocked the door to the flat, she heard his engine screaming as he drove away at high speed.

'Have you not heard from Paul yet?' Jenny asked.

'No and I'm not bothered about him any more. I can't live my life being possessed.'

'Don't be daft. You know he adores you. He was just afraid of losing you. When you're a couple you learn to compromise. I warned you of what would happen if you went out with Mark and Paul *is* right about him. He does enjoy a certain reputation.'

'It wasn't apparent when I went out with him.'

'Come on! He and Richard almost came to blows because Mark said something suggestive to you.'

'He knows I'm with Paul so there isn't a problem, other than what Paul's created. The only reason I'm going is to enjoy the concert.'

'But you have no idea what Mark's reason might be, that's my point. Still, you're going despite what I say and he'll be here soon so get your jacket.'

'He's here now. I'll see you later.'

'Enjoy!' Jenny called to her.

'How did you like the concert?' Mark asked as they returned to the car.

'It was brilliant and the acoustics are perfect but I imagine you'd have preferred something lighter.'

'Maybe but I enjoyed it. How's Paul?'

'Oh, same as ever,' she prevaricated.

'So when's the happy day?'

'We haven't decided yet. Right, I want to pay for the tickets now so tell me what I owe you.'

'I've already told you. The treat's on me. Just call it an early wedding present.'

'No I insist,' she said, finding her purse. 'Tell me or I'll have to go back inside to find out.'

Reluctantly, he accepted the payment. They were standing by the car and he kissed her cheek. 'Thank you and all the very best to you and Paul. I'm really happy for both of you.' he said. 'He's a good catch but he's very fortunate too to have found you.'

As they drove off, neither noticed the figure in the shadows watching them but Paul had witnessed the embrace and that vision would remain indefinitely at the very forefront of his mind.

Seven days had passed by since Alison and Paul's disagreement and there had been no contact.

'Why not give him a call?' Jenny suggested. 'You look so miserable.'

'I'll get over him.'

'So, you still love him then?'

'He doesn't love me so I try not to think of him.'

'What would you do if he turned up tonight while I was out? Would you let him in?'

'Probably but it's hypothetical because he won't.'

'Don't be angry. Paul *is* coming round tonight.'

'*What*?'

'He's phoned me a dozen times and he's frantic. Please be nice to him and make up. We'll stay away till twelve so you won't be disturbed. He's coming in half an hour. Try to stay calm and you'll be fine.

Tom's here now so I'll see you later Good luck!'

Alison was on tenterhooks as she awaited Paul's arrival. She didn't want another row or any further debate of the whys and wherefores of their quarrel. She wanted everything the same as it was before.

When the doorbell rang, she opened the door with nervous fear and gasped as she saw him. He looked exhausted and dark rings encircled his eyes.

'Can I come in?' he asked her in a barely audible voice. 'We need to talk.'

'Yes but I'm not going over old ground. It doesn't lead anywhere. We'll only end up arguing again.'

'We won't, I promise. I love you and I can't carry on without you around. I'm going out of my mind.'

'Let me get you a drink, although you smell as if you've had one already.'

'I've had quite a few. I was afraid you might slam the door in my face.'

'And you've driven here like this?'

'Yes, I'm irresponsible,' he replied ashamedly.

'Give me your keys. You can leave your car here tonight.'

He handed them over and she poured him a drink. 'Take a look at yourself Paul. You look dreadful.'

'I've been working night and day and I've had no proper sleep. I've missed you so much Alison and I didn't know what to do to make things right again.'

'I've missed you just as much but I can't handle the way you try to possess me. It's unnatural.'

'I'm sorry. I was terrified of losing you to Mark.'

'Don't be ridiculous. It was a concert. You can be so self-centred. Those arrangements were underway

179

before we ever met. I've always wanted to go there and when Mark offered to take me, I jumped at the opportunity. Because we were poor, I missed out on treats and I'd been looking forward to it for weeks and you tried to spoil it for me.'

'It wasn't like that. Mark has a terrible reputation where women are concerned and I was jealous.'

'It takes two to tango and you should have trusted me. I'm quite capable of keeping a man at bay, that is, I managed for eighteen years till you came along with your persuasive charms.'

'So are you saying you regret it now?'

'No. I loved you then and I love you now. That'll never change but something has to change. I won't be treated like a concubine.'

'You're right and I'm very sorry. I won't mention it again. Could I have another drink please?'

'No, you've had enough. I've never seen you like this before. Go to my room and sleep it off.'

'Will you come with me....please darling?'

'No Paul, I want you to rest. Have you eaten?'

'No. I've had nothing for days. I can't eat.'

'When I've got you into bed, I'll make you some sandwiches for later. Come on.'

As she helped him stand he put his arms around her. 'I love you so much that it hurts,' he mumbled.

She led him into her room and almost at once he fell asleep. As she closed the door she whispered, 'I love you just as much and you're right Paul, it *does* hurt. It hurts a great deal....'

Later, when she checked on him, he was sleeping soundly. She made his sandwiches and put them in

180

the fridge before relaxing on the sofa and writing in her diary, 'Everything's great now. Paul is back in my life,' and then she closed her eyes and fell into a deep sleep, still clutching her diary.

It was turned midnight when Jenny returned and when she saw Paul's car she assumed he and Alison had settled their differences. She was therefore surprised to see Alison asleep on the sofa. Gently, she shook her and asked, 'Is everything alright now?'

'I think so but I'll know better tomorrow. He was in a terrible state when he arrived. He'd been drinking heavily so we didn't have much of a discussion. I sent him to bed to sleep it off.'

'Get him to drop you off at work in the morning. Goodnight Alison.'

'Goodnight Jenny and thanks for everything.'

Paul was still sleeping soundly when Alison went to her bedroom. She got undressed and climbed in beside him. His body felt warm and comforting and she knew she would never leave him again.

When she awoke, his arms were around her and he looked content. She kissed his lips gently and he opened his eyes and returned her kiss.

'We're going to be alright aren't we?' he asked.

'Yes Paul, we're going to be just fine.'

'Look at the time. It's turned ten o'clock. I ought to have been at work an hour ago,' Alison exclaimed.

'Well, you've made me late too,' Paul protested.

'I've made *you* late? That's a laugh.'

'Are you complaining?'

'No, I'm not. Are you?'

He smiled at her lovingly. 'I'm happy as Larry!'

'Me too but hurry up and get dressed because I'll lose more time getting the third degree off Jenny.'

'You don't tell her *everything* do you?'

'I don't need. She reads me like a book. Come on. There are some sandwiches in the fridge I made last night. You can take them back to your Bordello.'

Paul roared with laughter. 'Bordello! If I told you how few women I'd had, you wouldn't believe it.'

'You're right, I wouldn't!'

'Seriously, you could count them on one hand.'

She laughed and quoted, 'And Little Red Riding Hood said, "What great big hands you have grand-mamma."'

'Honestly, I'm speaking the truth,' he insisted.

'Alright but if it's a contest, I can count *mine* on one finger.'

'I know darling and I'm the luckiest guy alive.'

'You won't be if we don't get out of here now.'

He checked his pocket. 'I can't find my car keys.'

'I took them off you last night. They're there.'

'I remember. I'd had a few too many hadn't I?'

'Yes and you wouldn't have counted those on one hand *and* you drove your car. That's terrible Paul.'

'I know but I'll never do it again,' he assured her.

When Paul dropped her off at work, he promised to call her later.

'Everything okay?' Jenny asked as she walked in.

'Yes, the wedding's back on,' she said and before Jenny could quiz her, she went into the back office.

Paul called her mid morning for a quick chat.

'Did you eat your sandwiches?' she asked him.

'Yes, thank you. They didn't even touch the back of my throat. I was ravenous and I could have eaten them twice over. I can't recall when I last ate.'

'That's silly. You'll be ill if you don't eat.'

'I was depressed and I couldn't be bothered going out, speaking of which, will you be free on Friday? I'd like to take you somewhere really special.'

'Where's that?'

'If I told you I'd have to kill you,' he joked. 'Wait and see but you'll have to dress up. Your new black dress would be very appropriate.'

'Won't you give me a clue? Please?' she begged.

'No, wait till Friday. You'll find out then.'

'Have you been there before?'

'I'm saying nothing so stop asking but don't have anything to eat. So you're free then?'

'Yes I am. Thank you and I'll look forward to it.'

'Me too. I'll talk to you later.'

Alison was delighted that they had resolved their differences and yes, she was free on Friday....a day she had been dreading following her tiff with Paul. Friday was the day of her eighteenth birthday. She hadn't mentioned it to Jenny as she hadn't felt able to celebrate it without Paul's presence and now he was taking her somewhere nice on her special day. It was strange how things worked out....

Unbeknown to Alison, there was nothing strange about the way things had worked out; the suspected heavy breather who wouldn't speak; the mysterious whispering conversations; the one purportedly from Tom that wasn't from Tom at all. Those incidents were relevant to an impending celebration of which

Alison knew nothing. In two days' time, she would have the shock of her life if the meticulous planning remained undetected.

'Was that Paul?' Jenny asked, dropping a couple of files on Alison's desk.

'Yes, he's taking me out on Friday.'

'I'm so pleased you're back together,' and with a straight face asked, 'Where's he taking you?'

'He wouldn't say but I have to dress up.'

'Well, you could never say Paul doesn't treat you well. He has his faults but then don't we all?'

'He's lived alone in that awful place for ages and he's very set in his ways but I'm changing that little by little. Maybe our argument wasn't a bad thing. It made us realise just how much we were giving up.'

It was Friday and Jenny suggested they finish work early as she was seeing Tom, and Alison had to be ready in time for her special date with Paul.

As far as Alison was aware, Jenny had no idea it was her eighteenth birthday.

Two items of mail were waiting for Alison when they arrived home. The first one she opened was an eighteenth birthday card from her grandparents and she smiled when she read the words, 'To our sweet granddaughter. Have a wonderful birthday. With all our love, Grandma and Granddad xxx.'

Alison stood the card on her dressing table and as she opened the second, Jenny appeared with a mug of coffee and asked, 'Is that your passport?'

'Yes and the picture doesn't look bad at all. See.'

'You wouldn't have said that about the originals.

Er....what's this?' she queried, picking up the card. 'It's not your birthday, is it?' When she'd read the words, she feigned disappointment. 'Why on earth didn't you tell me? It's your eighteenth birthday!'

Guiltily she said, 'I intended to but then Paul and I split up and I couldn't face celebrating.'

'Well, one night next week, we'll have to arrange a girly night out. Does *he* know it's your birthday?'

'No, I haven't told him. He knows it's this month but not that it's today.'

'Are you going to mention it to him?'

'I might, but don't say anything when he arrives.'

'Happy birthday you silly girl,' she said, hugging her. 'I can't believe you didn't tell me.'

She smirked, enjoying the farce she was directing so well. Alison hadn't any inkling of what to expect and there wouldn't be a dry eye in the house, metaphorically speaking, when she found out later.

'You look beautiful in that dress,' Jenny remarked when Alison was ready to leave. 'Paul certainly has a good eye for fashion and he's very generous too.'

'He loves me, that's why. So where's Tom taking you? You're not dressed yet or is your limited attire meant to save time when he arrives?'

She grinned. 'You don't miss a trick do you?' She didn't reveal that when Alison left, she'd just a few minutes to get dressed and hurry through the door. Everything had to work like clockwork. She wasn't even seeing Tom. In any event, he was on call.

'Is Paul staying over? I might stay at Tom's pad,' she lied. 'You could have the flat to yourselves and you won't keep me awake all night if I'm not here.'

'*Jenny*!'

She chuckled and checked her watch. Paul would be here anytime soon. She was ready apart from her dress. Her bag and shoes were tucked under the bed well out of sight.

When Alison answered the door, she felt weak at the knees. Paul was wearing an exclusive navy-blue suit, a white silk shirt and a blue and white striped tie. He looked amazing. The unsightly dark circles had vanished from around his eyes. 'Wow, what a sight for sore eyes. You look gorgeous,' he said.

'And I could fall head over heels in love with you again. That's a fabulous suit Paul....very retro.'

'Where are you off tonight?' Jenny interrupted.

'Sorry Jenny, I can't tell you. It's classified. Are you seeing Tom later?'

'Yes he'll be here soon,' she lied convincingly.

'Then get dressed you brazen hussy!' Alison said.

En route to the car Paul remarked, 'You look very sexy Alison. You don't know what you do to me.'

'Neither do you Paul. At times I wonder if other couples feel like we do about each other or whether we have something so special that it's unique.'

'I don't know but *I've* never felt like this before. Mine were temporary diversions to escape the humdrum events of daily life. Sorry, that sounds awful.'

'No, I had teenage crushes but they could change on a daily basis if there was a new kid on the block. It's to do with hormones and growing up I expect.'

He started to climb a steep hill and when he got to the top, he stopped. 'I want to show you something.

186

It's a very clear evening. See the millions of stars? Isn't it the most romantic place in the world? They look so tiny from here. I often wonder if some other form of life watches our planet like we watch theirs. We've still a great deal to learn about the Universe. Do you like to study the stars Alison?'

'Yes, but I don't understand them like you do.'

'Maybe it's because I am an artist. I look at things with greater intensity than the average person who merely scans the surface and I see colours that most people don't realise exist. I see beyond the obvious well into the depths. I wish everyone had my penetrable vision because they fail to see so much....'

In awe she gazed into his eyes as they scoured the skies, wishing she had the benefit of his perception.

He turned to face her. 'I want to do this properly.' Reaching in his pocket, he removed a small velvet covered box. 'Will you marry me?' he asked softly. 'I can't live without you.'

He opened the box containing a solitaire diamond ring and as he placed on her finger she kissed him and said, 'I'd be honoured to be your wife Paul.'

Beneath the stars, they embraced passionately and Paul smiled lovingly before saying, 'Now we really must hurry. I've a quick call to make first and then we can enjoy the rest of the evening.'

Wherever Paul was taking her, she knew nothing could compare to the magic of that special moment.

She was somewhat surprised when Paul drove to Maud's house. 'Why are we here?' she asked.

'I've a little quick business to settle. It won't take me a moment. You'd better wait in the car for me.'

'You're not going inside to lock horns with Mark I hope?' she questioned anxiously.

'All that's forgotten Alison. It's Harold I'm here to see and I'll only be a minute.'

As he hurried to the house, Alison inspected her ring in the light from the lamps on the driveway.

Paul returned looking restless. 'Now Maud wants a quick word,' he said irritably. '*Don't* let her keep you talking. I've told her we've no time to spare so keep it to a minimum or we'll be late.'

Tilly bobbed a curtsey as Alison dashed in. 'Good evening Miss Haythorne. Mrs. Taylor would like to see you in the drawing room Miss, if you please.'

'Thank you Tilly,' she replied. She had long since tired of advising Tilly there was no need to curtsey when she called to play the piano for Maud.

Tilly opened the door to the drawing room. It was in total darkness but instantly, lights illuminated the room. Alison heard voices shouting, '*Surprise*' and was conscious of Paul's arm round her shoulder but she couldn't work out what was happening. Though everyone was chanting, '*Happy Birthday*,' still she didn't realise it was directed at her. As she focused her eyes on the guests, suddenly it became obvious when she recognised all the familiar faces she loved and she began to laugh and cry simultaneously.

'Happy birthday, kid,' Jenny giggled in sync with the peal of laughter from everybody. 'Did you truly believe we didn't know today was your eighteenth birthday?'

Alison looked at Paul who grinned broadly at her. 'Caught you again! That's another one to chalk up.

I said you'd never beat me. Happy birthday Babe.'

'I'll never believe another word you tell me.'

'You'd better believe how much I love you.'

Everyone was hugging and kissing her. Mark and Richard were there as were Elizabeth and John, in fact all members of her adopted families were there. The only thing to mar her optimum happiness was the absence of her grandparents but she sensed that she would be in their thoughts.

'That went well,' Jenny remarked. 'You hadn't a clue and you branded me a brazen hussy! Now had that been *me*, I'd have known what was going on. I never miss a thing, ever.'

'Well you missed *this*,' Alison replied smugly as she held out her hand and Jenny screeched, causing Elizabeth and Maud to scuttle across to investigate before uttering superlatives about the beautiful ring and the size of the diamond, while the males could only speculate about the cause of the uproar.

'It'll be a girl thing,' Harold declared. 'Let them get on with it. At least, while they're across there, they're leaving us alone. Who fancies a drink?'

'Alison, my dear, come and see the table. We're almost ready to eat. You too Paul,' Maud said.

'Oh Maud, it's beautiful!' Alison gasped as Maud opened the door. 'Look Paul, doesn't it look superb. I'll never be able to thank you enough Maud. From the first day we met, you've been so kind to me and for you to do all this too....it's so unbelievable. This has to be the best day of my life.'

'Well, there's more yet my dear. You have lots of presents in the study,' she said, opening the door. 'I put them on the desk. You can open them later.'

Alison poked her head round the door and looked in the direction Maud was pointing and she blinked in total disbelief. Sitting at the desk were her grandparents. Tears flooded her eyes as she ran towards them and Maud went out, leaving the four together.

Alison heard from her grandparents how Paul had enlisted Harold's help in arranging their transportation from Brighton. They had arrived that afternoon and after a light lunch, had rested a couple of hours prior to the party. They had been invited to stay till Sunday, giving them plenty of time on Saturday to spend with their granddaughter and Paul.

'They're such friendly folk, every one of 'em an' they can't do enough for me an' yer granddad, an' i'n't it a posh 'ouse?' Joyce remarked excitedly.

She laughed. 'Yes, it's a *very* posh house and I'm so happy you're here. Thank you for the wonderful surprise Paul. I'll never forget this.'

'Anything to make you happy Babe,' he answered and kissed her tenderly.

'Did yer find the recipe for the sweetloaf lass?'

'I did Grandma and your cheque too. I was going to call you tomorrow. You are far too generous.'

'Nonsense, yer all we've got now an' yer'll get it all anyway when we've gone.'

'Don't say such things. I want you both forever.'

'If only that were possible lass but we're 'ere now so we should make the most of it.'

'Have you met everyone else?' Alison enquired.

'We 'ave. We just 'id in 'ere when you an' Paul arrived. They thought it'd upset yer too much if we

190

were in there as well as t'other folk. I bet yer were flabbergasted weren't yer?'

'Yes and more so to see you and granddad here.'

'Thanks, I don't mind if I do,' Alfred said. 'Aye, I could just manage a drop o' beer.'

'We're off,' Alison laughed. 'I thought it was too good to last. Come on, let's join the others. You sit next to granddad, Paul. He likes talking to you.'

'Not likely! I got a ticking off last time about the innuendo and I don't want to play footsie under the table with him. Well, not when you're here I don't.'

'Jenny was saying I should invite you to stay over tonight. She won't be there,' she said seductively.

'Great! Can we go now?' he asked with a glint in his eye and Alison slapped his arm.

'Carry on,' he laughed. 'I'm rather partial to a bit of slap and tickle first.'

Maud, in her own inimitable way at perfecting all the details had designated where everybody should sit. There were eleven diners and the prime position had been designated for Alison. Paul was seated to her right and her grandparents to her left and Jenny was to sit between Richard and Mark with the four parents occupying the remaining places.

Dinah and Tilly served out the food with dexterity and care. Hot food must never be served at Maud's table unless piping hot and everything had its rightful place on the plate. Maud wouldn't tolerate carelessness and one drop of sauce out of place would provide just cause for a raised eyebrow.

As expected, the food was scrumptious and at one point, Alison had to gesture to Alfred to stop, as he

191

attempted to scrape his plate as clean as it had been before the food was served.

'Would it be much trouble t'yer if I 'ad a glass o' beer 'Arold?' Alfred suddenly piped up. 'I'm not a wine drinker. Yer see, I were a bricky by trade an' when we cleared off for a drop of ale wi' our dinner if one o' t'lads 'ad dared to ask for a glass o' wine, 'e'd 'ave got thumped, if yer get my drift.'

Everyone found Alfred's remark highly amusing and laughed heartily, none more so than Paul who was bent double. He could well imagine the prejudice then towards a homosexual bricklayer and he guessed Alfred had witnessed noteworthy changes in attitude to sexual orientation during his lifetime.

To compound the outburst of laughter, though not with intent, Harold remarked that *he* would prefer a glass of beer too, whereupon Alfred responded that he hadn't been suggesting *Harold* was like that. His remark caused a tumultuous guffaw from the other men, causing Harold to wish that he'd kept his big mouth shut. Alison was horror-struck but Paul took hold of her hand beneath the table and advised her that everyone adored Alfred and there was no cause for concern.

The scene had been set for humour and so Harold took centre stage and began to narrate from his infinite script of amusing anecdotes.

A venerable raconteur, Harold spoke clearly and Alfred had no difficulty in understanding him and joined in the laughter as well. 'Yer tell a damn good tale lad,' Alfred called out to him regularly. 'I can't remember when I've ever laughed as much.'

When Harold finally sat down to enjoy his well-earned glass of beer, it was John's turn to speak. He initially proposed a toast to Alison on her birthday, then to the happy couple, who had become engaged to be married. He reminded everyone that although Alison had come into their lives just a few months ago, she had made a lasting impact on each of them and they regarded her as a family member.

'Hear hear!' they all replied.

Alison was about to respond with a few words of thanks when Mark stood up and tapped his glass for order. Alison and Jenny exchanged darting glances and Alison held Paul's hand, hoping there would be no unpleasant repercussions.

'The first time I met Alison, I was stunned by her beauty and charm and I felt fortunate to have made the acquaintance of such a sweet-natured creature. Unfortunately, I held back in showing my affection for her but Paul, a man of greater worth and experience than I, swept her off her feet the very moment he set eyes on her. Paul is Alison's Sir Lancelot and Alison is Paul's Lady Guinevere. They are so well-suited that they belong together and consequently, I am obliged to back out as the sorry loser.'

'And you'd better remember to stay out too,' Paul interrupted with a forced smile that only Jenny and Alison recognised as a warning. The others laughed at Paul's comment but Alison was furious with him and she kicked his ankle, causing him to wince and stare at her quizzically.

'Please raise your glasses to the lovely Alison.'

'To Alison,' they called in unison.

193

She arose to reply to Mark and John and thanked all of them for their kindness which would never be forgotten, and particularly for arranging her grandparents' presence at her celebration party.

Maud suggested it might be an appropriate time to return to the drawing room so Alison could open her presents and Richard seized the opportunity to offer to show everyone a new card trick.

They laughed when John declared he had saved a small fortune over the years by not having to hire a party clown when he had Richard for free.

Accompanied by Maud, Alison and Paul went to the study to collect the presents and when Maud left ahead of them, Alison turned to Paul who appeared angry and queried, 'Why have you got a face like a smacked arse?'

'I think that's a most inappropriate remark from a young lady,' he answered frostily.

'Now *there's* a strange coincidence because I felt exactly the same about what *you* said to Mark.'

'That's different. The bloody libertine was out of order paying you compliments. The only reason he said those things was to humiliate me.'

'Don't be so petty-minded. Besides, if that's what you thought, then you ought to feel triumphant that you've got what he wants. Put the parcels down.'

'Why?'

'Because I said so.'

Paul replaced his parcels on the desk and turned to face her. 'We agreed we wouldn't do this again, quarrel over stupid things,' she murmured softly as she began to unfasten the buttons on his shirt. She caressed his bare flesh while kissing him tenderly. 'So are you staying with me tonight?'

'I've no pyjamas,' he panted breathlessly.

'Don't worry about that…. You won't need any,' she said provocatively.

The moments of anger had passed and Alison felt victorious as they returned to the drawing room.

'Open that first,' Jenny said and Alison ripped off the paper excitedly to reveal two designer bikinis.

'They're beautiful. Thank you Jenny. You're determined to get me on holiday. First a passport and now the bikinis,' she said, passing them round.

'Open ours next,' Richard said. 'It's that big one. It's from Mark and me. We chose it together.'

As she attempted to remove the packaging, Paul knelt beside her to help. It was a set of travel bags.

'They're terrific. You won't believe it but I don't have a travel bag. I've never been away on holiday. Thank you Richard,' Alison said, leaping up to kiss his cheek. 'Thank you Mark,' she added and as she hugged him, Paul stared attentively to watch where Mark placed his hands.

Elizabeth pointed to their gift and that contained a flight ticket to Malaga and some foreign currency.

In response to Alison's baffled expression, Jenny told her they were Euros. 'Don't worry. You're not going alone. There's four of us….you, me, Antonia and Clare. Open that one from Maud and Harold.'

When she opened that package, she discovered a key but was at a loss to understand its significance.

'Maud and Harold own a huge four-bedroom villa on the Costa del Sol in Spain. It's even got its own pool and we can use it for a fortnight in April. What do you think of that?' asked Jenny excitedly.

Alison was speechless. 'I don't know *what* to say. It's unbelievable!' she cried and she ran round the room, thanking the four adults for their generosity.

'I'll explain it all in detail later but don't lose the key, the currency or your ticket. That's why I kept nagging you to get a passport,' Jenny advised her. 'Incidentally, did anyone *not* see Alison's original passport photos? I'm sure she'd be happy to show them you,' she added mischievously. 'Right, come on, there's another there from Paul.'

'But you bought me my beautiful ring,' she said.

'Not for your birthday. *This* is for your birthday,' he said, handing her a square parcel.

Alison quickly removed the paper and unzipped a leather bag containing a selection of sun protection and after-sun lotion. 'Thank you Paul. That's something I'd never have thought of buying.'

Jenny caught his eye and commented pointedly, 'In that case, it's a good thing Paul thought about it. One can never be *too* careful about protection, for there can be serious consequences. Right Paul?'

The inference of her aside was lost on the others, but Paul immediately grasped the significance and realised that if Alison had discussed such intimate concerns with Jenny, he had been foolhardy to dismiss those concerns so heartlessly.

He nodded in response though enraged that Jenny had chosen such a forum to make her point.

When Alison leaned across to kiss him, she was surprised how strongly he held her but Jenny didn't fail to notice and *she* knew the reason why.

As Harold went to pour everyone a drink, Alison collected up the wrapping paper and took it into the kitchen to throw it away.

Maud was hot on her heels. 'I'm making a pot of coffee,' she said. 'Would you like one Alison?'

'I'd love one please. Maud, I don't how to thank you. It's been such a wonderful evening. The food was superb as was the company and I've received the most wonderful gifts. I've never seen the inside of an airport. I haven't a clue what to do.'

'Don't worry, Jenny will take care of you. You'll have a great time. I always wanted a daughter and I feel as if I have one now. Life is so strange isn't it? Would you play the piano while I make the coffee? I can hear you in here. I'll call you when it's ready.'

'I'd love to,' she said, aware it gave her pleasure.

She walked in the music room and sat down at the piano and after practising her scales till her fingers were warm and supple, she chose a short medley by Maud's favourite composer. Her musical talent had been revived of late and she knew her pieces well.

In the kitchen, Maud listened carefully to her renditions while dabbing her eyes, as Alison, oblivious of everything but the music, continued to play.

Unheard, Paul had entered the music room and as he listened in amazement to Alison's interpretation of the music, it suddenly became apparent why the concert had meant so much to her and only when he placed his arms around her did her music stop.

'You never cease to amaze me sweetheart. I had no idea you were a talented pianist,' he said softly.

197

'Painting is your life and music is mine,' she told him with a smile as they left the room.

He gazed at her as she knelt by her grandparents, understanding her love for them, her two remaining relatives. He couldn't begin to imagine her distress at losing her mother with no one else close at hand.

He looked around the room at those who had befriended her; Jenny who was her rock; Richard who secretly adored her and Mark, who seldom missed an opportunity to go for the kill, yet who had mistimed his advances so badly on this occasion.

Paul's eyes were directed to Elizabeth and Maud who had competed forcefully to host the party but it had been Maud who was to win in the end, for she had the larger house and the requisite accommodation for Joyce and Alfred. Finally, there were John and Harold, currently arranging for Alison to manage one of their new ventures, although Alison was the only person unaware of that fact. Maud couldn't rely on Harold to maintain secrecy about the party and John had been similarly instructed to keep his distance. Maud and Elizabeth were determined that the loose tongue of either Harold or John would not scuttle their carefully prepared plans.

Again, Paul turned his attention to Alison, whose diamond ring flashed like a brilliant star. Very soon he would be placing another ring on her finger and that would be the happiest day of his life.

Richard called for quiet. 'Listen, I've got a brand new card trick. Who wants to see it?'

'There's no show without Punch!' John joked.

'Very funny but this *will* work,' Richard replied.

'It better had, Houdini,' John added with a laugh.

'Houdini wasn't a magician. He was an escapologist,' he corrected his father.

'I know that Richard, and that's what you'll need to be if this trick doesn't work!' he stated, knowing his son wouldn't take offence at his humour. 'Just get on with it and put us all out of our misery.'

'I'll bet you a fiver I get it right,' Richard replied.

'I'll do better than that. I'll bet *you* a tenner you don't,' John smirked.

He shuffled the cards and asked Alison to choose one and she removed the two of clubs and held it up for everyone to see before returning it to the pack. He shuffled them once more and placed them face down on the table. 'Give me a number between one and ten,' he instructed.

Each person called a different number, provoking further laughter. 'Paul, give me a number,' Richard demanded, becoming noticeably agitated.

'Five,' he answered, still laughing.

Richard removed the top five cards from the pack and placed them aside. 'So, *Doubting Thomas*,' he said to his father, 'Take the next card from the top of the pack please.'

John sighed and picked up the top card. 'Well I'll be damned. It's the two of clubs!' he exclaimed.

With a broad grin, Richard held out his hand for his father to settle his debt and John paid up. 'How did you do that? I'm very impressed,' John said as he picked up the cards while Richard was otherwise engaged, bowing and smiling victoriously at all the applauding onlookers.

'Every one's the two of clubs, you bloody cheat!' John cried....

It was well turned midnight and Joyce had prodded Alfred a couple of times for closing his eyes but the others were feeling weary too and had settled down to enjoy quiet conversation.

'I think we should take our leave, Harold. The old folks look exhausted. They've had a long and tiring day,' Paul remarked.

'You're right. I'll get Maud to take them upstairs. I assume you'll be round in the morning?'

'Yes but not too early, say about eleven and we'll take them out for the afternoon.'

'I'll take them up Harold, and Maud can relax for a change,' Alison said. 'She's done enough today.'

Joyce and Alfred left the room with Alison after making their way around the others with the usual pleasantries. 'What grand people they are. I were a bit bothered when we got 'ere an' saw this massive 'ouse but they couldn't 'ave made us no more welcome, an' for that young feller to drive all that way for us, I couldn't thank 'im enough, an' 'e wouldn't let us give 'im owt for 'is trouble, an' that meal, it were t'best meal we've ever 'ad. Me an' yer grand-dad are right suited to see yer settled wi' Paul. 'E's a well-mannered young feller. 'E kept comin' over talkin' to us. We've 'ad a right good time today.'

'Well now you can enjoy a good night's sleep. If you make your way to the kitchen in the morning, Tilly will attend to your breakfast. We'll pick you up around eleven o'clock. Goodnight.'

At the door, Alison clung to Maud and Elizabeth, thanking them once more for her tremendous party. Richard kissed her goodnight and Mark hugged her. 'If ever you need me, I'll be here for you,' he said.

Jenny took her in her arms and gabbled about the forthcoming holiday. 'I don't know how I've kept it quiet. We'll have an absolute ball. You'll love it.'

Paul put his arm round Alison in the taxi and she rested her head on his shoulder. 'Wasn't it a terrific party Paul? It was such a surprise and more so with granddad and grandma being there. It's been perfect and I'm so pleased you're staying over tonight.'

Though Paul made no audible response, the smile on his face confirmed his accord.

Saturday was an equally pleasurable day for Alison who was able to spend further time with her grand-parents when the four of them went out to lunch.

They returned via a country route, arriving back late evening after calling in at Elizabeth's to deliver some flowers, where they were then invited to stay for drinks and a snack.

The next morning, Alison bade a tearful farewell to her grandparents. 'We'll see you soon,' she wept.

'I do 'ope so,' Joyce said as her eyes welled with tears. 'You enjoy yer lovely 'oliday an' me an' yer granddad'll be thinkin' o' yer on that plane. Don't forget to send us a postcard will yer?' she added in a broken voice, while Alfred held her tight, fighting to contain his own tears.

7

Jenny had arranged a get-together with Antonia and Clare to discuss the forthcoming holiday.

Alison was in the kitchen preparing a snack when they arrived and they wandered in to ask if she had suspected anything about her party.

'Surely you had an inkling *something* was going on?' Antonia asked.

'Truthfully, I hadn't a clue. I didn't realise Jenny knew the date. I should have known it would be on my file. I'd fallen out with Paul the previous week so I was too upset to even think about my birthday.'

'How is he?' she enquired.

'He's great. He felt miserable too when we broke up but all that's behind us now and....'

Clare cut in, 'You've got quite a catch there you know. Paul's regarded as the most eligible bachelor for miles around but he's managed to remain out of reach of every female who's pursued him. You're a very clever girl to have snared Paul Trantor.'

'Clare, you can be such a cow sometimes!' Jenny said heatedly. 'Alison didn't *snare* Paul. *He* did all the running and he's the clever one to have found a fantastic girl like Alison when he *could* have ended up with a bitch like you if he'd dropped his guard.'

'Excuse me!' Alison said. 'I *am* in the room you know. She didn't mean any harm, did you Clare?'

'You'll soon get used to me Alison. I'm what folk refer to as, "all mouth and no knickers". I'm sorry. Paul *is* very lucky to have you. Look after him.'

'I intend to,' she replied.

They talked about the resort, the weather and the relative merits of the villa's close proximity to the night-life. Jenny, having been previously, was well-acquainted with the area. Though the villa was fully equipped, apart from breakfast, they would eat out, unless they were having a lazy day beside the pool, they agreed. Alison was excited and couldn't imagine what it would be like to be in a foreign country. She had already made a packing list, she told them.

'Right....well don't forget to pack enough of the necessities,' Clare laughed and Alison was puzzled.

'Take no notice....ignore her,' Jenny said. 'You'll not need any of those.'

'Well, you can still pack some in case I run out,' Clare added. 'A fortnight's a long time.'

Alison had already made up her mind that Clare wouldn't be *her* choice of friend but as she would be there, Alison would have to make the best of the situation. Perhaps when she knew Clare better she might change her opinion but she found her rather brash. If she wanted to sleep around for two weeks, that was her prerogative but she wouldn't be influenced to do likewise. She was more than happy to love Paul and she knew he would miss her as much as she would miss him.

She had expected Paul to kick up a fuss about the imminent holiday but he hadn't said a single word. She was unaware that Jenny had warned him not to put a damper on her first ever holiday that had been arranged before he appeared on the scene.

It was turned midnight when the girls finally went home. Alison started to clear away the supper plates and was about to leave the room when Jenny said, 'Don't feel intimidated by Clare. She has quite a lot of good points. She can be really good company.'

She frowned. 'I'll have to take your word for that but I promise I won't do anything to rock the boat.'

'Are you getting excited that we've only eight days to wait?' Jenny asked later in the week.

'*Excited* doesn't come close. I keep thinking it's a dream and I'll wake up because it feels so surreal.'

'Has Paul said anything derogatory about it?'

'Surprisingly not, although I expected he would, especially after the fuss he made about the concert.'

Jenny felt satisfyingly smug. Her warning to Paul must have been heeded. 'Are you seeing him later? Tom's coming round but you don't have to go out.'

'I can't get hold of him. I've tried his number two or three times but his phone's turned off.'

'Stay in with us then. We're only playing CDs.'

'It's going well between you isn't it? You're like a proper couple now....at ease and compatible.'

'Yes. Tom's sensitive and caring and he's forever phoning me, even if only for a moment or two and he says the sweetest things. I like him a lot.'

'It's a nice feeling to know you have a steady guy to rely on. We've a lot to thank Antonia for and to think I didn't want to go to her party. I was afraid it might end up a drunken orgy and look who I met.'

'Yes, Simon Ward!' she smirked.

'Ugh! Don't remind me.'

When it was time to leave work, Paul still hadn't contacted her and she was becoming concerned.

'Stop worrying. He's never missed phoning you,' Jenny said reassuringly. 'He'll call later.'

The telephone at the flat rang about seven o'clock and Alison rushed to answer it. 'Oh Paul, I've been trying to get hold of you all day. Are you alright?'

'Of course Babe. I've been out and about today. Are you free for an hour? I wanted to talk to you.'

'What about?'

'Wait and see. If I tell you now, I lose my excuse for having you all to myself later.'

'You don't need any excuse. I'll come anyway.'

'I'm still not telling you. Is seven-thirty okay?'

'It's fine. I've just had my tea so I'll get ready.'

'Dress casual. It's nothing fancy, just a drink.'

'Do you prefer a drink or a drive?' Paul enquired as they walked to the car.

'A drive would be a pleasant change. It's a lovely evening and I'm not really bothered about a drink.'

'Me neither. As long as I'm with you, I don't care where we are. I've missed you so much today.'

'Me too. Where have you been? I was worried.'

'There was no need, in fact, everything is perfect. I've been to visit my folks to tell them our news.'

She was surprised. 'Why didn't you tell me?'

He shrugged his shoulders and sighed. 'I suppose I was afraid to tempt providence because last time I arranged to go we ended up having a barney and I didn't want anything to go wrong this time.'

'So what did they say? Were they pleased?'

'Absolutely delighted. Mum ran round the house screaming. She was disappointed I hadn't taken you with me but she's invited us there for the weekend. She can't wait to meet you and she's very happy for us. There are however, two small drawbacks.'

'Tell me,' she said with an air of consternation.

'First, you'll get the third degree all weekend off mum and second, we'll be in separate rooms.'

'I can handle that.'

'I can't. I'll go mad knowing you're so near and I won't be with you. I'll have to think of something.'

'You'll do no such thing. I'm not tiptoeing about during the night at your parents' house. I would die of shame if we got caught. I don't even know your parents yet. Are they very straight-laced?'

'Mmm, that's a tricky one. I've been living away from home so long that I've had no adult life with them. I visit occasionally but rarely stay. I've never been in a situation where it's been tested but suffice to say I wouldn't risk coming to your room.'

'So you've not had any other lady friends there?'

'Alison, I haven't had any *lady friends* in the way you mean. Ours is the only meaningful relationship I've had. I've never been in love before nor ached with need for anyone before. Till I met you, art was my entire life. I can't bear to be separated from you for one day and I don't know what I'll do when you leave me for two weeks. I'll be counting the hours.'

'Me too,' she sighed. 'I wish you were coming.'

'So do I. For your next foreign holiday, we'll fly to Venice. It's the most beautiful and romantic city in the world. Couples can get married on a gondola. Did you know that?'

'Is that true?'

206

'It is. Would you like that, a romantic wedding on the Grand Canal, being serenaded by a gondolier?'

'Not if it means waiting. Anyway, I don't want a fuss. I just want you.'

'And I want you too but I expect there'll be some input from my mother. She'll want to make it a day to remember, so please don't cross her on that one. Just allow her to have her hour of glory.'

'Do you think your parents will approve of me?'

He laughed. 'Of course. They'll adore you just as I do. I fancy a beer. Where do you want to go?'

'Back to your place. I believe the guy living there has some fine wines and we won't be disturbed.'

'Good luck,' Jenny called as Alison left with Paul. 'Don't tell them anything about me if you want to impress your future-in-laws.'

Jenny closed the door and smiled, feeling content for Alison. Over recent weeks, Jenny's lifestyle had improved too. She enjoyed living and working with Alison and while she had helped Alison overcome her recent troubles, Alison had transformed her life too, though Jenny had been concerned of late when Tom had mentioned the possibility of his return to South Africa. She hadn't discussed that with Alison who had been dealing with her own problems then.

Tom had disclosed that he was homesick for his family and Jenny was devastated at the prospect of losing him. Since then, she had purposely avoided any mention of South Africa and she wished it had only been possible to discuss the matter with Alison who was so logical and level-headed.

After much deliberation, she decided she would seek Alison's advice on her return from Stafford.

'Tell me about your childhood Paul,' Alison said. 'I know so little about your life before I met you.'

He flashed a boyish grin. 'When I wasn't holding a paintbrush, I was holding a paintbrush. That's the measure of it. Nothing else is worthy of mention. I was a dreary sort of kid with tunnel vision. Art was all I ever wanted to do. Nothing else interested me.'

'That's not true. You were interested in me, so be serious.'

'I *am* being serious. I was a kid then but it was art at the forefront of my mind when I first saw you. I wanted to paint you. In my mind's eye, you were a magnificent canvas hanging on my wall.'

'This is another wind-up isn't it?'

'No it's not. I visualised you as a Gainsborough portrait, seated in your off-the-shoulder gown, your hair falling in curls over ivory-coloured shoulders. I still want to paint you like that and someday I will.'

'Surely you had other interests, like sport?'

'Not really. I was obsessed with painting from an early age. I went into the sixth form just to indulge my parents but the only subject to interest me was History and Appreciation of Art, though I somehow managed to pass three further A levels. When I said I intended enrolling at Art School, it caused uproar. My father was adamant I'd choose a reliable career but I wouldn't listen. It caused countless arguments so I left and rented a small flat with three other art students and didn't see my parents much after that.'

'It must have been hard without parental support.'

'There's an understatement if ever I heard one. I lived from hand to mouth. Food didn't pass my lips for days but I couldn't admit defeat. I had to prove I could be successful. I did whatever I could to earn a crust. Everything was legal but I had to stoop quite low at times. At one point I was even a donor for a fertility clinic. A few of us played crummy music in the market place and I can't recall how often we ran off when the police appeared on the scene.'

'And what did *you* play?'

'Nothing. I was the one who walked out with the cap for the money. We found that if we left it on the ground, everyone walked by but if I looked up with pitiful eyes, the ladies would spare a few coppers. Like you, they couldn't resist me,' he grinned.

'Imagine what you'd have earned as a Gigolo.'

'I know; that thought did cross my mind,' he said tensing his muscles as he awaited her disapproving slap. 'Look, there's a service area coming up. How about a coffee and a cuddle?'

'A coffee would be very welcome but I'll pass on the cuddle,' she replied snootily.

'I bet you don't.'

'I bet I do. Well, maybe not because I don't know when I'll get another. Gigolo indeed.'

As they drank their coffee she urged, 'Go on with the story. I want to know everything about you.'

'That's about it. I sold a few paintings that were on display in the Art School but it was a very competitive market. There were many talented students so I had to work night and day to deliver the goods.

209

We pooled our resources because some weeks we sold nothing but we still had to provide materials. I took a job at an all-night supermarket two nights a week shelf-stacking but I could barely drag myself to college some mornings so I had to pack that in.'

'How did you become the much sought-after Paul Trantor?'

'That was a lucky break. Some guy who knew my art teacher wanted a portrait painted of his children. He was a well-to-do guy and when it was finished, he paid me a hefty bonus. A few of his friends saw it and commissioned portraits of their children too, so for the first time in my life, I was earning a few quid. Then I was introduced to another guy with an exclusive furniture shop, so I did regular works for him. He bought my paintings and sold them on at a profit and soon my work was starting to be recognised. Around that time, the local rag ran an article about me with a photograph. It must have appealed to the readers because I got numerous commissions after that. From then on it all escalated to the extent that I needed an agent to market my work and plan exhibitions over a much wider field. It hasn't been a trouble-free passage, though it's been a rewarding one in many ways.'

'Do you ever tire of painting?'

'Never, though I often become frustrated because I set myself high standards. Don't you when you're playing the piano? It's no different.'

'It is, because I'm not a professional like you.'

'That's by choice. The only difference between a professional and an amateur is money. If you were to charge a fee then you'd be a professional pianist. Right, enough about me. It's time for my cuddle.'

'I feel anxious about meeting your parents.'

'Come here,' he said, taking her in his arms. 'You have nothing to worry about. They'll adore you.'

Paul kissed her reassuringly before they departed on the final leg of their journey.

Out of the blue she said, 'Your parents don't live in a big fancy house do they?'

'What possessed you to ask such a question?'

'Because everyone I've met recently does.'

'I don't Babe. I live in a fleapit.'

'Well yes but with the finest wines,' she laughed.

'What did you think of it last night when you saw it for a second time?'

'I didn't notice. We were otherwise engaged.'

With a mischievous grin he quipped, 'Indeed we were. I'd forgotten about that.'

Ignoring his response she pressed the point. 'You still haven't told me. *Is* it a big house?'

'It's semi-detached but you can see for yourself in a minute. We're coming up to it soon.'

She looked ahead as Paul turned his car into what could only be described as an imposing driveway to a stately home. Peering ahead she could make out a magnificent edifice in the distance but no ordinary houses were yet appearing in view. What a wonderful location, Alison mused. *She* would be overjoyed to live in a house in such a secluded spot where the gardens were so beautifully maintained.

As Paul proceeded down the drive, further houses still failed to appear in view.

Finally, he swung the car to the left and stopped outside the entrance to the gargantuan building.

'You *are* joking!' she exclaimed in horror. 'Your parents don't live here! They can't! I mean it Paul. If they do, I'm not coming in.'

'I'm sorry darling, I'm afraid they do.'

'Take me away, now,' she begged almost in tears.

'I can't do that. They're expecting us. It'll be fine, honestly. I promise not to let go of your hand. My parents are no different from Elizabeth and John or Maud and Harold. If you feel uncomfortable at any time, we'll leave. I can't be fairer than that, can I?'

'I don't understand. You struggled all through Art College, yet you have wealthy parents?'

'I needed to succeed without their help Alison. I had a point to prove.' He stepped from the car and opened her door. 'Please darling, come on now.'

Alison was visibly shaking as she approached the entrance although thankful she had decided to wear her cashmere suit. At least she would look present-able should they show her the door, she thought.

As they walked towards the double oak doors, she couldn't believe her eyes as a butler greeted them.

'Good morning Sir, Madam,' he said, bowing his head graciously. 'Sir Anthony and Lady Trantor are in the conservatory if you would like to go through. May I have your car parked in the garage Sir?'

'Thank you Charles,' Paul said, tugging Alison's hand as they stepped into the impressive hallway.

They had barely taken two steps before Victoria Trantor pranced hurriedly towards them. 'Paul my darling, you're early,' she cried and she gave him a

212

quick peck on the cheek. 'And you must be Alison. I've heard *so* much about you, though you're much more exquisite than Paul led me to believe. I simply *adore* your designer suit,' she gabbled loquaciously before kissing her on both cheeks. 'I'm thrilled Paul could bring you today. I couldn't wait to meet you. Follow me Alison. Tony's in the conservatory. I'm Vicky. Did you have a good journey? I want to hear everything about how you and Paul met. I'm such a romantic. Let me see your ring. Oh it's magnificent. Did you choose it yourself?'

Alison, who still hadn't uttered one word, looked over her shoulder to find Paul who was standing by the door. He flashed a reassuring smile to boost her confidence. 'Paul chose it for me. It *is* beautiful and exactly what I'd have chosen myself,' she replied.

As they reached the conservatory, Vicky called to her husband, 'Darling, Paul and Alison are here.'

Anthony Trantor stood up to greet her and Alison instantly recognised a striking resemblance between father and son.

Though he was of more distinguished appearance, Alison could clearly visualise how Paul would look in twenty or so years' time.

'I'm pleased to meet you my dear,' Tony said. 'I feel I know you already. Paul never stopped talking about you when he called. How are you?'

'I'm very well thank you. It's lovely to meet you too, both of you,' she answered politely.

'Make yourself at home dear. I'll summon some coffee, that is unless you'd prefer something a little stronger,' Vicky said.

'Coffee would be lovely, thank you,' she replied, though a brandy would have been more welcome to calm her nerves and settle her racing heart.

Paul appeared and stroked her neck momentarily before walking over to his father. 'Alright Dad?' he asked, shaking his hand.

'I'm fine son. I was just about to have a beer.'

'Make that two then. I could manage a beer. What about you darling? Would you like a proper drink?'

'No thanks. I'm having coffee with....' she replied hesitantly, looking flustered.

'Vicky,' Victoria reminded her.

'I'll sort out the beers,' Paul said.

'Be a darling and ask Betty to bring some coffee. Have you brought Alison's bag from the car?'

'Yes, it's by the door.'

'Right Alison, I'll take you to your room and you can freshen up. You can tell me how you met Paul. I want to know every little detail. We have so much to talk about. Come along dear.'

'I'll bring your bag up in a minute,' Paul said.

Alison followed her up the magnificent staircase. 'When was this house built?' she enquired.

'I don't really know. You'd have to ask Tony. It's been in his family for a zillion years. We don't own all of it; just the west wing,' she advised her.

Vicky led her along the broad impressive landing and opened a bedroom door. 'This is a pretty room and the view is unbelievable.' Turning to ensure no one could overhear, she whispered, 'I'm not expecting you to sleep here but remember to crumple the sheets please. I pay the maids to work not gossip,' she added on a shrill laugh. 'Paul would never dare come to you under our roof so you must go to him.'

Alison felt colour rising in her cheeks and Vicky laughed again. 'Now I've shocked you. Ignore me my dear. I speak first and think later but we're both women of the world aren't we? We must keep our men happy mustn't we? There, I've done it again. I'll leave before I say anything else I shouldn't. I'll see you later. Don't be long. I love talking to you. We'll discuss the wedding later. I'm so excited.'

Alison flopped on the bed, her mind in a whirl. Is this true, she asked herself, that in the last half hour, she had arrived at what could best be described as a stately home to be met by *titled* future in-laws? Had Vicky really said what she believed she had heard?

Alison was still reeling from the shock when Paul tapped on her door. 'Dare I venture in?' he enquired with a roguish beam. 'I've brought your bag.'

'I think you'd better. You've got some explaining to do. How *could* you throw me in at the deep end like that? I hate you!'

'No you don't, you love me. You said so earlier,' he said, taking her in his arms.

She closed her arms around him, wondering what other revelations might follow. 'Couldn't you have at least warned me? It was bad enough to see such an enormous house and then for a butler to open the door and to hear him refer to your parents as titled, I nearly burst out laughing. I thought it was a wind-up. I wanted to say, "Right, and I'm Lady Alison."'

Paul roared with laughter. 'Now *that* would have been hilarious. Mum would definitely have seen the funny side of that. She's not into all that pomp and circumstance that goes with the title. It's dad's title. It's hereditary so the day might dawn when you *will* be announcing that you're Lady Alison.'

'You're joking! I'd choke on the words. I want to be plain Alison Trantor, nothing else.'

'And you *will* be Alison Trantor, soon my sweet girl, but you will *never* be plain.'

'You still haven't answered me. What possessed you to keep it from me?'

'Supposing I'd told you, would you have believed one word of it?'

'No I wouldn't because you're persistently setting me up. Don't think I've forgotten those things you said to granddad and the way you embarrassed me.'

'You weren't allowed to mention that again. You promised,' he said, kissing her forehead. 'I've taken my punishment for that so, returning to my parents, if you wouldn't have believed it, then was there any point in my telling you?'

'I *might* have believed you. You didn't know for sure that I wouldn't.'

'So, if you had, would you have come today?'

'Definitely not!'

'So that's why I didn't tell you. Are you angry?'

'No, Paul. I don't know who you are but that isn't important because when all said and done, I'm only *marrying* you. Why mention something so trivial?'

'I love that cute face when you sulk,' he smirked.

'Shut up Paul and stop laughing. It isn't funny.'

'I can't see why you're so annoyed with me. Had my parents been serial killers, I could have under-

216

stood your concern but they're not....they're titled. That's no big deal Alison.'

She sighed with exasperation. 'I was greeted by a butler. I didn't think people *had* butlers nowadays. I was mortified and I almost died when he referred to your parents and then, when your mother whisked me off, you chose to desert me in my hour of need. I didn't even know what to call her. I felt like Tilly. I still don't know whether I ought to have curtsied or called her Ma'am. You're a horrible person, Paul Trantor. You really are....and it *is* a big deal!'

'Darling Alison, if you think I'm horrible now, I can't imagine what you'll say and do when I....' He couldn't even finish his sentence and he laughed so much that tears filled his eyes. When she glowered at him he laughed louder. 'I love you so much,' he said and he gripped her hands to restrain her before revealing, 'That was the *supreme* wind-up and you fell for it hook line and sinker. Charles the butler is actually Charlie the gardener and mum and dad are just Mr. and Mrs. Trantor. I persuaded mum to take part in this hilarious stitch-up and against her better judgment, I hasten to add, but my dad categorically refused to be involved. That's why he hardly spoke. If you could have seen the expression on your face when Charlie greeted us. I didn't abandon you my darling. I couldn't move an inch or I'd have blown it. I warned you I was better at wind-ups than you.'

'Do you know,' she shouted, 'I really *do* hate you Paul. I can't believe anything you say but this is the absolute limit and let go of my hands this instant. I shall never forgive you for this and don't imagine

217

you'll get away with it. I'll find a way to make you squirm like I did if it takes me the rest of my life.'

'Oh good....so you're going to hang around for a while then? Does that mean you love me really?' he asked with another burst of laughter.

'No I don't!'

'You don't mean that and you're thinking what a clever wind-up it was, aren't you?'

'No, I'm thinking how relieved I am now to know the truth. It is the truth isn't it Paul?'

'Yes, it is,' he murmured, taking her in his arms. 'You don't need any title darling. You'll always be *my* Lady Alison. I love you.'

'I love you too Paul but you'd better keep looking over your shoulder because it's your turn next and I'm working on it right now. You'll die squirming when I've finished with you.'

'I can't wait but it won't be half as good as mine.'

'Don't bet on it. You'll lose.'

When they went downstairs, Paul told his parents that Alison knew the truth. Vicky ran across to hug her. 'I'm sorry; it was Paul's idea. I hope you're not annoyed with me.'

'Of course not but I could have killed Paul when he told me. I felt so stupid.'

'Well, it broke the ice. It couldn't have been easy meeting the future in-laws but at least you can sleep easy now, knowing we're normal people.'

'There's nothing remotely *normal* about what the two of you did. It's bloody disgraceful,' Tony said. 'For what it's worth, I was dead against it from the outset Alison. Let me get you a large brandy.'

218

She laughed. 'A small one will be fine thanks.'

'Don't bother ringing for Charles,' Paul declared pretentiously. 'I'll attend to the drinks.'

'Don't push your luck Paul,' Alison snapped.

As Paul went to pour the drinks, Vicky sat beside her. 'We need to make plans for the wedding. Paul told me about your tragic loss. Life can be so cruel. It's at times like this that you need your mother but you can rely on us for whatever you need. Angela, Paul's sister, is calling round later to meet you. So, were you planning on having a huge wedding? I do hope so and so does Tony, don't you darling?'

'Whatever you say dear,' Tony answered without glancing up from his newspaper.

'You could show a bit more interest,' Vicky said.

'Why? You never take notice of anything I say.'

Alison laughed. 'We haven't discussed the details yet. We'd like it be sooner rather than later though,' she said, emphasising the importance of *sooner*.

'How romantic,' Vicky sighed dreamily. 'There's nothing quite like love but men aren't like we are.'

'Paul is. He's always planning romantic things.'

'When he's not planning his awful tricks on you.'

'Oh, but I have a cunning plan, to coin a phrase. I need your help though. He'll never try to set me up again if we can get it to work.'

'I'll look forward to it but he's coming back now. We'll talk about it later,' she replied quietly. 'We'll make it work, whatever it is.'

'Tell me about your grand plan,' Vicky said as she and Alison walked around the gardens after lunch.

219

'I don't know if you'll approve but it's to do with something you said earlier.'

It was easy to talk to Vicky and they enjoyed each other's stories, some of which were rather intimate. It was difficult to believe Vicky was Paul's mother. She had the flawless clear skin of a young woman and laughed as a girl would laugh. She was pretty in a youthful way and dressed as Alison would have loved to dress had she the financial means. The two of them had bonded the instant they met.

As Alison outlined her plan for retribution, Vicky added her own proposals so they could both derive pleasure from the trick to be played on Paul. 'He'll never suspect a thing,' Vicky chuckled. 'He's really quite a private person where we're concerned as we see so little of him. I can't wait for Paul's reaction,' she added as they laughed heartily in anticipation of his horror.

Paul watched through the window, pleased to see them together. Alison appeared composed, in spite of the harrowing experience, though he was worried he might have gone too far on this occasion.

They wandered through the gardens for almost an hour and returned when Alison felt chilly.

Paul held her close to warm her and he whispered a fond remark to which she responded with a loving smile. 'I'm sorry about earlier,' he said. 'I won't do anything like that again. Do you feel warmer now?'

'Yes, it went quite cold when the sun disappeared but I'm alright now.'

'What were you and mum laughing about? I saw you both giggling as I looked through the window.'

'It was just girl talk. Your mum's really great. We discussed the wedding amongst other things.'

'So have you arranged a date?'

'Not yet. We'll discuss the finer details later.'

When Angela and her husband Max arrived later in the afternoon, Alison observed that Angela was the image of Vicky as Paul was the image of Tony. She too had been thrilled to hear of Paul's engagement, she told Alison, especially, she added amusingly, as she had believed Paul to be gay as he never seemed to have a girlfriend.

'I assure you he's *definitely* not gay!' Alison said.

Angela and Max weren't able to stay to dinner as they had to collect their two children from a party.

During dinner, Alison discovered that Tony was a banker whose grandfather had formed the business seventy years ago. Tony's father had been initiated as it expanded into more diverse financial services and Tony's future career had been determined from the day he was born. It had been expected that Paul would follow suit but he had shown more interest in a paintbrush than a pen. 'I was saddened when Paul went away in his youth but he was passionate about art and I'm very proud of his achievements,' Tony stated. 'I regret we weren't closer in recent years as it was hard on Victoria who missed him terribly.'

After dinner, they relaxed by a roaring log fire to enjoy pleasant conversation. At eleven o'clock Paul announced he was ready for bed and Alison echoed his sentiment. After bidding goodnight, they left the room hand in hand and made their way upstairs.

They were standing outside Alison's room when Vicky walked past to hers. 'Goodnight. Breakfast at nine-thirty?' she queried.

'Fine,' Alison replied, 'Goodnight. Sleep well.'

'Alison, I'm going to miss you so much tonight,' Paul said. 'This is terrible.'

'Then why can't we sleep together? Your mum's gone to bed. No one would know.'

'Not a chance. Don't even think about it darling. I don't want to upset the apple cart, especially when we're all getting along very well. I'll see you in the morning. Goodnight,' he whispered.

'Goodnight,' she said, closing the door and with a wry smile, tittered, 'Every dog has its day.'

She waited some twenty minutes before opening her door after crumpling her bed sheets and turning down the covers as previously instructed by Vicky. Stealthily, she crept to Paul's room and cautiously entered. The curtains were drawn but she fumbled through the darkness to Paul's bed. She could hear shallow breathing, indicating he was fast asleep and she slid into bed beside him. When she wrapped her arms around him, he awoke with a start.

'Is that you Alison?' he asked in a loud whisper, sitting bolt upright.

'Why, are you expecting someone else? I missed you Paul. I wanted a cuddle.'

'My God, this is madness. You have to go back to your room immediately.'

'Then make me,' she taunted, her hands caressing his body.

'Stop that! Go back or you'll ruin everything.'

'Hush, I'm going nowhere. I'm staying here with you and that's an end to it. No one will ever know.'

Alison awoke around eight-fifteen the next morning and Paul was still sleeping. She stroked his hair and kissed him gently. He stirred and opened his eyes.

'I can't believe you're still here! You really have to go back to your room before someone sees you.'

'I will. Just a few more minutes and I'll leave.'

At precisely eight-fifty-five, she got up and made her way to his en-suite shower-room.

When Paul heard the running water he was aghast that she hadn't returned to her own room to take her shower. Everyone would be up and about soon. He checked his watch and it was almost nine o'clock. He felt overwrought and nauseous. What would his parents think if they knew? He hadn't taken a girl home before and there was Alison, taking a shower in his room. He was panic stricken. Suddenly, there was a knock on his bedroom door.

'Just a minute,' he cried out, as he looked around frantically for his robe.

The door opened and Vicky walked in. 'You did say *come in* didn't you Paul?' she asked, perching on the edge of his bed as Paul pulled up the sheets around his neck to cover his naked body.

'I....I was just about to get up,' he stuttered. 'I'll be down in a few minutes. You go and I'll see you downstairs,' he continued in a high-pitched voice as he coughed and tried to clear his dry throat.

'There's no hurry. I've just knocked on Alison's door but there was no answer so I expect she's still sleeping. I wanted to have a talk to you about her. She's such a lovely girl Paul. She's so sweet. You don't see what I call *nice girls* very often in this day and age. She's unspoiled and innocent and I am so pleased to see you are affording her proper respect until after the wedding. Moral values have declined so much in recent years. It's such a shame.'

He was positively squirming while silently urging her to leave the room but Vicky, who was enjoying every moment of Alison's retribution, had no intention whatsoever of ending her son's misery and she continued to punish him.

'Are you alright Paul? You look rather pale. Did you not sleep very well?'

'No, er... not too well,' he replied.

'Why is that Paul? You haven't been overtaxing yourself have you?' she enquired, her performance equal to that of a RADA professional. 'Er....what's that noise? Are you running the shower? Water is a *very* precious commodity and shouldn't be wasted. I'll just turn it off until you're ready.'

As she crossed the room, Paul leapt out of bed to prevent her opening the door, then realising he was naked, he cried, '*No!*' before leaping back into bed.

'Paul, you're not wearing pyjamas. You're going to catch your death.'

He was sweating profusely by this time and praying his mother would leave the room before Alison reappeared but suddenly the shower-room door was thrust open and his heart sank to his feet when she stepped out in her bathrobe, rubbing her hair with a towel.

224

With an egotistical shake of the head, she leered mockingly at Paul before transferring her attention to his mother. 'Good morning Vicky. I've just had a hot shower and it was so invigorating. By the way, I remembered to crumple the sheets like you said.'

They fell into each others arms laughing as they studied Paul's horrified expression.

'What's wrong Paul?' asked Alison. 'Surely you remember your advice to me? *If you can't stand the heat, get out of the kitchen*. Touché darling!'

As Paul agonizingly came to terms with the situation unfolding around him, Vicky, unable to contain her amusement, said, 'Breakfast in thirty minutes?'

'That's perfect. I'm ready for mine but I wouldn't makc too much for Paul. He appears to have lost his appetite,' Alison answered with a dry smile.

As Vicky left Paul's room, Alison told him, '*You* are playing an extremely hazardous game with me Paul Trantor. There's *nothing* to beat girl power so you just remember that.'

'I surrender,' he replied. 'You win! I promise I'll *never* set you up again. I've just had the worst day of my life and it's still only nine o'clock. I thought I was going to have a coronary attack and....'

'Shut up whinging,' she interrupted. 'Get up now or I'm getting back in with you and you'll be even more embarrassed if you're caught a second time.'

They laughed about their action-packed weekend as they journeyed home.

'Your parents are fantastic. Your mum's so open-minded. I like her a lot,' Alison said.

'And she certainly took to you and she's so happy for both of us and dad is as well. What do you have planned when you get back?'

'I'm letting my guard down and relaxing for a bit with Jenny. It will take all night to relate everything that's happened.'

'Not everything I hope,' he replied.

The moment Alison arrived home, Jenny burst into tears and rushed into her room. Alison hurried after her and knocked on her door. 'Let me in Jenny and tell me what's happened,' she said with concern.

'It's Tom,' she blubbered, opening the door. 'He says he's going back to South Africa. I don't want him to go. I don't want him to leave me.'

'Slow down and start from the beginning. Tell me everything. Come on, don't get upset.'

'I've had a rotten weekend. I've been crying most of the time,' she told her. 'Tom says he's homesick and there's nothing to keep him in England now.'

'Haven't you told him how you feel about him?'

'Not in so many words. I don't want him to think I'm making him choose between me and his family Every time I try to broach the subject I can't speak.'

'Do you think he might be fishing to find out how you feel?'

'I doubt it but I don't know.'

'Would it help if I spoke to him? I wouldn't make it obvious. I could casually bring South Africa into the conversation. Tom might open up to me.'

'I don't know what to do. I don't want him to hate me for the rest of his life because I kept him here.'

'Listen to me. If he really wants to go back, then nothing you or I say will alter that but if he knows how you feel he might reconsider his options. Has he been here this weekend?'

'Yes, he came today but it wasn't mentioned.'

'When the time's right, I'll have a word with him. You can't carry on like this or you'll make yourself ill. I'm sure he loves you as much as you love him. He's never away. I'll get to the bottom of it.'

'Thanks. I knew you'd make me feel better. Let's change the subject and tell me your news,' she said, blowing her nose noisily. 'Did you get on with your prospective outlaws?'

'Yes but I think we'll leave that story for another time when I have your undivided attention. It was such a battle of wits that I'm exhausted.'

'Oh, come on, I need a diversion. Is there a good laugh in the story?'

'Several. You'll have hysterics when I tell you.'

'Let's sit in the lounge with a stiff drink then and you can tell me everything. I need cheering up.'

Alison sat beside her and described their weekend in detail as Jenny listened in disbelief.

'I bet you wet yourself when a butler opened the door. That was an ingenious hoax of Paul's and his mother sounds great.'

'She is and she helped me to get my own back on Paul. I didn't know until she told me later that Paul actually leapt out of bed starkers to dash over to the shower-room before she could get to the door. Paul isn't aware I know about that. He really fell for it.'

'Let's hope he's learnt his lesson,' Jenny laughed.

227

'He has. He won't try anything like that again.'

'When we go on holiday, tell Antonia and Clare. They'll have such a laugh. Poor Paul. He must have been frantic. You're so lucky. You have a gorgeous bloke who loves you. I wish I felt half as secure.'

'Life is what you make of it. Everyone gets a raw deal at some point in time but you have to move on. There's a reason for everything but we can't always figure it out at the time. When mum died, my whole world fell apart but then I started working with you and moved in here. Later, we went to a party and I met Paul. Life is a tangled web. We have to unravel it a little at a time and if you're destined to be with Tom, you will be. Why don't we ask Tom and Paul round for a meal on Wednesday? We could have a few drinks and they could both stay over.'

'That sounds great if you'll cook. I'll wash up.'

'It's a deal and whilst you're washing up, I'll try and get Tom to open up. A few drinks might loosen his tongue. Paul can help you as further punishment for his mean trick. He'll be repentant for a while for setting me up in Stafford. He'll be all over me.'

'Paul's *always* all over you but it bothers me that he's so possessive.'

'He'd never do anything to hurt me.'

She said nothing further to back up her concerns. Alison was blinded by passion and the force of that passion was so powerful that Jenny firmly believed it could ultimately destroy Alison and Paul. She had been apprehensive since Mark had taken her to the concert and she prayed that her intuition proved to be wrong.

Alison left work early on Wednesday to organize the meal for Tom and Paul. The previous night, the girls had repositioned the furniture and had bought candles to create a romantic mood. Cleverly folded napkins and a floral arrangement as centrepiece for the table added the finishing touch.

She had prepared a fresh salmon and dill pâté the previous evening. For entrée, she had chosen boeuf en croûte, broccoli, snow-peas, pan-seared corn and baby new potatoes and for dessert, there was fresh fruit salad and chocolate gâteau. Alison hardly ever ate dessert but of late, she had found that particular brand of gâteau irresistible and would have a slice at every opportunity.

At seven o'clock, she wrapped the beef fillet and brushed the pastry with egg white before placing it in the hot oven, having first decorated the top of the pastry with hearts made from pastry trimmings.

'You're so artistic,' Jenny said. 'I could never do anything like that.'

'Of course you could if you tried. It's easy.'

Jenny tidied up when Alison went for her shower and with their combined efforts, all the chores were completed with plenty of time to spare before Tom and Paul arrived.

As Jenny answered the door, Tom instantly made reference to the appetizing aroma they had followed down the corridor. 'I'm absolutely ravenous. What are we having?' he asked.

'You'll have to wait and see, though I can tell you it looks delicious. Alison's cooked the meal.'

'Are you a good cook too, Jenny?'

'I'm good at beans on toast,' she replied jokingly. 'Where are Alison and Paul?'

'Locked together in the hall when I left them.'

'I'll get you a drink. Would you like a beer?'

'Yes please. *Come on, I'm starving*,' Tom yelled down the hall and Alison and Paul appeared hand in hand with eyes for no one but each other.

The young men were impressed by the romantic candlelit atmosphere. 'You've worked hard,' Paul remarked. 'The salmon pâté was delicious. Did you really make it Alison?'

'Yes but it's easy to make,' she told him modestly as she cleared the plates away.

She tested the vegetables that were cooked to perfection before checking on the beef. The pastry was golden brown and crisp.

After transferring the beef to a serving platter that she'd garnished with parsley and orange slices, she carried it to the table along with a carving set.

Jenny followed with four hot plates.

'Would you carve that darling? Each slice should be about an inch thick. I'll fetch the vegetables and the sauce. Put at least two slices on each plate.'

He stood up and began to carve. 'It looks fantastic Babe. Is there no end to your talents?'

She pondered fleetingly. 'No!' she said blithely as she arranged the tureens on the table.

Barely a word was spoken as they listened to soft background music and enjoyed their delicious meal.

When Paul had finished, he sat back in his chair and exhaled vociferously. 'That has to be the most delicious beef I've tasted,' he said. 'I'm positively stuffed. Thank you both very much. You must have spent hours producing a meal like that.'

'It was nothing,' Jenny stated, glancing at Alison who raised her eyebrows in disbelief. 'I carried the plates and sauce boat in didn't I?'

'I had to learn to cook when mum was ill. It was by necessity, not choice and I made some dreadful blunders in the early days,' she admitted.

'Well, you certainly made up for it this evening. I totally agree with Paul. I've never tasted better beef either,' Tom affirmed

'You're both too kind but you can carry on if you like. I'm wallowing in the praise. It's not every day I get the chance to cook for my two favourite men.'

'Well, we could make it *every* Wednesday if you like then? What do you say Tom?' Paul asked.

'That sounds good to me.'

'And pigs might fly,' Alison quipped. 'So, who's ready for dessert? There's fresh fruit salad, luscious chocolate gâteau and I've also done a cheeseboard.'

'Fruit salad without cream,' Tom said eagerly.

'Darling?'

'I'll have the same and a little cheese if I may.'

'Jenny?'

'Same as Tom. I'll help. What would you like?'

'Daft question! Chocolate gâteau of course.'

When Jenny slanted her gaze towards Alison, she made no comment, doubtless too late for words she concluded as she began to clear away the dishes but time would tell.

As she continued to stack the plates, she was recalling an enraged Paul who telephoned her the day after Alison's party, demanding to know what right she had to publicly humiliate him on the matter of safe sex. He had *never* put Alison in danger; he had *never* had unprotected sex with any girl before her and he could *never* father a child he had screeched down the telephone like a madman.

Jenny was shocked and asked whether Alison was aware she would never have children and he yelled that it was none of her bloody business and that he would tell her when he was good and ready and that she should keep her interfering nose out of matters that didn't concern her. Never before had she heard Paul react so angrily.

Jenny prayed there was a simple explanation for Alison's recent obsession for chocolate gâteau. She couldn't be pregnant; Paul was adamant about that, so God help her if she were, because if Paul wasn't able to father a child, then somebody else had to be responsible and that could only be Mark....but then she hadn't been with Mark....or had she?

'I'm talking to you Jenny. Are you alright? You look a bit pale,' Alison remarked.

'I'm fine. I was just thinking about our holiday.'

She tried to rid Paul's revelations from her mind but found it impossible to dismiss her deep concern for Alison. She helped her serve dessert and turned on the coffee maker.

When everyone had finished, Jenny asked Paul to help with the dishes. They had resolved their differences the day after his angry telephone call when he called again to apologise, accepting that she'd had Alison's best interests at heart and admitting he had overreacted. He accepted she'd been right to show concern for Alison and on the matter of children, he promised to talk to her on her return from holiday. Other couples lived a fulfilling life without children but if Alison wanted children, then they would go to whatever lengths were necessary, even adoption. He requested Jenny's promise to withhold details of either conversation from Alison.

'Am I missing something? It's blatantly obvious we've been banished to the kitchen. What's going on?' Paul asked.

'Alison wants some time with Tom. She's trying to find out if he's going to return to South Africa.'

'Wouldn't it be easier to ask him yourself?'

'No, because if I ask him, I'll beg him to stay and that could ruin everything if he has to choose. She won't be long now. She'll call us when she's done.'

As Alison removed the final items from the table she asked, 'Where in South Africa are you from?'

'Johannesburg,' he informed her.

'Is that nice? I know nothing about South Africa.'

'It's nice where I used to live but there's a fair bit of trouble but then there's trouble everywhere these days. It doesn't seem to matter where you live but it's my homeland and I miss my folks. I often think of going back but then I love England too.'

'When did you last see your family?'

'Two years ago. I went for a three week holiday.'

'Was it hard to tear yourself away to come back?'

'No. I had good reason to return. I hadn't finished my studies but there's nothing to stay for now.'

'What about Jenny? I thought you loved her?'

'Look, we both know Jenny. Everyone's warned me that she changes boyfriends like blokes change their socks. I do love Jenny but it's only a matter of time before she moves on. My work colleagues are amazed we're still together.'

'If you're going to listen to everyone else's opinion, there's no hope for you and Jenny. You should try talking to her rather than listening to others. She *has* had many boyfriends but none of them satisfied her high expectations of what she wanted in a man until you came along, so take that as a compliment. She passed on the others but she's been seeing you for some time. Doesn't that tell you how she feels?'

'If I thought there was any future here with Jenny, I'd stay. We could visit South Africa for holidays. Jenny would love it and she'd love my family too.'

'Then talk to her for heaven's sake. Tell *her* what you've told *me* and I guarantee you'll be delighted.'

'You mean….?'

'I've already said far too much. You need to work this out with Jenny so don't be afraid to talk to her. Remember, faint heart never won fair lady. You're staying over tonight so don't waste the opportunity. We're going away in a few days' time.'

'Thanks. I can't tell you how much better I feel.'

'Then tell Jenny,' and walking to the kitchen she asked, 'Haven't you finished those dishes yet?'

'We're coming,' Paul said. 'We've done now.'

'Same here,' Alison said and whispering to Jenny added, 'Everything's alright. If you play your cards right, Tom's going nowhere. He's waiting for you to make the first move, so start talking later.'

234

With an expression of utter relief, Jenny sighed. 'Thanks Alison and when you need me, I'll be here for you, so don't forget. I *will*,' she repeated and for a split second, Alison sensed some hidden message in her remark but when Paul approached she erased it from her mind.

'What are you two whispering about?' he asked.

'Nothing that need concern you,' Alison said.

'In that case, come and sit here with me. I haven't seen you for twenty minutes and I'm missing you.'

He kissed her affectionately while Jenny and Tom were sorting through CDs at the back of the room.

'Are you looking forward to your holiday Babe?'

'Yes, I'm getting excited now. It was so generous of Maud and Harold to allow us to use their villa. I can hardly wait but tell me, is it scary on a plane?'

'No and it's the safest way to travel. Once you've settled down, you'll love every minute and it only takes two and a half hours to Malaga. How will you get to the villa? Are you hiring a car?'

'We discussed it and decided against it because if we go out, the driver won't be able to have a drink, so there's not much point if it's going to stand idle.'

'I guess not. So, will you miss me darling?'

'More than you'll ever know. Will you call me?'

'Every day and I'll text you too, although you'll soon forget about me when you arrive in Spain.'

'I won't. I'll be thinking about you every waking moment. I wish you were coming too.'

'So do I sweetheart. I'll go crazy when I can't see you for two weeks. Do you fancy going somewhere special for a meal tomorrow night?'

'I can't. I'm going to Maud's straight from work.'

'Oh?' he questioned. 'Why are you going there?'

'I go to play the piano. She enjoys the music as it reminds her of her mother.'

'How often do you go?'

'We've had this conversation before Paul. I try to go twice a month.'

'Right, I remember now. Will Mark be there?'

'I don't know. Sometimes he's there but he's not interested in classical music.'

'Why, what kind of music does Mark like?'

'Modern noisy stuff. The kind I don't like.'

'But you listen to it all the same?'

'Is something bothering you? If you have a point to make, then make it and we can move on.'

'I'm not making *any* point,' he stated cynically. 'I was making conversation. How do you get home?'

She shrugged her shoulders. 'Usually Harold will drive me home but if he's out, then Mark drives me home and if they're both out, I take a taxi.'

'I see,' replied Paul, staring ahead.

'Oh, for God's sake grow up or I'm off to bed and you can go home.'

'Is that what you want?'

'No Paul, I don't. I want to make the most of the few days we have left before I go away but you can be positively obnoxious at times. I don't understand why you can't trust me. Will it always be like this?'

'I do trust you Babe,' he replied, kissing her head. 'It's Mark I don't trust. He's an opportunist.'

'You're obsessed with Mark! You should talk to a shrink about your silly paranoia. Shut up or leave.'

Realising he had well and truly crossed the line, he didn't retaliate. When Alison glanced at Jenny, she raised her eyebrows and Tom looked shocked.

It was Alison who ultimately broke the silence by asking, 'Who'd like a drink? I'm having one.'

'I wouldn't have any more alcohol,' Jenny said.

'Is that right?' she snapped angrily.

Cautiously she continued, 'I only thought....'

'Not you too! Everyone professes to know what's best for me. I'm eighteen and I've come of age!'

'I'm sorry Alison, I didn't mean....'

'Jenny, I'm not annoyed with you. It's *him*!' she cried, nodding in Paul's direction. 'He's impossible at times. I don't know what's wrong with him.'

Paul jumped up instantly, walked towards her and took her in his arms before making his apology. 'I am so sorry. I'm a bit edgy because Alison's going away. I would hate to spoil what has been a superb evening but I'm alright now, really. I'd love a drink please sweetheart,' he said, brushing his lips against hers. 'I'm going to miss you so much.'

'We're all a bit jumpy at the moment. There's no harm done,' Jenny said. 'I'll have another drink too. What about you Tom?'

'Yes er....thanks. I'd like a beer please.'

As Jenny went for a can of beer, he followed her.

Paul was remorseful and pleaded, 'Don't send me away tonight. I want to be with you and I'm really sorry Babe. I love you. Are we friends again?'

She heaved a sigh. 'I suppose so.'

Nothing more was said about the former unpleasant incident as they enjoyed the rest of the evening.

On Saturday night, Paul turned up without prior notice at the flat. 'I'm not staying,' he told Alison. 'I know how busy you are but I wanted to wish you a happy holiday. I've bought you a present. Please don't open it until I call you tomorrow night.'

'I promise I won't but you shouldn't have. You're always buying me things Paul.'

He kissed her tenderly. 'I like buying you things. I'd buy you the world if I could.'

His remark brought a smile to her lips. 'And why would I want the world when I have you? I'm glad you decided to call round, if only for a little while.'

'So am I. Where's Jenny? I wanted a quick word with her before I left.'

'She's just finishing her packing. I'll fetch her. I won't be two ticks.'

As soon as Alison left the room, he looked for her bag and opening it quickly, he slipped an envelope beneath the rest of her things, hoping she wouldn't find it before she arrived in Spain. He was standing by the window when Jenny appeared.

'Hi Paul. I didn't think I'd be seeing you today. Is everything alright?'

'Everything's great. I didn't want to leave before wishing you a happy holiday.'

'Thanks and don't fret over Alison. I'll take good care of her and bring her back with a golden tan.'

On an audible sigh he forced a smile. 'I'll be sure to look forward to that as I'm counting the days.'

When she returned to her packing, he took Alison in his arms and hugged her. 'You have no idea how much I'm going to miss you,' he said. 'Don't forget

I'm calling you tomorrow night and thank you once again for the excellent meal on Wednesday and for afterwards....which was *very* special. You take good care of yourself Babe.'

With tears welling in her eyes, she said, 'It's only for two weeks Paul. I'll be waiting for your call.'

He kissed her goodnight. 'Have a great time. Bye darling.'

'You take care too. I love you,' she called to him.

As she locked the door she shivered, experiencing an inexplicably eerie sensation that she was closing the door on a chapter of her life. She was perturbed as a sudden rush of adrenaline pumped through her body. Never before had she suffered such a strange, scary feeling. Could it be some kind of premonition she questioned?

She was being stupid, she told herself as she tried to eradicate the emotive thoughts from her mind. It was obvious she was overreacting to the thought of being apart from Paul for two weeks. She would be asleep in another hour or so and when she awoke, she would be off to the airport with Jenny, Antonia and Clare for her first foreign holiday.

8

'Move it Alison! Just stop gawping about and keep up or you're going to get lost,' Clare said sharply.

She giggled and quickened her pace. That was an expression she hadn't heard for years, not since her piano teacher had censured her for gawping about if she wasn't paying attention. 'I've never been inside an airport before so I'm trying to absorb everything, she explained. 'It's enormous.'

'There'll be enough time later. Look at the queue! If there's only one desk open we'll be here all day.'

'What do we do at the desk?' Alison asked.

'We check in. You'll need to find your ticket and your passport. We'll show you what to do.'

When they spotted Jenny and Antonia, who were standing in line, a few people had joined the queue behind them. As Clare was inching past to join her friends, someone shouted out, 'Hey, there's a queue 'ere! Get to t'back yer cheeky buggers!'

'We're together,' Clare advised the chap wearing the silly hat and who was glaring at her angrily.

'Some folk 'ave a bloody nerve,' he announced to anyone who might be listening.

'Take no notice Alison. Everyone's bad-tempered when they're checking in. Once that's over, they'll settle down, waiting for the delay to be announced.'

'What delay?'

'Ah that's the sixty-four thousand dollar question. They keep you in suspense and then you learn your plane still hasn't left where it's coming from. Okay I might be exaggerating but I bet we *are* delayed.'

'So what happens then?' Alison asked.

'We wait. We can get a drink and a bite to eat and there are a few shops. At least we can all relax once we've finished here. This is always the worst bit.'

'We won't miss our flight, will we?'

She grinned at her anxious expression. 'When it's time to go to the gate, they'll call us. Don't worry.'

Clare was pleased to take Alison under her wing, even though Alison had succeeded with Paul where she had failed miserably. She was a considerate girl and Paul was a private kind of guy who clearly disapproved of raucous brash girls. Clare had to admit they seemed well suited. Antonia had informed her of Alison's misfortune and so was delighted to hear she now had Paul. The poor girl deserved a break.

'We're moving up. It won't be long now. Are you excited about your first foreign holiday Alison?'

'Very....though I'm a bit uptight about flying.'

'You'll be fine. Remember to flap your arms and the plane won't drop from the sky. I'm joking!' she laughed when Alison stared at her wide-eyed.

'Do you like swimming Clare?'

'Yes but I'd rather sunbathe. I like to have a tan.'

Eventually they reached the desk, checked in their luggage and Alison moved aside.

'Put the Boarding Pass with your passport. Zip up your bag and keep your hand on top of it. That way, no one can nick anything.'

The furious man wearing the silly hat approached the desk. 'About time too! I've been stood here in this bloody queue for an hour,' he grumbled as the two girls walked away laughing.

'Thank you for helping me Clare. I wouldn't have had a clue what to do,' Alison said gratefully.

'You're very welcome. Right, I'm having a large brandy after that performance. How about you?'

'I'll just have orange juice. It's a bit too early for me but I'll be having my fair share in Spain.'

'And we'll have a terrific time. You never forget your first foreign holiday. It's magical.'

As they ambled along behind Jenny and Antonia, Alison brought to mind a similar remark by Jenny about never forgetting the first time, although that had been on another topic. She would never forget her first time with Paul. *That* had been magical. She wondered what he would be doing now. It was still early so he could be asleep. She loved to watch him sleep. She was missing him already and yet she had seen him only a few short hours ago.

'Listen to me!' Jenny said, digging her in the ribs.

'Sorry. I was on another planet.'

'With Paul, I don't doubt. I was just saying, shall we find a café and get something to eat?'

'I'll do whatever you're doing.'

'I only want a slice of toast and a cup of coffee to tide me over till we get our breakfast on the plane.'

'Fine, I'll have the same as you then.'

'Alison, would you like the window seat?' Antonia asked.

'Don't I have to sit where my ticket says I must?'

'It doesn't matter between us four. Hurry up and make up your mind. You're holding everybody up.'

'Yes, I would if no one else wants it,' she replied.

242

'Then will you sit down for heaven's sake as I'm getting dirty looks here. That's your seat belt. Keep it fastened when that light's on.'

Alison fastened her belt and with an apprehensive expression remarked, 'It's far too big. It's no use.'

'See, you just tighten the strap. Is that better?'

She heaved a sigh of relief. 'Yes, it fits now.'

Antonia grinned. 'You're hard work aren't you?'

'I suppose I am but everything's new to me. Are we setting off now?'

'We shouldn't be long. I take it you've switched your mobile phone off?'

Timidly, she stammered, 'Er....no....I didn't know I had to.'

Expelling an exasperated grunt, Antonia glared at her. 'Where is it? *Don't* say up there in your bag.'

'Yes, it is I'm afraid,' she answered red-faced.

With another audible sigh, she unbuckled her belt and ferreted through everything in the overhead bin for Alison's bag that was buried beneath the others. 'Right, where's your phone?'

'In the pocket at the side. Just turn it off.'

'Is there anything you need before I sit down?'

'No and hurry up please. I don't want the plane to take off while you're standing up.'

'If it takes off now we'll be in trouble. The doors are still open. Somebody must be missing. There's always one.'

'I'm glad it's not me. I'd die of embarrassment.'

'Right, they're closing them. We'll be off soon.'

Alison listened to the male voice coming over the speaker. 'Good morning ladies and gentlemen. This

243

is your Captain speaking. I'd like to welcome you aboard your flight to Malaga. Our flying time today will be two hours and forty minutes and the weather in Malaga is favourable at twenty degrees Celsius. We will be flying at an altitude of....'

Alison felt a little movement and stared restlessly out of the window. Antonia took hold of her hand. 'Don't worry. You'll be fine,' she said reassuringly. 'Within minutes, we'll be over the clouds and then we can have a drink. Malaga here we come.... Lots of sun, sand and the unmentionable.'

'What's the unmentionable?'

'I can't say. I've been told not to lead you astray.'

'You won't lead me astray. I love Paul.'

'You're a sweet girl. I wouldn't dream of leading you astray. I hope he's worthy of you.'

'He is. We're getting married. Did you know?'

'Yes, I heard and I'm pleased for you Alison. I'm delighted you met at my party. Initially, I wouldn't give Paul your number. I thought maybe you didn't want to see him but he was very persuasive and he called me again later to thank me. Right, off we go! Did you hear the change in engine noise? We're on the runway now. Are you ready? Any second now.'

Timidly, she peered out of the window, gripping Antonia's hand. Then, like a bird soaring, they left the ground and took to the sky. Within seconds the buildings below were like tiny models. 'It's great,' Alison cried. 'We're flying.'

'Make the most of the view because soon there'll be nothing to see. When we get off we have to stay together. We need to locate our bags and there'll be hundreds of people milling around so if you *do* get lost, don't leave the baggage hall.'

When a member of the cabin crew handed her the breakfast tray, Alison felt nauseous as she lifted the foil cover. She quickly covered it up and moved it aside. Following a half-hearted attempt to chew her bread roll, she abandoned that too when it stuck in her throat. Her eyelids felt heavy and soon she was asleep. Later, when she awoke, the cabin crew were serving hot drinks and a snack.

'I'm hungry now. How much longer will we be?' she asked Antonia who checked her watch. 'I'd say fifty minutes or so. Are you enjoying the flight?'

'It's terrific. I can't think why I was so worked-up about it and I haven't had to flap my arms once.'

'What?'

'Nothing. It was just a yarn Clare spun earlier.'

Despite her earlier unease with Clare, Alison now liked her tremendously. Jenny was right. Clare was a great girl and Antonia was too. They would have a fabulous time together she thought as she watched the aircraft touch down. 'I'm in a foreign country,' she gabbled excitedly under her breath.

'Alison, you carry the small bags and I'll pull your big one along with mine.' Jenny said.

'It's alright; I'm fine with the big one.'

'I'd rather pull both. It helps me to keep balance.'

'Okay, if it's what you want but shout if you can't manage.'

'It's amazing how there's never any trolleys when you need one,' Jenny grumbled. 'Flaming typical!'

She didn't want Alison to lift a heavy bag and at Manchester airport she had insisted that the others wait with the bags until she returned with sufficient trolleys. Throughout the flight, she had thought of nothing else but Alison. For the last few mornings she had heard her vomiting but had decided that at this early stage, she had better not interfere. It was feasible Alison regarded her nausea as a nervous re-action to flying though Jenny had no such thoughts. Alison was likely pregnant, but Jenny didn't intend to spoil the holiday by raising the matter, and since she would be unable to hide it for much longer, she knew Alison would have to confide in her once she realised her dilemma. Maybe she wouldn't see it as a dilemma; she might even be delighted. After all, she didn't know Paul was incapable of fathering a child and would assume it to be his.

Throughout Paul and Jenny's angry exchange and consequent apology, she had learned nothing of his medical history. Could Paul have had a vasectomy, she wondered, but then dismissed that thought. That would have been an absurd procedure to undergo at his age and would any self-respecting surgeon have even contemplated such drastic action, unless there existed some family history of genetic illness which could be passed on to his issue?

She was unaware that Paul had received the dev-astating report of his infertility at the donor clinic. She was also unaware that some years later, he had discussed the matter with his GP who had told him it was most likely to be a consequence of mumps he had contracted at the age of fifteen.

Jenny was worried because if Alison were indeed pregnant then all hell would break loose. Jenny had seen how Paul could react when he felt threatened by Mark and she was anxious for Mark too. It was a desperate situation. Jenny was damned if she didn't raise the matter yet equally damned if she did, but whatever the eventual outcome, she would be there for Alison to pick up the pieces. Alison had served as *her* rock at the time she had been troubled about Tom and thanks to her intervention, things had been resolved once Tom realised she loved him.

Jenny and Alison hailed the first available taxi and Clare and Antonia jumped into the one behind.

'I hope you've remembered the key,' Jenny said.

'It's in the bottom of my bag. It was the first thing I packed. Just look at that view. Isn't it lovely?'

'It's beautiful and you can see the coast from the villa. It's spectacular at night when it's illuminated. We should be there in forty minutes.'

Alison made reference to the outdoor cafés. 'Will we have those where we are?'

'Yes. Unless it rains, everyone eats *al fresco*.'

The driver turned off the road and started to climb a hill. Fifty yards or so along that street, he stopped.

'Right, we're here. I'll attend to all the bags. You pay the driver from the communal purse, then go to the one behind and pay him too,' Jenny instructed.

'How much please?' Alison asked him slowly.

'Treinta Euros por favor señorita.'

She didn't understand and held out some notes on her open hand. He took three ten Euro notes.

'Treinta....thirty. Muchas gracias,' he said.

She gave him a tip before repeating the procedure with the second driver.

They trudged wearily into the beautiful house and flopped down on the sofa. 'Look at the size of this place and what gorgeous furniture,' Alison shrieked before scampering off to view the rest of the house.

'The bedrooms are lovely too,' she made known on her return. 'Each one has a bathroom or shower.'

'Well, it's your holiday kid so you can have first pick of the rooms,' Jenny said.

'Then may I have the large one on the front over-looking the sea? Does no one mind if I do?'

'You take which you want,' Clare chipped in. 'As Jenny said, it's your holiday.'

'Thanks, I'll take my case in and start unpacking and then I'll have a shower.'

'Go and get your shower and I'll bring your case when my feet stop screaming at me,' Jenny offered.

Alison shot to her room, although not specifically for her shower. She needed privacy to see what was at the bottom of her bag. She had spotted something unfamiliar while searching for the door key.

She tipped the contents of her bag on the bed and removed an envelope on which was written, 'To my darling Alison. I miss you already. Love, Paul.'

Inside the envelope was a sheet of paper. She un-folded it to discover a pressed red rosebud, together with a photograph of Paul. Resting her head on the pillow she murmured, 'I'm missing you too Paul,' as she held it to her lips and kissed his face.

Her contemplative reverie was halted by Jenny.

'Here's your bag. I'll leave it on this stand where it's easy to unpack. Don't try and lift it. It's heavy,' she panted, hoisting it into position.

'Thanks Jenny. Look what I've found in my bag. Paul must have hidden it there last night.'

Jenny perched on the edge of the bed, attempting to force a smile as she studied the photograph. 'It's a good likeness. When was this taken?'

'I don't know. This was in the envelope too,' she said, showing her the rosebud.

Though she uttered no words, her thoughts raced ahead towards what the future might hold in store for Alison, who observed a worried look and asked, 'Are you alright Jenny? You look anxious.'

'I'm tired. I'll be alright when I've had a shower.'

'Where's the pool? I'd like to have a look at it.'

'Go out the way we came in and follow the path to the right and you can't miss it.'

'I might take a dip. Is there a shower at the pool?'

'Yes but the water will feel chilly so brace yourself,' she said, watching her rummage through her case for her bikini. Then she chuckled. 'You put me in mind of a kid at his first Christmas. Go and have a swim. You'll enjoy it. There's a debate going on in the lounge about our plans for the rest of the day. I might just have forty winks by the pool. Tom said he'd call at lunchtime so I don't want to miss him.'

Alison took her mobile from her bag and turned it on. 'Paul's not calling me until eleven tonight. I'm already missing him,' she sighed. 'Are you missing Tom?'

'Yes, though I never thought I'd see the day when

'I'd be pining for a bloke. I must be going soft in the head.'

'Do you think you'll get married soon?'

'We haven't got around to that yet. I'm thankful he's staying for now. He's not impulsive like Paul. He's careful and methodical in love like he is in his job. I'd definitely accept though if he asked me.'

At that point, Alison's mobile rang. 'That will be Paul,' she said excitedly.

'That's my cue to go then. I'll leave you in peace to whisper your sweet nothings. Give him my best.'

'I will.... Hi Paul. How are you?' she asked.

'Crazy with loneliness. How are you Babe?'

'Missing you very much. What are you doing?'

'Eating my lunch....a bag of chips and a pie.'

'Oh Paul, you do eat such rubbish. Is it good?'

'Not particularly. Nothing will taste good till you come home. Your lips taste like a rich ruby wine.'

She sighed. Paul said such romantic things to her.

'So how was your flight?'

'It was great. I was a bit nervous so Antonia held my hand as we were taking off,' she laughed.

'Lucky Antonia. Next time you go anywhere, I'll be holding your hand.'

'I wish you were here now.'

'Me too Babe. How's the villa?'

'Fabulous! I chose the best room. It overlooks the sea. It has a king-size bed and an en-suite shower.'

'Very nice. Have you been swimming yet?'

'No, we've only just got here. I was just about to put my bikini on and go for a dip when you called.'

'Stop it. I don't want to hear about such things.'

'Why not?' she laughed.

'You know perfectly well why not. Don't tease.'

'Alright. Have you been painting?'

'Yes, I've had a decent morning. I woke up early. Incidentally, have you anything to tell me?'

'I'm sorry. Thank you Paul. I found the envelope a few minutes ago. It's a lovely photo. I've put it on the pillow next to mine and I adore the red rosebud. It went right out of my head when you called.'

He exhaled noisily. 'Out of sight out of mind.'

'Never. I've thought of nothing else but you.'

'Then promise you'll never leave me again.'

'I definitely won't leave you again....ever. Would you like me to open the present you gave me now?'

'No, save it until later. I'm phoning again tonight at eleven. Enjoy your day. Tell me everything then. I'm off now. Bye darling.'

'Bye Paul.'

Moments later, Jenny barged in. 'Tom's phoned. He's missing me and counting the days, he says.'

'Aren't we all?' Alison replied.

'I'm joining you for a swim. The other two have decided they're coming in too.'

For the rest of the afternoon, they swam and dried off in the hot sun with a glass or two of Bacardi and coke, which Alison hadn't tried before.

'Everyone drinks it here,' Clare told her. 'We can get it in the supermarket a lot cheaper than at home. We'll get some when we go shopping.'

'Are we eating out tonight?' Alison asked.

'Yes, Jenny knows of a nice restaurant down the road. We're going in an hour if everyone's ready.'

'I'll be ready. I'll be starving by then. I'm having a great time and we've only been here half a day,' she informed the others.

'It gets a lot better than this,' Clare told her.

'Take a cardigan with you Alison,' Antonia said. 'It goes cool at night at this time of the year.'

Clare hobbled along the uneven street in her high-heel shoes trying to keep up. 'I'm hungry enough to eat a mattress stuffed with bugs!' she declared.

'Ugh, the thought of that's enough to put anybody off. You say some charming things,' Jenny grunted.

They opted for an inside table as there was a cool sea breeze.

'Where are *you* four staying?' a voice called out.

Jenny turned to see four young men at an adjacent table. 'Up that street,' she told them, pointing in the direction from where they had come.

'Did you get here at lunch-time?' another queried. 'You look like four girls we saw getting out of two taxis and who are staying in a pink villa near ours.'

'That's us,' she said. 'How's the weather been?'

'Brilliant,' yet another replied. 'It's been *too* hot. Mike here got burned. We're having a barbecue on Friday night. There are loads of folk coming and so if you fancy it, it starts at seven. You have to bring booze and some food to shove on the barbie. We're off to Puerto Banus now. Don't forget Friday.'

'Well, he didn't waste any time,' Antonia said. 'I wouldn't mind dressing Mike's burns. He's a dish.'

'For God's sake, we've only just got here!' Jenny complained. 'You're man mad!'

252

Alison expelled a shrill laugh. Neither Clare nor Antonia ever missed an opportunity so she was glad to have an ally in Jenny who wouldn't be hounding every guy in Spain.

Touchily, Antonia responded, 'I *like* barbecues.'

'No, it's all the *guys* at barbecues you like,' Jenny corrected her.

'Well....I'm on holiday. I want to enjoy myself.'

'And so you shall. Are we all ready to order?'

Following an enjoyable meal they went for a walk along the beach. There was a clear sky and Alison looked at the stars, wondering if they were the same ones she had studied with Paul.

'Where's Puerto Banus?' she asked Jenny.

'It's not far. It's great at night and you get to see the posers in their fancy cars. It's a bit artificial but well worth a visit. It has a lovely marina and there's some fabulous yachts. Many belong to the stars.'

'I'd love to go there,' Alison remarked dreamily. 'Can we get close enough to see the yachts?'

'You can walk right by them.'

'Have you ever seen anyone famous there?'

'I saw Sean Connery once. Many celebrities have houses there. It's very classy and upmarket.'

'I'm going to enjoy this holiday. I'm so happy we came. Can we get a coffee? I'm parched.'

'Yes, come on. Let's catch up with the others.'

Alison's mobile rang in the coffee bar and it was Paul again. 'Hi darling, have you eaten?' he asked.

'Yes, we've just had a lovely meal. I had chicken fillet cooked in a mushroom and wine sauce. What have you had?'

'Fish and chips.'

'I ought to come straight home to sort you out.'

'I wish you would. I've had bad news today.'

Startled she asked, 'Why, what's happened?'

'I've had two months' notice served to vacate my studio. The building's being demolished.'

'Oh Paul, whatever will you do?'

'I'll have to find somewhere else. It's a nuisance because it will waste time and I was hoping to catch up on my work while you were away. I made a few calls today but there's nothing worth looking at and then I had a thought. We need a house when we're married so I intend talking to the agents tomorrow who might be able to find a suitable property with outbuildings so I could work from home. There are lots of houses like that in the country but they don't come on the market very often. I'll view anything that sounds promising and keep you posted.'

'You wouldn't buy anything I hadn't seen would you? I'd like some input into where we'll live.'

'Do you doubt my judgment Alison Haythorne? I only ever choose the best. I chose you didn't I out of all the girls in the world?'

'Yes darling, you did and I'll be eternally grateful for that.'

'Don't be silly. I don't want gratitude. I want you to love me....forever.'

'I already do and always will.'

'I know, so it's I who should be eternally grateful. Are you enjoying Spain?'

'Yes Paul, it's incredible. We're just having a cup of coffee at a beach bar.'

'Is it a warm night?'

'It's breezy but not cold. It smells of the sea.'

'Are you getting along alright with the others?'

'Yes, they're great. We're having such a laugh.'

'And you haven't run off with any Gigolos yet?'

She giggled. 'They wouldn't stay long with me. I'm skint. Besides, the only Gigolo I want is you.'

'Have you opened your little box yet?'

'No, you said I had to wait until you called. May I open it now please?'

'Yes you may,' he replied with a faint laugh. She was always polite except for when he played tricks on her and then she could have a fiery temper.

'I'm just trying to take the paper off it. Right, I'm opening it now.' A few moments of silence elapsed before she cried, 'It's beautiful,' and she removed a gold bangle from its box. The other three looked on in admiration. 'Thank you darling. I love it.'

'Have you looked inside? There's an inscription.'

She held it to the light and read, 'Darling Alison, I'll love you forever, Paul.'

'Yes, I've read it Paul. You're so thoughtful. I'll give you a hug and a kiss when I see you.'

'I'll want much more than that after two weeks' absence. Can't you think of anything better?'

'Of course but there are people listening.'

'Whisper then nobody will hear.'

'No I won't!'

Seductively Paul whispered, 'You know precisely what I want to hear. I want *you*.'

'I think I'd better hang up.'

'No, don't. Have you put your bangle on?'

'No, I need two hands. I'll put it on when I get off the phone.'

'Always think of me when you're wearing it.'

'I do anyway.'

'I'm missing you so much. I'll call you tomorrow at the same time. Sleep well.'

'And you Paul. Bye darling and thank you.'

The girls passed Alison's bangle around the table. 'You're so lucky,' Clare remarked. 'Paul thinks the world of you doesn't he?'

'I suppose he does. He's one in a million. He'd do anything for me,' she sighed.

Jenny didn't speak the words aloud but under her breath she answered, 'He'll never forgive you.'

It was Wednesday and the girls were organising an outing to Malaga. 'So how do we get there and are there lots of shops?' Clare asked Jenny.

'By train....and there are hundreds of shops.'

'Excellent! I could just do with a few hours' retail therapy,' Antonia chipped in.

'There's a department store too, *El Corte Ingles*.'

'So it sells clothes and the like?' Clare asked.

'Everything. You name it, they sell it. Right, let's get this show on the road. Is everyone ready?'

Alison enjoyed the short train journey, expressing surprise at the abundance of greenery they passed.

'It's unusual to have a water shortage here. Most of it comes from Artesian Wells,' Jenny told her. 'It isn't like at home where, if it stops raining for five minutes, there's a hosepipe ban. A large amount of produce is grown for export. Tomorrow, when we

256

go to Fuengirola market, you'll see spring onions as big as leeks and you'll not find bigger cauliflowers anywhere and everything's so cheap.'

Within minutes of their arrival, the four girls were scrutinising the shop windows in the narrow streets.

'There's some fabulous bags here. Look at that,' Clare drooled. 'Can we go in and have a look?'

'Feel free to look where you want. Just make sure no one gets lost. Yell out if you're going in a shop,' Jenny announced as if she were team leader.

'I'm looking in this shoe shop,' said Alison. 'I'm after some new sandals.'

Alison was delighted with her purchase, knowing she couldn't have bought such a lovely pair of gold leather sandals in England at that price.

'There's a tea shop at the end selling scrumptious cakes and pastries if anyone's interested,' Antonia said and they all agreed a drink would be welcome.

'Did you buy that bag Clare?' asked Alison.

'Actually, there were two I liked so I bought them both. See,' she said as Antonia went for the coffees.

'Clare, they're beautiful. I love the black one and it'll match anything but the white one's lovely too, especially for holidays,' Alison stated, stroking the leather. 'Look, I bought these gold sandals.'

'They're dainty. They'll look nice with shorts or a dress. I hate trainers. They're clumsy aren't they?'

'Well, I suppose they're comfortable, though I've never had any. I prefer sandals.'

'Does anyone want a cake?' Antonia called out.

'I'll have a nice chocolate cake if they have one,' Alison called back to her.

257

'There's a dozen different ones. Come and choose and you can help me carry the coffee.'

Alison eyed up the gorgeous chocolate cakes. 'I'll have that one,' she said licking her lips.

'You'll throw up if you eat all that,' Antonia said.

'No I won't. I love chocolate cake.'

Jenny didn't miss the moment and she felt sick to her stomach. She would have to find some way to broach the subject before the others realised too.

By the time they had walked the streets of Malaga and every floor of El Corte Ingles they were tired. It was six o'clock when they headed for the train and it was turned seven when they arrived at the villa. Following a vote, they decided to relax for an hour and eat around nine.

Jenny went for a word with Alison in the privacy of her room. 'Did you enjoy Malaga?' she asked.

'Oh yes, I love shopping and I enjoyed my lunch too. I was starving. I've gone off breakfast lately.'

'Why is that?' Jenny quizzed. 'You always used to eat a good breakfast.'

'Maybe it's because I'm tired in a morning. I feel a bit sickly some mornings. I'm fine by lunchtime. I could eat a horse then.'

'I was thinking that the four of us should perhaps buy a small gift for Maud for allowing us to use her lovely home. I have when I've stayed here before.'

'Good idea. How often have you stayed here?'

'Twice. I came once with a friend and again with Mark but he got on my nerves,' she lied as she tried to get Alison to open up. 'All he thought of was sex but don't repeat that. He's very pushy isn't he?'

258

Innocently she asked, 'How would I know?'

'Well, you've been out with him. You know what he's like. He thinks he's God's Gift doesn't he?'

'We only went out twice. We went to dinner once and then to the concert. He was fine with me.'

'Didn't you find him a bit, er....touchy-feely?'

'No, I found him charming. He was good fun and he made me feel special.'

'How do you mean....special?'

'He paid me compliments. He was....er....nice.'

'You liked him quite a lot then didn't you?'

'I suppose I did. I was very disappointed when he didn't ask me out again. I felt used.'

'How do you mean, used?'

'I thought he was just trying to score points over Richard and I didn't like that.'

'Well, we both know what men want....sex.'

'You're right. Women can be vulnerable. A bloke flatters you and before you know it, you've been to bed with him and he doesn't want you anymore.'

'Is that what happened with you and Mark? You can tell me. We don't have secrets. He can be quite irresistible and you're only human Alison. Anyone can make a mistake. Nobody would blame you.'

'What *are* you prattling on about? You asked me about our date at the time. It wasn't a date when we went to that concert. We went as friends and he was a perfect gentleman. He never touched me, then or ever. Are you jealous?' she asked indignantly.

'Of course not, I'm curious, that's all. I just find it odd that a guy as er....horny as Mark would be so well behaved. He never misses an opportunity.'

'There *was* no opportunity! I didn't lead him on and he didn't try to take advantage of me. Can we drop this now? There's only one man in my life and it's Paul. I've never been with anyone else, nor will I ever go with anyone else. Is that plain enough for you to understand?'

'Yes, I'm sorry. I wasn't trying to pry. It's none of my business anyway. I shouldn't have asked.'

'Off you go again. I don't know what it is you're asking. Let's make it clearer. Did Mark and I ever have sex? *No*! Did Mark *try* to have sex with me? *No*! If that answers your questions, can I have some peace now and can we forget about Mark?'

'I'm sorry Alison. I meant no harm. Have a sleep and we'll go for a nice dinner later. I won't mention him again. I promise.' At that, Jenny scuttled to her room like a scolded dog, regretting her interference. She hadn't intended to offend her but if Alison had admitted that there had been something between her and Mark, then she would have revealed what Paul had told her. She simply wanted to protect her from Paul's wrath when he discovered she was pregnant.

She was in a quandary. She had to believe Alison who insisted she had been with nobody else so what was Paul up to? Why had he said he couldn't father a child? There was no doubt at all that Alison was pregnant and Paul *had* to be responsible, but Jenny feared Paul would never accept that fact. This was worse than Jenny had first thought and it was only a matter of time before the proverbial bubble would burst and she dreaded that day. Jenny had witnessed Paul's anger and it wasn't a pretty sight.

Clare's voice echoed around the house. 'Are you all ready? I'm ravenous.'

There was a united response of, 'Yes!'

'Why don't we go back to that place we went on Sunday?' Alison suggested. 'It was great there.'

'Well I'm game if everyone else fancies that. It is a nice restaurant,' Jenny agreed, locking the door.

'It's far enough for me to walk,' Antonia groaned. 'I've got a blister on both feet.'

'I have some plasters in my bag,' Alison said.

'You're an absolute angel. I'll put two on now if I may,' she said thankfully. 'We'll catch up with the others in a minute.'

She removed both sandals. 'Ouch, they don't half burn,' she winced, pressing one on each blister.

'They should help. I've plenty more,' Alison said.

'Thanks. You're a life saver.'

'Good evening,' a voice from behind called.

Alison turned round and recognised the four boys they had seen on Sunday. 'Hi, are you going out for the night?' she asked.

'No, we're just off for something to eat. Have you eaten yet?' Mike questioned.

'No,' Antonia said. 'That's where we're off. The others are in front. Where did you get to today?'

'We went Go-Karting in Fuengirola this morning. Then we went to the beach,' Mike informed her.

'You didn't get burned again I hope?'

'Definitely not. I'll not be making that mistake a second time. Have you been anywhere interesting?'

'Nowhere you would regard as interesting. We've been shopping in Malaga.'

261

'Right, here we are,' Mike said. 'I hope there's a table free for us soon. We've eaten nothing all day.'

'There's Jenny and Clare. They've got one for us. We'd better go in. I hope you don't have to wait too long,' Alison commented.

'See you Friday,' Antonia added with a smile.

'Good. So you're definitely coming?' Mike asked returning the smile.

'You bet! Wild horses wouldn't keep me away.'

'I've ordered the drinks,' Clare said as Alison and Antonia took their seats. 'What kept you?'

'Blisters! I had to stick plasters on my toes. The four lads from next door caught up with us. They're just waiting for a table,' Antonia told the others.

'How are your feet now?' Jenny asked.

'Not bad. I'll live. What do you fancy tonight?'

'I'm having chicken again. I couldn't face eating red meat,' Alison replied.

Clare looked concerned. 'Are you alright?'

'Yes, I'm just a bit tired so I don't want anything too heavy and the chicken was delicious last time. What are you having Jenny?'

Jenny was relieved when Alison addressed her as they hadn't exchanged one word since their earlier discussion, and her appetite returned immediately.

'I fancy steak. Yes, that's what I'm having.'

'Me too,' said Clare.

'I'll have the same,' Antonia added.

'Right, that's three steaks and a chicken. How do you like your steak?' Jenny asked.

'Medium,' Clare and Antonia said simultaneously and giggled.

262

'You two are like Tweedledee and Tweedledum,' Jenny remarked.

'Then I'll be Tweedledee,' Antonia laughed.

Disgruntled, Clare retorted, 'What a cheek.'

'Well, you had every opportunity to pull a bloke back there and you wandered off with Jenny. I seem to have clicked with Mike. I've told him we'll be at the barbecue on Friday. He was delighted we were going so that's me sorted and if you play your cards right, you're in with a chance 'cos they're coming in now. *Don't* look round! You don't want to make it obvious,' Antonia told her.

'That's rich coming from the likes of you. If you threw yourself under a speeding train you'd be less conspicuous than when you see a bloke you fancy,' Clare attacked furiously.

Alison turned to Jenny who was enjoying the entertaining repartee. 'Aren't you glad we don't have these problems? It's great that we're in stable relationships, don't you agree?'

'I do,' was all she could bring herself to say.

The four young men took their places at a nearby table and one called out, 'We have to stop meeting like this. People will start to talk.'

Clare immediately seized on the opportunity and said with a broad smile aimed at the speaker, 'Let them talk. I can stand it if you can.'

The young man beamed back at her, stood up and walked across to their table. Directing his attention towards Clare he said, 'I'm Matthew.'

'I'm Clare,' she answered. 'And these three girls are my friends Antonia, Alison and Jenny.'

'I'm happy to make the acquaintance of four such lovely ladies,' he replied. 'That's Mike with blonde hair; next to him is Simon and the end one's Dave.'

'How long are you here for?' Clare asked.

'We arrived on Wednesday for two weeks. We've another week left yet.'

'That's plenty of time to get to know each other,' she replied provocatively.

'I guess so,' Matthew smiled, his eyes focused on hers.

When he returned to his table, Antonia remarked, 'Did you hear her? And *she* has the cheek to accuse *me* of being conspicuous. I thought she was going to strip off there and then.'

Alison laughed heartily. However uneasy she had felt about Antonia and Clare earlier, spending time in their company had definitely altered her opinion. In some ways, she envied them their audacity.

'Right, that's us two fixed up,' Clare announced. 'I'll have Matthew, Antonia can have Mike and the two of you can squabble over Simon and Dave.'

Jenny laughed. 'I don't want either thanks though I expect Alison will want Simon. She has a bit of a fetish for blokes called Simon don't you Alison?'

Having heard about Alison's unwanted encounter with Simon Ward, Clare giggled impishly. 'What's all this I hear? Come on and tell Auntie Clare about your inclination towards men called Simon?'

Coldly she said, 'It was Simon Ward who had the inclination when he inclined his slimy body against mine at the party, the obnoxious creep. I definitely *don't* want another Simon, thank you.'

'Right,' Clare replied, unwilling to let the matter drop as she capitalised on the moment. 'You'll have to have Dave and Jenny can have Simon, so we're all sorted now.'

'*No we're not,*' Alison protested. 'I don't....'

'She's winding you up Alison,' Jenny interrupted.

'Oh, right,' she blushed, feeling stupid. 'I'm more than happy with Paul,' she added, trying to hide her embarrassment. 'I don't want anyone else.'

'I know but I couldn't resist the joke when I heard one was called Simon. I'd heard about Simon Ward but at least you managed to escape. You were very lucky. He's like the Venus Fly Trap,' Clare said.

'Somebody ought to trap *his* fly. It might cool his ardour for a while,' Alison said smugly.

Antonia howled. 'I must remember that when I go back to work. It'll go down well in the canteen.'

The waiter arrived with the food and the ravenous girls tucked in greedily.

'It's market day tomorrow,' Jenny reminded the others. We need an early start as it gets busy later.'

'I wake early,' Alison said. 'I'll call you at eight.'

Matthew reappeared at the table. 'Can we get you a drink ladies?'

Instantly Clare stated, 'Thanks. We drink Bacardi and coke.'

'Ice and lemon?'

'Please,' Antonia replied.

Alison was anxious, not wishing to feel obligated in any way but Jenny read her thoughts. 'It's only a drink. You don't get your kit off for one drink.'

'Oh, right,' she answered with a watery smile.

'You do for two though,' she added, then laughed at her shocked expression. 'Loosen up. We're only having a laugh. If we stick together, I'll take care of you while you keep me out of temptation.'

'You wouldn't….'

'Get my kit off? No, I'm like you. I would never do anything to hurt Tom.'

'Did he call you today?'

'Yes but only for a couple of minutes.'

'I got a text message earlier. Paul's calling around eleven again. Although I miss him, I'm glad we're here. I wouldn't have missed it for anything and we have such a laugh. Antonia and Clare are terrific.'

'What about me? Am I not terrific too?'

'Yes….even when you cross-examine me, I can't get angry with you. I hope we'll always be friends.'

'We will,' she said, squeezing her hand.

The waiter arrived with the drinks from the young men and the girls turned to face them, their glasses held high. 'Cheers,' Antonia announced, making a point of looking straight at Mike.

'Cheers,' they called and Mike acknowledged her gesture with a wink and a suggestive smile.

They were enjoying girlish gossip when Alison's mobile rang.

'It's Paul. I'll take it at the door. It's a bit noisy in here,' she said, excusing herself. 'Hi Paul, have you had a good day?'

'It's been fairly productive I suppose but I'm lost without you Babe.'

'I know. I miss you as well. I've been waiting for your call so I could talk to you.'

'Why what's wrong darling?'

'Nothing, I wanted to hear your voice. We went shopping today in Malaga. I bought some sandals. There's a splendid Cathedral there. You'd like it.'

'Never mind that. What did you buy for me?'

'Nothing. I haven't decided what to get you yet.'

'I'm joking. Don't spend your pennies on me. All I want is you and you couldn't afford to buy Alison Haythorne. She's priceless. Anyway, I've got you.'

'Yes Paul, forever.'

'And we'll grow old together, just like Joyce and Alfred won't we?'

'Yes we will and I'll never leave you again.'

'I won't let you leave me again,' he said. 'I heard it said that absence makes the heart grow fonder but then it goes on to say that gone too long it makes it wander. Yours won't ever wander will it darling?'

'I've got the man I want for the rest of my life.'

'And do you really love him to distraction?'

'He's my life!'

'That's a sweet thing to say. You're my life too.'

'So tell me what you've been doing today.'

He cleared his throat. 'Looking at houses.'

'*Paul*! Weren't you going to tell me?'

'After I'd listened to all your compliments. I like to hear how you love and miss me,' he laughed.

'You're impossible. Did you see anything nice?'

'I looked at two. One was alright I guess.'

'And the other?'

'Absolutely fabulous. I put in an offer and before you go off on one it's not legally binding but if they accept my offer, I'll delay things until you get back.

It's exactly what I wanted to buy for you but if you don't like it, although you will, we'll just say we've changed our minds. I didn't want to lose it.'

'Does it have an out-building to use as a studio?'

'There's a huge barn. It wouldn't take much effort to convert it to a studio.'

'Where is it?'

'In a small village in Cheshire.'

'I can't wait to see it Paul.'

'And I can't wait to see you darling. Just imagine, a home of our own together. Right, I'm going now. I'm running out of credit.'

'And I'm running out of compliments. So are you calling me tomorrow?'

'Yes Babe. Same time. Take care of yourself.'

She returned as the girls were about to leave.

'Here's the bill. Will you see to it?' Jenny asked.

As the others walked towards the door, they were quickly followed by the young men. Alison paid the bill, zipped up her bag and followed them outside.

'Move yourself, slowcoach. We're walking down the coast together,' Antonia said.

Uneasily, she asked, 'Are they coming too?'

'We're only *walking* like we walked down to the restaurant earlier. Don't be so soft.'

'I thought you had blisters?'

'Bugger the blisters! I'll limp if I have to. I want to get to know Mike,' she told her.

They started off as a group but within fifty yards, Antonia was walking with Mike and Clare was with Matthew. Jenny was chatting to Simon, which left Alison and Dave together. Alison broke the silence as she felt uncomfortable. 'I'm Alison. It looks like we're the hangers on,' she remarked.

He grinned. 'I was just thinking the same thing.'

'Where are you from Dave?'

'Congleton. That's in Cheshire.'

Alison wanted to make her position clear from the outset. 'There's a coincidence. I was just talking to my fiancé and he's been viewing some properties in Cheshire today. We're getting married soon.'

'I thought that was an engagement ring. I have to say it's quite a rock. He must be well-to-do. Laura, my girlfriend and I got engaged a couple of weeks ago. So where was he looking at properties?'

'I haven't a clue. He said it was a small village in Cheshire. It's a house with a large barn. That's all I know about it. He's an artist so he needs a studio.'

'Does he call you every day?'

'Yes and he texts me too.'

'Same here. We booked this holiday months ago before Laura and I met. Can I ask you something? Don't be offended but are you looking for a holiday romance before the big day?'

'Certainly not!' she protested.

'Good, me neither. I like to know where I stand. I love Laura and it's very awkward for me when I'm here on holiday with three hormonal lads.'

'My sentiments entirely. I'd never look at anyone else. Jenny, my friend just ahead with Simon is also involved with somebody but Antonia and Clare are both footloose and fancy free.'

'I feel better now,' Dave said with a broad grin 'I thought I might have to fight you off.'

'Fat chance. There's only one man for me, so tell me about Laura. Tell me how you met.'

'I met her at work. She's a lot like you. She's tall and pretty too. I worked with her for ages before I plucked up the courage to talk to her. I'm backward at coming forward if you understand what I mean.'

'I do and I'd be afraid of rejection if I were a lad.'

'That's exactly how I felt. There were dozens of giggling girls there, so I didn't want to make a fool of myself. Girls can be very cruel you know.'

'I know. I happen to be one. We do giggle a lot.'

'It was at the work's party in November where I saw her giving me the eye, or that's what I hoped, so I went across to talk to her. She was pleasant and responsive so I asked if I could take her home at the end and she agreed. I was the happiest guy there.'

'And it blossomed from there?'

'Yes it did I'm pleased to say. She's a lovely girl. When I offered to cancel my holiday, she wouldn't hear of it. She trusts me so I'd never let her down.'

'Well, you're safe with me. Have you fixed a date for the wedding yet?'

'No but we're working on it. We've been looking for somewhere to live but we might have to rent for a few months until we've saved a bit more money. Have you fixed the date yet?'

'No. It's the top item of my list once I'm home.'

Jenny turned her head when she heard Alison and Dave chatting easily. 'Are you okay?' she enquired.

'Yes, we're just swapping notes. Dave's engaged as well so we're taking care of each other. We don't feel like gooseberries now do we Dave?'

270

'That's right,' he nodded in agreement. 'I believe you're involved too Jenny. Are you engaged?'

'No, Tom hasn't popped the question yet. I might have to give him a bit of a push.'

'He must be an idiot. Er....I'm sorry,' he stuttered looking embarrassed. 'I didn't mean that the way it came out. What I meant was he's a very lucky guy.'

'I'll take that as a compliment then,' she laughed.

They meandered for some time before stopping at a beach bar for coffee. 'The unattached appear to be hitting it off well,' Dave said.

'I was thinking exactly the same. Look at Antonia and Mike; it's like a match made in heaven,' Alison remarked and he nodded in accord.

'Were you all at school together?'

'I wasn't. I think the other three were. I only met Antonia and Clare twice before the holiday. Jenny and I went to a party at Antonia's apartment. That's where I met Paul so we haven't known each other long. He pursued me from the minute he saw me.'

'That's nice. I'm glad I met you tonight. I feel out of place with the lads. I'd hate to spoil their holiday but it's a tricky situation.'

'Keep a clear head and you'll survive. In a week you'll see Laura but I've longer to wait before I see Paul. It looks like we're making a move now.'

'It's been good tonight Alison. It's the first night out for a week that I haven't felt threatened. You'll come to the barbecue won't you?'

She nodded. 'Who owns the villa you're in?'

'It belongs to a work colleague of Simon's. It has four bedrooms and a pool.'

'So has ours. It belongs to some friends who said we could use it for a fortnight. It was my birthday a few weeks ago and it was my birthday present.'

'That's a great present. Was it your twenty-first?'

'My eighteenth actually.'

'Oops, sorry. I thought you were older than that.'

'Don't apologise. Everyone thinks I'm older. The others are twenty-two so I'm the baby. Paul will be twenty-nine next. Now that sounds old doesn't it?'

He laughed. 'Actually, *I'm* almost twenty-nine.'

'Now it's my turn to put my foot in it. You look younger than that.'

'What's Paul's last name. You say he's an artist?'

'Paul Trantor.'

'That rings a bell. I'm sure when I was a student, we worked together stacking shelves. He was at Art College....tall with blonde hair. He didn't last long.'

'That has to be Paul. Imagine you knowing him.'

'Small world,' Dave said. 'Well, thanks again for everything. You're off to the market in the morning I hear. There's a Churros Café at the far side of the market. Nip in and order enough for two with your coffee and they'll fill all four of you. You dip them in sugar to eat them. Goodnight Alison.'

'Goodnight Dave. It's been nice talking to you.'

Alison checked her watch. It was one o'clock and she had to wake the other girls at eight, so she went straight to bed after locking and bolting the door.

9

Alison awoke soon after eight. She jumped out of bed and ran to Jenny's room. 'Come on. It's time to get up,' she called to her.

'What time is it?' she asked sleepily.

'After eight. Come on, I'll wake the others.'

'*No, don't….*' Jenny started to say but it was too late. Alison had already closed the door.

Alison tapped on Antonia's door and barged right in. 'Are you up?' she called, then stopped suddenly when she noticed two people in bed. She turned and rushed out almost knocking Jenny over.

'Sorry Alison, I did shout to warn you but you'd already closed the door.'

'This isn't on, Jenny! I don't have a problem with Antonia's behaviour but it's a bit much to bring her bloke back here. She should have gone to his place and I'm not having it. I shall speak to her about it. Paul would go mad if he knew blokes were here.'

'Well, he doesn't know does he?'

'Oh, so you're condoning it are you? I might have known. After all, it takes one to know one doesn't it? I could have darted in there completely starkers.'

'Alright, you have a point. I'll speak to them both about it.'

'What? You mean Clare's got Matthew in hers?'

'Er….yes, they both stayed over.'

'I don't believe it! What about yours? Is he here?'

'Mine, as you call him went back to his villa. I've no intention of making it with Simon. Anyway, he isn't my type.'

'You're very fussy all of a sudden. I thought anything in pants was your type.'

'I'm sorry. You're right; it won't happen again.'

'So what do we do now....sit at the breakfast table playing happy families?' she asked sarcastically.

'I'll ask them to leave. I'll say we're going to the market so calm down. You've never bothered when Tom's stayed and you've let Paul stay a few times.'

'That's totally different. He's your boyfriend and Paul's mine. They've only known these guys for a couple of hours. I'd have plenty to say if you were bringing different guys home every night. Imagine if Maud walked in and surprised us.'

'Well, if that happened, it would be Maud getting the surprise wouldn't it?' Jenny howled.

'It's not funny. Why, it's bordering on obscenity.'

'Come on, it isn't that bad. It won't happen again. They can go to the lads' villa in future. It's as much my fault. I should have considered your feelings.'

'Sort it out then. I don't feel comfortable.'

'Consider it done. Have a shower and by the time you're ready, they'll be gone, I promise.'

'They'd better be gone!'

Alison took her time getting ready and when she went into the kitchen, Antonia was there. 'I'm sorry Alison. I was out of order. You're shocked that I'm promiscuous,' she said apologetically.

'Correction! I'm well aware you are promiscuous but shocked that you had the audacity to practise it here, where not everybody shares your enthusiasm for anything in trousers. Why didn't the two of you go back to their place?'

'So what's the difference between their place and ours? The end product's the same.'

'Maybe, but I wouldn't have been there to barge in would I?'

'I'm sorry. It won't happen again. I never wanted to embarrass you. I realise how shocked you must have been. I know you're different.'

'I'm *different*? What's the hell's *that* supposed to mean....that I'm mentally retarded or something?'

'Of course not. Let me make you a cup of coffee. I'm sorry but I can't undo what's been done.'

Clare poked her head around the kitchen door. 'I believe I'm in the dog house. Is it safe to come in?'

Alison flashed a scathing look and didn't answer.

'I'm really sorry Alison. It won't happen again. I promise I'll be celibate from now on.'

'When hell freezes over perhaps but not before,' Alison grunted. 'It's okay to come in. I won't chuck anything at you. It's not that I'm judging you Clare. I just don't like you shoving it in my face.'

'That's fair comment. I can't argue with that,' she said. 'Am I forgiven?'

'I suppose so,' she replied with a forced smile.

By the time they arrived at the market it was almost ten o'clock. Alison was mesmerised by the number of stalls. There were hundreds. 'Why don't we split up and meet up later for a coffee,' Jenny suggested.

'Good idea,' Clare said. 'We'll see more then.'

Alison looked round for the Churros Café. 'Look, across there, where it says, *Churros*. Why not meet up there at eleven-thirty? That gives us an hour and a half and if we haven't finished, we can start again afterwards.' Everyone was in agreement.

Alison wandered between the stalls. She bought a leather belt for Paul and a boxed ceramic mug with a humorous relief picture of an artist on the front.

The tea-stained mug in his studio was crazed and chipped and she had intended to get him a new one.

At another stall she bought six postcards and the stallholder even had stamps for England.

When strolling past the fruit and vegetable stalls, she was amazed. Jenny hadn't overstated either the quality or value. She bought a big bag of pears and ate one while continuing to pore over the articles on sale. It was very hot and the fruit was refreshing.

She could feel the hot sun on her back and wished she had brought something to cover her shoulders. The deeper she walked into the market, the busier it became. She was fascinated by the elderly Spanish women gabbling incessantly to one another as their men folk stood silently like statues.

Young boys in long shorts were kicking a football around in the arid dust behind the stalls and dozens of wild cats darted from under the stalls in different directions in their search for food.

Stallholders called out to passing tourists, leaping forth with tablecloths held high if anyone dared to cast a fleeting glance in their direction. Alison was spellbound by everything as still the bustling crowd increased in number. By eleven o'clock, barely able to move she took minute steps, inching forward by degrees. Gasping for a coffee, she exited at the next opportunity to make her way across the dusty path.

Arriving at the café just before eleven-thirty, she found a table in the shade and waited for the others who arrived in quick succession shortly afterwards.

'I'm glad we're shaded,' Jenny sighed, throwing herself in the chair. 'Phew, it's so hot today!'

The waiter came to take their order. 'Four coffees and Churros for two,' Alison articulated clearly.

'What's that you've ordered?' Antonia asked.

'I've no idea. I'm following Dave's instructions. It's something you dip in sugar and it's supposed to be delicious so we'll give it a try.'

The waiter quickly returned with four coffees and a plate of Churros that he placed in the centre of the table with two smaller plates.

'Those look tempting,' Clare stated as she picked one up and dropped it again. 'Ouch! They're hot!'

Alison tipped two sachets of sugar on each of the small plates. 'We're supposed to dip them in sugar so let's do it properly,' she said.

Each girl took one and dipped the long thin piece in the sugar before taking a bite. Jenny was first to speak. 'They're scrumptious. They taste like crispy doughnuts. I've seen them many times but I didn't know what they were, so I never tried them.'

'You should have asked someone. We could have had them each morning with our coffee. Remember to thank Dave for that bit of advice Alison,' Clare said. 'Did you remember to tell Alison we're going to Puerto Banus tonight, Jenny?'

'No, it slipped my mind,' she said apologetically.

Alison's eyes lit up. 'Great, I wanted to go there,' she said and when she learned the four lads would be going too she was delighted, as that afforded her protection from roving eyes and she could enjoy the sights in peace....and so could Dave.

Within moments the Churros plate was bare. The four girls licked their sticky fingers and sighed with contentment. 'I'm washing my hands,' Jenny said.

As she walked inside, Alison took a deep breath. 'Listen both of you, I'm really sorry about earlier. I shouldn't have reacted like I did. It's nothing to do with me what you do. If we'd arrived back together last night, I'd have known the lads were staying and I wouldn't have made a fuss, so if you'd like them to stay over again, it's fine. I wouldn't have thought twice about letting Paul stay, had he turned up.'

'No Alison, it was our fault. You must have come in only seconds after us and we should have waited and run it by you first. This holiday is for four, not two and we have to be conscious of other people's feelings. We discussed it this morning and we both understand how shocked you must have been.'

'I'm no angel, Antonia. I sleep with Paul. I'm not shocked. I was taken aback when I barged into your room and I overreacted, not having expected that.'

'We can always stay at theirs,' Clare interrupted.

'There's really no need. I'm fine with it now,' she assured them. 'I suppose I'm in their bad books?'

'No, we made the excuse that we were late for the market and shoved them through the door,' Antonia explained and with a throaty chuckle, Clare butted in, 'Well, they'd served their purpose!'

Alison burst out laughing. 'You two really are the limit!'

Alison went into the kitchen when they returned to rummage in the fridge, feeling hungry following their exhaustive walk around the market.

Having decided to make a light lunch by way of apology for her outburst, she set to, slicing a block of cheese into thin slices that she arranged neatly on a platter. She prepared a tossed salad of lettuce, raw onion, tomato, cucumber and green pepper, adding a liberal shake of black pepper and sea-salt. When she had finished, it smelled lovely.

She placed the salad platter in the fridge with the cheese while she sliced and buttered the hot crispy baguette that had been in the oven for ten minutes.

Adding ice and a wedge of lemon to each of their drinks, she carried them to the patio table. Then she returned with the food. 'Luncheon is served ladies!'

'Brilliant, I'm famished,' Antonia said, rushing to take her seat with the others. 'That looks appetizing and doesn't salad always smell lovely when you're on holiday? Look at that bread. I could eat the lot!'

'Just make sure you don't,' Clare said. 'There are four of us here.'

'Alison, you're amazing,' Jenny informed her.

'Who's having a brilliant holiday?' asked Alison.

'Me,' they replied in unison.

'That was delicious,' Antonia declared when they had finished their lunch.

'I almost bought strawberries this morning. I wish I had now,' Alison sighed. 'They looked absolutely delicious but I had lots of bags to carry.'

'That would have been lovely. A big bowl of cool strawberries with ice-cream,' Clare fantasised.

'I bought a massive bag of pears, if anyone would like one. The juice ran up my arm when I ate one at the market.'

'Go on then, you've tempted me,' Jenny said.

The remaining pears went instantly. 'I'll get some fruit when I go shopping tomorrow to buy meat for the barbecue. We are still going I take it?'

'Of course,' Antonia replied. 'It should be good.'

'We'd better top up the communal purse too. We haven't much left.'

'What do you want?' Jenny asked.

'Another fifty each should last us until weekend. I don't want too much in case my bag gets nicked.'

'Where's your passport,' Jenny asked.

'It's in my bag. Why?'

'Don't carry it round in your bag. If you lose your passport, you'll be in big trouble. You'll be trailing about all week to get another. Lock it in a drawer.'

She stood up. 'I'd best do it now before I forget.'

As Alison walked away, Antonia remarked, 'Isn't she terrific? She'll do anything for anybody. I'm so sorry we upset her this morning.'

'Don't worry. Alison can stand her corner,' Jenny said. 'She'll tell you straight what she thinks.'

'Paul Trantor's a lucky guy. I hope he appreciates what he's got,' Clare remarked pensively.

'So do I,' Jenny responded with a sigh, reflecting deep concern known only to her.

'So, what's the plan for later?' Alison asked when she returned.

'I think we're meeting about seven. The guys are coming here. We'll have a drink first and then we'll go down to the bus stop. We haven't been on a bus yet so that should be quite a novelty,' Antonia told Alison. 'I'll call Mike later to confirm the time.'

'What's special about a bus ride?' Alison asked.

'You'll see. I'm going for my shower now.'

Alison felt peeved. Whenever she asked anything, rarely did she get a straight answer. Paul was full of surprises and would never tell her where they were going and the girls were even worse. What possible mystery was there about a bus ride? She was treated like a child and was furious earlier when described as *different*. If being faithful to one man and having high moral values meant she was different, then she was glad. She'd rather be decent any day.

Once she was standing beneath the gently flowing shower, all thoughts of her earlier irritation quickly faded. It felt exhilarating to take a shower after such a hot day. She was looking forward to her night out where she would see the yachts of the stars.

When Alison was ready, she wandered across the garden to gaze at the sea. It looked beautiful in the evening just as the sun was setting. The remaining sunlight illuminated the water and the lights along the coastline added a further sparkle to the halcyon evening. The fragrance of *Lady of the Night* almost overpowered the still air, the modest breeze of two days, now departed, having left a serene tranquility. It was a perfect evening to walk round the marina.

She wondered what Paul would be doing. When she was there, he had at least two decent meals each week when they went out. She studied her beautiful diamond ring. He was so generous and loving….

'A penny for your thoughts,' Jenny interrupted.

'You know who I'm thinking about. I miss him.'

'I'm the same. I never thought *I'd* miss a guy but I miss Tom. I lie in bed at night and sometimes I'm afraid because I can't picture his face.'

'I'm fortunate. I have a photo of Paul. Once we're home I won't ever leave him again. I can't bear for us to be apart,' she sighed meditatively.

'Have you heard from him today?'

'No, he'll call later. Have you heard from Tom?'

'Yes, he just rang. He's counting the days too.'

'You never know, he might just pop the question when you go home.'

'I doubt that. He's a guy who needs a good push.'

'Well, he knows how you feel now and he made it pretty clear to me how he feels about you so don't be too sure. Would you really accept if he asked?'

'Definitely. We're great together. We enjoy doing the same things and….'

'And he's a doctor too,' Alison cut in. 'You'll not associate with me once you're married to your posh affluent doctor and I'm married to a lowly artist.'

'Paul, a lowly artist? He's loaded but then you're well aware of that. You'll never be poor as long as you live. Here's Antonia with Clare in hot pursuit. I wonder what's up with them.'

'Alison, do you have any more plasters please? I don't know how I've done it but I think I've rubbed the top off one of my blisters,' Antonia complained.

'It's probably a friction burn off the bed sheets,' she replied dryly and Clare howled with laughter.

'You had that one coming,' Jenny remarked.

'I guess I did,' she acknowledged.

'Here, keep them in your bag. I won't be getting any friction burns. Leastways, not this week.'

'You never know your luck,' Antonia quipped.

Jenny heard voices. 'Right, the guys are on their way down. Clare, will you open the gate please?'

'I'll get some glasses. Do they all drink Bacardi?'

'It's that or nothing Alison. We've no beer.'

'Give me a hand. I can't carry eight glasses.'

'Two of them will have to stand up. We've only got six chairs,' Antonia said looking round.

'Well, blokes don't bother. They stand at a bar all night like they're terrified somebody might steal it,' Alison laughed.

By the time they returned with the drinks, the lads were in the garden and Dave ran over to help. 'You look lovely Alison. Laura wears dresses like yours.'

She smiled courteously and thanked him. 'Would you hand the drinks round please Dave. Have you had a good day today?'

'Yes, we went to Torremolinos. The others went off together and I went round the shops looking for something for Laura. I got her some perfume.'

'Well, you can't go wrong buying a girl perfume. Have you spoken to her today?'

'Yes and I told her about you and the way we'd rescued each other.'

'And what did she say to that?'

'She laughed. I told her you were getting married soon and that I remembered Paul from my student days. She thought that was some co-incidence.'

'I'll ask him tonight where those houses are.'

'Yes, do that and before I forget, I've written my phone number down. Give it to Paul when you get home and ask him to call me sometime. It'd be nice to hear from him. So he really made it as an artist?'

'He did. He's quite well-known in the art world.'

'Can't be bad. A rich husband and no worries.'

'I know. I'm very fortunate. He's a great guy and I think Laura's done well. She has a great guy too.'

'Are you ready for off?' Clare interrupted.

As they made a move Dave enquired, 'Have you been to Puerto Banus before Alison?'

'No, but I'm looking forward to it. Everyone says it's fabulous.'

'It is, though the restaurants are rather pricey. The atmosphere is great. You'll love it.'

'And we won't be bothered by opportunists,' she laughed. 'How did Simon react when he found out Jenny was attached?'

'He wasn't bothered. He plays the field. We had a talk before we came away as I didn't want to be left on my own and he agreed to hang about with me if Dave and Mike connected. You're aware of course that they didn't come back last night?'

'I am! I found out when I charged into Antonia's room. I wasn't happy and I let the girls know.'

'Oh dear, so you had words?'

'It was over in a few minutes. I was shocked. I'm inexperienced with men. I could never be anyone's one-night stand but we're all different aren't we?'

'We are but it's easy talking to you as we're alike in many ways. I'm caring too. The lads I work with think I'm soft in the head because I respect girls.'

284

'I think that's an admirable quality. Paul's caring but he has a short temper. He's very jealous. If he saw me talking to you, he'd be furious. Lately he's mellowed but still has a way to go. He's possessive and it wears me down but that's his only fault. Still, nobody's perfect.'

'What do you mean? I am,' Dave laughed.

'Well, you come close,' she concurred.

'What are you two laughing about?' Jenny asked.

'Oh nothing. Is there no sign of that bus yet?'

'It's like back home. You wait an hour and then three come together.'

'What if it's full when it gets here?' Alison asked.

'It won't be full.'

'How could you possibly know that?'

''Cos they never are! I'll give you a tip. When it comes, push and shove like hell 'cos nobody knows what an orderly queue is and they'll all fight to the death to get on. Right, it's coming now. Get ready.'

As the bus slowed down it certainly appeared full and when the driver released the door, Alison could hardly believe her eyes. It was absolute mayhem.

Dave pushed her ahead into the jostling mob and when they reached the door, he blocked the opening with one arm and with his other arm heaved her on the bus before scrambling on behind her.

The stairwell was jammed and the driver shouted to everyone to move down but they were packed so closely they couldn't move. Finally, they made it to the aisle as more people rammed them forward.

Alison glanced through the window when the bus pulled away from the stop and the queue had gone.

She looked round for Dave and smiled with relief to find him standing behind her. 'Do you know where we get off? I can't see the others.'

'Don't worry, when you see lots of people getting off, we'll be there,' he told her reassuringly.

After an uncomfortable journey during which she had been elbowed and pushed more times than she cared to remember, they arrived at their destination. 'If I never see another bus again, it'll be too soon.' she panted breathlessly. 'That was horrendous!'

Dave smirked, 'Yes, it was rather an ordeal. Let's wait over here for the others.'

She watched as dozens of passengers stepped off the bus and then Antonia appeared.

'Was that a bus ride or what?' Antonia gasped.

'It was awful,' said Alison, looking relieved when the others showed but on their arrival at the water's edge, she was stunned and felt the trip worthwhile.

Quickening her pace to follow the others who had wandered off ahead, she tried to absorb everything in sight as she hurriedly skimmed past restaurants, bars and exclusive fashion shops.

'You should bring Laura here. She'd love it,' she told Dave. 'It's fabulous and look at those boats.'

'*Yachts*, Alison,' he corrected her.

'I've never been abroad before so I didn't know what to expect. I wish Paul could see it.'

'Has he not been here?'

'I don't think so. He often goes abroad because of his work but usually to Italy. He doesn't talk much about his work and I've only seen his studio twice. Paul's passionate about art but when we go out, he forgets it completely. I don't understand art the way he does. He sees what other mortals don't, he says. That's probably why he's so temperamental.'

'He sounds a complicated guy.'

'He's not really. He wears his heart on his sleeve and is passionate about everything he does. He lives a very simple life with no frills and fancies despite his wealth but that will change when we're married. Do you know how long I'd been seeing Paul when he proposed to me? A week.'

'So he's impulsive too?'

'When he knows what he wants, he goes for it so I suppose he *is* impulsive. He doesn't stop to think. If he sees me talking to another male, he intervenes instantly and as I won't tolerate being controlled by him, we finish up arguing. He's a lot better than he was and I'm still working on him to show me more consideration. We'll get there eventually.'

'He never hurts you does he, physically I mean?'

'No, Paul's a pussycat. He's possessive but that's his one and only fault. He's wonderful. You knew him when he was young. How was he then?'

'Easy going and agreeable as I recall but *I* wasn't engaged to him,' he laughed.

She halted by one of the yachts. 'Look at the size of that. Isn't it magnificent? I wonder who owns it.'

'Someone very wealthy. That's like a small cruise ship. There's a fair bit of brass moored around here. There's one over the other side that's three times as big. I'll take you over to see it before we leave.'

'I can't see any of our lot.'

'Don't worry. They're in front. We'll find them.'

287

Before they had walked more than a dozen yards, Antonia called out to them, having found an outside table at a restaurant fronting the marina.

'We're eating here. Are you hungry?'

'Starving,' Alison said. 'How about you Dave?'

'Famished. I've had nothing since breakfast.'

'From here, we can see the posers,' Jenny advised them. 'You won't half see some sights. Hollywood has nothing on this place.'

Whilst awaiting their meal, Alison watched as the same prestigious cars repetitively cruised past their restaurant. 'You were spot on about the posers,' she remarked. 'Do they just drive round all night?'

'They're weighing up the talent like a tiger stalks its prey and when they see someone enticing, they pounce,' Jenny explained.

'That's horrible,' Alison said earnestly.

Dave howled with laughter. 'You'd better watch out Alison as you might be the next victim.'

She shuddered. 'I'm glad you're here. I've never seen anything like this in my life.'

After the meal, they continued up the waterfront, leading to the enormous yacht Dave had mentioned earlier. 'What kind of person owns such a luxurious yacht as this?' she questioned.

'Probably royalty from overseas. Stand close to it and I'll take your picture. Write your address down after and I'll send you a copy.'

Alison moved towards the yacht and sat sideways on a capstan. 'Is this okay?'

'That's perfect. Now turn to face me and I'll take another. Would you mind taking one of me? I'll tell the lads at work that I won the yacht on the Spanish lottery. They're stupid enough to believe anything.'

'I'll make it a good one then. Smile naturally.'

Antonia, Clare, Matthew and Mike decided they were ready for home and said goodnight.

'It's okay if they stay over with you,' Alison said.

'Are you really sure about that? Clare queried.

'Yes, I know them now and if I'm expecting them to be there then I won't come barging in your room. Here's the key. *Don't* lose it. Leave it unlocked.'

'I don't think we'll be far behind you. It's turned eleven now,' Jenny told them.

Alison looked at her watch. 'I didn't realise it was that time,' she said with concern. 'Paul didn't call.'

'He's probably asleep,' Jenny said reassuringly.

'I'm going to text him. I'm worried. How do you do it from here Dave?'

'Give me your phone. What do you want to say?'

'"RUOK?" If he gets it, he'll call me back.'

'Right, it's done so stop worrying now. Shall we meander back? Are you ready for home Simon?'

'Er....yes. I bet we've missed the last bus though.'

'I'm sure I can sweet-talk a taxi driver into taking all four of us. I'm definitely not walking. My poor feet are killing me. I'm having a sun day tomorrow and then I'll be fit for the barbecue,' Jenny said.

'Me too,' Alison said with a sleepy yawn.

As they made their way to the taxi rank, Alison's mobile rang and she answered it quickly. 'Oh Paul, I've been worried to death. Are you alright?'

'I'm sorry darling. I've been busy. I didn't realise what time it was. I do apologise.'

'Did you hear anything more about the house?'

In jest he asked, 'What house?'

'Will you stop that and *tell* me. I want to know.'

Paul laughed. 'They accepted my offer....almost. I had to go up two thousand quid but I'd have raised my offer by ten, so I guess I'm the winner.'

'So what happens now?'

'Nothing till you've viewed it. Nothing is legally binding before Contracts are exchanged.'

'Where exactly is it Paul?'

'On the outskirts of Alderley Edge. It's way out in the country away from other houses.'

'Tell me about it. What's it like?'

'I'll do better than that. I'll take you the moment you get home. You'll love it.'

'Won't you tell me anything at all?'

'No, as I don't want to spoil your surprise. We'd never find another so perfect for the two of us.'

'I can't wait to see it and you too. It's not a week yet. I don't know how I'll survive ten more days.'

'The second week always goes faster when you're on holiday. Are you in bed?'

'I'm in Puerto Banus. There's a beautiful marina. I wish you could see it. We're just heading back.'

'How's Jenny?'

'She's missing Tom as I'm missing you. Antonia and Clare have trapped off so they're with them.'

'So you're there alone with Jenny?'

'Yes,' Alison replied dishonestly, not wishing to provoke a confrontation over the telephone.

'Be very careful. Call me when you get back then I know you've arrived home safely.'

'I will Paul. I love you.'

'And I love you too. Bye darling.'

Alison tried to imagine what the house would be like, hoping she would like it as much as Paul did. She fancied the idea of living out in the country but wondered if there would be a school close by. They hadn't discussed having children but she knew Paul liked children because he talked very affectionately about his sister's and would often kick a ball for an infant in the park, or pass a witty comment about a cute toddler in a buggy.

They arrived back at the villa at midnight, having arranged to be at the barbecue at seven o'clock the next evening. Alison offered to take salad and some jacket potatoes, additional to the pork ribs that had looked most appetising in the supermarket butchery department earlier in the week.

Feeling exhausted, Alison went straight to bed but not before stopping and smiling at the amateurishly prepared 'no entry' signs on two bedroom doors as she passed by.

'There but for the grace of God go I!' Jenny said, laughing at the home-made notices.

'That chapter of your life has ended now,' Alison reminded her. 'Are you sorry? Do you miss it?'

'Not in the least. Tom's everything I want.'

Alison was on the verge of sleep when her mobile rang. She answered it quickly to avoid waking the others. 'Are you home yet?' Paul asked.

'Yes Paul, I'm so sorry. I forgot to let you know. I got back at midnight.'

'It's like I said before, out of sight out of mind.'

'If only you knew how untrue that was.'

'Did I wake you?'

'Not really. I was just about to drop off.'

'Sorry, I was worried. Did you take a taxi?'

'Yes, we had to because we'd missed the last bus but I wasn't sorry. The journey there was absolutely horrendous. We were packed like sardines.'

'I wish I'd been standing close to you Babe.'

She laughed. 'You never miss an opportunity, do you?'

'Not if I can help it. Are you off out tomorrow?'

'No, we're relaxing by the pool. We walked our feet off today and we're off to a barbecue next door tomorrow night. It should be a good night.'

'How did that come about?'

'I'll tell you if you promise not to overreact.'

'I don't think I'm going to like this am I?'

With irony in her voice she answered, 'Anybody normal wouldn't bother but then you aren't. You're such a drama queen.'

He laughed heartily. 'Point taken. I promise.'

She explained that four young men were staying in the next villa and that two of them had connected with Antonia and Clare, resulting in an invitation to their barbecue. There was a lengthy silence. 'Don't do this Paul, please. It's a barbecue. It's harmless.'

'I can't help it. I'm sorry darling. I'm just envious that other people are enjoying your company.'

'I wish you weren't so possessive. In every other way you're amazing. If you can't learn to trust me, we'll end up apart. You must stop being like this.'

'I know. I'll try harder. I'd be lost without you.'

292

'I've told you a dozen times, I'll never hurt you, I'll always love you and I'll never leave you Paul.'

'I'll make it up to you when I see you. I promise.'

She sighed. 'Just trust me Paul. That's all I want.'

'I'll call you tomorrow darling. Sleep well.'

'I would if you were here with me.'

He laughed suggestively saying, 'I guarantee you wouldn't.'

'I like that. That's more like the Paul I love,' she giggled. 'Bye darling.'

Matthew and Mike didn't stay for breakfast. By the time Alison surfaced, they had already left.

After clearing away the breakfast plates, the girls flopped down on sun loungers and remained there until Alison announced their lunch was ready.

'You spoil us. You're quite the little housekeeper. With barely a morsel of food in the fridge you still manage to conjure up something nice for our lunch. I don't know how you do it,' Clare said.

'If I don't get some more, I won't be conjuring up any food tomorrow. The fridge is empty now. After lunch I'm off shopping to restock and I need meat, potatoes and salad for tonight.'

'Get a litre of Bacardi and two big bottles of coke too. We have to take some booze,' Clare said.

'Hey, I've got to hump that lot up the hill!'

'I'll come too,' Jenny stated protectively. 'You'll never carry it all on your own. It's far too heavy.'

'I'll manage,' she replied. 'You get some sun.'

'I'm coming with you so stop arguing.'

'We'll clear away and wash up,' Antonia offered.

As Clare and Antonia began to clear away, Jenny and Alison went indoors to freshen up.

Alison changed out of her top and trousers into a pretty sun frock and put on her new sandals. After applying a little make-up she brushed her hair.

When Jenny saw her she was surprised. 'I didn't know you were getting dressed up. Look at the state of me. Hang on; I'm not going out looking like this when you're all dolled up. I'll be two minutes.'

Minutes later, Jenny returned in a silky two-piece trouser suit, looking like the front cover model of a fashion magazine and they left for the supermarket.

'It's further than I thought,' Jenny complained.

'I enjoy walking,' Alison replied. 'It doesn't seem to take long when I come alone and it's alright once you're inside. It's air-conditioned.'

Jenny studied the building. 'This wasn't built last time I was here. There were dilapidated apartments on this site. It's quite smart that, isn't it?'

'Wait until you've been round it. It's much bigger than it appears. I need a ticket for the meat counter first. The other day I heard such a row. This woman thought everyone was pushing in until the assistant behind the counter pointed out the ticket machine.'

Alison ripped off a ticket. 'Two hundred and four and it's on one hundred and eight-five presently, so there are nineteen in front of us.'

'We'll be here all afternoon!' Jenny exclaimed.

'No, we'll start our shopping and I'll keep an eye on the number until it's getting close.'

They started by selecting a dozen big potatoes. 'If we cut them in half, that'll be plenty,' Alison said.

294

From the dishevelled box that contained lettuce of dubious freshness, they managed to find one decent one. Walking past the racks, Jenny got a cucumber, a dozen salad tomatoes and a bag of onions. Packs of mixed peppers were ridiculously cheap so Alison dropped one into the trolley and added some apples and pears, lemons and a punnet of strawberries.

She called at the bread counter for two baguettes and added cream, butter and a good-sized block of cheese to her trolley. 'All we need now is Bacardi and coke but we'll go for our meat first.'

At the meat counter there were still four in front of them. 'I'd never have thought to do this. I'd have stood about like a lemon waiting my turn. You're a very astute individual Alison,' Jenny declared.

'I hate queuing. I always find a short cut. I had to do the shopping when mum was ill and it annoyed me so much that when the till assistant was making small talk with customers, I'd yell out, "Excuse me, some of us have to go to work!" It always worked.'

She laughed. 'I've heard you telling Paul off. You don't stand any nonsense do you?'

'Not if I can avoid it. Right, our number's coming up now. I hope she understands what I want. Yes,' Alison said, handing over her ticket as her number was revealed. 'Can I have a pound of ham please?'

The assistant looked confused and pointed to the sliced cheese.

'No....ham....there on that tray,' she said.

At the third attempt, the assistant understood.

'Si, ham,' Alison repeated. 'A pound please.'

Once more the assistant appeared puzzled.

'Medio kilo por favor,' a lady nearby translated.

'Gracias señora,' the assistant replied.

Alison turned to the woman and thanked her.

'They work in kilos here,' she told Alison. 'You get used to it in time. I ordered half a kilo for you. That's slightly over a pound.'

'¿Algo mas?'

'She wants to know if you want anything else.'

'Yes, I want a dozen pork ribs. Those large ones.'

The woman kindly ordered the ribs for her.

'That's everything, thank you,' Alison said.

'Nada mas,' the woman said to the assistant.

The assistant wrapped up the meat, stuck a price label on the package and passed it to Alison.

'Well, that could have gone better,' Alison said.

'Stop grumbling, you got what you wanted didn't you? If I'd come on my own we'd have been eating barbecued pigs' toe-nails tonight,' she laughed.

'When we've got the booze, we'll have a coffee. There's a coffee-bar over there,' she told Jenny.

They collected two litres of Bacardi and two large bottles of coke on their way to the checkout and the trolley was overflowing. 'You'd never have coped on your own,' Jenny remarked, imagining the likely consequences had Alison tried to carry that weight back to the villa. 'We'd better take a taxi back.'

They left the checkout, lumbering the heavy bags to the coffee bar. 'That's settled it,' Jenny groaned. 'We'll definitely get a taxi. These are far too heavy to carry. I'll get two coffees. Watch the shopping.'

As she walked away, Alison's mobile rang. It was Paul. 'Hi Babe, what are you doing?' he asked.

'I'm with Jenny in the supermarket. We've been shopping for tonight. She's just getting two coffees. I'm glad you called. Are you okay about tonight?'

'Of course I am. You go and enjoy the barbecue.'

'I wish you were coming. I can hardly wait to see you again. I miss you so much,' she whispered.

'Speak up, I can't hear you. What did you say?'

'I can't. There's a bloke sitting right beside me.'

'I'll have you a bet that he's wearing a blue shirt.'

She turned her head. 'You're right, he is. How did you know that?'

'Call it a calculated guess. Actually, it's the most popular colour,' he replied on a laugh. 'Wasn't that much better than any of Richard's card tricks?'

'Had you not stated how you knew, it would have been but you can redeem yourself if you can tell me what colour of shirt the guy next to him is wearing.'

He hesitated momentarily. 'Well, the second most popular colour is er....white, so I'll settle for white.'

She laughed. 'You're right again. I'm impressed.'

'What are *you* wearing? Are you in shorts, showing off your gorgeous sexy legs?'

'I'm wearing a white dress with yellow flowers.'

'Very summery. I wish 1 could be with you Babe. I can just picture you in your lovely summer dress. I bet it would look even nicer with gold sandals.'

'I *am* wearing gold sandals....the ones I bought in Malaga.'

'Is there a photograph booth in that supermarket? They're usually by the door.'

'Yes, it's just by the café where I'm sitting now.'

'Can you see it properly?'

'Yes I'm looking straight at it now, why?'

'Then you'd better look again.'

His remark could only mean one thing and with a pounding heart she fixed her eyes on the booth.

'*Paul*!' she screeched as he stepped into view.

'Hi Babe! I couldn't wait a moment longer to see you,' he laughed as she raced towards him, hurling herself into his arms.

'She's glad to see me,' Paul announced to anyone watching. A few applauded and Jenny looked round to seek the cause of all the commotion.

She was happy for them, though downhearted that Tom wasn't there too.

Alison gave him a lingering kiss. 'Darling, this is unbelievable. Tell me I'm not dreaming.'

'I'm here until Sunday. That's two days and two very long nights,' he whispered sensually.

'I suppose you want a coffee?' Jenny said, giving him a welcoming hug.'

'I wouldn't say no,' he replied.

'Alison, go and queue up for a coffee for Paul. I'll keep him amused till you get back,' Jenny said with a straight face and Paul howled with laughter.

'Get lost Jenny!' she retorted indignantly.

'Okay if you insist, I'll go,' she said, walking off smugly at her having made Alison rise to the bait.

'I still can't believe it,' Alison sighed. 'How did you know where to find me?'

'Antonia told me. She said you'd only been gone ten minutes and that it would be an hour before you were back, so she showed me to your room where I took a quick shower. I've been stalking you for the past half hour. At one point, you turned round and I was sure you must have seen me but you hadn't. I watched you struggling with your order at the meat counter and queuing at the checkout and how I kept myself from giving the game away on the phone, I don't know. You are so gullible Alison. I could *see* what those guys were wearing,' he laughed.

'Well, I didn't know that, did I?' she said tetchily.

'Are you really pleased I'm here? You don't mind me gate-crashing your holiday?'

'Paul, I couldn't describe my feelings. You've no idea how much I've missed you.'

'Listen,' he whispered. 'Don't breathe a word but Tom's at the villa with his own surprise planned.'

'That's fantastic! Jenny will be ecstatic. So when was all this arranged?'

'We went for a drink on Monday and hatched the plan then. We would have come tonight after Tom finished work but there were no flights, so he took the day off. I'm shattered though because we had to be at the airport at six this morning.'

'Don't worry. You can rest over the weekend. I'll sleep on the sofa,' she said with a glint in her eye.

'Thanks darling. I knew you'd understand,' Paul said and she slapped his arm playfully. 'Watch out, Jenny's on her way back. Not a word.'

'That's yours. We drank the others,' Alison said.

Jenny smiled warmly at Paul. 'I'm pleased you're here. Alison's been really crotchety all week.'

'*I have not!*' she protested strongly.

Jenny disregarded her response. 'Have you heard anything from Tom this week, Paul?'

'Yes, I called him on Monday. He was fine.'

'Poor Tom. He hasn't had chance to call yet today *and* he has to work all weekend.'

'That's a pity,' he sympathised and Alison almost choked as she avoided eye contact with them.

'Has Alison mentioned the barbecue tonight?'

'Yes, it should be a good night.'

'Well, I don't think my night will be brilliant. I'm the only one now without a partner.'

'Don't worry. Hang out with us. We won't leave you on your own will we Alison?'

'No,' she croaked, keeping her head bowed.

'I'll nip to the loo before we go,' Jenny said. 'Are you coming Alison?'

'No, I'm not letting Paul out of my sight.'

As Jenny walked away Alison said, 'I'm hopeless at this. I'm going to let something slip.'

'You didn't have a problem when you set me up at my parents' house in the bedroom.'

'Ah, that was sheer determination, which reminds me, you didn't tell me you were running round the bedroom starkers in front of your mother!'

'Did *she* tell you that?' he asked looking shocked.

'Of course! That was the best part and I'd missed it,' she laughed.

'Not for me it wasn't, I assure you. I almost died of embarrassment. I wasn't sure if she'd seen me.'

'Believe me, she saw *everything*, in fact she told me what a sexy physique you had.'

'*You're lying*!'

On a shrill laugh she replied, 'You're right, I am.'

He sighed. 'I'll never live that down, will I?'

'Not if I've anything to do with it.'

Jenny came back and finished her coffee. 'Are we ready?' she asked.

Paul picked up the shopping effortlessly. 'I have a hire-car in the car park, so we don't have to walk.'

As he walked on ahead, Jenny remarked, 'I'm so pleased for you Alison.'

'Thanks. I'm sorry Tom couldn't be here as well.'

'Don't be daft. I'll be fine.'

Antonia and Clare were anxious to hear all about Alison's surprise and laughed as she confessed that she still hadn't grasped he was there, even when he described what people nearby were wearing. 'It was the last thing on my mind,' she said. 'I was talking to him on his mobile and I really believed he was in England. I went crazy when I spotted him and....'

'I'm off for a shower,' Jenny butted in desolately and no one spoke as she left the room.

'Where's Tom?' asked Alison in a whisper.

'In Jenny's bed. Wait for it....'

The next moment, they heard an almighty scream.

'I think she's found him,' Antonia remarked.

Jenny raced from her room screeching like a barn owl, much to everybody's amusement and directing her question at Alison yelled, 'You knew Tom was here you little bugger, didn't you?'

Alison's grin answered her question and she shot back to her room, banging the door behind her.

Paul carried the shopping through to the kitchen. 'It's a beautiful villa. There's a fabulous view from your window *and* you have a king-size bed too,' he whispered to Alison.

301

'Can we help with anything Alison?' Clare asked.

'I want everything in the fridge. You can wrap the salad please. I'll part-cook the ribs then we'll finish them off on the barbecue.'

Alison removed the meaty pork ribs from the bag. 'Aren't those great? I'll make a marinade and soak them and then they'll need an hour in a slow oven.'

'I hope you're not going to spend the entire afternoon cooking,' Paul whispered, kissing her ear.

'Had you something else in mind?' she asked and the passion in his eyes answered her question. 'I'll be finished in a few minutes,' she promised.

She prepared the marinade and tossed all the ribs in the bowl. 'You have my undivided attention now Paul Trantor,' she murmured provocatively.

He kissed her gently. 'Come on,' he said, leading her from the kitchen. 'I want to show you just how much I've missed you.'

They paused briefly outside her room, laughing at the shoddily-made 'no entry' sign to which, across the top had been added the word *definitely*.

10

Alison prepared the salad while Antonia, Jenny and Clare hovered by the cooker, tantalized by the smell of roasting ribs. Everyone was ravenous and Clare dipped a finger in the sauce as Alison removed the tray from the oven. 'That's delicious,' she drooled, licking her finger. 'I hope we all get one of those.'

'Make a point of it. Imagine you're getting onto a Spanish bus and elbow everybody out of the way,' Alison said dryly and they howled with laughter.

She took one partially baked potato from the oven and pierced it with a skewer. 'They're fine. They'll finish off nicely on the barbecue. Let's get the food to the door. It's turned seven already.'

Earlier, when Alison informed Paul about Dave's friendship, he reacted angrily, causing her to shout, 'Why don't you just listen instead of jumping to the wrong conclusion every time I speak? I've told you Dave doesn't want anyone else either, so we protect each other from unwanted advances. I thought you would have been grateful, especially when we were in a place like Puerto Banus.'

'It's *my* place to protect you,' he yelled angrily.

'*But you weren't there!*' she bellowed.

Although he sulked for a short while, their quarrel was soon forgotten. Alison didn't tell him that Dave was an old acquaintance but she insisted he should thank Dave, which he reluctantly agreed to do.

It was time to leave and Paul offered to stack the food in the car to take it next door.

'We'll help you load up then,' Antonia said. 'It's

all by the door and there's a lot. Alison has been a busy bee as usual. We'd all have died of hunger this week had it not been for her. She's quite a magician in the kitchen.'

'I'm pretty good at magic on my mobile, isn't that right darling?' Paul said, winking at her.

She gave him a withering look. 'If you say so.'

They carried the food and drink to the car and the four girls walked to the lads' villa. There were half a dozen strangers already there when they arrived. Matthew and Mike greeted Antonia and Clare while Dave went to talk to Alison. 'You won't believe it,' she told him excitedly. 'Paul flew out this morning and Jenny's boyfriend's here too. They'll be here in a minute.'

'I'm delighted for you Alison. I wish they'd have brought Laura too,' he sighed.

'I know but you'll see her in a few days.'

Paul and Tom headed for the patio, carrying some of the food. 'Hi,' Paul smiled, directing his greeting at Dave who was standing beside Alison. 'Show me where you want this lot will you?'

'Paul Trantor! I don't believe it,' Dave laughed, removing the tray from Paul's right hand which he proceeded to shake vigorously. 'How are you mate? It's been years. Don't you remember me?'

'I can't place you at the moment. Let me think.'

'Nasty Norman! Does that ring any bells?'

'From the supermarket? Now I remember, you're Dave er....Maxwell. Well, I'll be damned. It has to be ten years since we worked together and Norman was never off our backs,' he laughed. 'He watched us like a hawk. Do you know who this is Alison?'

Impassively she answered, 'This is Dave. I know all about him. He's engaged to Laura....remember?'

'Right! So *you're* Dave who Alison relies on for protection? She couldn't have found anyone better. It's great to meet up with you again. We'll catch up as soon as I've brought the rest of the food in.'

Alison took hold of Paul's hand. 'Thank you,' she whispered with a heart-warming smile.

'Let me give you a lift with it Paul,' Dave offered as they hurried away together, happily reminiscing about their student days.

As the two of them continued to catch up, Jenny and Alison prepared the table. Three further couples arrived making a total of twenty-two.

Alison returned to the kitchen to cut the large ribs in half to make twenty-four pieces. Paul appeared at her side and clasped his arms around her. 'I'm such an idiot. I'm pathetic at times aren't I?'

'You're better than you were. Dave's a decent lad and I'll be sorry when he leaves on Wednesday.'

'I know and I'm sorry about earlier. Fancy Dave Maxwell being here. I can't get over that.'

She placed the ribs between the burgers, sausages and chicken pieces for Simon who was in charge of the barbecue and very soon, everyone was enjoying the delicious food.

'This is great Alison. I'm pleased we came now,' Paul said.

'I was always coming Paul, with or without you. You have to grow up,' she told him pointedly. 'You have to learn to trust me.'

'I know but you'll straighten me out. I've been a bachelor too long. I really hate it when we quarrel.'

'Who's quarrelling?' she asked, kissing his cheek with greasy lips.

'Unhand me wench,' he protested light-heartedly. 'I'm worn out.'

At that point Dave sidled across. 'I almost forgot. I got these photos printed today,' he said.

She removed them from the envelope and found the usual shots of drunken lads fooling around. The last three were taken at Puerto Banus, two of Alison and the one she had taken of Dave.

'Terrific camera Dave. Is it digital?' Paul asked.

'No, it's a standard thirty-five millimetre. It takes great shots so I'm loath to part with it.'

'May I keep this one? It's perfect for what I want and I don't have any photographs of Alison.'

'Be my guest. I was going to have both copied for Alison. I'll still get them done and I'll post them on when I get home.'

'Thanks Dave,' Alison said. 'It's a very good one of you that I took. It really captures your mood.'

'You're becoming very art critical,' Paul told her. 'You'll have to start delivering my lectures so I can catch up with my backlog at the studio.'

'Do you have a large studio?' Dave questioned.

'Yes and if you give me your number, I'll be sure to give you a call next week. I'll show you. Maybe we can have a drink and catch up some more?'

'Great....I'd like that.'

A couple wandered over. 'I believe we have you to thank for the delectable ribs. Would you tell me how you made the sauce please? I buy mine in a jar and it always tastes bitter. Your wife is so talented,' the young woman told Paul.

'I'll write it down for you. It's as easy as opening a jar. I'll pop over with it later,' Alison promised.

'Thank you so much,' she said and moved on.

'That sounded amazing when she referred to you as my wife,' Paul murmured.

'Yes it did and I'm going to call Vicky as soon as I get home and get things moving for the wedding.'

'Well when you do, do you mind restricting your dialogue to the wedding arrangements, as opposed to my physical attributes?' he asked.

'What physical attributes would those be Paul?'

'I didn't hear you complain earlier,' he remarked, taking her in his arms. 'We're so good together and I want to be with you always. I have a nice surprise for you when we get back to the villa.'

'I thought you were worn out?'

'The house brochures! I have them with me. With all the commotion from screeching women, I forgot and by the way, I'm not worn out. I was joking.'

Alison shook her head in disbelief. 'You forgot to show me? You *knew* I wanted to see them.'

'More than you wanted me?'

She smiled forgivingly. 'No, I wanted *you* more than anything in the whole world.' Changing topic she laughed, 'Look at Jenny and Tom. They've not let go of each other yet. Let's wander over.'

They ambled across the patio hand in hand, 'Have you two had any food yet?' Alison interrupted.

'No. I'm far too excited to eat. Look!' Jenny said,

stretching out her hand to reveal a diamond cluster. 'Tom's asked me to marry him and I've accepted.'

'Well done Tom! Congratulations to both of you,' Paul said, shaking his hand heartily. 'I hope you'll both be very happy.'

'Come here,' Alison cried, wiping tears from her eyes. 'I'm so happy. Have you told the others yet?'

'No, I'm still in shock. I was really dreading this barbecue earlier and now, I'll never forget it.'

'We'll leave you alone and we're thrilled for both of you,' Alison told them and as they moved away she said to Paul. 'Isn't everything turning out well? It's been an unusual evening hasn't it?'

'It's been fantastic and it isn't over yet,' he said, tightening his grip around her. 'Let's see if there's any food left. I could do with some sustenance.'

'I'm afraid we're out of oysters,' she laughed.

'Who needs oysters?' he grinned. 'Come on, let's get another drink.'

All the food had gone apart from a solitary burger and a couple of slices of bread. Paul made himself a sandwich and taking a huge bite he remarked, 'It's worked out just right hasn't it? I don't think there's anything else left.'

'That would probably have gone too had someone not dropped it on the floor and stood on it earlier,' she replied with a straight face.

'You're joking!' he spluttered.

'Yes I am,' she laughed. 'And you have the nerve to call *me* gullible. Do you honestly think I'd have let you eat it had it been on the floor?'

'It's what I deserve. I don't deserve you Babe.'

308

'Maybe not but you're stuck with me Paul, just as I'm stuck with you, for better for worse. No matter what happens, always remember that.'

'You're very serious. Is something wrong?'

'No. I get upset when we fall out over silly things. Life's too short. My mother's death taught me that.'

'I know sweetheart.'

'Come on, let's look for Antonia and Clare,' she said and they went indoors where they found them in the kitchen with Matthew and Mike.

'It's been good tonight and the ribs were superb,' Dave, who was washing up, said.

'I got them from that new supermarket on the left. There was plenty of meat on them, unlike the ones at home that are all bone.'

Simon cut in, 'Everybody got a piece which was great. Did you part-cook them in the oven first?'

'Yes, slowly for an hour. It tenderises the meat.'

'Can I interrupt the cookery class for a moment?' Paul asked. 'Are you lot doing anything tomorrow night? If not, there's a very nice restaurant I'd like to take you to if I can book us a table....my treat for tonight and for taking care of Alison and Jenny.'

'We've nothing planned yet. Thanks,' Mike said.

Everyone else nodded in agreement.

'It's my last night and Tom's so we might as well go out with a bang. Is there a phone book here?'

'Yes, there's one in the sideboard but the phone's disconnected,' Mike advised him.

'It's alright, I have my mobile. It's a table for ten isn't it?' he questioned, counting up.

Mike counted up too and verified the number.

Paul returned within minutes. 'I've booked a table for eight-thirty. I'll take Alison, Jenny and Tom. It takes about fifteen minutes and there's a taxi rank just down the road. Leave about eight and you'll be there in plenty of time.'

Simon handed Paul a sheet of paper on which he scribbled, *Restaurante Val Paraíso*.

'Thanks a lot Paul. I'm really looking forward to that,' Mike said.

'Yes thanks,' the others echoed.

'Help yourself to a drink Paul. It's still early and we're going to turn the music up now,' Simon said.

'Could I have a couple of sheets of paper please?' Alison asked. 'A lady wants a recipe from me and Dave wants my address and phone number.'

When she went outside, Dave was standing by the railings with a faraway look in his eyes. 'A penny for your thoughts,' she said.

'It's Laura; I'm missing her so much.'

'I know, it's rotten. The timing worked out badly for both of us but at least I have Paul for two days.'

'He's a great guy Alison. It's hard to imagine he can be so moody.'

'I've told you, he's possessive that's all. It might take a while but he'll change.'

'He worships you. He told me earlier.'

'I know. I feel the same about him. Did you speak to Laura today?'

'Yes, I went inside earlier. Everybody was paired off and I was fed-up so we chatted for a while.'

'Perhaps I'll meet her sometime. You never know what the future holds.'

A few people had started to dance and Paul asked Alison if she would like to dance.

'I can shuffle but very little else,' she said.

'Let's give it a whirl. We'll have to dance in front of everyone at our wedding.'

'Won't that be something?' she sighed as he held her close. She could hear his beating heart and felt happy and secure in her lover's arms.

'We'll have to leave soon darling. It's almost two o'clock and I've been up since six yesterday.'

'Okay, I'll tell the others. Wait here,' she said.

Jenny and Tom prepared to leave too as Tom was falling asleep.

Paul wandered over and said goodnight to Dave. 'It's been great. Thank the others for me please. I'm ready for bed now. I'm pleased we've met up again after so long and in such unusual circumstances.'

Wearily, they made their way to the villa. 'I could murder a cup of coffee,' Paul said.

'I'll see to it,' she offered. 'You get ready for bed. You look shattered.'

When she returned with Paul's coffee, on the bed was a note saying, 'excellent for friction burns' and beside it the box of plasters she had lent to Antonia.

Alison laughed and murmured softly, 'I'll not be in need of any,' as she placed the mug of coffee on the table by Paul who was sleeping like a baby. She slid in beside him and wrapped her arms around his warm and comforting body and fell asleep too.

Paul slept until ten the next morning and when he awoke Alison wasn't there. The bathroom door was ajar and he could hear her vomiting. He ran to her aid. 'What's wrong darling?' he asked. 'What can I do to help?'

'I'll be fine in a minute. I think I had too much to drink last night.'

'But you hardly had anything. I was there.'

'Would you make me a cup of tea please and I'll get back into bed for a few minutes?'

He nodded and hurried to the kitchen.

'Alright Paul?' Jenny asked in her normal bubbly manner as Paul appeared in the kitchen.

'No, Alison's been sick. She'd like a cup of tea.'

'I'll attend to it,' she said. 'You go back to her.'

Jenny felt concerned and her heart went out to her friend whose morning sickness had now continued for some days. She must realise she was pregnant. No one could be *that* naïve, she told herself.

Jenny took the cup of tea to her. 'What's up kid?' she asked, trying to act normal in Paul's presence.

'Something must have upset me a bit but I'm fine now,' she replied without looking up.

'Stay in bed darling. I'll sit with you,' Paul said.

'I'll do no such thing. I'm going to have a shower when I've finished my tea.'

'She'll be okay now,' Jenny remarked, giving her a knowing look. 'Just give us a few minutes Paul. I wouldn't say no to a cup of coffee.'

'I'll see to it then. I won't be long Babe.'

Jenny shut the door and turned to face her, 'Right lady, start talking and no bullshit! This is *me*!'

Tearfully, she spluttered, 'I can't tell him Jenny!'

'You've got to tell him. Paul has a right to know. You can't keep it hidden ad infinitum. That's why I

312

wouldn't let you carry your heavy bag but nobody else suspects anything. You have to tell him.'

'Paul assured me I was safe and I believed him. I don't want to force his hand. That's why I'd rather get married quickly before he finds out.'

'That's ridiculous! You can't marry Paul and not tell him you're pregnant. To try to build a marriage on deceit would be disastrous. Whatever he's going to say or do, you *must* tell him. If you keep holding back, he'll think you're hiding something.'

'What could I possibly be hiding?'

'Alison, I'm going to ask you a question now and I don't want you to get upset or angry. Is it possible anyone else could be the father?'

'*No*! You know I haven't been with anyone else!' she exclaimed before bursting into tears. 'I've never looked at anyone else. That's the truth. I swear.'

'Listen, I know you're speaking the truth because I know you wouldn't hurt Paul. I'm asking because you said he'd promised you would be safe but how could he make any such promise when you weren't careful? Did he explain the reason why?'

'No, he just told me not to worry when I tried to raise it with him after you and I had talked. He was angry with me for doubting him. I never got around to asking him. He knew why I was concerned and he got angry because he said I couldn't trust him to take care of me. I *did* trust him Jenny and now I'm pregnant and I don't know what to do.'

Jenny remembered her heated exchange with Paul vividly but by some miracle, Alison was pregnant. She doubted however that Paul would believe it to be a miracle. Jenny was distressed for both of them. Paul would be livid and would undoubtedly suspect Mark. Poor Paul, she thought. He was a caring guy who would rather cut off his arm than hurt Alison. The revelation would totally destroy him.

Jenny couldn't disclose the information Paul had shared albeit Alison was her best friend. This was a tragedy without solution, as Paul, being jealous and strong-willed, would walk away when he knew the truth. Even Paul's undying love for Alison couldn't hold them together now.

'You should have been more persuasive in asking what he meant. It was wrong of him not to discuss such important issues with you.'

'I didn't want to prolong the discussion as I'm not comfortable discussing such matters. I've heard of male contraceptive pills so I just assumed Paul was referring to something like that when he said it was safe. I'm not ruining our weekend so I'll find a way to tell him when I'm back home.'

'Do you promise?'

'Yes, I do. Let's just forget about it now. I'd like Paul to come back in please.'

'Alright, I'll find him.'

Paul returned carrying a tray that he placed on the bed.

'Be careful darling. I've brought another hot cup of tea and I've made you a slice of toast. Try to eat something and I'm sure you'll feel better.'

'That's lovely,' she said, referring to the sprig of vivid pink bougainvillea he had placed on her tray. 'You're so thoughtful. Where did you find that?'

'Poking through the railings next door. Hey, have you been crying? What's wrong Babe?'

'It's nothing. I'm much better now you're here.'

'Are you upset because I fell asleep last night?'

'Don't be silly. You don't have to prove anything to me. I was more than happy just to curl up beside you and fall asleep. Will you lie here with me now? I want to hold you.'

Paul turned back the covers, slipped into bed and wrapped his arms around her. 'How's that darling?'

'That feels nice. I love you so much Paul.'

He kissed her. 'I love you too.'

Alison slept for an hour and when she awoke, she was still in Paul's arms.

'How are you feeling now?' he questioned.

'Much better. I don't know why I felt so weepy.'

'Do you still feel sickly?'

'No, I really am fine. I must have been overtired. I'm going to take a shower now.'

'Do you mind if I do too?'

'No, I won't be very long.'

'I meant with you.'

She smiled. 'I'd like that very much.'

'Would you like to go out for an hour or so when you've had your shower?'

'Yes, if you'd like to Paul. Where shall we go?'

'I'll drive you to Granada and we can take a stroll round the Alhambra Palace. It's well worth a visit.'

Jenny was in the hall when they appeared, ready to go out. 'You look a lot brighter,' she made known.

'I'm fine now so we're off out. Where's Tom?'

315

'He's in the pool. Where are you going?'

Paul sighed impatiently. 'Granada, if we go now.'

'Enjoy yourselves. I'll see you later,' Jenny said.

Alison sat on the wall while Paul went next door for the car and soon they were in the country, away from all the noisy traffic.

'Look at the sun on the mountains. They look like cardboard cut-outs,' Alison remarked.

'The sunlight plays very odd tricks. It can change the whole appearance of something.'

'Am I getting another art lecture?'

He laughed. 'If you like.'

'Do you realise, I'll be as clued-up as you soon?'

'That's what I'm working towards. Do you fancy stopping for a quick snack? You've still not eaten.'

'Yes, I could manage something now.'

'Right, I'll stop at the next place I see.'

A mile or two along the road he came across a bar offering food and he pulled in and parked the car. They chose a shaded table and the waiter appeared immediately.

'May I have a coffee and some toast please?' she asked but the waiter didn't understand.

'Una cerveza pequeña….y una café con leche por favor. ¿Tienes tostados?'

'¿Jamón señor?'

'Jamón y queso por favor.'

'¿Para dos?'

'Si.'

'Gracias, señor.

'I don't believe it. You speak Spanish,' she said.

'Just a few words,' he said modestly.

316

'A few words? It was an entire conversation. I'm very impressed.'

'Save it till the order comes. I might not get what I tried to order. I make a lot of mistakes.'

'What did you order?'

'A pick-me-up, after taking that shower with you this morning,' he laughed.

'Don't you go blaming me. That was your idea!'

'I know Babe. Actually, I ordered two cheese and ham toasties but we'll have to see what he brings.'

The waiter returned with the two toasties, a milky coffee and a small beer.

'That's spot on,' Paul announced. 'Enjoy.'

Another car pulled up alongside theirs and Alison watched with interest as a young couple exited their car and lifted a toddler from his car seat.

The child's mother strapped him into a buggy and the couple sat down at the table next to theirs. They pushed the buggy into the shaded part close to Paul.

Paul turned his head and smiled at the young boy and his parents. '¿Cuantos años tiene?' he asked the child's mother.

'Dieciocho meses,' the child's mother replied.

'El es muy guapo,' Paul replied with a smile as he touched the child's hand.

'What was all that about?' Alison asked.

'I was telling her how handsome her son is. He's eighteen months old.'

She saw this as an opportunity to raise the subject of children. 'You like children, don't you Paul?'

'Yes, I love kids. I wish I saw more of my sister's two. They're great.'

'Hopefully, we'll have our own before long. You would like to have children wouldn't you?'

Paul shuffled uncomfortably in his chair. 'What's brought this on Alison?'

'It's not unusual for couples to want a child Paul. Why are you being so tetchy?'

'Tetchy? We're not married yet!' he snapped.

'I'm only asking for your views. It's a reasonable enough question to be asking,' she persisted.

'We'll discuss it later,' he stated disparagingly.

'I want to discuss it now. Please don't be angry.'

'I'm not angry,' he said. 'It's awkward to discuss at the moment when there are people around.'

'There's no one here except the Spanish couple.'

'Alison, can we *drop* it....please? We'll talk about it next week when you're home.'

She felt disheartened, unable to understand Paul's cavalier attitude towards what she felt was a normal topic of conversation between two people who were planning to get married. She knew if she continued to pressure him, they would finish up having a row. In any event, it was obviously not the time or place to tell him she was pregnant. That bombshell would have to be put on hold. She hoped she wouldn't feel nauseous again the next day to raise any suspicion.

'How was the toastie?' she asked, changing topic.

'Fine,' he said restlessly. 'Let's make a move.'

Alison returned to the car as Paul went to pay the bill. She knew he would relax again shortly, just as he always did when left to his thoughts.

'Have you been to Granada before?' she asked as they left the car park.

318

'Yes but I always enjoy it. You'll be amazed,' he said taking hold of her hand.

That made her happy. The man she loved dearly was back with her again.

On their arrival in Granada, Paul managed to park close to the Alhambra. 'We've only got two hours,' he advised her. 'How are you feeling now Babe?'

'I'm perfectly alright thank you.'

'That's great,' he said, squeezing her hand. 'You were doubtless overtired. I definitely was. Come on and I'll show you some truly veritable architecture. You'll think you are living in the fourteenth century when you enter The Lions' Courtyard and see some of the finest Arab art in the whole of Spain. It's an amazing ensemble of palaces and fortresses.'

She held Paul's hand as they ambled through the ruins. The mosaics were astonishing and he led her through what had once been glorious gardens with pools and fountains.

'I didn't realise it was so old. It's beautiful Paul. I didn't know what to expect but I never imagined a spectacle so well-preserved, considering its age.'

They meandered to the car and he chose a shorter return route by motorway, then diverted, following the signs for Mijas. 'I want you to see this,' he said. 'It's called Mijas and aptly labelled the Essence of Andalucía. It's one of the nicest villages you'll see. It's quite small with around fifteen thousand inhabitants many of whom are foreigners. People arrive in their hundreds every day by car, bus or coach. It's quite commercialised now which is a pity. I doubt I would find a place to park so look around as I drive through. Watch for a line of donkeys. It's the *burro* taxi. They plod around the streets so their riders can take in the sights. It's lovely here at night and there are vantage points overlooking the coast. It boasts its own small bullring, unique because it's square.'

Alison craned her neck from side to side as Paul continued to drive very slowly through the village.

'It's so picturesque,' she sighed. 'Just look at the brightly coloured geraniums in the window boxes. Aren't they lovely? The houses are so quaint and so clean. Look there's a donkey with a floral hat on.'

'You'll see a lot more of those before we've gone through the village,' he told her.

As he circled the car park to return, a driver was reversing out. Paul waved him out and shot into the space before anyone could beat him.

'Half an hour maximum!' he said earnestly. Then smiling at her glee added, 'I mean it. Half an hour!'

The shops were just yards from the car park. 'The best buys are Lladro figurines and leather, like bags and belts,' he advised her.

'Here's a Lladro shop. Look, aren't those figures beautiful? Can we go in please?'

'It comes off your half hour so choose wisely.'

Spellbound, she wandered around the shop. Some of the pieces cost thousands of Euros and she took great care not to knock a piece over.

One particular cabinet displayed many variations of a Bride and Groom and her nose almost touched the glass as she studied every detail.

'Do you like those, sweetheart?' Paul questioned, encircling her in his arms.

'Yes and I was thinking how happy I would be on my wedding day. Study the faces, especially on that piece there....there's so much detail. It's exquisite.'

'Then you shall have it,' he said.

'No, I don't expect you to buy it. I only said....'

'It's for me too....a memento of our trip to Mijas,' he cut in, beckoning the assistant for service. 'Are you sure that's your favourite piece?'

'Yes, I do prefer that one. Do you?'

'No, I prefer you to any of them and you will out-shine any bride on *your* wedding day Alison,' Paul replied, kissing her tenderly.

The shop assistant understood his complimentary remark and smiled at both of them.

'That's the price I have to pay for behaving badly earlier. I know I'm an idiot and I could kick myself afterwards. There *is* something we must discuss but not this weekend. It's something we can resolve, so please don't worry. Just remember I love you.'

Alison was happy. Who wouldn't be, she thought with someone like Paul?

'And now I have some *very* bad news for you,' he said solemnly as he passed her the parcel.

'Why, what's wrong?'

'Your half hour is up. We have to go,' he grinned.

'I don't care. I have everything I want. I have my Lladro Bride and Groom and best of all I have you.'

Paul took her back by the lower road. 'Those are restaurants,' he stated, indicating elevated buildings with sea views. 'My intention was to bring you here last night had we not gone to Dave's barbecue but at least you've caught a glimpse of it today.'

'I'll never forget Mijas. I didn't realise you were so well acquainted with Spain.'

'I've painted for many a day on that hillside and I sold my work to tourists to pay for my keep. I also painted at Puerto Banus and that's the reason I was worried when you were alone there with Jenny.'

'Dave and Simon were there as well. We weren't alone but had I told you, you'd have hit the roof.'

'No I wouldn't. Dave's a great bloke.'

'You didn't know who he was then. You'd have gone mad like you always do if I speak to anyone.'

'I don't go mad when you speak to Jenny.'

'You know perfectly well what I mean Paul.'

'Yes Alison.'

'You can be really annoying at times.'

'Yes Alison.'

'And stop saying *yes Alison*.'

'Yes Alison,' he laughed, moving aside hurriedly before she could slap him.

'Why are we slowing down?'

'First, I want to hug you,' he said. 'Then, I'd like you to look up there at that restaurant. That's where we're eating later. The views are really spectacular but that's all I'm telling you. You'll see everything else later. We really must make our way back now.'

When they arrived at the villa ten minutes later it was turned seven o'clock. 'We've only got an hour. We must hurry now or we'll be late,' Paul told her.

The girls were frantic when they hurried in. 'We were worried something had happened,' Jenny said.

'We've had a great day but I'll tell you all about it later. I need to get ready now,' Alison said.

When she went to her bedroom, Paul was already in the shower. 'If you want to save time, jump in,' he yelled to her.

'That won't save time! We'll *never* be ready if I get in there with you. Just hurry up,' she demanded irritably and Paul howled with laughter.

She hurriedly chose what to wear. He had earlier described it as a restaurant where the diners dressed elegantly, so she was delighted she had packed the black dress Paul had bought for her. She found her shoes and jewellery and took out her make-up purse in readiness.

Paul dressed swiftly. 'Do you want a quick coffee Babe? I'm having one.'

'Please.'

When Paul left the room she ran to get showered. She felt lucky to have a manageable hairstyle that she quickly dried and brushed.

Stepping into her dress, Alison smiled diffidently, recalling the consequences of her putting it on for Paul in Brighton when she had given herself to him completely for the very first time.

She remembered how she had struggled with the zip then and how Paul had eagerly gone to her aid. She was struggling again now but not because her hands were clammy as previously. She couldn't be gaining weight so soon, she told herself, tugging at the zip and she felt relief when it suddenly cleared her waistline and slid up. She studied her reflection in the mirror. She adored that dress and much more so the man who had bought it for her.

'Wow, you look fantastic,' Paul exclaimed when

he returned. 'I've never seen you look so radiant. Is that the dress you bought in Brighton?'

'Yes, or rather, no. You bought it for me.'

'Well I definitely have a good eye for fashion.'

'You do but your memory's poor. I wore it at my eighteenth party but you were so preoccupied with Mark that you probably didn't notice me at all.'

He laughed. 'I always notice you my precious girl but when you look like that I'm obliged to keep my eyes on Mark and all other males for miles around.'

She turned to face him and straightened his tie. 'If I wasn't in love with a fine-looking man called Paul Trantor, I could really fall for you. It's that *boys in uniform* thing we girls have but with me, it's men in ties, especially gorgeous hunks like you. You look just like Richard Gere in *Pretty Woman* but you are much more handsome and I prefer your hair to his.'

'In other words, I'm nothing like Richard Gere.'

'Nothing at all,' she giggled. 'By the way, do you happen to know his middle name?'

'I haven't a clue. Why would I?'

'It's *Tiffany*. He's called Richard Tiffany Gere.'

'*Tiffany*!' he howled. 'You are joking!'

'I'm not. It was on a quiz show. Maybe it was his mother's maiden name but it's definitely his name.'

'Fancy name….but he's not as cute as me.'

She laughed at that. 'You're right there Paul. No one is as cute as you. I'd give you a sloppy kiss but I'd ruin my make-up,' she whispered intimately.

'You're extremely provocative tonight. You're in a very strange mood.'

'Am I?' she asked with a glint in her eye.

'You know you are. Please don't do this all night. You'll drive me crazy.'

'That's the idea so you won't fall asleep tonight.'

'Let's go. I need some fresh air, you temptress.'

Jenny and Tom were waiting in the hall. It was a little before eight. 'Doesn't everybody look dashing tonight?' Alison chirped. 'It's nice to get dressed up properly. I simply adore your tie Tom.'

'What's up with her?' Jenny asked Paul quietly.

'Search me. I think she's been on the happy pills. She's been like that since we got back.'

Jenny laughed. 'Well it's an improvement on this morning. I think you might be in for a long night.'

'That's what's worrying me,' he sighed.

Paul caught up with Alison at the end of the path. 'Hey, hang on Alison. What's all the rush? Are you alright Babe?' he asked.

'I've never been better.'

'Stop! Come here and tell me what's wrong?'

'*Nothing*. Why, what's the matter with you Paul?'

They reached the wall where the car was parked and Alison looked round but Jenny hadn't appeared in view. She placed the flat of her hand in the centre of Paul's chest and pushed him against the wall. I intend to be in control tonight,' she whispered in a sultry voice. 'I'm usually the conservative lover but all that's about to change. I want to be er….what do they call it….yes….dominatrix! I love the tie. It's a real turn on,' she added huskily.

He stared at her in bewilderment.

'You look a bit peaky. I hope you aren't going to disappoint me. I have so much planned for later.'

'Er….what do you have planned?' he questioned.

'You'll have to wait and see. That's what you're always telling me. What a surprise I have for you.'

'Alison, tell me what's wrong, please. I've never seen you like this before.'

'It's because you haven't worn a tie before when I've had you all to myself. You're driving me crazy Paul. Will we be able to slip away somewhere for a while when we get to the restaurant?'

'Look, I'll take the blasted tie off if it'll calm you down,' he offered frantically.

She fought to contain her laughter at his anguish. 'No! I don't want your tie to come off but I'd love everything else to come off. Please, just leave your tie on. It's so sexy.'

'Jenny and Tom are on their way. Behave Alison. I don't know what's come over you tonight.'

'That's a shame. Now I'll have to wait till later,' she replied huskily.

Paul stalled the engine twice while attempting to turn the car round.

'Is something wrong with the car?' Alison asked.

'No, it's fine,' he said, sounding agitated.

'Where did you get to today?' Jenny enquired.

'Granada and then to a pretty place called Mijas.'

'I've been there, it is nice,' she agreed.

'Paul was saying we could get there by bus from Fuengirola. He bought me a Lladro ornament today in Mijas. I've got to think of a special way to thank him for that. He's so good to me.'

'Well, I'm sure you'll think of something,' Jenny said. 'You're very intuitive.'

Paul cut in, 'We'll be there shortly. I'll drop you at the door and someone will park the car for me.'

'You're having things easy tonight Paul,' Alison smirked. 'By the way Jenny do you like Paul's tie?'

'Yes, it's very chic. It's so rare for a man to wear a tie in this day and age which is a shame. It seems to alter his whole appearance doesn't it?'

'I said the very same thing didn't I Paul?'

He was squirming in his seat as he stopped the car outside the entrance to the restaurant and when the others got out, he turned to her and said anxiously, 'Will you stop this now! This isn't like you at all.'

'I know Paul, but I can't help myself. You're very sexy when you look at me like that,' and with a toss of the head, she stepped from the car.

The taxis bringing the other six pulled up directly behind and after brief pleasantries were exchanged, everyone went inside.

Alison decided for the moment to let Paul recover a little. The night was young.

As they entered the reception area, a photographic display of the many celebrities who had dined there caught their eye and between them, they were able to put names to most faces.

They were led to a table on the florally decorated patio overlooking the coast of Fuengirola and none of them failed to comment on the prize location of the restaurant.

Alison ordered a Bacardi and coke and when Paul raised his eyebrows, she said, 'Don't worry. I won't drink too many as I need to remain in total control tonight.'

He swallowed hard and she laughed. 'Maybe you should order oysters. Would you excuse me please? I need the little girls' room.'

Ever the gentleman, he stood up too when Alison rose. The others were involved in conversation and no one appeared to notice as he swiftly followed.

When Alison reappeared, he led her outside to the car park. 'What the hell's the matter with you?' he asked fractiously. 'You're a totally different person tonight. I don't even know how to talk to you.'

She started to laugh, unable to contain her mirth a moment longer. It was confession time. 'I'm sorry; I'm winding you up. I wanted to test your reaction if I took control and you responded so unexpectedly that I let it run on for a while.'

Paul heaved a huge sigh of relief and took her in his arms. 'You just reminded me of Glenn Close in that fear-provoking film, *Fatal Attraction*. I thought we'd promised there'd be no more wind-ups?'

'I don't recall making any such promise. *You* did following the bedroom scene at your parents' house but I'll give you my word, I won't do it again. Were you scared to see me like that?'

'Scared? I was bloody petrified,' he laughed. 'It's great to have you back. I love you just as you are.'

'Had we better go back inside to the others?'

'Yes and my appetite has suddenly returned.'

Everybody enjoyed a memorable night at the Val Paraíso and a Flamenco show added the final touch. Alison gazed intensely into Paul's eyes, assured he would love her always as she would love him. He was leaving the next day and she believed her heart would break when the time came to say goodbye.

It was an emotional moment as Paul shook hands with Dave and thanked him again for his concern. 'It's been a fantastic weekend,' Paul said and added quietly to Alison, 'There's only been one better.'

'Er….this one's not over yet Paul,' she answered in the sultry voice she had used earlier.

He laughed. 'For God's sake, *Bunny Boiler*, don't start that again. Come on, let's make tracks.'

When Alison went to her room, Paul's tie was on the bed and with a smile, she slipped it in her bag.

As Paul came out of the bathroom, Alison went in to remove her make-up. She returned in her scarlet underwear, Paul's tie draped around her neck.

Paul was packing his overnight bag as she waited provocatively, her back against the door casing.

As he closed the wardrobe, he turned and caught sight of her. Overcome with excitement he paused, remaining motionless for some time as he cast his ravenous eyes over her shapely body. Then, panting hotly he whispered, 'Alison, I want you so much.'

Her smile in response echoed his feelings….

11

Paul slipped out of bed quietly the next day. Alison was still sleeping and he didn't wish to disturb her.

He removed his overnight bag from the top of the wardrobe and took out the envelope containing the house brochures.

It was a glorious morning. He went to the kitchen to make Alison a mug of coffee, hoping they could go for a final stroll along the beach together before he left at midday. He didn't want to waste a second of their remaining time together.

She was still sleeping as he returned with the tray and he stooped to kiss her, awaking her slowly.

'Hi darling, you're up early,' she said and seeing the steaming mug she smiled. 'Is that for me?'

'Yes, it'll wake you up and then maybe we could go for a walk along the beach.'

'Oh yes, I'd like that. Is it a nice morning?'

'It's beautiful so I thought it'd be nice to have our breakfast at a beach bar.'

Alison showered and dressed quickly and before long they were strolling hand in hand on the beach. She took off her sandals to feel the soft silken sand as it trickled between her toes. The water was very calm and short waves lapped the shore-line gently. Few people were about as it was still early but soon the beaches would be full.

They walked for over a mile, much of the time in deep thought and from time to time he would draw her close and kiss her tenderly. Another seven days without Alison would be an eternity, he thought.

It was Paul who broke the silence. 'See, there's a beach bar coming up. Are you ready for breakfast?'

'I'll just have a cup of coffee. I'm not hungry.'

He ordered a full English breakfast with toast and asked for two coffees to be brought right away.

'Good heavens!' Alison commented at the size of his breakfast. 'You'll never eat all that!'

'Don't bet on it. You'll lose,' he stated, attacking his food eagerly. 'Do you want a sandwich?'

'I'll just try a bit of toast so you won't nag me.'

'I know you're sad darling but it will pass for you much quicker. Enjoy yourself. Don't spoil your last week fretting,' he begged. 'If you like I'll stay over next Sunday night and you can tell me all about it. I bet Tom wouldn't refuse either. He's a great guy.'

'Yes, he's very caring like you. Jenny and I are so lucky,' she said. 'I *would* like you to stay over Paul. We should arrive home around six in the evening, subject to there being no delays but I'll give you a quick call when we arrive in Manchester.'

'Eat your toast then or I won't stay!'

Obediently she ate her toast. 'Will you call Maud when you get back and tell her we're having a good time? By the way, I keep forgetting to ask; did you know Tom was going to propose to Jenny?'

'Yes but I was sworn to secrecy so I couldn't tell you….sorry. Right,' he said, replacing his cutlery. 'I'm absolutely stuffed. I can't eat another thing.'

'Not even me?'

'Not even you. How about another coffee?'

'If you like. What time is it?'

'Ten-thirty. I must leave at twelve,' he sighed and

Alison started to cry. 'Please don't. It tears me apart when you cry. I'll call you tonight, I promise.'

'Can I come to the airport Paul? I can come back on the train.'

'No, it'll only make you feel worse darling. Let's say goodbye here, please.'

'I don't want to say it at all. I have a very uneasy feeling I won't see you again. I had the same awful feeling before I came on holiday,' she sobbed.

'Well, that was wrong because I'm here now,' he answered, taking hold of both of her hands. 'Listen, I love you so much I could never put it into words. I will always be here for you. Remember that Alison. That'll never change and if you stop crying, I might even promise to wear a tie next Sunday.'

She smiled at him through her tears. 'I'm going to miss you so much.'

'Come on, finish your coffee. We'll have a laugh about this once you're home.'

As they retraced their steps along the beach, she seemed less preoccupied with her sadness.

'Do you fancy a June wedding? You could plan it with mum once you're home. You'll have to choose your bridesmaids and make out a guest list. There's lots to arrange but don't worry. I'll pay for it all.'

'Thank you Paul. Actually, I've chosen my three bridesmaids. I'm having Jenny, Antonia and Clare.'

'Well I must admit they're good-looking girls but none of them will outshine you,' he said, giving her a loving kiss. 'And I promise to talk about children too once you're back home. It has been an amazing weekend darling. I've enjoyed every second.'

'Liar!' she laughed wildly. 'You were scared witless when I was playing the scarlet woman.'

'If I'm perfectly honest, I was concerned because others were about. I actually found it both alarming and exciting but as I didn't know what you had in mind, I was afraid I might disappoint you.'

'You have never disappointed me Paul but I know exactly what you mean because I felt the same that afternoon in Brighton. I was scared then but when I asked you to stop, you did. You made no attempt to coerce me and for that I respected you. I knew from that moment how much I loved you and I promise I will never be a scarlet woman again,' she said with a reserved smile.

'Now I'm really disappointed. *Please* be a scarlet woman again,' he implored with a shrill laugh. 'I'll take you to my Bordello if you promise.'

'How can a girl refuse an offer like that?'

'That's better. Are you feeling okay now Babe?'

'No but I'm trying to be positive. As you say, it's only for a few more days.'

When they got back, Jenny and Tom were sitting outside eating breakfast. 'I didn't know you'd gone out,' Jenny remarked.

'We went for a walk on the beach. It's a beautiful morning as you can see,' Alison said.

'Have you packed everything?' Jenny asked Paul.

'Yes, I finished it early before Alison awoke.'

'That reminds me,' Alison said. 'Come with me.'

Opening her dressing-table drawer, she removed the two presents she had bought for Paul. 'I thought this might amuse you.'

Paul unwrapped his mug carefully and laughed at the comical artist. 'Very appropriate,' he remarked. Where did you find that?'

'On Fuengirola market. I couldn't resist it when I saw it and you needed a replacement.'

'Why? What's wrong with the one in my studio? It serves its purpose. I happen to be very attached to it and I rinse it out occasionally.'

'It's disgusting. It's filthy and chipped. For a man of means you live like a tramp.'

'Then we're well matched, Lady and the Tramp.'

'Throw the other away. It must be full of disease.'

'What do you mean? There's years left in it yet.'

'*Throw it away*! You've got a nice new one now. Here, I've got you something else.'

Paul removed the belt from the bag and fastened it around his waist. 'It's perfect. I brought two with me but as we eat out a lot, I've gained some weight and they were too tight.'

'You're telling me you had two belts I could have used last night to strap you to the headboard! You might have mentioned it Paul,' she teased.

'I'd have died had you suggested that, though on reflection I might just fancy that,' he grinned.

'Gigolo,' she giggled as he pushed her on the bed and threw his arms round her.

'Give me a hug Babe. It has to last for a week.'

Tom tapped on the door. 'Are you ready mate?'

'Give me two minutes,' he called.

'Will you take the Lladro with you Paul? It's less for me to carry.'

'I will and I'll be careful with it. Keep safe sweet

334

girl and enjoy the rest of your holiday.' He kissed her fondly and left the room with his bag.

Antonia and Clare were waiting for them by the door and Clare threw her arms around Paul's neck. 'Have a good flight and if you ever tire of Alison, give me a call. You're one terrific guy,' she said.

'I know,' he laughed. 'I'll bear it in mind but I'm afraid you'll have a very long wait.'

'Come here,' Antonia said, giving him a hug.

'Bye Tom,' Alison said. 'Please look after Paul.'

'See you soon Paul. Keep in touch,' Jenny added.

Paul turned to face Alison as the others discreetly wandered out of earshot. He took a deep breath and his eyes were misted over. 'Don't come with me to the car. Let's say our goodbyes here,' he whispered.

She was sobbing uncontrollably as Paul continued to hold her, his own tears but a blink away and in a broken voice he said, 'I can't bear this darling. I'll never leave you again, ever.' Then he picked up his bag and walked out without looking back.

As Alison heard him drive away she felt her heart would break….still fostering a nagging feeling that something inexplicable was lurking.

'Come on, sit outside and you'll feel better. I've poured you a nice cool drink,' Jenny said. 'I take it you didn't enlighten Paul about you-know-what?'

'I did try Jenny but he refused to talk about it but he's promised we'll discuss it next week when I'm home. He still doesn't know I'm pregnant.'

'Try to put it out of your mind. It's been a great weekend hasn't it? Tom was quite nervous when he asked me to marry him.'

'I'm happy for you Jenny. Tom's a sound guy.'

Alison fell asleep and only awoke when Antonia yelled that someone's mobile was ringing.

'It's mine,' Alison called as she hurried to find it, knowing it would be Paul. 'Hi, is everything okay?'

'Yes, we're boarding now. There was a delay but we're on our way now. I'm sorry about earlier but I was upset too. I have to go now. Tom's calling me. Tell Jenny he sends his love. Bye darling.'

'Bye Paul and thanks. Enjoy your flight.'

She returned to the terrace. 'They're just boarding and Tom sends his love Jenny.'

'That's nice. Tom adores everything about Spain. He thinks it's a fabulous country,' Jenny remarked pensively and Alison burst out laughing.

'What? What's funny about that?'

'He's scarcely left the bedroom all weekend. The furthest he went was next door. He's seen *nothing*!'

'He went to the restaurant last night, didn't he?'

'Well that hardly qualifies Tom as an aficionado of Spain you nutter. I bet he knows a lot more about pillows, sheets and duvets,' she howled.

Caustically she snarled, 'Are you making lunch?'

'Maybe, when I've done laughing. How's it going between you and Matthew?' she asked Clare.

'Alright. He's a cute guy but not really my type. I find him rather dull….not a bloke I'd describe as an extrovert like me. I prefer more dynamism in a guy. Having said that, he's pretty good in the sack!'

'Too much information!' she said censoriously. 'I wasn't enquiring about his sexual prowess. Do you intend seeing him when you're back home?'

336

'I might if nothing better turns up. He's okay but the earth doesn't move if you get my drift.'

Jenny laughed. 'I often wonder if guys discuss us like we discuss them. All we seem to do is compare notes and find fault.'

'They're worse than us. They discuss every little detail,' Clare remarked and Alison was horrified.

'I'd hate to think Paul shared our intimate details with anyone. That's horrible, Clare.'

'You tell Jenny everything so how's it different?'

'No I don't,' she contradicted. 'I've discussed one or two things that might have been of some concern but I've never given her a blow by blow account.'

Clare seized on the opportunity for a wind-up and placing both elbows on the table, rested her head in her hands, looking straight at Alison. 'Well, give us a blow by blow account now. I've often wondered what Paul Trantor was like in the sack so spit it out! Is he as talented on a mattress as he is on a canvas?'

'You're repulsive Clare! I'm telling you nothing!'

Jenny and Antonia were hysterical. 'She's joking Alison. Ignore her. She doesn't really expect you to tell her anything,' Antonia advised.

'Like hell I don't! Come on, spill the beans,' she insisted with an expression of anticipation.

'You can get lost Clare! *You'd* be the *last* person I'd tell,' Alison retorted angrily. 'What's more....'

'You didn't ask me about Mike,' Antonia cut in.

'I'll not be bothering after that,' she said huffily.

'I'm sorry,' Clare said. 'You should try to lighten up a little. We're just having fun.'

'Well have it at someone else's expense. I happen

337

to love Paul very much and it would be disloyal to tell *you* how absolutely fantastic he is in the sack as you call it,' she disclosed with a sassy smile.

'*I knew it*,' Clare squealed.

'Well, keep it to yourself. I mean it and that's all you're getting to know.'

Antonia interrupted again. 'If anyone's interested, I'm rather smitten with Mike. We get on very well and we intend to see each other when we get home. He's taking me out to dinner tonight at the Casino at Torrequebrada.'

'Great,' Jenny enthused. 'Don't forget your passport or you won't get in. You'll enjoy it, especially if you win something. Set yourself a limit though. You can soon lose a hell of a lot of money.'

'I'm pleased for you Antonia. Mike's a nice lad,' Alison remarked cheerily.

'He's also caring and that's a quality I've seldom experienced in a bloke,' she said wistfully.

'Huh! You barely have time to weigh up a guy's qualities. It's simply a quick in and out of bed with you and then you shove them through the door. I'm not surprised they aren't caring. They're doubtless relieved to escape,' Clare attacked mockingly.

'That's rich coming from you. I've never had two in one night like you have!'

'That was *once*! I couldn't decide which I fancied more so I had them both but I don't make a habit of it.' Addressing Alison she explained, 'I didn't have them both together. There was a gap in between.'

Alison couldn't stand any further revelations. 'I'll wash the glasses,' she said hurrying from the table to avoid more embarrassment and under her breath she mumbled, 'Thank God I've led a sheltered life.'

After lunch the girls lazed by the pool. Simon and Dave wandered down later and arranged to meet up to go to the usual restaurant.

As they returned from the restaurant, Dave asked if Paul had arrived home safely. 'I imagine so,' she said. 'He's phoning at eleven. That's Paul's regular time and he's fastidious about time-keeping. When you sent him that text at Puerto Banus, he'd fallen asleep. He must have apologised ten times for that. One night, he was picking me up at seven o'clock, so I altered my watch and informed him he was five minutes late when he arrived, just to irritate him.'

On a laugh, Dave asked, 'What did he say?'

'He marched to the phone and called the speaking clock. I couldn't believe my eyes. I think it's called *obsessive compulsive disorder*.'

'He's a great guy. We had such a laugh about old times, reminiscing about the lads who worked with us. I hope he rings me when I'm home.'

'If he said he would then he will. If you see him before I'm back, give him my love. We'll be seeing you again before you leave on Wednesday I hope?'

'You certainly will. Goodnight Alison.'

Alison was in bed before eleven and was writing her few remaining postcards when her mobile rang at precisely eleven o'clock. She smiled as she found Paul's little idiosyncrasies quite appealing. He was such a dependable guy.

'Hi Paul. Are you tired after the trip?' she asked.

'I don't know about tired. I'm fed up!'

339

'I am too. How was your flight?'

'Okay but the meal was diabolical. It had melted cheese all over it and it smelled like vomit.'

She chuckled at his descriptive account. 'It seems ages since you left. I hope the remaining days pass more quickly,' she sighed.

'Don't wish your holiday away Babe. Have you been anywhere nice today?'

'No, we lazed around talking by the pool.'

'What on earth do you find to talk about all day?'

'You don't want to know, believe me Paul.'

He laughed. 'Did I feature in your conversation?'

'Yes Paul you did, as did every other bloke Clare and Antonia ever knew.'

'I hope you don't mean *knew* in the biblical sense. I've been with neither of them, perish the thought.'

'That wasn't for the want of trying on their part.'

'Tell me about it! Still, I can't help being utterly desirable and irresistible to females that they fight to the death over me,' he replied self-righteously.

'I would too darling,' she sighed.

'But you don't need. You already have me, so the others must learn to live with their disappointment,' he joked sanctimoniously.

'I hope I'll always have you Paul,' she said with consternation in her voice.

'Hey, what's wrong? I'll love you forever. By the way, we forgot to look at the house brochures.'

'Oh Paul! I really wanted to see them,' she sighed with disappointment.

'Then I suggest you look under your pillow.'

Alison rummaged under her pillow and pulled out

340

a large envelope. Opening it quickly she exclaimed, 'Oh, it's incredible,' when she saw where Paul had written, *this is ours*, under the glossy photograph on the front cover. 'It's enormous. Are you really sure we can afford to live there?'

'You might have to work a spot of overtime but if we're careful, we should just scrape by,' he teased.

'Listen, you can jest but I wouldn't mind at all.'

'My wife won't be working at all. I intend to keep her in luxury forever as long as she wears that sexy red underwear from time to time. Have you looked inside the brochure yet?'

'No, I'm still looking at the front cover.'

She opened up the brochure and fingered through the pages which highlighted all the major rooms. 'I can't take it in. I need to study it. It's magnificent!'

'So, do I go ahead or do you want to see it first?'

'No, I don't need to see it first. I wasn't expecting anything like this Paul. You're full of surprises.'

'You like it then?'

'I love it....if the barn is okay for you as a studio.'

'It's perfect. It's very spacious with lots of light. It's exactly what I was looking for.'

'What did I do to deserve you Paul? Sometimes I wonder if all this is real.'

'Trust me, it is. I'll arrange a viewing next week.'

'Did you get the Lladro back in one piece?'

'Yes and I'll keep it safe. I'll call you tomorrow. Meanwhile, you study the brochure. Bye darling.'

Alison decided to say nothing to the others about the house. Paul was obviously much wealthier than she had imagined. To even consider buying such a property, he had to be a millionaire she mused, yet he drank his tea out of a grimy chipped mug!

Monday turned out to be another relaxing day with a meal at the regular restaurant but on Tuesday the lads invited the girls to join them at the Val Paraíso for *the last supper*. They had enjoyed that particular restaurant the most, having found the setting superb and the ambience second to none.

On the stroke of eleven, Alison got her customary call from Paul. 'How was the meal?' he asked.

'Excellent but I wish you could have been here.'

'Me too and it's raining here to add to my misery. I've been remembering our evening there when we stood by the railings looking down at the coast. The moonlight was shining on your face and you looked so radiant. I'll never forget that night.'

'For more reasons than one,' she reminded him.

'What? Oh yes, you little minx, the wind-up and I can't even get my own back because I promised not to play any more tricks on you.'

'I promised too. Are you busy?'

'Yes, I'm getting my studio into some semblance of order ready for moving out and my agent called. He wants me to do an exhibition in Los Angeles in a couple of months.'

'So does that mean you'll have to go Paul?'

'Yes at some point but definitely not without you. I'm never going to leave you again.'

'But Paul, I can't just take time off work.'

'When we're married, I don't want you to work. I want you here with me twenty-four-seven.'

'I need space Paul. I like to look round the shops, see my friends and do girl things.'

'Of course and as long as I know precisely where you are, I can live with that.'

Alison felt her hackles rising but now was not the time to argue with him. Maybe he didn't mean that the way it came out. With no intention of becoming any man's prisoner, she would definitely clarify his remarks when she returned home.

'Are you still there Babe?'

'Yes, I'm still here. Something distracted me.'

'What did you eat tonight?'

'I had chicken and it was lovely. I'm avoiding red meat at the moment.'

The instant she uttered those words, she regretted it, knowing Paul would pick up on her remark.

'Why is that? Are you not well Babe?'

She hated to lie to Paul but she couldn't disclose that red meat made her feel nauseous as that would give rise to additional questions. 'I'm worried they won't cook it enough. I feel safer with chicken.'

'All that matters is that you enjoyed it. I'd better let you get back to your friends. I'll call tomorrow.'

'Don't forget Dave leaves tomorrow. Give him a call later in the week. You have his number.'

'I will. Sleep well darling. I love you.'

She felt annoyed when the call ended, wishing he was less possessive. Though his remarks were aired innocently, she felt mistrusted and it offended her.

'Come on Alison. We're all dancing,' Dave called and when she joined them, her irritation at Paul was quickly forgotten.

At the end of the night, Alison thanked Dave for his friendship. 'I hope your flight isn't delayed and I wish the very best for you and Laura. I'm going to miss our little tête-à-têtes when you've gone.'

Everyone bade a final farewell before returning to their respective villas.

'What a terrific foursome they were,' Jenny said. 'I've thoroughly enjoyed their company and wasn't it kind of them to pay for our meal? Did Paul ring?'

'Yes, but we didn't speak for long. Shall we go to Mijas tomorrow? I think Antonia might welcome a distraction. She's upset because Mike's leaving.'

'I'm game for that. Nothing's been organised and we haven't been out much during the last couple of days. They'll be back early so we could have breakfast and be on our way. The shops open around ten. It'll be quiet then. I know just the place for lunch.'

The next morning, the girls were having breakfast outside when two taxis arrived next door. They ran to the railings and waved goodbye to the lads.

'Don't forget to keep in touch,' Alison yelled to Dave. 'Give my regards to Laura.'

As the taxis passed their villa, Antonia burst into tears. 'Well, I'll be damned,' Clare sneered. 'That's definitely a first!'

'Just shut your gob Clare! You can be so bloody insensitive at times,' Jenny admonished her angrily. 'You never know when to keep quiet!'

Within minutes it was forgotten and an hour later, they were meandering through the narrow streets of Mijas by burro taxi.

Afterwards they climbed the host of steps leading

344

to the finest vantage point to enjoy the magnificent views and take photographs.

For lunch, they made their way to the restaurant recommended by Jenny. Entering from a back street they clambered up the precipitous narrow staircase. Lacking enthusiasm, Antonia trudged wearily after the others until they reached the outside terrace that was adorned with attractive tablecloths and colourful floral decorations and they stared in disbelief at the amazing panoramic vista.

'How's this for a place to enjoy our lunch?' Jenny stated smugly. 'I bet you weren't expecting this.'

'It's fantastic,' Alison said and the others agreed.

'They do a varied menu too. The seafood is really amazing and we can stay as long as we want. They won't throw us out,' Jenny informed them.

They enjoyed a leisurely lunch as the sun became hotter and Alison scanned the hillsides, scrutinizing every detail of the villas dotted around below.

The restaurant was full to capacity as more people came in to escape the midday sun. The terrace had no empty tables either and they decided to leave to make room for new arrivals.

After a final shopping spree, they made their way to the bus stop and took the next bus to Fuengirola.

By the time they arrived, the shops were about to close for afternoon siesta.

Clare was thirsty. 'How about a long cool drink?' she suggested and the others needed no persuasion.

They came across a pavement café where Antonia went inside with Jenny to order as Alison sat down beside Clare.

'I love Mijas. Paul took me on our way back from Granada but we were in a hurry to get back, so I'm glad we were able to go today,' Alison told Clare.

Clare nodded. 'I enjoyed looking round the shops and I love this leather bag. I have an obsession for bags and shoes. It's very noisy here. What's all the commotion about?'

At that point, Jenny appeared in the doorway and called to Alison, 'Do you want ice and lemon?' but she couldn't hear because of the noisy traffic.

'Hang on a tick, I can't hear you,' Alison yelled, standing up to walk towards Jenny.

Suddenly Jenny screamed, '*Alison, look out*!' and for several seconds, Jenny observed silently as the ensuing events unfolded in seemingly slow motion. Horror-stricken, she held her breath as Alison took first one then two steps towards her.

An articulated vehicle had skidded out of control and Jenny's eyes were fixed on the driver who frantically attempted to manoeuvre his rampant vehicle out of the path of an approaching bus. The lorry and bus collided with a deafening impact and there followed a multitude of sounds of screeching brakes, skidding tyres and the noisy clanging and groaning of twisting metal as the lorry tore through the side of the bus with such great force that the bus, which was still travelling at speed, started to topple.

Bystanders were screaming as the bus, appearing to gain momentum, skidded at an angle, producing luminous flashes of friction sparks as the crumbling crunching mass of metal scored its way through the footpath it had mounted by the café.

The unsuspecting clients had little opportunity to escape as the irrepressible bus ploughed through the tables wantonly before smashing into the wall with such force that it ripped through part of the building before finally coming to rest, blocking the entrance where Antonia, standing beside Jenny, had watched the events unfold in horror and disbelief.

Jenny watched powerlessly as Alison was hurled through the air by flying debris, and with the speed of a discharged bullet, her head hit the wall where she fell motionless to the ground.

A short eerie calm presented before the screaming recommenced but these were no longer cries of fear like the ones Jenny had just witnessed. These were the screams of pain, of anguish and of panic.

Lacerated limbs poked through smashed windows as injured victims strove to escape from the twisted remains of the bus. When Antonia looked across to where Clare had been sitting, one arm was the only visible part of her body, protruding from the jagged heap of crushed and twisted metal that had formerly been a bus filled with lively passengers.

As every second passed, pools of blood increased in intensity. It was utter carnage.

Antonia screamed out to Clare as she attempted to scramble across the wreckage-strewn pavement that had been transformed from a happy meeting place to a graveyard. With her bare hands, she tore at the debris to free her, gashing her hands and wrists on the jagged metal but her efforts remained futile.

Jenny cradled Alison who lay motionless, willing her to wake up as blood pumped from a deep head-wound and tiny fragments of splintered bone were clearly visible in her hair.

Workmen close by rushed to the scene, smashing windows while showering the wounded with shards of glass as they grappled relentlessly to release the victims from the bus. A whimpering toddler with a hand missing was hauled out barely alive and while workmen and passers-by transferred the rescued to a place of safety, fractured limbs hung loosely from limp casualties barely able to draw breath, many of whom would certainly lose their lives as a result of their horrific injuries.

Sirens screeched as emergency crews approached. Impatient drivers beyond sight of the chaos, honked their horns in frustration as traffic backed up. Jenny screamed for assistance but nobody came to her aid. Others stood about helplessly not knowing what to do. Gripped with fear, Antonia stroked Clare's hand while begging her not to worry though she knew in her heart of hearts that her friend was dead.

Carefully Jenny laid Alison on the ground and ran to a man in uniform, tugging at his sleeve, pulling him to where Alison lay bleeding. He lifted up her hand to check her pulse and yelled to a colleague.

'Is Alison alive?' Jenny screamed hysterically but he didn't understand her.

A smartly-dressed man was standing nearby. 'Do you speak English?' Jenny shrieked but he failed to answer. Instead, he just stared ahead with a vacant expression. '*Answer me!*' she yelled, punching his arm frantically, '*Do you speak any English?*'

'Yes,' was all he replied.

'Ask him if my friend's alive,' she begged. 'You have to help me....please!'

The stranger spoke briefly to the paramedic then said softly, 'Yes, she's alive,' before walking away.

Jenny hurried to Alison where the paramedic was talking on a two-way radio and within seconds, two men in white coats appeared, running towards them and after strapping Alison to a stretcher, they lifted her into a waiting ambulance as Jenny grabbed her shoulder bag and followed. She yelled to Antonia, 'I have to go with Alison. You take care of Clare.'

Jenny scrambled into the ambulance and held her hand. 'Please don't die,' she sobbed. 'You mustn't.'

The paramedics worked diligently to keep Alison alive. As one monitored her respiration and blood pressure, the other attached a drip to her arm. Blood continued to seep from her heavily bandaged head and her face was as pale as death.

Jenny wanted to wake up. This was a horrifying nightmare. She felt to be floating and tried to stand still but everywhere was so dark. She groped for the light switch and suddenly there was utter terror as she tumbled headlong into an endless chasm.

When she awoke, she was in a hospital side ward. A woman in a blue uniform was talking to her but she couldn't understand one word of what she was saying, then everything suddenly made sense to her. The woman was a nurse and Jenny was in hospital. As memories of the terrible accident came flooding back Jenny began to weep uncontrollably. 'Where's Alison?' she cried.

The nurse left but returned instantly with a junior

doctor. 'Are you feeling better?' he enquired of her.

'Yes! Where's Alison? She was in the ambulance with me.'

'Miss Haythorne, she go for a scan. She has head injury and perhaps broken bones. We need to check with er….X-ray.'

'No you can't....you mustn't. She's pregnant!'

'I see. I speak with doctor in charge. Excuse me.'

The nurse called in frequently to check on Jenny. She brought her a cup of tea but no one brought any news about Alison. There was an empty bed next to hers and Jenny had a vague recollection that Alison had been there earlier but she was confused.

Later, the senior doctor appeared. 'Good evening. How are you feeling now?' he asked.

'I think I'm alright thank you. What happened?'

'You had a terrible shock and you passed out.'

'How's my friend? How's Alison?'

'I regret she has suffered brain trauma. Her brain is distended because she bang her head. Her brain bang against skull....you say ricochet? Your friend is unconscious. She's very sick. She has fracture of skull but we clean and dress it but there were loose bone fragments to outer skull. Very severe bang to skull!' he tutted. 'We have put sutures in laceration. Now there is no bleed which is good.'

'Will she get better?'

'Hopefully, yes. We have to wait now. For forty-eight hours is critical. After that, brain should start to return to normal. We monitor regularly.'

'Will she have permanent brain damage?'

'Maybe yes, maybe no. It's not possible to know.'

'And the baby? Is the baby alright?'

'Again I cannot say with certainty. Your friend is ten weeks into her pregnancy. Just hope for her.'

'Thank you doctor. How long must I stay here?'

'I'll see you tomorrow and I'll decide then if you can be discharged.'

'Am I allowed to walk about?'

'Yes, but not too far.' He smiled sympathetically. 'Try not to worry. We're doing all we can.'

Jenny was traumatised and the doctor had told her not to worry! Whatever the nationality, each doctor must learn those four words early in their training, she concluded and what ridiculous words they were too. She was frantic with worry for Alison and very concerned for Antonia and Clare who couldn't be at the villa as the key was kept in Alison's bag. Jenny remembered having Alison's bag in the ambulance but what happened to it after that? She had no idea.

When the nurse came to check her blood pressure, Jenny asked, 'Where's my handbag?' but she didn't understand. 'My *bolsa*?' she repeated in Spanish.

She nodded and smiled before removing two bags from the locker by Jenny's bed that she gave to her.

Jenny rummaged through Alison's bag to find her mobile and called Paul's number immediately.

He answered instantly. 'Hi Babe! What's up?'

'Paul, it's Jenny. Just listen to me as I only have a moment. Alison's in hospital. She's unconscious. I don't know which hospital we're in but there was a serious accident when a bus mounted the pavement. Paul I'm scared. Alison has brain trauma and also a skull fracture. I'm frantic. I don't know what to do.'

'Tell me she won't die. Is she there? I want to talk to her,' he cried, unable to digest Jenny's words.

'She's gone for a scan. You must *do* something.'

'*Have you spoken to the doctor*?' he yelled.

'Yes but he can't say whether she'll wake up. He said the next forty-eight hours were critical. I don't know where Antonia and Clare are either. It looked like a battleground with bodies everywhere. Please call Tom and my parents and tell them I'm alright. Someone will know where the injured were taken. I remember the ambulance driving towards Marbella and then I passed out and woke up here. No one but the doctor speaks any English and I think he's gone off duty now. Alison really needs you. I have to go now. I'm not allowed to use a mobile here.'

'I know where you are. I'm coming over. I'll see you as soon as I can. I can't take this in Jenny. I'll kill myself if anything happens to Alison,' he wept.

Jenny held Alison's mobile to her face. It smelled of her perfume and tears gushed from her eyes.

The nurse returned and stroked Jenny's hair while speaking words of comfort and though Jenny didn't understand her words, she appreciated the gesture.

Everybody was kind and showed concern but she wanted Alison, sweet Alison who would never hurt anybody and who had suffered such major tragedies during her short lifetime. Why was life so brutal?

Summoned by the nurse, the junior doctor turned up to see her. 'You need to sleep. You are in shock and this will help,' he said, giving her a sedative.

She closed her eyes and in her thoughts she had a flashback of the accident. She could smell the burning rubber tyres as the bus hurtled towards her, and in a further vision she saw Clare's arm protruding from the wreckage, holding the bloodstained handbag she had bought only hours earlier in Mijas, but as Jenny cried out, no sound emerged from her lips. She remained in a deep sleep for several hours....

It was dark when Jenny next opened her eyes. As she focused through the darkness, she was startled by Alison's presence. Intravenous drips, wires and monitors were attached to her motionless body, her head was bandaged and her arms lifeless at her side.

Raising herself up she looked closely as Alison's slender frame moved slightly with each breath she took. She could make out a form in the darkness by the bed. 'Paul? Is that you?' she whispered.

Paul walked towards her and took her in his arms.

'I'm so sorry Paul,' she said. 'It wasn't anybody's fault. It was an awful accident and Alison was flung against the wall. 'Have you spoken to the doctor?'

Paul wiped his hand across his wet face. 'Yes, but there's little he could tell me. They're taking Alison for another scan tomorrow. Tom called me before I had chance to call him. He'd seen it on TV and the news bulletin was very explicit. I said you'd called and he's trying to get leave to fly over. Maud says we can use the villa as long as we need and I spoke to your family and Richard will be here soon. God Almighty, I can't believe this,' he groaned.

'I don't know where Antonia is. She doesn't have a key. I keep having flashbacks and I think Clare's dead. I can see her buried under the wreckage with Antonia telling her everything was okay. Blood was running down the street Paul. It was unbelievable. I screamed out for help for Alison but everyone was rushing about in a state of panic not knowing how to help. I grabbed a man in uniform and pulled him towards her. We were obviously brought here in the ambulance but I passed out,' she stuttered tearfully.

'Well we're in God's hands now. There's nothing further the doctors can do. They're monitoring her every few minutes and she isn't deteriorating.'

'We have to be positive Paul. Alison is young and healthy. That has to count for something.'

'I pray you're right. I can't live without her. I'm going outside for a few minutes for some air.'

He stood outside silently for a while before walking to the far end of the building where he could be alone. He stared at the sky praying as tears scalded his eyes. Alison looked so helpless and he could do nothing for her. The doctor had not been optimistic. She had suffered severe brain trauma, caused when her brain ricocheted against her skull at the moment of impact. They had treated her for shock but there was little else they could do. If her brain continued to swell, she could haemorrhage and further blood loss could be fatal, yet in her present unstable state, surgery was out of the question.

Paul walked back to the main entrance where the reception area was empty apart from a lone cleaner mopping the floor. His footsteps echoed eerily as he approached the ward where Alison looked so serene yet remained so critically ill.

Impassively staring into space, Jenny was sitting on her bed, unable to believe the day's events.

354

A hospital night worker brought Paul and Jenny a cup of tea. There would be no restrictions on visiting until the crisis had passed, Paul was told.

Jenny opened Alison's bag and gave the door key to Paul. 'Go back and get some rest. I'll call you on your mobile if there's any change,' she told him.

'I'm staying here,' he answered abjectly.

'Paul, you can't *do* anything. Have something to eat and come back here in the morning. That's what Alison would want. There's some ham in the fridge and bread in the ice-box. I bet you've not eaten.'

'How can I face food at a time like this?'

'You have to. Go and try. I'll call with any news.'

'If I go, I'm coming back early,' he said.

'You do that. I'm here to watch over Alison.'

He gave her an appreciative hug. 'You are such a loyal friend,' he said. 'I'll be back in a few hours.'

When he left, Jenny got up and feeling steadier on her feet, she walked along the corridor.

A young nurse smiled and asked if she would like a hot drink and Jenny was thankful to have finally found someone able to speak intelligible English.

The Spanish nurse had an English mother she told Jenny and they discussed Alison's condition, which still remained unchanged.

Jenny related that two of her friends were missing but that one had not been involved in the accident, although she thought the other could have died.

The nurse referred to the admissions' sheet. There was no mention of Clare's name. 'I'm so sorry,' she said. 'All the injured came here. I don't have names for the deceased but I know that twenty-two people died and around forty were badly injured. Many on the bus died and most of the people at the café died as well. I did see an English girl yesterday who had severe lacerations to both arms. She had an unusual name for an English girl....er....Antonia.'

'That's her,' Jenny said excitedly. 'Where is she?'

'She's here. She severed a main artery and needed sutures and a blood transfusion. Both her arms were badly injured. She was trying to help her friend but I'm afraid her friend was dead when the paramedics went to her aid. I can arrange for you to see her for a few moments. She had to be sedated for shock but she's in no danger now.'

'I'd like to see her. I've been frantic with worry.'

'Come along then but only for a moment or two.'

She escorted Jenny to Antonia's ward and Jenny caught her breath when she saw her.

'Is this your friend?' the nurse asked.

'Yes, this is Antonia,' she answered choking back her tears because when she saw her, she knew Clare hadn't survived that appalling tragedy.

'Can I touch her?' she asked, tears coursing down her cheeks. The nurse smiled caringly and nodded.

Jenny stroked her hair soothingly. Her wrists and hands were heavily bandaged and Jenny brought to mind the frenzied screams as Antonia had tugged at the jagged metal while trying to release her friend.

Antonia opened her eyes. 'Is it really you Jenny?' she asked tearfully.

'Yes and you mustn't worry. You're doing fine.'

'Clare's dead isn't she?' she sobbed, blinking the tears from her eyes and the nurse nodded her head.

356

'I'm sorry Antonia. Clare didn't make it,' Jenny said, throwing her arms round her as they both wept uncontrollably.

'Is Alison going to be alright?' Antonia asked.

'We're praying she will. I have to go now but I'll see you later. You rest,' she said, embracing her.

'She had to hear the truth. She can begin to grieve now,' the nurse counselled as she led Jenny back to her ward. 'It's tragic to lose such a young life. My job is so stressful. I see so much pain and suffering. I'll pray that both your friends recover soon.'

Paul returned early the next morning. He looked terrible. His hair was uncombed and he appeared to have slept in his clothes. He kissed Alison softly on the lips. 'I love you,' he said with grief in his eyes.

'There's been no change yet,' Jenny advised him. 'The nurse has been in and out all night.'

'I phoned earlier. They described her condition as critical but stable. They said they might be moving her to a hospital with more specialist equipment but they didn't elaborate further. I want a word with the doctor. I haven't missed him have I?'

'No, he hasn't been yet. Antonia's here. She's on a different ward. She cut her wrists and hands very badly, trying to pull Clare from the wreckage.'

'Is there any news of Clare?'

She swallowed hard but was unable to contain her tears and sobbing bitterly she told him, 'She's dead. Clare's dead, Paul.'

'Oh Jenny, I'm so sorry,' he sighed, taking her in his arms. 'I don't know what else to say to you. Has anyone been in touch with her parents?'

357

'I doubt it but they have to be told today. Antonia should have their number. I can't believe this. Only yesterday we were all laughing and joking and now Clare's dead and Alison's fighting for her life.'

'If Antonia wants me to make any calls, I will.'

'Did you know that twenty-two died? If only I'd called out to her a second earlier Alison might have escaped. She was only inches from me. I screamed as the bus mounted the footpath but she just walked slowly towards me as she couldn't hear…'

'Stop that! Don't torture yourself! You probably saved Alison's life. Had she stayed with Clare, she would definitely have been killed.'

'Look at her. Take a long look. I've done nothing else all night. She's never moved at all.'

'Jenny, the doctor said it could be a while before she wakes up. Help me to be strong, please. You're scaring me. I have to believe she'll get better.'

When the junior doctor arrived to check Alison's records, Jenny introduced Paul as Alison's fiancé.

They exchanged several words in Spanish, which Jenny didn't understand. 'Is there any improvement Doctor?' she questioned optimistically.

'I am afraid not but is early for change,' he stated in his broken English. 'That is not too bad because she not any worse and she could have go worse in the night. Her blood pressure is a little high but that is expected. That is not the first concern. We cannot assess damage to brain and we not know until your fiancée is waking up but that is unlikely soon. The consultant, he talked with neurologist yesterday at University Hospital in Málaga. He make his rounds

358

at eleven o'clock and I shall be with him. We might tell you more then. Please, try not to worry.'

Paul sat with his head bowed after the doctor left. There was little likelihood of Alison regaining consciousness soon, the doctor had advised and he was distraught. 'Were there other injuries? Were there any fractures when debris was flying around, or any internal injuries? Did they examine her properly?'

'I'm sure they did Paul. They worked very hard.'

'What about X-rays for broken bones?'

'I'm not sure,' she lied.

'When he arrives I intend to have a long talk with the consultant. I need to know everything.'

The moment of truth had finally arrived but such a revelation would have been better delivered from Alison's lips. Paul would have been angry but she would have been there to answer all his questions. Jenny took the bit between her teeth. 'Paul, there's something I need to tell you and I don't want you to start yelling. Now isn't the time and here isn't the place for that. I need you to listen carefully. Alison is ten weeks' pregnant with your child.'

She gripped his hand firmly as he looked back at her open-mouthed. 'Trust me Paul; it *is* yours.'

Paul snatched his hand away and glared at Alison with hatred in his eyes.

'I'll kill that bastard. Whatever the consequences, I'll bloody-well kill Mark Taylor, do you hear me?' he cried angrily.

'Please Paul, it's nothing to do with Mark. I know what you said about the clinic's findings but it can't be right. She's never been with anybody else. She'd have told me. I was shocked too till I thought about it,' she explained, but he wasn't listening to a word.

'So between you, you cooked up a scheming plan to provide a suitable father who would be grateful?'

'Of course not. I only found out a day or two ago. I'd suspected for a couple of weeks as I'd heard her being sick and I was very worried about what your reaction might be. I told her to tell you and she tried the day you went to Granada but you wouldn't talk about it. I didn't breathe one word to her about your tests. She's never loved anyone but you Paul.'

'What's that got to do with it? Did you love every guy you copulated with?' he queried judgementally. 'I blame you and the other two trollops for leading Alison astray. I should never have permitted her to associate with lowlife trash. Well, Mark Taylor can have her. It's about time he made an honest woman of someone. God knows he's had more than his fair share. No wonder Alison wanted to get wed quick! What a fool I've been. I would have laid down my life for her and she's betrayed me with that moron.'

'Paul, calm down. Get the test done again, if only for your own satisfaction….please.'

'There's no need. I'm more than satisfied with the first one. It was conclusive. I'm definitely not going through that again to prove the child's not mine. I know it isn't and as you enjoy sticking your oar in, *you* can tell Alison if she recovers that she was my life. You can tell her how she's destroyed me.'

'You can't walk away now when she needs you. Hasn't she suffered enough? If you leave, she's lost everyone she's ever loved. She'll have nobody.'

'She'll have her child and she's got *him* and that's more than enough for anybody but he'll never love her as I did. He's a womaniser who'll never change. Do you remember that concert they went to? Well you can tell Alison I followed her and I waited near Mark's car and I watched them come out. I saw her in his arms. He was kissing her, so that's your loyal friend. I stayed away for a week but I loved her so much that I forgave her but never in a million years could I forgive her for having his child. You are so naïve Jenny. Alison tells you what she wants you to hear, unless you're a liar who's covering for her.'

'Please don't go. I know you're angry and jealous but you're mistaken and by the time you wake up to what you've done, you'll have lost Alison for ever.'

His eyes filled with tears. 'I've already lost her. I truly hope she recovers. I wish her no harm and I'll never stop loving her as long as I live but I refuse to be manipulated by any woman, not even Alison. I'll leave the villa key under a stone by the door. Don't ever try to contact me and that goes for Alison too. I don't ever want to see or hear from you again.'

Paul glowered at Alison with loathing in his eyes before storming away without another word.

He returned to the villa and put the key in the lock. Feeling angry and flustered he tried unsuccessfully to unlock the door. He tried once more but his eyes were blurred with tears and as he fumbled with the key it fell to the ground.

As he stooped to retrieve it, the door opened and Richard was standing ashen-faced in the doorway.

'Hello Paul. I've just got here. How's everybody doing?' he asked with concern.

'Jenny's fine. She has no injuries. She'll probably be discharged later. Alison is in a coma. She's very ill. Antonia's injuries should heal with no lasting ill effects but I'm afraid Clare died in the accident. We received confirmation this morning,' Paul told him.

'My God! It's worse than any nightmare. I can't believe they just happened to be in that place at that moment in time. Her parents must be devastated.'

'They haven't been told yet. Would you speak to Jenny and deal with it please? I'm heading off now. I presume that's your hire-car by the gate. Hospital Costa del Sol is on the right. Stay on the main road to Marbella for about thirty minutes. It's enormous and well signposted.'

Paul put the key on the hallstand. 'That's Alison's key. If or when she recovers, she'll need it to return for her things. You've obviously got your own.'

'Yes, Maud gave it to us. We didn't know where you'd be when we arrived.'

'We?' Paul asked. 'I thought you'd come alone?'

'No, Mark's here too. He's just getting changed. He'll be out in a moment when....'

Angrily Paul interrupted, 'Which room is he in?'

'Er....the end one. Is something wrong Paul?'

Just then, Mark appeared in the corridor buttoning up his shirt. 'Hi there Paul,' he greeted him affably. 'How's Alison? Is there any change yet?'

Without any warning, Paul drew back his arm and thrust it forward at speed, landing a heavy blow in Mark's face, knocking him to the floor. Mark lifted his hand to his face and blood trickled through his fingers as Richard looked on horrified.

'*You scheming manipulative bastard. Get up so I can kill you*!' Paul bellowed at the top of his voice.

Mark was dazed and made no attempt to stand as Richard intervened anxiously. 'Paul, for God's sake what's the matter with you?'

'Ask your interfering sister,' he told him heatedly and turning his attention back to Mark he shouted, '*Get up you slimy git. I won't tell you again.*'

'Stop it Paul! Don't hit him again. You've really hurt him,' Richard pleaded on Mark's behalf.

'*Hurt him? Hurt him did you say*? I'll bloody-well *kill* him,' he yelled. 'Get up you….you disreputable opportunistic, lowlife bastard! Bloody lothario!'

Mark attempted to stand but slumped to the floor again, blood pouring from his nose and staining his white shirt heavily.

'Keep looking over your shoulder Taylor, for you haven't seen the last of me,' he warned as he glared at him and after storming to his room to collect his bag, he left the villa slamming the door behind him.

Richard went to Mark's aid. 'What's going on?'

'I've no idea. He's one crazy guy. That's for sure. Somebody's obviously rattled his cage.'

'That's an understatement if ever I heard one. I'd stay well away from him if I were you. Get changed and I'll drive us to the hospital. It sounds like Jenny knows what's wrong,' Richard remarked pensively.

12

Jenny looked at her watch to check there was time to visit Antonia prior to the consultant making his rounds. Since her run-in with Paul, she had been in tears. Although she had predicted an angry reaction, she had nonetheless expected Paul to be much more sympathetic towards Alison in her present state.

Jenny ambled down the corridor at a snail's pace, peering through open doors at the casualties of the horrendous accident. Two further victims had died during the night and more fatalities were expected. Furthermore, there were many victims who had lost limbs. Remembering the ill-fated child whose hand had been completely severed, Jenny shuddered and others would retain traumatic memories for life. As a mere spectator she knew the effect it had had on her. She remembered the well-dressed man with the vacant expression who had given her such welcome news that Alison was alive and though wanting to obliterate her agonizing memories, she felt a strong sense of duty to remember the victims' suffering.

Antonia beamed as Jenny approached. 'I thought I'd been hallucinating yesterday when you visited. I'm glad you're here. I can't stop crying for Clare.'

'Same here. I'd give anything to bring her back. I doubt anyone will have contacted her parents yet.'

'I never gave that a thought. Perhaps they've been trying to call her. This is awful. Could Paul help?'

'Paul's left and he won't be coming back but that story can wait. There must be someone with whom we can liaise about Clare. I'll make some enquiries.

Why don't you come and see Alison? They put us together but I'm warning you now, she's hooked up to all kinds of equipment. It looks scary but most of the machines are monitors.'

'Will you help me out of bed then? I can't use my hands. They looked terrible when the nurse came to dress them. Every time I look at my hands in future, I'll think of Clare.'

'We don't need scarred hands to remember Clare. We'll never forget her,' Jenny sighed.

Mark and Richard were at Alison's bedside when they reached the ward and Jenny burst into tears to see their familiar faces.

'What's happened to you Mark?' Jenny asked.

'I ran into Paul back at the villa, or rather his fist I should say. No doubt you'll fill me in on the details but first things first. I can see you're okay. Is there any news about Alison?'

'No, nothing's changed but the consultant should be round soon. Alison hasn't moved a muscle since she was admitted.'

'And he's sure it's brain damage?'

'Well, he called it brain trauma. The scan showed swelling to her brain so we have to wait for that to subside. It doesn't mean she'll wake up though. It's too complex for my understanding and then there's the language difficulty too.'

Richard kissed Alison gently. 'I'm here for you,' he whispered, though he knew she couldn't hear.

Richard, desperately in love with Alison, knew he was bottom in the pecking order behind Mark and Paul and he had spent many an hour chastising himself for his failure to make a further move after their first and only date. Jenny had been right about procrastination. He had hesitated, afraid of losing her if he acted too quickly and in so doing had lost her to Paul but until today, he had been content for Paul to be loved by Alison as Paul worshipped her too.

'So what's wrong with Paul then? He was like a madman when he saw Mark,' Richard asked Jenny.

'Oh that's a long story I'd rather not discuss at the present time. He's very distraught about Alison and doubtless looking for some outlet for his anger. He always thought there was an element of competition for Alison's affections and sadly, Mark was in the wrong place at the wrong time,' she prevaricated.

Richard seemed content with her explanation and she felt there was no reason for him to know about the pregnancy. There remained uncertainty it would continue to full term, though Jenny hoped it would for Alison's sake. Whilst being a lone parent would present difficulties from every perspective, the loss of her child could push her over the top. There was a limit to the anguish any individual could endure.

The consultant had no new information to impart. Alison was neither better nor worse but he saw that as a positive sign, he remarked. Jenny could leave hospital immediately and Antonia could leave when someone could be found to provide the care needed for all aspects of her daily life.

Jenny said she'd be agreeable to be her carer until Antonia regained the use of her hands and her offer satisfied the criteria for Antonia's discharge.

Antonia was anxious to visit Clare's parents soon

but first she had the unenviable task of breaking the tragic news to them of their daughter's death.

Mark and Richard were to stay on in Spain for the time being to report back on Alison's progress and also to liaise with the hospital authorities about the transportation of Clare's body back to England.

Later that afternoon, Tom arrived at the villa. He was shocked by Jenny's news of Paul's unexpected departure though relieved that she was fit and well.

Around the same time, Paul's flight was touching down in Manchester. He had thought long and hard about Jenny's disclosure but would never take care of Mark Taylor's child. His liaison with Alison was over though it broke his heart to lose her.

Before she left Spain, Jenny wrote Alison a letter. With reference to Paul, she said he had returned to England and that she would return to Spain as soon as she was well enough to receive visitors. She told her how greatly she valued their friendship and that she would pray for her speedy recovery. She made no mention of Clare's tragic death before slipping the letter and the door key in Alison's bag.

She kissed Alison goodbye and sobbed as she left the ward, turning at the door for one last look at her friend, not knowing if she would ever see her again.

As she packed her bag in readiness for her flight, Jenny reflected on their catastrophic holiday. Clare had been killed; Alison was at death's door and had lost Paul; Antonia would be physically scarred for life and she and Antonia would remain emotionally scarred for life, not to mention Mark's undeserved beating. The holiday had been a horror story of unbelievable magnitude, the one happy outcome being her engagement to Tom.

Tom had been given a ticket to join Jenny on her return flight to England after he had earlier notified the appropriate authorities of Clare's death.

As they waited to board their flight, he turned to her and stated earnestly, 'If this holiday has taught me anything, it's taught me that life is too short and I don't want to wait any longer. Let's get married as soon as we get home. What do you say?'

Tom's words brought an instant smile to her face. 'I say *yes* Tom, one hundred per cent *yes* and while the arrangements are being made, why not move in with me? Besides, I don't want to live there alone with Alison's things serving as a constant reminder of what happened. When she comes home, she can stay with us until she's well enough to move on.'

'I think that's a brilliant idea and we'll both take care of her then. I'm confident she'll pull through,' he said reassuringly.

Jenny was relieved Antonia was there when Tom left. The flat appeared so empty and lifeless without Alison's presence and when she led her to Alison's bedroom, she sobbed pitifully for her friend.

Jenny removed Alison's things to accommodate Antonia's. She felt intrusive when bundling up her Family Bible and papers. They had never interfered with each other's belongings previously.

As Jenny placed them on the top shelf of the hall cupboard, a sheet of paper fluttered to the floor.

It was a letter that Jenny had not intended to read but she was intrigued by the old and tattered item.

It might be from her grandparents in Brighton, she thought and she needed the address to inform them of Alison's accident.

When she unfolded the letter, Jenny was incensed to read the contemptible words of Alison's paternal grandmother who vehemently attached all blame to Alison's grief-stricken mother for her son's demise. It was a nauseating letter and Jenny wondered how many times Alison and her mother had read it from its worn and ragged appearance.

The sight of that letter troubled her for the rest of the day, unable to rid her mind of it and although it had been sent sixteen years earlier, Jenny could not resist the burning desire to respond in similar vein.

Antonia was sleeping and Jenny sat silently with her thoughts before penning her reply.

She tore up her first two attempts and threw them angrily into the waste bin beside her as she couldn't decide how to address such a despicable individual. Never in a million years would she address such an evil woman as *Dear* Mrs. Haythorne.

She began with a flourish, writing her address and mobile telephone number at the head of the letter.

Mrs. Haythorne,
It is with great sadness that I write to you today.
You may recall that you have a granddaughter, not that you have acknowledged her existence since the day she was born. Her name is Alison and she is my dearest friend. She came into my life a few months ago, following the tragic death of her mother who was married to your son, the son you acrimoniously

banished from your life when he disregarded your demands by choosing to marry the woman he loved. I cannot comprehend how, as a mother, you could behave in such a despicable way towards your only child nor can I understand how as a grandmother, you could turn your back on an innocent child who was blameless in your family feud.

Alison was one of many who met with a disastrous accident last week in Spain and she is presently in a coma and might never recover. If she dies, this will be the end of your family line and you will be able to eliminate them all from your thoughts forever as if they had never existed.

You are indisputably a contemptuous and bitter old woman and I wonder why I write to you, as you are totally unworthy of my concern but should you have one remaining spark of decency in your body, you may contact me at the above address if you require any further information.

Jenny Joyce.

The tiny wrinkles of age in the poor quality paper made the address barely legible. Jenny didn't know whether Mrs. Haythorne was still alive, whether she still resided at that address or whether the property was still standing as she copied the address onto the envelope.

While Antonia still slept, she hurried out to post the letter, praying the old witch would soon receive it and that her words would cause her consternation.

Richard telephoned her later. 'It's good news,' he told her excitedly. 'Alison appears to be making a little progress. The consultant was pleased when we spoke to him earlier. She's not out of the woods yet but her vital signs are improving. She's still being monitored on a regular basis and even though she's still unconscious there's some hope now.'

'Richard, you can't imagine how relieved I feel. I wish I'd stayed now,' Jenny sighed heavily.

'Why? There's nothing you could have done for her. We're here and I'll call again with any updates. Did you manage alright on the flight?'

'Yes, everybody was really helpful and Tom was great. We're getting married soon so Tom's moving in at the end of the week. I couldn't bear to be here alone without Alison.'

'I can imagine. By the way, be sure to phone Paul with the news. He's bound to be very anxious.'

'Of course,' she answered although Jenny had no intention of telling *him* anything. If Paul wanted to know anything, he could make his own enquiries.

Antonia was awake when Jenny went to give her the news. 'I'm so relieved. I know it's not much but at least she's making progress. I feel better already. Can I ask you a favour Jenny? I don't like being a nuisance but could I call Mike please?'

'Of course! Come in the lounge. You should have mentioned it sooner.'

Jenny dialled the number for her and propped the receiver under her chin.

'Hi Mike, it's Antonia. We've just got back from Spain and I wanted to talk to you.'

'I wasn't expecting to hear from you,' he replied coldly. 'I've been calling since Wednesday but your phone was always turned off so I could only deduce that we were over.'

'You obviously haven't heard what's happened. I take it Paul didn't call Dave?'

'What are you going on about? Are we over?'

'No Mike, we're not!'

'Thank heavens for that. Do you fancy going for a drink? I'll come to yours and you can tell me then.'

'I'm at Jenny's place. Write the address down and get here as quick as you can. See you soon.'

Jenny replaced the receiver and gave her a milky mug of coffee with a straw. 'Mike will be shocked to learn what's happened. It sounds like Paul didn't call Dave,' Jenny said, not having expected him to.

'Great place!' Mike stated cheerily as he bounded in. 'Have you lived here a while Jenny?'

'Not long,' she said, leading him to the lounge.

'Hi Antonia,' he said, rushing towards her and he stopped abruptly when he noticed the bandages on her hands. 'What's happened to you?'

Jenny poured Mike a beer while Antonia tearfully related the details of the accident and Mike listened ashen-faced as he learned of Clare's death and that Alison was critically ill in hospital. 'I can't take this in. So how's Alison doing now?'

'There was a little improvement today though it's early days yet. We're trying to be optimistic but it's far from easy,' she sighed.

'The other lads won't believe this and Dave will be absolutely devastated. It's like a horror story.'

'It *is* a horror story!' Antonia corrected him tearfully.

372

Though Alison continued to make daily progress she still remained in a coma, causing the consultant grave concern.

Richard telephoned Jenny the following Thursday after speaking with the consultant who had advised that the longer Alison remained in a coma, the less likelihood there was of a total recovery. They were trying various medications to help bring her round.

Jenny felt depressed and it hadn't helped her state of mind when earlier, the postman had returned the letter sent to Alison's revolting grandmother noted, 'Gone away. Not known at this address.'

Richard and Mark stayed in Spain for another two weeks before returning home. Two days before they left, Richard was surprised to learn that Alison was pregnant. He had visited her alone that morning and when a nurse came to perform an ultra-sound scan, he was told it was to confirm that everything was in order with the pregnancy. She had assumed Richard to be the father when divulging that information.

Richard decided not to discuss it with Mark as he quickly put two and two together about Paul's swift exit from Spain, though he found it hard to believe Mark was the father. There and then he made up his mind he would be there for her when she recovered as there would be no one else to pick up the pieces now that Paul had moved on. By any stretch of the imagination Mark wasn't the settling down kind, so there should be no further obstacles in his way.

The ultra-sound scan revealed no abnormality and Richard felt very emotional to see the tiny foetus on the monitor.

Peggy Walker, *the book lady*, as she was known, walked across to talk to him later.

'How's your friend today dear?' she asked with a friendly smile. 'Is there any news yet?'

'No, there's no noticeable change,' he answered.

'Aren't you off back to England soon dear?'

'Yes, I'm going the day after tomorrow but I wish I could stay longer.'

'Well, I promised to keep an eye on her and when she wakes up I'd be happy to call you in England if you give me your number. I'm here most days.'

Richard scribbled his number on a scrap of paper. 'I'll give you my sister's too.' Alongside he wrote, *Jenny*. 'You'll catch one of us during the evening.'

'Are you coming again tomorrow?'

'Wild horses wouldn't keep me away,' he blushed with a boyish smile.

'I take it this young lady er….Alison, is your girl-friend?'

'Not exactly but I'm hoping she's going to be.'

'I hope so as well. You're a very agreeable young man,' she told him as she walked away.

Richard smiled as his eyes followed her from bed to bed. Peggy was a voluntary worker who lived in Spain with her husband for six months every year. They owned an apartment close by the hospital and she visited the wards four mornings a week where she distributed books and a selection of magazines from her overflowing trolley.

When Richard enquired where all her books came from, she laughed and answered, 'I beg, borrow and steal them dear. People are so kind when I tell them

374

what I do. It's such a long day in a hospital bed so I provide the dear souls with a little light relief.'

Richard was happier about leaving, knowing that Peggy would be keeping a watchful eye on Alison, and when, three weeks later, she called to tell him Alison was awake, he was elated and wept with joy.

Accompanied by Jenny, Richard left for Spain on the next available flight.

'I know Alison's pregnant,' he advised her during the flight and he went on to explain about the ultra-sound scan. 'I didn't tell Mark. Is he the father and is that why Paul punched his lights out?'

'*Paul* is the father but it's complicated and I don't want to betray a confidence. The problem is, Paul believes that *Mark's* the baby's father, so yes, that's why he thumped him.'

'Well he must have caught them in the act to even think that,' he continued trying to force the issue.

Furiously she reprimanded him. 'I don't want you bad-mouthing her! She's *never* slept with Mark.'

'Well, she's definitely slept with Paul. Is he crazy or what?'

'He says he's infertile! There, you know now and if you *ever* repeat that to *anybody*, especially Mark, I'll give you worse than he got so be forewarned!'

Richard looked puzzled. 'I don't understand you.'

'I'm not going to draw you a picture. You should know about things like that. You're a big boy now.'

'I meant, why does he believe he's infertile?'

'Because he's stupid, bad-tempered and he won't listen to reason and now I have to break the terrible news to Alison that he's never coming back to her.'

'I would never have given her up like that. I agree with you that he's stupid.'

'That makes two of you! If *you* had played your cards right, *you* could have had her, but then we've all seen you with a pack of cards, haven't we?'

Richard didn't answer. He was still trying to take on board what Jenny had said and plan how best to win Alison over. He was in the same position of not wanting to rush things and he was glad Mark hadn't accompanied them to Spain. He was eager to outwit Richard at every opportunity and though they were the best of friends, Richard found this characteristic of Mark's to be extremely churlish and infuriating.

When Jenny had called Dave with the news about Alison, it had been an emotional conversation. Was it not amazing, Jenny thought, how everyone loved Alison apart from Paul who had abandoned her so callously? Jenny would be more than ready for Paul Trantor if their paths ever crossed again.

Jenny and Richard collected a hire car and drove straight to the hospital. They ran down the corridor to her ward and Alison's face lit up when she saw them. Jenny burst into tears, while Richard battled desperately to choke back his own tears of joy.

'I'm alright. At least I'm going to be. Please don't get upset Jenny,' she pleaded.

'Do you know what happened?' Jenny asked her tearfully.

'They haven't told me much. I know there was an accident and I banged my head. That's all.'

'That's about the measure of it,' Jenny answered. 'Are you in any pain?'

'No, but I can't walk yet. My legs are very weak and the physiotherapist came today. If I'm able to walk properly by the end of this week, they might discharge me if there are no issues with my bodily functions but I'm not allowed to travel home for a while. I need more physiotherapy. So how are Clare and Antonia? Were they there too? You'll be going home soon won't you?' Alison asked fervently.

'Listen. You've been here six weeks. That's why you can't walk as you haven't been out of bed. You fractured your skull and you were unconscious. We were all involved in a traffic accident and you were hit by flying debris. I'm fine. Antonia had cuts on her arms but she's okay now. We all went home the following Sunday, then the book-lady Peggy, called Richard to say you were awake,' Jenny explained.

'I know Peggy. She's a lovely lady. She sits with me sometimes and we talk about all kinds of things, my childhood, my mum, what I liked at school, my job, who my friends are....I told her all about Paul. Where *is* Paul? Why isn't he here?' she asked.

She glanced at Richard but said nothing. Though Alison had not picked up on the absence of Clare's name during Jenny's account, she had remembered to ask about Paul. Jenny changed the subject. 'Your ultra-sound scan shows the baby's fine,' she said.

Alison glanced uncomfortably at Richard.

'It's alright. He knows you're pregnant. When he was last here, he watched the baby on the monitor. He said it was wonderful to see your baby Alison.'

'Has Paul seen our baby? Does he know now that I'm pregnant?'

'Yes, I told him because I'd had to tell the doctor you were pregnant when he was going to send you for an X-ray and Paul was going to speak to him.'

'Was he happy?' she asked hopefully but Jenny's face told her otherwise. 'He was angry wasn't he? I thought he would be. I don't think Paul wants us to have children but he likes other people's children.'

Richard opened his mouth to speak. 'Keep it shut, she doesn't know,' Jenny murmured brusquely and turning to Alison, she chirped blithely, 'You know Paul. One minute he's down, the next he's up.'

She stared at Jenny questioningly. 'I know when you're hiding something. He's left me hasn't he?'

Jenny took a deep breath. 'Yes Alison and I'm so sorry. I really did try to talk some sense into him.'

'I'm sorry too,' Richard added.

'When did he leave?'

'Over five weeks ago.'

'So he's not coming back then! Jenny, what am I going to do? I'd rather die than live without Paul.'

'I know,' Jenny sympathised, taking Alison in her arms as she sobbed uncontrollably.

Changing the subject once more Jenny asked her, 'Have you had anything to eat yet?'

Alison dried her tearful eyes. 'Only a tiny bowl of soup. I'm not allowed any solid food yet. The nurse explained that they would build up the amount each day. Does Paul know I'm awake?'

'No. I've seen nothing of him since he left.'

'When you go home, would you call him please and tell him I need him and would you remind him that he promised he would never leave me again?'

'If that's what you want, then that's what I'll do,' she replied, suffocating on her words.

Alison seemed more settled in the knowledge that Jenny would speak to Paul. She recalled how Jenny had promised she'd be there for her no matter what, as if she had known this would happen. How could Jenny have known how Paul would react? Anyway it didn't matter as Jenny would resolve the problem and Paul would be back in her life soon. She had to rebuild her strength now. She was fourteen weeks' pregnant and she wanted her baby so much.

Jenny and Richard visited Alison each day and on their second visit, Jenny met Peggy who was a kind and gentle soul. She embraced Peggy warmly while thanking her for her kindness in conveying the very welcome news of Alison's progress. Peggy related that she and her husband wintered in Spain and then usually went home in June when Spain became too hot but they travelled back to Spain each November before the cold weather returned in England.

When living in Spain, they had a hectic schedule, she continued. When they had completed their daily chores, Wilfred, her husband went bowling and she came to the hospital to make her rounds.

It was apparent to Jenny as she watched her going about her business that everyone loved Peggy. Most foreigners had few visitors and Peggy never tired of being a friendly companion. She had without doubt taken kindly to Alison and had even offered to take her to their apartment on her discharge because she would need a carer. Alison could travel to England with them at the end of June, she advised Jenny and she could be back home in Manchester again before she was too far into her pregnancy to travel.

Jenny was happy as she could now go home with Richard, knowing Alison was in safe hands.

With the holiday season fast approaching, Jenny's father was having difficulty in trying to find cover for everyone's job, especially Richard's.

Antonia had moved temporarily into her parents' house during Jenny's overseas absence and she was now making excellent progress.

Jenny packed Alison's case and took it to Peggy's apartment a few days later.

'You have a lovely apartment,' she told her when Peggy proudly showed her around. 'The swimming pool will provide excellent therapy for Alison who is still rather unsteady on her feet.'

'I'll have to be her feet,' Peggy replied.

'You'll do no such thing!' Jenny said. 'Make her do things. I would. She must learn to walk again.'

'You're a very good friend to Alison. You let folk know what you think don't you? I admire a woman who stands up for herself. I was always a doormat when I was married to my first husband. He had me doing some terrible things but all that's in the past. I have a truly wonderful husband now. We've been married for fourteen years. Are you married dear?'

'No but I soon will be and I can't wait!'

'Well, I hope you'll be very happy Jenny.'

'I'll tell you what. Write me down your address in England and we can keep in touch.'

'I'll write it down for Alison. She'll be talking to you before long no doubt and if there's a problem, which there won't be, I'll call you. Have a safe trip home.'

'Thanks for everything Peggy. They threw away the mould when they made you.'

'Get away with you,' she laughed.

Jenny and Richard left for England the next day following a poignant farewell with Alison but they were happy with her progress and the prospect that she would soon be back home amongst friends.

'Isn't Peggy fantastic?' Jenny remarked.

'She's the best,' Richard replied.

It was Clare's funeral on the following Friday. Her remains had been flown home two days ago. Jenny and Antonia were dreading the day. Clare's family, friends and work colleagues would be in attendance as would the four young men they'd met in Spain.

Clare's parents were making plans for a memorial service to be held at the end of July and hopefully, Alison would be home in time for that.

It had been a distressing time for Clare's parents who had found it impossible to ascertain what was going on in Spain. An inquest had been opened and adjourned but only after a lengthy investigation into the cause of the crash. The bureaucracy had seemed endless as they waited for her body to be released.

Meanwhile, Antonia's lacerations had healed very well. The scarring though visible would fade given time. She had regained the use of her hands but she hadn't returned to work because of her mental state. Jenny believed she would feel a lot better once the funeral had taken place.

381

Having ineffectively tried to fulfil her obligation to Alison as Paul's number was unavailable, Jenny asked Tom if he knew of Paul's whereabouts but he was reluctant to help. 'I don't want to get involved. He's a mate,' he said.

'Some mate!' she scoffed contemptuously. 'Just tell me what you know Tom.'

'I know he left his studio and he said he might be going to America. Truly, that's all I know. He was very distressed to learn about Alison's pregnancy.'

'It's definitely his baby,' she insisted.

'Paul's adamant it's not and it isn't our business. I don't want *us* to quarrel about that. I haven't a clue who the baby's father is and neither have you. The only person who knows the truth is Alison.'

'Oh, let it drop. You're a bloke. You always stick together. I've done what I promised. I can't contact him, so that's an end to it. She's better off without him. He was forever ranting and raving.'

Tom took her in his arms. 'I know you're on edge darling but I'm sure you'll feel better after Friday. I love you and I don't want you to be angry with me. It's not my fault.'

It rained heavily all day Friday. It was a miserable day for a miserable event.

Clare's mother had to be supported as she walked into the small church that was packed to capacity.

The Minister delivered an emotional service that touched the hearts of the entire congregation. Most people were in tears for the entire duration.

'Why does everybody have to choose, *Abide with me*?' Jenny asked. 'It's such a depressing hymn.'

'Everything is depressing about a funeral service, especially so when the deceased is a young woman like Clare,' Tom answered. 'We're here to pay our respects. It'll be over soon darling. Try to be strong for Clare's parents. They need the support of both you and Antonia.'

Jenny was relieved to breathe fresh air again. She exchanged a few short words with Clare's parents who persuaded her and Tom to go home with them for refreshments.

The four lads they had met in Spain offered their condolences to Jenny, and enquired about Alison's progress. They were glad to hear she would shortly be coming home, none more so than Dave.

It was early evening when Jenny and Tom arrived home and Jenny was exhausted. The funeral service had been much more solemn than Clare would have wanted, Jenny reflected. Clare had been happy and lively yet the day she went to her final resting place had been anything but that. She would certainly not have approved.

Alison was benefiting from her sojourn at the apartment and Peggy and Wilfred were extremely kind. She continued with her physiotherapy for a further two weeks and it was a day of mixed feelings when she finally said goodbye to the dedicated staff.

She travelled to England at the end of June with Peggy and Wilfred, still unaware of Clare's death.

Alison was delighted to be back on home territory and could hardly wait to call her grandparents.

Joyce sobbed when she heard her granddaughter's

voice. ''Ow's Paul? I bet 'e's relieved that yer 'ome i'n't 'e?' she blubbered.

'I might as well tell you, we're not together now,' she said, explaining what had transpired.

Joyce, who didn't shock easily, told her, ''E'll be back lass for you an' yer baby. Mark my words.'

'No, he won't, Grandma. It's weeks since he left and there's been no contact. I won't see him again.'

'D'yer still want 'im back?'

'I don't know what I want anymore. I know I still love him. That won't ever change.'

'Then wait for 'im to come to 'is senses. Trust yer grandma. Paul's a good lad. 'E'll do what's right in the end. You just take care o' yersel'.'

Peggy brought her a cup of tea. 'Have you spoken to your grandma?' she asked.

'I have and she told me how relieved she was to hear from me. She didn't bat an eyelid when I said I was pregnant. She's all the family I have now and granddad of course. I lost my dad first but sadly, I never knew him and then I lost my mum, then Paul left me and I almost lost my baby too,' she sighed.

'You're a good girl Alison and I'm sorry you've had such sadness in your life. Hopefully things will soon get better. Wilfred and I would like to keep in touch when you leave. We'd like to know all about the baby when he's born. I hope we get to see him.'

'I'll be taking driving lessons soon after he's born so I'll bring him to visit you. I was thinking earlier that your husband's name's Wilfred and granddad's name's Alfred, so I shall call my baby Freddie but his registered name will be Paul, Michael, Anthony,

Trantor, Haythorne....Paul after his father, Michael after mine and Anthony after Paul's father.'

Peggy expelled a shrill burst of laughter. 'Wilfred will be thrilled to bits when I tell him.'

When Alison offered to help prepare the meal, her help was refused. 'You watch the telly,' Peggy said.

'If you're sure, I'll write to Paul's mum then. I've no idea whether Paul has told her about the accident but I think she should be aware she'll be a grandma again soon. Her daughter has two children though I don't think that will detract from her excitement. I don't want to phone her because I'd be tongue-tied. I can write everything down so much easier.'

'There's plenty of paper and envelopes in the left hand drawer of the dresser. You just help yourself to whatever you need dear and I have some stamps too.'

When she opened the drawer and poked around to find the paper she suddenly froze, unable to believe her eyes as she came across a framed photograph, as familiar as her own reflection. She had seen that photograph daily throughout her childhood. It was a photograph of her late father, Michael, but what on earth was it doing in Peggy's drawer?'

With tears blurring her eyes, she lifted it from the drawer and was holding it in her trembling fingers when Peggy appeared, drying her hands. 'Have you found it dear?' she asked and halted abruptly when she saw Alison holding the photograph.

The look of horror on her face answered Alison's unspoken question. 'You're my grandma aren't you Peggy?' she then asked ashen-faced.

Peggy began to sob. 'Yes, but I never wanted you to find out like this. I'm sorry. I hid the photo when we got home. Someday I would have told you but I wanted you to get to know me. I'm not, nor have I ever been evil....weak yes! I adored my son and you too when you were born and God knows I've tried to find you over the years but you moved and....'

'Stop it. Please don't cry. I can't take this in. How did you find me when I wasn't even in England? I don't understand.'

'It was your friend Jenny who set this in motion. I assume she found the letter I wrote after your father died. Your granddad made me write that. He was an evil man who used to hit me, and Michael was glad to get away. I should have left him but I'd nowhere to go. When I put my coat on to post the letter, your granddad snatched it out of my hand and knocked me to the floor. He knew I wouldn't have posted it so he stormed out and posted it himself. I'm deeply sorry for allowing myself to be bullied into writing it. I left him two months later. Wilfred helped me to get away. I wrote to your mother but the letter was returned as you'd moved. Wilfred owned an apartment in Spain and so he took me there, where your granddad couldn't find me and after your granddad died, I got married to Wilfred. I'm not a bad person, Alison. Truly I'm not,' she sobbed.

'Jenny wrote me a scathing letter following your accident and she sent it to my previous address but Wilfred's sister's living there now. As soon as she opened it, she phoned me in Spain as she knew how I'd searched for you. I told her to mark it *not known* and return it because I wanted to find you without you or Jenny knowing who I was. I hoped that over a period of time, when you'd got to know me, you might forgive me. I just wanted to be your grandma especially so when I knew you'd been injured. I'd heard about the terrible accident that Jenny referred to in that letter and it took me only minutes to find you. I visited you every day Alison, please believe me and I prayed you'd recover. I didn't want to lose you when I'd found you. I owed that to your father. He was a good man. Can you ever forgive me?'

'Oh Peggy, Grandma, there's nothing to forgive. I didn't understand why you could have sent such a letter when my mother told me. I didn't even know I had the letter so I don't know how Jenny found it but she did and I'm so happy that we've found each other. I've lived my life losing people but now I've got you, my other grandma. You couldn't begin to imagine how much that means to me.'

Peggy touched Alison's face. 'You look like your dad. When I first saw you I recognised you.'

'Does Wilfred know who I am?'

'Yes, and he agreed it might be better for us to get acquainted before telling you I was your grandma.'

'Well, you're going to be a great-grandma now. I have to call Jenny to tell her. She won't believe it,' she laughed, wiping her tear-stained face.

'She's very protective of you isn't she? The letter she sent was as bad as the one I wrote to your dear mother and when I knew she was coming to Spain I was scared stiff she'd discover who I was. Do you reckon she'll still be angry with me?'

'Not when I tell her the whole story, in fact, she'll be embarrassed about the things she said now she's met you. She couldn't praise you enough.'

'She only spoke the truth as she saw it. There was no other way of reading that dreadful letter. Fancy your mother keeping it all those years.'

'I wasn't aware she'd kept it and I'm at a loss to know how Jenny found it. She never touches any of my things. I'm going to call her now.'

Jenny was pleased to hear Alison's voice. 'How's it going? Are you walking any better?' she asked.

'I'm doing great. I'm on a high at present but I've got a bone to pick with you,' she told her playfully. 'Have you been messing with my stuff at the flat?'

'What's brought this on? You know I wouldn't do that. Antonia came to stay for a short while, so I put her in your room and I shifted your things into the hall cupboard until she'd gone but I fail to see how you could have known about that.'

'Did you find anything er….unusual amongst my things....anything that disturbed you?'

'Like what?'

'Like the letter to my mother from my grandma?'

'Well yes er....I did find that but I didn't discuss it with anybody. I think it must have been inside your Family Bible, because when I was placing it on the shelf in the hall, it fluttered to the floor and landed at my feet. It was as if I was meant to read it but I still don't understand….'

'I love you Jenny Joyce,' she interrupted. 'I don't deserve a friend like you!'

'Will you tell me what's wrong? Are you alright?

388

You're worrying me. Can I have a quick word with Peggy?'

'Are you sure? You might not want to when I tell you she's my grandma....the one you wrote to.'

There was a deathly silence as Jenny attempted to collect her thoughts. 'You're joking! That kind lady is your grandma? But the letter came back to me.'

'It's a long story and I'll tell you all about it when I get home. I'm hoping to be back next week. I've found her. After all this time I've actually found her and she's wonderful,' she cried, smiling at Peggy.

'Let me speak to her. I must apologise.'

'I told her exactly what you'd say. Hang on,' she laughed, passing the telephone to Peggy.

Before Jenny had chance to speak a word, Peggy remarked, 'Don't apologise to me. I'm the one who should apologise. I'm so happy you sent that letter or I'd never have found Alison and I'll be grateful to you for the rest of my days. It has to be fate. I'm sure Alison wants to tell you everything so I'll say nothing more. I'm passing you back to her now.'

'You can't believe it can you Jenny?' Alison said.

'I might when you've told me the full story. I'm really thrilled for you because you've lost so many people in your life.'

'Speaking of which, did you contact Paul?'

'I'm afraid I didn't. His number's unobtainable. I don't think he wants to be found, Alison. I'm really sorry. I did try and Tom knows nothing either.'

'I hope he comes back Jenny. I want him to be a father to his child and I want him too. I'm writing to Vicky to find out if she knows anything.'

'I hope she can help. Returning to something you said earlier, are you fit enough to come home next week? Richard will collect you but I don't want you home before you're well enough. You'll be on your own when I'm at work,' she said with concern.

'I'm fine now but I want to spend some time with grandma. We've lots of catching up to do. Listen, I must go. I'll call you soon and if you hear anything from Paul, let me know won't you?'

'Of course I will. Bye Alison.'

Alison wrote a lengthy letter to Vicky, telling her about her accident, that Paul had walked out when he learned she was pregnant and that she had found the grandma she had not previously known. It was a very moving letter in which she pleaded with Vicky to ask Paul to get in touch with her.

Vicky called her at Peggy's the very next day to apologise for Paul's behaviour and she promised to support her every step of the way.

Vicky was excited about her new grandchild and assured Alison she would pass her message to Paul should he contact them. She was unaware Paul had left his studio as he hadn't been in touch for about two months but she stated it was typical of Paul to disappear for months on end.

Vicky asked how she would be fixed financially and to that she curtly stated she would manage. 'No grandchild of mine is going short of anything, not while I've breath in my body,' Vicky retorted. 'I'm furious with Paul. Tony and I will support the baby until he turns up. Have you no idea why he left?

'I haven't a clue. I was still in a coma at the time.

When Jenny told him I was pregnant, Paul stormed out of the hospital and never came back. I'd tried to talk to him about having children a few days before my accident but he wouldn't discuss the subject and we had a row because I persisted. Because of that, I didn't tell him I was pregnant so maybe that's why he was angry. I just don't know.'

'Why don't you come and stay with us until your baby's born?' she suggested.

'Thank you Vicky. That's very kind but I want to go home. Besides, Paul might suddenly turn up.'

'Well, if you change your mind, let me know and Tony will collect you and do call if you need us.'

'I will and thank you.'

Alison felt relieved following her talk with Vicky. At least she had an ally in her.

The following Saturday, Richard and Jenny went to collect Alison from Peggy's. While Peggy made a pot of tea, Alison showed her father's photograph to Jenny and described her disbelief at finding it in the drawer. 'It's such an amazing story,' Jenny said, 'But one with a very happy ending.'

When it was time to go, Alison kissed Peggy and Wilfred goodbye and thanked them for their help.

'Get away with you,' she chuckled. 'For eighteen years I didn't even know you. I'll never be able to make up for eighteen years lass. Your mum and dad would be so proud of you if they were here.'

13

During their return journey, Alison made numerous references to the Spanish holiday but each time she raised the subject, Jenny changed it. Though Alison remained unaware of Clare's death, Jenny knew she must enlighten her at the earliest opportunity.

When they entered the flat, Alison was justifiably emotional though delighted to be back.

Jenny poured her a celebratory drink to mark her return and asked her to sit down. There was no easy way to break the devastating news. First of all, she told her about the accident and then explained how Antonia had rushed to Clare's aid. With tears in her eyes she then revealed that Clare was dead.

Alison sat quietly with a faraway look in her eyes before bursting into tears and Jenny comforted her. 'I didn't tell you sooner because you were too ill to go to her funeral. There's a memorial service in two weeks and her parents would like you to be there.'

Alison went to lie down after she heard the heart-breaking news. In her thoughts, she pictured Clare's smiling face as she recalled the outrageous conversations that had made her laugh until she cried. She would never see her again and she was beleaguered by memories of her dynamic and vivacious young friend whose life had been so tragically terminated.

Jenny later revealed that Tom had moved into the flat but she promised Alison she could remain there too, at least until after her baby was born.

Alison was six months into her pregnancy when Clare's memorial service was held. She had spoken to Clare's distressed parents to enquire if she might say a few words at the service and her mother had replied that she would take comfort from her words.

The church was packed to capacity with relatives, work colleagues and friends and when the Minister gestured to Alison, she took her position before the hundred or so people awaiting her words. Clearing her throat, she smiled timidly at the congregation.

'I'd like to talk to you about a young woman who was beautiful in mind as well as in body. Her name was Clare and she was my special friend. It was an honour and a privilege to be her friend, if only for a few short months but I learned so much from her in that time that I feel compelled to share my fondest memories and feelings with you. I'm not here today to express sadness but rather to invite you all to join with me in the celebration of a life that was joyful. Clare epitomised the words *joy* and *happiness* and all who knew her, adored her. Your presence here today must be of great comfort to her parents. Clare was thoughtful, witty, gifted and very special. She lived life to the full. She was the proverbial life and soul of any party and wherever she is now, I'm sure she'll be smiling down on us. She would want us to be cheerful today and her message to each one of us would be to face up to the everyday tragedies of life and move on to confront any subsequent challenge, for that was how she lived her life. Clare's dictum was love and be loved and don't dwell on the past.'

Alison paused to look round the congregation. A few of the women were drying their eyes and some were smiling caringly. The men looked meditative, their heads bowed reverently, apart from one who was standing at the rear and whose eyes were fixed intently upon Alison as he listened to the heart-felt words she delivered so skilfully. Catching her eye, he nodded in acknowledgement. The man was Paul.

Her heart skipped a beat but she found the resolve to continue. 'I feel honoured to have known Clare. I shall never forget her kindness and compassion and I ask each and every one of you to remember her as she lived her life, self-assured, joyful and content. Finally I would ask that you continue to cherish her memory in the manner she so richly deserves.'

Alison stepped down and as she made her way to her seat there was quiet murmuring throughout the congregation. Several nodded and smiled at her and Clare's tearful mother briefly took hold of her hand, while attempting to force a smile.

When the service had ended, Alison walked with Jenny to the door. She whispered, 'Paul's here,' but Jenny made no verbal or visual response.

Outside, Alison went to talk to Clare's mother.

'Thank you for the lovely words Alison,' she said sorrowfully. 'We miss her so very much.'

Alison hugged her and as she was walking away, Paul approached her and stated quietly, 'It probably isn't the time or place but could you spare me a few minutes please? There's something we must discuss and I didn't know where else I'd find you.'

Before she had time to reply, Mark appeared and putting his arm around Alison's shoulder, he smiled mockingly and exclaimed, 'Well well! It's amazing what crawls out of the woodwork isn't it darling?'

Angrily, Alison reprimanded him. 'Stop it Mark! I don't need this today of all days.'

'It's alright Alison. I'm not here to cause trouble,' Paul said. 'I just wanted to fill you in about where I've been and why I've been unable to contact you.'

'Fill her in? *Fill her in*? You're not man enough to fill a bloody pram according to my information!' Mark laughed scornfully.

As Paul stormed off rubbing his bruised knuckles, Richard rushed to Mark's aid and tried to help him up from the ground. 'I don't believe it! Look at the state of you again. Your jacket's covered in blood and everybody's looking. You told Paul what I said didn't you after promising you wouldn't breathe a word?' Richard yelled. 'I shouldn't have told you!'

'Is somebody going to tell me what's going on? I can't believe such disgraceful behaviour at Clare's memorial service,' Alison cried, hurrying after Paul with Richard in hot pursuit.

As she reached the exit to the car park, Paul's car was heading towards her at speed. She stood in his path forcing him to brake abruptly. Paul opened his window and shouted, 'You stupid girl! I could have killed you. Let me pass!'

'Turn off your engine Paul. I want to talk to you,' she replied aggressively.

'There's nothing to say. I've seen all I need to see and I hope you'll be very happy with Mark though I doubt you will be. The last thing I needed was to be ridiculed in front of everyone,' he replied bitterly.

'Hang on Paul. That was my fault,' Richard stated apologetically. 'I was the one who told Mark about your problem. It's not Alison's fault. Alison doesn't know anything about it.'

'Would somebody tell me then? What problem?' she asked looking confused but neither Richard nor Paul enlightened her.

'It was my mistake coming here today but I'll not make the same mistake again,' he bellowed. 'This time it really *is* over. I must have been mad to even think we could pick up the pieces and begin again. I've never stopped loving you and I always will but I won't try to come between you and Mark again.'

'Don't do this Paul,' Alison pleaded. 'You've got everything wrong. Why can't we discuss it like two sensible people?'

'What else is there to say? You made your choice when you slept with Mark Taylor. I was prepared to forgive you and….'

'Slept with Mark? What the hell are you talking about? I've never slept with Mark,' Alison laughed sarcastically. 'You need your head examining Paul. Is that what all this is about? You walked or rather you ran away because you think I'm having Mark's child? It's time you grew up Paul!' she continued, shaking her head in disbelief.

'Well it certainly isn't mine is it Richard? You're the man with all the answers. Whose is it then? Is it yours?' he yelled but Richard was too astounded to respond. 'In the absence of a denial, I'll take that as *yes*,' he scoffed as he started to drive away, almost touching Alison as he did so.

Richard dragged her out of harm's way and Paul moved off swiftly without uttering another word.

As he looked through his rear view mirror, he saw Richard holding Alison in his arms as he attempted to console her, and Paul's heart had been broken for a second time as he disappeared from sight.

Richard took Alison back to the church by which time most of the congregation had departed. Jenny, Antonia, Mark and Tom were still there, together with another male who Alison recognised as Dave Maxwell when she drew closer.

Dave wrapped his arms around her. 'I'm so sorry. It's my fault. Paul phoned me out of the blue from America to ask how he could contact you as he was anxious to see you. I knew you'd be here today and I was trying to help. I had no idea where you were before you returned to the flat and I saw no harm in his coming here. I never imagined he would make a scene in front of everyone. I didn't think it right for other people to be interfering and turning him away but I've really messed up and I apologise Alison.'

'It's not your fault. What you did was with good intent. Evidently, there are things the others haven't bothered to tell me. Jenny has plenty to answer for and I'll be talking to her when I'm home. Between them, my friends have wrecked any likelihood I had of resolving matters with Paul. It wasn't anybody's decision to make but mine and Paul's and I should have been told he was looking for me. I'm grateful to you Dave. Unfortunately, your efforts backfired but it wasn't your fault and you mustn't feel guilty. I always believed Paul and I would work things out but now we'll never be reconciled. He glowered at me with revulsion in his eyes as he drove away. I'll never forget that look on his face and I still have no idea what's wrong. Did he tell you?'

'No. He simply said he'd had time to think about everything and that he'd forgiven you, but he didn't elaborate further and I didn't like to ask.'

'But I've done nothing to require his forgiveness. First Paul accused Mark then Richard of fathering my baby but I've never given him cause. I'll get to the bottom of this if it's the last thing I do because I know for certain that it's Paul's.'

'He should trust you. I'd trust Laura with my life. Maybe you'd be better off without him and maybe your friends believed that when they wouldn't tell Paul your whereabouts. I'm certain they were only trying to protect you but at the end of the day, it's your decision, not theirs,' he said sympathetically.

Alison promised to keep in touch with Dave and asked that he inform her if Paul made contact again.

Alison and Jenny stared through the car window in total silence as Tom drove them home.

Richard had made an excuse to leave but Alison insisted that Richard, Mark and Antonia's presence was required as she needed to talk to all of them.

When they arrived home, Alison broke the silence as the others hovered around fidgeting and looking agitated. 'Right, I'd like to know what's been going on! I want no lies or half-truths,' she insisted. 'You can start first Jenny by telling me when Paul made contact with you and why you didn't tell me.'

She looked anxious and replied, 'It was soon after you left hospital. I didn't want him upsetting you so I wouldn't disclose your whereabouts. I told him to

398

call you here in a week or two. I was disgusted with him for being so aggressive and inconsiderate.'

Antonia chipped in, 'Hey, he's great. I like Paul.'

'Do you now?' Jenny sniggered scornfully. 'Well perhaps you'll cool your ardour when I tell you he referred to you as a strumpet or something equally offensive....a trollop. Yes that was it. Clare too!'

'Never mind that! What happened at the hospital when he stormed off? He wouldn't just get up and leave without cause after traipsing all the way from England to see me. Was it something you said?'

'Paul was going to speak to the consultant about your X-rays and I didn't want him to learn from the consultant that you were pregnant.'

'And what did he say when you told him?'

Jenny sighed. 'Paul said he wasn't the father.'

'Right, let's clear this up once and for all. Mark, you first! Have you and I ever had sex?'

Grinning widely he replied, 'I wish!'

'I'm not asking for your smart mouth Mark. *Have we had sex?*' she asked heatedly. '*Speak the truth!*'

'No Alison, we haven't.'

'Thanks. Now you Richard. Have *we* had sex?'

Looking perturbed he answered, 'No we haven't.'

'So what about you Tom? After all, it's only right that I ask everyone I know since I have to wash my dirty linen in public. Have we had sex?'

'Don't do this Alison, please,' Tom said.

'You'll be prime suspect if you refuse to answer.'

He heaved a sigh. 'No Alison, we haven't.'

'Right who else could it be? Ah, now I remember, it must have been Doctor Simon Ward. I do recall

399

he slipped me one on the sofa at Antonia's party so that clears up any confusion now we know who....'

'Stop this! Just stop this!' Jenny interrupted.

'*No I won't*! There's got to be a reason why Paul thinks he's not the father and I've never given him grounds so someone here must have said something and this will continue until we get to the truth about why I've lost the love of my life, so tell me Jenny. I know that Mark knows and Paul knows that Mark knows. That's why Paul struck him isn't it? *Tell me before I go mad*,' Alison screamed.

'You won't like the answer Alison but you have a right to know since everyone else does.'

'I don't know,' said Antonia.

'You will shortly,' Jenny remarked and turning to Alison she inhaled noisily. 'Paul's infertile, Alison. He's incapable of fathering a child.'

She looked stunned. 'That's ridiculous!' she said. 'Who on earth told you that pack of nonsense?'

'Paul did, ages ago, long before I knew you were pregnant. I'd censured him at your eighteenth party about unprotected sex and he was furious with me. He yelled that you were not at risk of anything and above all of becoming pregnant as he was unable to father a child. Paul swore me to secrecy because *he* wanted to tell you when the time was right.'

She was close to tears. 'So that's why he reacted so angrily when I raised the subject in Spain?'

'I guess he didn't want to spoil the weekend.'

'But he's wrong Jenny. You have to believe me.'

'I do, in fact we all do,' she said, looking round at the others who nodded in accord.

400

'I owe you an apology,' Mark said. 'I've been an idiot. I admit I was jealous of Paul but I just wanted to irritate him to make sure he appreciated you.'

'I'm sorry too,' Richard sighed remorsefully. 'If I hadn't told Mark about Paul, he might still be here. The last thing I wanted was to hurt you Alison.'

'No, it's my fault,' Jenny stated. 'I shouldn't have turned Paul away nor should I have told my brother what Paul had divulged in confidence. Richard isn't fit to know anything. There's another thing though. When you went to that concert, Paul followed you and he saw Mark kissing you in the car park.'

'I was congratulating Alison on her engagement,' he protested. 'I only kissed her on the cheek.'

'Paul didn't see it like that and when he found out Alison was pregnant, he wrongly believed you were responsible,' Jenny told him and turning to Alison she continued, 'I pleaded with you not to go to that concert. I knew it would cause trouble.'

'Does anyone know where Paul is now?' Richard queried. 'I don't mind going to see him to explain.'

'He's probably on his way back to America. No one knows where he lives now,' Alison replied.

'We're equally to blame,' Tom interposed. 'It was none of our business and the one innocent person is Alison who's lost Paul because of our interference.'

'I wish you'd told me Jenny. I would have talked to Paul and perhaps I'd have been able to reassure him. Do you know what he told me earlier? He told me that he would always love me,' she wept.

As Mark, Richard and Antonia prepared to leave Alison went to her room and cried herself to sleep.

401

Jenny's father turned up the next morning to talk to Alison. Jenny had talked to him earlier about the commotion at the memorial service where Elizabeth had diplomatically succeeded in dispersing most of the onlookers, her having made the excuse that the two young men had been resolving a long-standing dispute and things had got out of hand. Her account had satisfied the curiosity of the vast majority of the spectators who had taken their leave with no lasting damage caused to the reputation of either Maud's or her family, though Elizabeth was furious at Richard whom she held wholly accountable for Paul's show of anger. Conversely, John had found Mark's quip to be sharp and hilarious, *if* somewhat offensive.

As always, Alison was pleased to see John. After explaining he was there to discuss her rented house, he advised that her tenants had left her house while she was still in hospital and he had taken the liberty of using it for his Property Management Company. He had converted one bedroom into an office with a computer and related accessories so she could work from home with hours to suit when the baby came. He would pay a commensurate salary for her hours, additional to an annual rental on the property.

'When you have your baby, I know you will want to move from the flat. Besides, your house is better suited to rearing a child. The work won't be overly taxing for a single parent and you can organise your routine around your other commitments,' he said.

Alison was delighted and expressed her gratitude to John for his help and support.

'Good, that's settled. I'll have that cup of coffee

you didn't offer me now Jenny,' he said with irony.

Alison stood up. 'I'll see to it John.'

'Er, aren't you supposed to be resting?' he asked.

'I'm pregnant, not infirm,' she laughed. 'I'm still capable of making a cup of coffee.'

'So when's your baby due?'

'I've been given the thirty-first of October so I've about three months to go yet.'

Jenny did a quick calculation and determined that Alison must have conceived the weekend she went to Brighton. That was no mean achievement from a supposedly infertile lover, she thought.

'I intend going back to the Agency next Monday,' she told John.

'Is that wise?'

'Yes, I'll be fine for another few weeks yet.'

By the time she returned to work, she had settled her former dispute with Jenny. Remarks that Jenny had earlier made, that she would always be there for her, now made sense. Jenny had correctly predicted Paul's angry reaction to the news of her pregnancy. Jenny knew Paul as well as she did.

Alison also felt sympathy for Paul who genuinely believed he wasn't the baby's father and she could imagine how betrayed *she* would have felt in Paul's position. He had such an irrepressible temper. Had he been mild-tempered, she might have stood some small chance of convincing him he was wrong but now she must try to put him out of her mind.

Alison continued to work for another nine weeks but the effort of getting up early and working a full day gradually became too demanding and she took maternity leave. Her baby was due in four weeks' time and she was excited about her future.

Vicky had contacted her daily over recent weeks and she and Tony had insisted they would provide financial assistance for their grandchild. Vicky had finally talked Alison into providing her bank details and had instantly transferred two thousand pounds into her account to buy essential items for her baby.

Alison listed the telephone numbers of her friends and grandparents who Jenny had to notify and who eagerly awaited news of the birth.

Dave called Alison two weeks before the due date for an update. 'Are you still hanging in there?'

'Nothing's happening. I'm fed up,' she grumbled.

'It won't be long now. Is Jenny there with you?'

'No, Tom's taken her out for the day. It's the first Saturday he's had off for a month so I told them to go out and enjoy the beautiful sunny day rather than sit gawping at my miserable phizog.'

'Listen, we're going out for lunch so why don't I pick you up? You still haven't met Laura and she's dying to meet you, that's if you're well enough.'

Her eyes lit up at his suggestion. 'That would be a pleasant change if you're sure it's no trouble.'

'None whatsoever. We'll be there within an hour. I'll bring Laura up to the flat and you can meet her.'

When Alison opened the door, she greeted a very attractive Laura who smiled pleasurably at her. 'I'm so pleased to meet you at last,' Alison said.

'I am too, though I feel I know you already. I was sorry to hear of your horrible accident and the death of your friend. How are you feeling now?'

'I'll feel a lot better when I get rid of this gigantic lump,' she laughed. 'You'll know exactly what I'm talking about when it's your turn. Come on in.'

Without thinking Dave cut in, 'Er....hang on a bit. We'd like to get married first.'

'Wouldn't we all?' Alison quipped with a cursory glance at Dave whose expression changed to one of horror. 'It's okay. I'm getting used to the prospect of being a single parent.'

'I take it you haven't heard from Paul?' he asked.

'No, not a word.'

'I have the number he called me from in America. I never gave it a thought at Clare's service but when he originally called me, I saved his number.'

'I don't want it Dave. I'm not running after him. If he wants to find me, he will. Unless he can learn to act responsibly, I don't want anything to do with him. I'll have my baby soon and I don't need Paul spoiling everything. He'd never want anyone else's child and I'd never convince him the baby was his.'

'It's such a sad story Alison,' Laura said caringly. 'I wish things had turned out different for you. It's not going to be easy coping on your own.'

'I have lots of support. Jenny's brilliant and she'll spoil him rotten and as a lone parent, there'll be no interference from Paul.'

'Well, that's one way to look at it but you're very brave. Come on, let's go for lunch.'

As they walked to the car, Alison enquired, 'Have you finalised your wedding plans yet Laura?'

'No, we need to save a decent deposit for a house first and then we'll get married, maybe next year.'

'I hope I get an invitation to your wedding. You'd never have found a more thoughtful guy than Dave. He was so kind to me on holiday.'

'Well, that worked both ways. Dave was having a rotten time till you arrived with your friends.'

'Yes, and mine was considerably worse after he'd left, a total disaster in fact.'

Dave parked up at the pub and called, 'Everybody out, I'm ravenous.'

'And so am I,' Alison concurred. 'Did he tell you about the Val Paraíso in Spain, Laura?'

'Yes, he did. I'd like to visit Spain sometime.'

'You'd enjoy it but *don't* sit at a pavement café. I still shudder when I see a bus,' she grimaced.

They enjoyed a tasty lunch but afterwards Alison felt uncomfortable. 'I think I've eaten too much.'

'Are you alright?' Laura asked with concern.

'Yes. I shouldn't have had that crème brûlée but I love it. Perhaps Freddie doesn't like it,' she laughed patting her bump. 'He's kicking up a right fuss!'

'I think we'll head back when you've drunk your coffee,' Dave said, exchanging glances with Laura.

Dave was apprehensive. The baby was due in two weeks and sometimes babies did arrive early.

When they arrived at the flat, Alison felt better.

'It's probably nothing,' Laura said reassuringly.

Jenny and Tom were delighted to meet Laura who was still there when they arrived home.

'We had a brilliant time together in Spain,' Jenny told her. 'When Dave and his three friends held the barbecue, Tom had made an unexpected trip for the weekend. It was there that he proposed to me. I'm

406

glad you came today and I know Alison is pleased to meet you at last. I'll make us all some coffee.'

Laura followed her into the kitchen and closed the door. 'Listen, I don't want to be alarmist but Alison felt odd when she'd eaten her lunch. She appears to be fine now but at one point I was worried the baby was coming so keep an eye on her will you?'

'Right, I will,' Jenny replied.

'I'll help with those,' Laura said as she picked up two of the mugs. She gave them to Tom and Dave who were in deep discussion about the holiday.

'Where did you go today?' Alison asked Jenny.

'That pub in Cheshire you and I found. We had a really nice day....it was a pleasant change.'

'From me!' she laughed.

'No, I didn't mean that,' she said apologetically.

'I'll move back to my own house once the baby's born, then these two young love birds can have a bit of peace,' she explained to Laura.

'You're no trouble Alison....in fact we like having you here, er, don't we Tom?' Jenny said red-faced.

'Don't answer that Tom!' Alison cried and Laura and Dave laughed. 'The thing is, it'll get worse for a while when the baby's crying for his feed during the night and you have to get up for work,' she said, directing her remark at Jenny and Tom.

'We'll pull together,' Jenny said. 'Besides, it'll be good practice for me. It might be my turn next.'

Tom swallowed so hard he almost choked. 'Relax I'm joking,' she laughed, winking slyly at Alison.

Jenny had make known to her that she would like a baby but Tom wanted to get married first and take

407

Jenny to South Africa to meet his folks. They were hoping for a spring wedding in six months' time if everything went to plan.

It was time for Dave and Laura to go and Alison thanked them for a most enjoyable afternoon.

During their journey home, Laura confessed, 'I'd go out of my mind if you left me. What kind of man would leave a sweet girl like Alison?'

'Only a madman!' he sighed.

It was three in the morning when Alison banged on Jenny's door. 'What's up?' Jenny asked anxiously.

'I think the baby's coming,' Alison stated looking alarmed. 'I keep having pains and then they subside for a bit and then they return and it's going worse.'

'*Tom*!' Jenny screeched. '*Wake up. I don't know what to do.*'

'What's wrong?' Tom asked as he appeared at the door rubbing his eyes.

'It's Alison. She thinks the baby's coming.'

'Right, just relax both of you,' he ordered, taking control and fully awake. 'Let's go to your bedroom Alison where we can discuss things quietly. There's no cause to panic,' he told her reassuringly. 'People have babies all the time.'

'Men don't!' she snarled brusquely, clinging hold of Jenny as her knees suddenly gave way during the next contraction. 'I *hate* Paul Trantor.'

As the pain eased, Tom helped her back into bed. 'How long have you been having contractions?'

'About an hour but they're getting worse. They're every few minutes now. I didn't like waking you.'

408

'Alright, Jenny would you call an ambulance, tell them the birth's imminent and ask them to hurry,' Tom requested calmly. 'Right Alison, do you mind if I take a look. I'm not unfamiliar with childbirth. I've delivered quite a few babies. You'll be fine.'

'Just make it go away!' she yelled as another pain started to surge.

'Keep panting. That ought to help. Remember the breathing exercises you were taught. You've quite a bit to go yet,' he advised as he covered her with the sheet. 'You mustn't push until I tell you.'

'But I *want* to push!'

'I know but you mustn't. It isn't time and you'll need all your strength for later.'

'They're on their way. How is she?' Jenny asked.

'She's doing very well. I need to get scrubbed up. I don't think Freddie intends waiting much longer. When Alison's had her next contraction, go and put the kettle on and find some towels please.'

Alison screamed out with the strength of the next contraction and Jenny gripped her hand. All earlier thoughts of it being her turn next quickly dispersed as she dried the rivulets of sweat off Alison's brow. Never before had she witnessed childbirth and she found it to be a fear-provoking experience.

As the pain subsided, Jenny ran to the kitchen and filled the kettle to the top. She might discover now, she thought, why everybody ran amok with gallons of boiling water in the films she had watched. She collected four towels and ran back to Alison just as another contraction was lifting her off the bed as it surged through her body. Tom returned then.

Jenny was surprised by Tom's composure, though she had never had an opportunity to observe him in a professional capacity previously.

'Alright Alison, I need to check again,' he stated, then added, 'It's time. Jenny, stand there and offer Alison some moral support. She's got her work cut out for the next twenty minutes or so. We can't wait any longer.' He smiled reassuringly. 'It's Freddie's birthday. When you get the next contraction, I want you to push as hard as you can. Jenny, unlock the front door so the paramedics can come straight in.'

She pushed intensely for the duration of the next contraction and then fell back exhausted.

'Good girl! Very well done!' Tom praised. 'Relax now. You're doing fine. Do the same again with the next one. It won't be too long now.'

'Paul should be here,' she cried and Jenny's heart went out to her, feeling overwhelming compassion for her friend at this momentous time.

'Right, there's another coming. Get ready to push as hard as you can when you have the urge. Really hard this time, come along harder….harder….good. Right, stop now until I tell you to start again. Okay, off you go again,' Tom encouraged her calmly.

Alison was exhausted but she puffed and panted robustly on Tom's commands before bearing down vigorously on his final order. At that moment they heard voices and someone called, 'Hello?'

'In here, quick!' Jenny yelled and the paramedics ran in at the precise moment Freddie was delivered into the world by the driving force of Alison's final thrust.

'Okay mate we'll take over,' one said and recognizing Tom, humbly added, 'Sorry Dr. Garfield.'

'Be my guest,' Tom replied, placing the new-born baby in Alison's arms. 'I've done my bit now,' and smiling at Alison he asked, 'Wasn't he worth it?'

Laughing and crying simultaneously, she held her screaming child close. 'Oh yes, definitely.'

'He's adorable,' Jenny cried, purposely omitting to state the obvious, that Freddie was the absolute image of Paul. At that moment, Jenny detested Paul for the misery he had inflicted on Alison.

'Would you take her in mate? I'd like everything checking over. It was my first ever delivery,' Tom admitted. 'Text-book stuff!'

'Well, you seem to have done an excellent job Dr. Garfield,' the paramedic told him.

'Beginner's luck, that's all! I observed a delivery once and I've read Medical Journals on childbirth. Actually, I'm quite delighted with my efforts,' Tom announced proudly.

Astonished by his confession, Alison asked, 'Are you saying you haven't delivered a baby before?'

'Freddie is my first,' he replied with a broad grin.

'I can't believe that Tom. You were so calm and composed.'

'Don't kid yourself,' he guffawed. 'I was bloody petrified and I won't be doing it again in a hurry so don't get any ideas Jenny. Give me time to get over this trauma first. I need a stiff drink now!'

Jenny passed Alison's ready packed bag to one of the paramedics and said goodbye to Alison and her enchanting baby as they prepared to leave.

'Say thank you to Uncle Tom and Aunty Jenny,' Alison whispered to Freddie but the contented baby merely closed his eyes and yawned as he lay warm in the arms of his loving mother who would always protect him.

Jenny joined Tom in a brandy when everyone had left. 'Wasn't that something?' she asked. 'Were you really nervous?'

'Yes but I had to act composed for Alison's sake. They'll look after her on Maternity for a day or two before discharging her. What time is it?'

'Just after four. Let's go back to bed and get some sleep. We won't be getting much when Freddie gets home with those lungs. What are you grinning at?'

'I'm tickled pink. It's an incredible experience to deliver a baby. Later, I'll phone the hospital for an update and enquire what Freddie weighs. He looked a whopper to me and he's the image of Paul.'

'Yes, I felt guilty when I saw him. He's definitely Paul's. By the way, in films where babies are born, why do they always boil gallons of water?'

'Search me,' Tom laughed. 'I've never known the answer to that one. Perhaps you ought to ask Simon Ward. He's the gynaecologist.'

'Shut up and go to sleep. The very thought of that creep makes my flesh crawl,' she shuddered.

'Freddie weighs eight pounds three ounces and both mother and baby are doing fine,' Tom announced.

'That's a decent weight, considering Freddie was two weeks early. I'm going to phone everyone now. I'll start with her relatives,' Jenny said.

Alison's grandparents were delighted and Peggy wept when she heard the news. 'I'll ask Wilfred to drive me to the hospital tomorrow. Just think, I'm a *great*-grandma now. I'm so thrilled. Thank you for everything and please thank your young man for all his help too,' Peggy said.

Antonia was still half asleep when she answered the telephone but awoke quickly when Jenny gave her the good news. She too was overjoyed as were Jenny's parents and Maud and Harold.

'I'm going to ring Paul's mother now,' Jenny told Tom. 'I've not spoken to her before. I hope she and Paul's father are equally delighted.'

Jenny needn't have worried. Vicky was overjoyed and she too promised to visit later that day. During their conversation, they discussed Paul briefly and Vicky was saddened to learn that Alison had cried out for him during the birth.

'He can be a strange lad at times,' she told Jenny. 'He's very withdrawn and insecure. His grandfather was the same but he'll come back. He's devoted to Alison. He hibernates when things go wrong but he always bounces back when least expected. I'm sure things will work out for them when he comes to his senses. I disapprove of what he's done. It's such a cowardly act to desert your own child. His father is absolutely furious.'

'Freddie's the image of Paul,' Jenny advised her. 'He's gorgeous and Alison's so proud of him.'

'Hopefully, we'll see him today. I can't wait.'

'I might see you later then. I'm off to the hospital with Tom when I've called everyone on this eternal

413

list. I didn't realise how many people Alison knew. I'll look forward to meeting you.'

The last person Jenny called was Dave Maxwell. 'Laura was right, *Uncle Dave*. Alison's got a divine baby boy who was born at three-thirty this morning. He came so quickly that Tom had to deliver him.'

'We'll be at the hospital later. I can't wait to see them,' said Dave, eagerly taking down the details.

Alison was inundated with visitors throughout the day. Each one brought a gift for Freddie and Alison didn't tire of opening the numerous parcels of baby clothes and soft cuddly toys from all her friends and relatives who agreed Freddie was the most beautiful baby they'd ever seen. Vicky wept to see the replica of her son as she remembered him at birth.

Alison was exhausted when the guests finally left but she told Jenny it had been an incredible day and one she would always remember.

'So will Tom,' Jenny chuckled. 'I was very proud of him. When we're alone, he's simply Tom but he was so professional and you were very brave too.'

'Until I heard Freddie cry, I was tense. I suppose my accident caused the anxiety. When you think of it, it's something of a miracle that he's here at all.'

'In more ways than one,' Jenny said to herself as she imagined what Paul's reaction might be should he ever to see his son.

Three days later, mother and baby arrived home. Tom had assembled the cot in Alison's room during her absence and though Freddie would use a carry-cot for three months, Alison wanted to place that in the large cot so Freddie would become used to it.

414

After two or three disruptive nights, Freddie slept soundly after his late night eleven o'clock feed until Alison awoke him at six the next morning. Though it was contrary to convention to allow a young baby to wait so many hours between feeds, Alison felt no desire to follow convention. Freddie was happy and he was sufficiently strong-minded to let her know if he needed attention and if he was prepared to sleep through the night, she saw no harm in that. She felt that the sooner she had a strict regime in operation, the sooner she could return home, affording Jenny and Tom their well-deserved peace and tranquillity.

Three weeks later, Alison joyfully returned to her refurbished terraced house with Freddie.

Meanwhile, Tony had set up a standing order into Alison's bank account for seven hundred pounds a month although Alison had been unaware of Tony's generosity until her bank statement arrived and she contacted Vicky immediately.

'Tony insists,' Vicky told her. 'He's embarrassed about Paul's absence so there's no point in arguing. Freddie's our grandchild and Tony is aware of your financial circumstances. Please allow him to do this small thing to ease his conscience. He's devoted to Freddie and he wants him to have as much from life as any other child. Sadly, there's nothing we can do about Paul's absence but we can make life easier by providing a little financial help. We never shirk our responsibilities. Though you're not married to Paul, we nevertheless regard you as our daughter-in-law.'

'But I'll be working soon and I'll have rent from my property so I should manage,' Alison protested.

'Have you learned to drive yet and what will you do about a car? You'll need something reliable. The money isn't just for Freddie. It's for both of you. If you buy a car, you'll be able to visit us at the weekend and stay over. That way we all benefit as we'll be able to spend time with Freddie. Seven hundred pounds a month is nothing to Tony. Don't deprive Freddie because of your pride. It's very challenging being a single parent.'

'Alright, you have a point but I didn't want you to think I was looking for handouts. I've always been independent. I admit I was very naïve to allow Paul to convince me I wouldn't get pregnant but I'm not sorry anymore. Paul is the loser here. He has a son he'll never know because of his stupidity.'

'I can understand how you must hate Paul but....'

'I don't hate Paul,' Alison interrupted. 'I love him as much as I ever did. There'll never be anyone else for me. I was handling his juvenile tantrums before my accident and I've no doubt he's as miserable as I am because he really did love me. It's hard for me when I look at Freddie because he's so like Paul but I won't chase after him. It has to be his decision to come back and be a father to the baby he denies is his. Only then could we begin to build bridges, but that's unlikely to happen after so long.'

'Well, I don't know what the future holds Alison. I wish he'd come to his senses and come home. It's not easy for me. Paul's been running away since he was a youth. It's about time he grew up into a man.'

'Please thank Tony for his support. I appreciate it and I will start my driving lessons very soon. Jenny

416

will baby-sit for me anytime. She can't get enough of Freddie since we moved from the flat. I believe she's getting broody,' she laughed.

'He's a gorgeous boy. Who wouldn't want a baby like Freddie? He's adorable. I'll call you soon and I'll pass on your message to Tony. Bye Alison.'

Three months later, Alison took her test and passed first time.

'You did better than me,' Richard told her as they toured the second-hand car lots. 'I took mine three times before I passed. I just went to pieces.'

She turned to check on Freddie in his car seat. At five months old, with his mop of blonde hair he was even more like Paul.

Richard was pleased that Alison had asked him to advise her about a car. He loved Freddie as much as he loved Alison though he was still reluctant at this early stage to make his feelings known. She knew however and her heart went out to him.

Dave and Laura visited Alison regularly and they had met Richard several times. Laura remarked that he was one of the nicest young men she'd ever met and was sorry Alison couldn't return his feelings.

Now living in rented accommodation, Laura and Dave had invited Alison and Richard to dinner the following Friday. Laura had also invited Amanda, a work colleague, who was a quiet caring girl….a girl Laura felt would be the perfect match for Richard.

'I'm looking forward to Friday,' Alison said.

'Me too, I like Dave and Laura. It was thoughtful of them to invite me too,' Richard replied.

'It was a necessary evil,' she joked. 'I couldn't go if you weren't taking me. I don't have a car yet.'

'Well, hopefully, we'll resolve that soon,' he said pulling into another car lot. 'I bought a second-hand car from here once so let me do the talking and I'll try to get a good deal if there's anything you like.'

'As long as it's reliable and in my price range, I'll be happy with anything. I know nothing about cars. I even thought Paul's Porsche was a BMW.'

'I take it you still haven't heard from him?'

'No, he could be anywhere.'

Changing topic he stated, 'That car's economical for fuel and the insurance will be lower too. You'll pay a hefty premium at your age for your first car.'

'I've put money put aside for that and I shouldn't spend much on petrol as I don't intend going too far except for occasional trips to Paul's parents and my grand-parents. I hate imposing on other people.'

'I don't mind Alison. I'd do anything for you.'

'I know you would. You're very sweet Richard.'

After much deliberation, she selected the Peugeot she had first fancied. Richard took it on a test-drive and negotiated a huge price reduction after arguing that she was a single parent.

She was irate and as they returned home, she told him in no uncertain terms he had embarrassed her.

'What are you worrying about? That's the way to do business,' he explained. 'You'll likely never see the guy again. They expect you to haggle.'

'I don't take advantage of people,' she snapped.

'Well, if Paul hadn't taken advantage of *you*, then you wouldn't *be* a single parent,' he retorted. 'And if you'd let *me* take care of you, then you wouldn't *remain* a single parent. There….I've said it now. I think the world of Freddie and you must know how I feel about you Alison.'

'Please stop the car Richard. We need to talk.'

He pulled into a lay-by, turned off his engine and turned to face her. 'I do know how you feel Richard and if I could return the feelings you so deserve, I would but I can't. I love Paul and I always will but if there was any other man I would want to love, it would be you Richard. That's the truth. Somewhere out there, there's a charming girl looking for a man like you and when she finds you I'll be the happiest person alive. I do love you Richard but not the way you want me to. If I never ever see Paul again, my feelings for him won't change. I'm sorry because I know how it hurts to lose somebody you love.'

He looked downhearted and replied. 'Er….thanks for being honest. I've lived in hope for the past few months and I hope it doesn't affect our friendship. I was willing to lose you to Paul because at the time, I thought he was the better man. He made you very happy and you deserved some good fortune but despite what's happened since, you have Freddie.'

She kissed his cheek tenderly. 'I don't deserve a friend like you. I do hope you find happiness soon.'

Dejectedly, he answered, 'I hope you do too.'

Despite their earlier awkward discussion, Richard was still looking forward to dinner with Laura and Dave and they arranged to leave at seven on Friday.

When Richard called for her, Jenny answered the door, thrilled to be baby-sitting for Freddie and she took Richard upstairs where Freddie squealed with delight to see him.

Jenny told them not to rush back. 'Tom's coming here after work and we'll have a take-away so don't be back before midnight. Freddie will be fine and I have your number if I need you.'

'Are there just the four of us or will there be other couples there?' Richard enquired en route.

'As far as I know there's no other couples going,' Alison answered with a half-truth, not wanting him to think she was playing Cupid. 'Dave tells me they have a nice house,' she added, changing the subject. 'It's a three-bedroom semi and they've rented it at a good price. Dave's a handy lad who's made quite a few improvements and redecorated everywhere.'

Laura was thrilled with the colourful house plant from Alison. Richard gave Dave two bottles of red wine and they followed Laura into the living room.

'There's been a change of plan. We have another guest. This is Amanda,' Laura said.

Richard bounded over in his typically jovial style and shook hands with Amanda. 'I'm happy to meet you. This is my best friend, Alison.'

The two girls exchanged greetings and Alison sat at the opposite end of the sofa from Amanda, leaving Richard with no choice but to sit between them.

'Do you work with Laura?' Richard asked.

'Yes, we've worked at the same bank for a couple of years,' she replied with a pleasant smile.

Amanda's perfect complexion and her flaxen hair gave emphasis to her radiant blue eyes that Richard didn't fail to notice as he returned her smile.

420

Laura called, 'Come and see the kitchen Alison. Dave has fixed a new worktop and it's made such a difference.' When she walked in, Laura closed the door leaving Richard and Amanda alone.

'Richard's a good conversationalist,' Alison said. 'He'll chatter happily to Amanda all night. Are they seated next to each other for dinner?'

'Yes, and I haven't forgotten what you said about American football. She's crazy about it so I'll bring it into the conversation at an appropriate time.'

'Good. Let's hope it works. I'd love him to find a suitable girl but he does need a bit of a push.'

During dinner, Amanda was entirely at ease with Richard. Having been primed prior to her arrival, at first she was reluctant to attend and told Laura she felt she was being fed to the lions but Laura assured her that Richard came from good stock, that he was a sensitive young man and a very good catch.

'Never in a million years would you guess what Amanda's mad about, Richard. *American football*,' Laura told him. 'What do you think about that?'

'I don't believe that,' he said in amazement. 'I am too, in fact Alison bought me a book on American football one Christmas, didn't you?'

'Yes I did,' she confirmed.

'I have a video collection of the most memorable games,' Amanda told him.

'Wow! I'd give anything to watch them,' Richard replied. 'Which ones do you have?'

They became embroiled in deep discussion. Laura and Alison exchanged glances and smiled. This was going much better than expected and then, suddenly

Amanda surprised them by inviting Richard to her flat to choose any he'd like to see.

'I'd love that Amanda,' he said. 'I've never met a girl before who likes American football.'

Alison felt smugly satisfied. It was clear Richard enjoyed Amanda's company as they were planning to meet again and she prayed it would develop into something more meaningful.

Later, Laura overheard Richard invite Amanda to dinner when he called to view her videos and when she accepted his invitation, Laura was delighted.

On their way home, Richard remarked that he had thoroughly enjoyed his evening. 'It was such a nice surprise to meet Amanda. She's really pleasant and very pretty too.'

'I thought so as well and you seem to have a great deal in common. You appear well-suited.'

'Hang on Alison. I've only known the girl for two or three hours,' he laughed.

'She's charming and she has no baggage. All I'm saying is that you should follow your heart and see where it leads you.'

'I did that with you Alison but it led nowhere.'

'Then learn from your mistakes. Don't dilly-dally this time. If you like her, then get off your backside because someone will snap her up. She's lovely.'

Richard took Alison's advice and followed his heart and his relationship with Amanda flourished.

Six months later, Amanda proudly displayed her new diamond engagement ring at Jenny and Tom's wedding reception, much to everyone's delight.

14

Alison tried to make at least one weekend's visit a month to Stafford. She and Freddie would leave at around seven o'clock on Friday after the rush hour traffic had subsided and they would stay there until Sunday afternoon.

Freddie, almost eighteen months old, and with an above-average vocabulary, coupled with a matching appetite for learning, enjoyed his visits to his grand-parents, *Pops* and *Nana*. Tony would play football with him and when Freddie tired of that, he would drive him to a Petting Farm a couple of miles away, a venue Freddie always enjoyed.

It was also a relaxing time for Alison, who would sit in the garden whenever possible, enjoying one of Vicky's extra-special cocktails. They were as close as sisters and often they would leave Freddie with Tony and go shopping together.

'Have you given any thought to a nursery school for Freddie?' Vicky asked one weekend. 'Children learn so much from each other.'

'I have thought about it though I'd miss him now I'm used to having him around.'

'Sometimes you must put the child's needs before your own. We're very over-protective as mothers,' Vicky counselled. 'You could try him for say, three sessions a week and see how that goes. I did it with both mine and it certainly made a difference.'

'Maybe in another few months I'll try to find him a place. I think he's too young at the moment but I am serious about nursery as a learning process. Just look at the two of them! I don't know which one is the child,' she howled and Vicky joined in as Tony fell into a flower border while Freddie hooted with laughter at Pops who was covered in mud.

'Would you ever consider letting us have Freddie for the occasional weekend when you can't come?' Vicky asked. 'We'd take very good care of him.'

'I know you would and I'm sure it would be fine when I've got used to the idea.'

'You're such a wonderful mother Alison. Freddie couldn't have better. You do so much with him.'

'I've nobody else to devote my time to, have I?'

Vicky felt a pang of guilt and believed the remark was directed at her absent son but she could understand Alison's acrimony.

On the Saturday evening, the family settled down when Freddie had gone to bed. Nobody was paying particular attention to the television as Tony flicked the remote control to find something of interest.

Suddenly Alison yelled, 'Tony, turn back quickly to that news programme.'

Tony changed the channel back immediately and Alison froze to see Paul attempting to escape from a reporter on an American news channel. Vicky and Tony watched silently as another reporter elbowed his way through the surging crowd to speak to him. As the camera moved in close, Alison felt weak as she saw Paul in close-up, wearing formal dress and with his arm around a beautiful young woman.

'Would you answer a couple of questions please before you leave Mr. Trantor? There'll be hundreds of disappointed young ladies today who have heard that one of L.A.s most eligible bachelors is to marry Miss Annabelle Fisher. Do you care to enlighten us about the rumours circulating sir?' he asked.

'I do not. No comment!' Paul replied abruptly.

'What about you Miss Fisher? Would you care to make a short statement please?'

'I said *no comment* and that goes for Miss Fisher too,' Paul snarled rudely, trying to hurry Annabelle Fisher into a chauffeur driven limousine as security guards placed their arms round the couple to protect them from the heaving crowd of screaming women. The car moved away slowly and gathered speed as it escaped from the horde of spectators and photographers whose cameras continued to flash until the car was out of sight.

'I'm sorry about that folks. I guess you'll have to keep watching this space to see if there's going to be any official confirmation of the news we've been hearing all day. You will be aware of Mr. Trantor's unprecedented popularity as a British artist of great status among the Hollywood stars who have spent millions of dollars over the past couple of years for his services. I'll keep you updated as I continue to find out more. Meanwhile girls, keep hoping. This is Tom Maynard reporting from the opening night of Mr. Paul Trantor's latest exhibition here in L.A.'

Alison was too shocked to speak; Vicky burst into tears and Tony stood up to get them both a drink.

'I don't know what to say. This isn't easy for the two of us either,' Tony commented sympathetically as he handed Alison her drink. 'I'm so sorry. I can't even begin to imagine how you must be feeling.'

'I just hope she loves Paul as much as I do,' she answered almost inaudibly. 'I really want him to be happy but I can't stop loving him because he loves someone else. It saddens me that he'll never see his son but you have to promise if he contacts you, that you won't tell him. Paul was adamant that Freddie wasn't his as he believes he's infertile, so it's better he never knows. He would be distraught to discover later that Freddie was his child.'

'I didn't know about that,' Tony said. 'Why does Paul believe he's infertile?'

'I've no idea. I was in a coma when Paul learned I was pregnant. Before my accident, he would never discuss children, then he left me because he thought I'd betrayed him with someone else. I never had the opportunity to say there hadn't been anyone else.'

'I'm very sorry,' Vicky said. 'I'd no idea. If that's what you really want then we'll respect your wishes but we want to continue seeing Freddie.'

'And you shall. I'm not vindictive. None of this is of your making and I wouldn't dream of punishing you. Freddie loves you. You're his grandparents. If you would excuse me, I think I'd like to go to bed. I don't feel very sociable but I'm sure I'll feel better in the morning. Goodnight.'

'Goodnight darling,' Vicky replied.

As Alison left the room, Tony declared, 'I could kill that bloody lad even though he's my own son. I don't know how that poor girl will handle this lot!'

Alison stayed in her room with Freddie until ten the next morning and only appeared when Freddie made it clear he wanted his breakfast.

426

Vicky looked worried when Alison walked in the kitchen. 'How are you feeling now?' she asked.

'I've had a good cry but I'll get over it. I've had a lot of practice at coping with disasters,' she replied, trying to force a smile. 'Freddie's hungry.'

'Come here darling. Sit up here and I'll make you some breakfast. What about you Alison?'

'Just coffee please. Do you mind if I go outside?'

'Not at all, Freddie will be fine with me.'

Alison was relieved when it was time to leave. She thought about her poor mother's grief at the age of twenty-nine and Alison felt the same at the age of twenty. While Paul had been the absent parent there had been hope he would return but now that he had Annabelle Fisher, she would never see him again.

'Drive carefully Alison. I know how unhappy you must feel. I'll call in a couple of hours,' Vicky said.

'Thanks. I know it's difficult for you and Tony as well. I'll see you in two weeks when you come up,' Alison replied as she drove away.

She decided not to go straight home. She needed to pour out her thoughts to Jenny; she also needed a shoulder to cry on.

Jenny was surprised to see her and made the usual fuss of Freddie as they walked in.

'I've something to tell you Jenny but first I have to call Vicky to let her know I'm back.'

'Come on Freddie. Let's see if we can find you a choccy biccy in the tin,' Jenny said, taking his hand and leading him into the kitchen.

Alison made a short call to Vicky before tearfully

427

outlining the events of the previous evening. Jenny was shocked and she comforted Alison who sobbed bitterly when she reached the end of her story.

'I'm so sorry. I don't know what else I can say to you. I know how much Paul means to you.'

'I wanted to tell someone how horror-struck I felt when I saw him. Paul looked so handsome and his hands were all over that floosie who was with him. I wish I'd never gone to Antonia's party.'

'Hey! You don't mean that. If you hadn't known Paul, you wouldn't have Freddie and you'll always have him. You're distraught but you'll get over him in time. Do you want to stay for your tea?'

'No, we're going home. I want to be alone.'

'I understand. I'll call you later,' she promised.

As Alison walked in the house, Dave called her.

'I've been trying to call you all day,' he told her.

'We were at Paul's parents for the weekend.'

'I thought you might be there. There's something I need to tell you but I don't want to upset you....'

'If it's about Paul, I watched the news bulletin on the television,' she cut in.

'That's partly what I wanted to talk to you about. I saw the interview early in the evening and I tried to call you then but this morning, Paul rang me. He made no mention of the news item but he sounded rather dejected and he asked about you. He wanted to know how you were, if you were with anybody meaningful as regards a boyfriend or partner and he mentioned your child but only in passing. I tried not to give anything away during the conversation but he did seem genuinely concerned about you. I kept

428

changing topic and I told him Laura and I had fixed the date for our wedding thinking it might prompt him to say something about his but he didn't. Twice he asked me to repeat the date of our wedding and I think he wrote it down. Then he told me something about anger management sessions he'd been having for some time and that he was much better now but I didn't understand what he was talking about and I didn't want to question him about it. Then he asked if you were still with Richard, which I thought was odd. I told him Richard was engaged to be married because he seemed convinced that you and Richard were an item. He didn't ask where you were living nor did he mention Jenny and Mark. I'm not sure if he intends to come to our wedding but as he doesn't know where it's taking place, he'll need to contact me again if he does. I just wanted you to know, in case there's anything you'd like me to say to him.'

Alison's head was spinning. After more than two years, why would Paul suddenly make contact with Dave? Perhaps he realized the news bulletin might be shown on British television or maybe he thought as he was getting married, his conscience would be eased, knowing she had someone in her life.

'I can't get my head around this Dave. One thing though, if he calls again and wants to come to your wedding, will you ask if he's coming alone? I don't want to meet his floosie under any circumstances. If he intends bringing her, I'll have to stay away.'

'If he says he's coming alone, will you be there?'

'Of course. I can handle Paul Trantor but I'm not going to be within a hundred miles of that woman.'

'If he asks, do I tell him your number or address?'

'Definitely not! If our paths cross at the wedding, so be it. I can't run the risk of him seeing Freddie. He can choose his own destiny but I have to decide what's best for Freddie and I don't want Paul to be a part of his life. He turned his back on me when I needed him and I don't want him harassing me for access when he discovers I was speaking the truth, especially not when he's living abroad.

Dave sighed. 'I understand Alison. I'm just sorry things didn't work out for the two of you.'

'Well, let's see what happens at your wedding but there won't be any conflict I promise and thanks for telling me. I'm meeting Laura next Saturday. We're looking at wedding dresses….she's so excited,' she said, trying to sound enthusiastic.

'So am I! I'll talk to you soon. Bye Alison.'

She thought long and hard about Paul and Dave's telephone conversation. Paul would know she was in contact with Dave and his comment about anger management sessions implied that Paul wanted her to know though she couldn't think why. She tried to erase it from her mind after discussing it with Jenny who thought it rather strange too.

Three months later, Alison approached a nursery and within a few weeks a place had arisen for three half-day sessions a week. Freddie was almost two and she thought it time for him to spread his wings.

The first time she left him at the nursery, she was distraught but Freddie quickly adapted to become a respected leader of less gifted children, Alison was informed at the end of his second week.

430

Freddie's birthday, the nineteenth of October fell four days after Dave and Laura's wedding.

Tony had arranged to collect Freddie the previous Friday to take him to Stafford until Sunday. He and Vicky had organised an early birthday party for him on Saturday the fifteenth and Angela's children and several of their young friends would be there. Tony was borrowing a pony from a neighbouring farmer for the children to ride.

One week prior to the wedding, Dave rang Alison with disturbing news. 'Paul's just phoned again to say he's coming to our evening reception. He'll be here on Friday for four days and he'll be alone. Are you alright with that? I'll call him back if it bothers you but it might be wise to settle your differences. Twice he enquired if you'd be there and he seemed very preoccupied during the conversation as if he'd a lot on his mind. He asked if I'd advised you about his earlier call and I stated I'd mentioned it briefly but I didn't elaborate about what we had discussed. I told him to talk to you himself at the reception as I wasn't prepared to get involved. That was about the measure of it. His call lasted no more than a couple of minutes.'

'Thanks Dave. I'll handle it somehow. It won't be easy but we must make our peace and he can get on with his life. It will be nice for you to see him and I don't want you to feel inhibited because of me. You were friends before I knew him. I only knew him a few months. Don't say anything about Freddie if he asks, will you?'

'My lips are sealed on that subject. I promise.'

431

When Jenny called round, she was astounded by Alison's revelations. 'He's got a bloody nerve!' she remarked. 'How do you feel about seeing him?'

'Excited but anxious. I was always excited at the prospect of seeing Paul and until we've finally said goodbye, that won't alter. I'll get upset and I might make a fool of myself....that's why I'm anxious.'

'Do you want Richard there if Paul talks to you?'

'No, it's something I have to face by myself with Paul. I owe him that.'

'You owe that man *nothing*!' she said scathingly.

'Jenny....I have Freddie....and I owe Paul *big time* for Freddie. He's my life now.'

'You're only twenty years old for God's sake. It's inconceivable to give up on life on account of Paul. I know you'll find a new guy soon and move on.'

'I never think about that. I'd only want somebody who could love Freddie as much as I do and it'd be impossible to find anyone like that.'

'Are you never going to tell Paul about Freddie?'

'No. He's made a new life for himself in America and I don't want Freddie to be part of that. Whether I'll change my mind at some point, I don't know. I don't expect to see or hear from him anymore after Saturday. I believe he's coming to make his peace.'

'Or pick up the pieces and rebuild what you had, like he's tried to do previously.'

'That won't happen. He's been away far too long. I only knew him for three months Jenny.'

'But you still love him?'

She sighed heavily. 'I'll always love him.'

'Have you decided what to wear on Saturday?'

432

'I haven't a clue. I feel like being bold and daring. If I look confident then maybe I'll act confident.'

'What about the red dress you wore at Maud's?'

'Right!' she laughed. 'That'd make a statement!'

'I'm being serious. It's perfect. Let Paul see what he's lost and he can spend the remainder of his life regretting his folly. Come round after tea. Tom can look after Freddie while we root through my stuff.'

'You've persuaded me. I'll come about six, then.'

'By the way, how's Freddie doing at nursery?'

'He loves it there but the only problem is, he sees men picking up their children and wonders why he hasn't got a daddy and I don't know how to explain it to him. He's too young to understand.'

'Why is that a problem then?'

'Because he approaches men and asks if they are his daddy. He did it at the supermarket yesterday. I was so embarrassed I could have died.'

Jenny howled. 'I can just imagine how you felt.'

'Believe me, you can't. It was horrendous.'

Alison arrived at six as arranged and she and Jenny disappeared into the bedroom. Many of her dresses felt tight and Alison couldn't find anything suitable.

'My boobs are the problem. I think they doubled in size after Freddie was born,' she moaned.

'Try the red one. It's low-cut so you might have a bit more room in that.'

Alison slipped it on but it felt tight across the bust line when she fastened the zip.

'Then yank 'em up a bit,' she grinned. 'If you've got it, flaunt it! You look terrific it that.'

433

'I don't want to look like a tart,' she scowled.

Jenny ignored her petulance. 'It's lovely. Low-cut necklines are in fashion. Show Tom.'

When she walked into the lounge, Tom exploded. '*Wow*! You look amazing. Very eye-catching.'

'Be honest. Am I showing too much cleavage?'

With a throaty chortle he stated, 'There's no such thing as too much.'

'Right, that settles it,' she grunted with irritation. I'm not wearing that!'

He expelled a hearty laugh. 'I'm joking. You look gorgeous.'

She regarded him dubiously. 'Are you absolutely sure?'

'I'm positive. You look a million dollars….truly.'

'I'm not used to exposing myself like this.'

'You really do look stunning,' Jenny confirmed.

Finally convinced, Alison went to get changed as Jenny went to put the kettle on. Richard and Mark turned up a few minutes later.

'Uncle Mark,' Freddie screeched jumping into his arms.

'Hi,' he said. 'Have you been a good boy today?'

'I don't know,' Freddie tittered, glancing round at his mother. 'Uncle Mark, are you my daddy?'

Mark looked uneasy as Jenny and Alison laughed.

'Ignore him. It's just a phase he's going through. He sees daddies collecting their children at nursery so he wants one too,' Alison explained.

'No Freddie, I'm not your daddy,' Mark replied.

Freddie directed his attention to Richard. 'Uncle Richard….are *you* my daddy?'

434

'No darling, I'm not,' he answered apologetically, feeling compassion for the lovable boy who wanted so much to have a daddy like other children.

'I'll be thankful when he grows out of this phase. It's so embarrassing. He posed the same question to a complete stranger in the queue at the supermarket checkout yesterday and everyone glared critically at me. I was absolutely mortified. I didn't know where to put myself.'

Everyone howled with laughter at that.

'Right, I'm off home now,' she said, gathering up her bags. 'It's way past Freddie's bedtime. It's been great to see you,' she added, kissing them all good-bye.

'See you!' Freddie shouted to peels of laughter.

15

It was Saturday, the day of the wedding, and Alison had spent a restless night as her thoughts repeatedly returned to Paul. She was also missing Freddie who had left with Tony the previous evening.

Freddie hadn't shown the slightest concern about leaving her as he clambered into Pops' car with his favourite teddy, but she had been unable to contain her tears as the car disappeared from sight.

She had arranged an early hair appointment for a cut and re-style. Her hairdresser had persuaded her to try highlights and her new look was rather more sophisticated she felt.

An hour before she was due to leave, she applied her make-up with care, paying meticulous attention to her eyes. She changed into her dress just minutes before Richard and Amanda were due to arrive. She had bought a pair of very high-heeled shoes, adding a couple more inches to her already generous height and made a final check in the full length mirror.

When Richard and Amanda arrived, they said she looked amazing. 'Are you nervous?' Richard asked.

'Let's just say I'll be glad when today's over.'

'Don't worry, you'll be alright,' he reassured her. 'You've dealt with worse than this. I think Paul will suffer more. He has to face everyone. Let's be off.'

The wedding ceremony was delightful and Alison had to fight back her tears during the wedding vows as she reflected on what might have been with Paul. Laura looked beautiful in her bridal gown and Dave looked very distinguished in his grey morning suit.

The Old Hall, where the wedding reception was held boasted a wealth of historical features and after the meal, Alison meandered slowly down the many corridors to admire the building's impressive architecture, antique paintings and artefacts.

She called in the ladies' room to tidy her hair and refresh her make-up and as she continued to admire the archaic structure, her thoughts repeatedly turned to Paul. She wondered whether he would put in an appearance later or whether instead he might have second thoughts and stay away.

As she studied an antique painting hanging above the old oak staircase, a familiar voice stated, 'Hello Alison,' and she turned to find Paul standing beside her. 'I'm sorry if I startled you. I spotted you earlier but like the first time we met, you were surrounded by young men so I thought I'd better wait my turn,' he added with a friendly smile.

She felt a flush of colour as he kissed her cheek.

'It's good to see you again Alison. How are you?' he questioned and though she felt close to tears she managed a weak reply, 'I'm fine thank you Paul.'

'You look absolutely amazing,' he declared as his eyes searched her face. 'You're even more beautiful than when I last saw you.'

With irony she responded, 'When I was linked to monitors and tubes with a bandaged head?'

'No, I didn't mean that,' he said calmly but with a pained expression. 'I've seen you since then.'

'I'm sorry Paul. I shouldn't have said that. I really didn't intend to be unpleasant this evening. How's America?' she asked, changing topic.

'Very impersonal. I much prefer England's green and pleasant land. People are more sociable here.'

She smiled. 'Present company excepted.'

'That's better. I like to see you smile. 'You look so different, very sophisticated, in fact I have to say positively ravishing.'

'Thank you and you've been working out I see. It suits you,' she remarked, feeling weak at the knees as she cast her eyes over Paul's broad shoulders, his muscular body and his golden tan.

He laughed and went on to elucidate, '*That's* my escape. I work out to keep the vultures at bay.'

'Vultures?' she repeated quizzically.

'Women. They're crazy in Los Angeles.'

'Yes, I saw you on television fighting them off.'

He seemed surprised. 'You did? When was that?'

'A month or two ago. I believe it was the opening night of your latest exhibition.'

'I'm amazed it made British television. I hate the media. I didn't want to talk to that reporter.'

'Clearly….so did you ever answer his question?'

'Yes, he followed me and foolishly I believed if I gave him a few words he might leave me in peace. I told him we were hoping to be married soon.'

'And did he leave you alone then?'

'No,' he guffawed. 'The irritating fool continued to hound me. So, what are you doing these days?'

'I still work for John and Harold. Whilst I was in hospital, John converted one room of my house into an office so I could work from home after my baby was born. I run their vast property empire now that continues to expand. I took a legal course and I'm a

Licensed Property Lawyer now so I handle all their legal transactions. I have a couple of girls there who deal with the rental side.'

'Mmm….I'm impressed. You've done very well.'

'I suppose I have,' she answered tongue-in-cheek. 'One has to move on and it keeps the wolf from the door. I'm appreciated too and that's worth a whole lot more than any amount of financial reward.'

He recognised a bitter undertone in her words but thought it better to make no flippant comeback and pausing for thought, he carefully structured his next question. 'Is there someone in your life important to you? Please don't answer if you prefer not to.'

'I don't mind answering and yes, there is. There's Freddie now. He's wonderful. He's my life now.'

Paul looked dejected. 'You said that to me once.'

'Correction….more than once but that was a long time ago Paul.'

He paused briefly. 'So do you love er….Freddie?'

'Very much. I told you, he's my life.'

'Then I'm happy for you Alison. You deserve the best. I was never good enough for you. I was self-indulgent and jealous and the moment I left you, I knew I was wrong but it wouldn't have worked out had I come back. I was too pig-headed and I wanted to rule and possess you, besides which, I withheld an important matter from you because I was afraid of losing you.'

'You would never have lost me Paul. I loved you passionately then. I thought you understood that.'

'I did when it was too late. I was angry for a time and when I wanted to come back, everybody closed ranks when I enquired about you. Where did you go when you left hospital?'

'I went to my grandma's house. I found my other grandma....or rather she found me.'

'Not the one who abandoned you? I can't believe you would ever have wanted to see her.'

'It's a long story but unlike you, she was there for me when I needed someone. Can you imagine how I felt when Jenny said you'd walked out on me?'

He bowed his head in shame. 'I'm sorry. I didn't deserve a sweet considerate girl like you and by the time I came to realise that your pregnancy was the best thing for both of us, I'd already lost you.'

'I don't understand what you mean by....'

'Well,' he interrupted, 'I couldn't give you what you wanted, so we might have ended up adopting a child we knew little or nothing about, whereas with your baby, only the father's identity would remain unknown to me and I would never have questioned you about him, I swear.'

'That's very magnanimous of you,' she said with a perfunctory smile but the insincerity of her words was lost on him. Her head was spinning. Paul still didn't believe it remotely possible that he could be Freddie's father. If only he had come to her sooner they might have been able to resolve matters.

'Do you think I could have a drink please Paul?'

'Certainly. I'd like one too. We'll have them here where we won't be disturbed. Is it still Bacardi and coke with ice and lemon?'

'Yes, thank you.'

'I won't be long. Please don't go away.'

440

He returned swiftly with the drinks. 'You used to drink this in Spain,' he reminded her.

'I did. I liked a lot of things then but I seldom go out now. It's difficult with a two year old son.'

'I can't believe he's two already.'

'*Tempus fugit* Paul. He'll be two on Wednesday. He's very intelligent with an outgoing personality.

He smiled. 'Does he look like you?'

'No, not in the least. He's the absolute image of his father,' she advised him and for a moment, Paul looked pensive.

'So is Jenny baby-sitting today?'

'No, he's with his grandparents for the weekend. He's coming home tomorrow. So, what was it you found so difficult to tell me back then Paul?'

'I had mumps when I was about fifteen. It left me infertile. It was a devastating discovery.'

'Well, that wasn't hard to say! Who told you?'

'They told me at the donor clinic.'

'Did you bother to check whether your infertility might be temporary? After all, you might have little Trantors all around Los Angeles if you've regained your fertility. From what I saw on television you've certainly had plenty of opportunities.'

He looked at her with sadness in his eyes. 'Don't do this Alison, please. I came back once before to beg your forgiveness but Mark Taylor had to get in the way of my fist and I'm here today for the same reason. Have you forgotten what I said to you?'

'"*I'll always love you*,". I'll remember those four words forever. I said the very same words to you a hundred times but it didn't keep you here.'

'I've said I'm sorry. Sadly, I can't rewrite history. What's done is done. This guy you have now, have you known him long?'

'Almost two years.'

'Does he love you as much as I did?'

'He needs me much more than you ever did Paul and yes, he loves me very much.'

'Then I'm happy things worked out for you,' he stated sorrowfully. 'I just hope that someday you'll find it in your heart to forgive me. I never meant to hurt you.'

'And I never meant to hurt you Paul so I think it's time we both moved on. You have Annabelle now and I sincerely hope you'll be very happy together.'

'*Annabelle*?' Paul snorted. 'I'm not involved with *Annabelle*. I employ her to keep the vultures at bay. That's why I wouldn't answer that news reporter's question but you have someone and I'd never try to come between you. If you love him, I'm happy for both of you. I just hope he's worthy of you.'

'Did you mean it when you said that if things had been different, you would have taken on my child?'

'I did. That's the truth,' he stated, looking deeply into her eyes. 'That's the reason I came back and to say sorry for not telling you that I was infertile but I could never find the right time and place. You must agree it was hardly a suitable topic of conversation for a first date and after that I was too much in love with you to risk jeopardising what we had. I would have told you eventually but things got in the way. Try to imagine how devastated I felt when I found out. I was a mere youth and my manhood had been stripped away forever. I couldn't have a meaningful relationship because there'd come a point I'd have to disclose that fact. Just when would that point be Alison? Would it be early on in the relationship or later when we felt committed? Either way, I ran the risk of humiliation by way of contempt, or walking away with a broken heart if I were dumped. Neither option appealed to me so I chose to remain single. I threw myself into my work instead and then, some years later, I allowed myself to be sweet-talked into attending a party, where I spotted a beautiful young woman who stole my heart instantly. At that special moment, my previous resolve was totally defunct. I think you know the rest,' he sighed.

Alison was totally overwhelmed. Everything was moving far too quickly for her to grasp. Adrenaline pumped through her body and she didn't know how to react to Paul's body language. 'I think we should go downstairs and join the others,' she said quietly. She needed time to collect her thoughts.

'I'd rather stay with you. Is Freddie downstairs?'

'No, Richard brought me.'

'Does that mean I have you all to myself for the evening if I promise to behave?'

She smiled at his optimism. 'Yes, I guess it does.'

'It's going to be hard because I still love you. My life has been meaningless without you. I've been so lonely and miserable for the past couple of years.'

She took a step back. 'I must go downstairs where there are other people. I'm not comfortable here.'

'Tell me why?' Paul whispered with deep burning passion in his eyes.

'Because I won't be responsible for my actions if I stay here alone with you.'

Filled with emotion he took her in his arms, kissing her passionately and she returned his passion as they clung to each other. 'I'm sorry, I should never have done that but I couldn't help it,' he whispered softly. 'I love you more than you'll ever know, but I'd hate to ruin the relationship you have now.'

'You would never do that....Freddie's my son.'

He stared at her in total disbelief. 'What? You're saying there's no other man in your life?'

'There's only been one man I've ever truly loved. That's you Paul, and I never stopped praying you'd come back to me. Are you here to stay this time or is this another nightmare I have to contend with?'

'Alison, I promise I won't leave you again as long as I draw breath. I'm back forever if you'll give me another chance. Please darling. I realise how hard it is for you to believe me but I'm speaking the truth.'

'Certain things would have to change. I won't be controlled anymore. I've grown up over the last two years. I have my independence now and I won't be subjected to your juvenile tantrums. I must consider Freddie so I'll only take you back on my terms.'

'I've grown up too. I've had a lot of time to think about everything and I know I'm to blame. I created most of the problems out of jealousy and mistrust. I was so scared of losing you but I finished up losing you anyway because of my stupidity but I won't let that happen again. I give you my word.'

'And will you love my son unreservedly?'

'He's *our* son now, and yes darling, I'll love him

444

as much as I love you,' he pledged earnestly. 'God, I don't deserve you.'

'Well, I can't argue with that,' she rejoined with a wry smile. 'Come on, let's go downstairs.'

Richard was astonished when Alison returned to the reception hall with Paul and shook his hand as a matter of courtesy. 'Good to see you Paul.'

'Likewise,' Paul enthused. 'Many congratulations on your engagement. I'm happy for you.'

'This is Amanda, my fiancée. Amanda, I'd like to introduce you to Paul Trantor, Alison's friend.'

'Pleased to meet you. I've heard a lot about you.'

'Obviously nothing good but I hope to rectify that very soon,' he told her as they moved on. 'Another drink darling?'

'I'll have the same again please.'

When Paul returned with their drinks, Alison was fiddling with the engagement ring she had worn on her right hand since leaving hospital in Spain.

'Have you seen Dave and Laura yet?' she asked.

'No, I haven't. Where are they?'

'In the middle of that crowd of people.'

'Then I'll wait until things quieten down. I'm not waiting in line when I can spend time with you.'

'I'm still worried Paul....worried you won't stay.'

'Trust me, I *will*! I don't care what anyone says to me. I'm very self-disciplined now. Mark can be as caustic as he likes and will you please stop playing with your ring and put it back where it belongs.'

'Where should it be Paul?'

He smiled and taking the ring from her, he looked deeply into her eyes. 'This is like history repeating itself. Will you marry me darling? I really want us to be a family. I won't ever disappoint you again.'

'If we can resolve certain issues, I will,' she said, watching him slip the ring on her finger.

'Can I come home with you tonight?'

'I don't see why not if you promise to behave and sleep on the sofa,' she said with a glint in her eye.

'Not a chance! I have over two years to make up.'

'And whose fault might that be?'

'It's mine! You can't imagine how relieved I am. I never expected things would turn out like this.'

At that moment the DJ made an announcement. 'I have a special request now for Paul who would like to dedicate this next song to Alison. You're such a romantic,' he stated and Alison listened attentively as Chris de Burgh began to sing, 'Lady in Red.'

'May I have the pleasure?' he asked, offering her his hand and all eyes were upon them as they made their way to the dance-floor.

Alison fought back the tears as she listened to the poignant words. She lay against him until the song ended, then with a loving smile whispered, 'Thank you for that Paul. It was....'

'Paul, I'm delighted you made it,' Dave Maxwell interrupted and shaking Paul's hand, he continued, 'Doesn't Alison look absolutely gorgeous tonight?'

'She certainly does and we'd both like you to be the first to know. We're getting married. I've been a bloody fool long enough.'

'I can't disagree with that,' Dave replied joyfully. 'I'm delighted for you. Laura, *this* is the infamous Paul Trantor. He and Alison are getting married at

446

long last. He's finally come to his senses. Isn't that wonderful news?'

'I'm pleased to meet you Paul and it *is* wonderful news. Congratulations!' Laura said.

'Please don't tell me you've heard all about me. I couldn't stand any more criticism this evening,' he laughed. 'Thank you for allowing me to be here and you look beautiful Laura. Dave's a very lucky guy.'

Flippantly she replied, 'And so are you Paul.'

'Catch you later,' Dave said as they moved away.

At eleven-thirty Alison looked at her watch. 'I'm exhausted. I hardly slept a wink last night. I tossed and turned all night thinking about you. I need to go home now. Are you coming back with me?'

'You know what will happen if I do. I don't want you to have any regrets tomorrow. I'm prepared to wait till you've had time to think about everything.'

'I've already thought about everything. What will happen about America? Will you have to go back?'

'No, my agent's still over there so he'll attend to the exhibition. I'm here to stay now.'

'I'd like to see you with Freddie. I need to know that everything is alright between the two of you.'

'Don't worry, it will be. I can't wait to meet him. I love kids and I'll be a good father to him. It's rare to be given a second chance when you've let some-body down as badly as I have but I'll never let you down again. That's a promise I *will* keep. Trust me. All I want is for us to be a family....truly.'

'That's what I want too Paul, in fact that's all I've ever wanted. I'll just tell Richard you're taking me home.'

She wandered across to Richard to explain.

'Are you sure of what you're doing?' he asked.

'Yes, I am this time. Paul doesn't know Freddie's his son but he will by this time tomorrow. We love each other Richard. It's what I want so please try to be happy for us.'

'I am happy for you and I hope it works out.'

'It will. I'll call you soon. Bye Richard.'

He gave her a hug. 'Good luck Alison.'

As they walked hand in hand to Paul's car, Alison remarked, 'Look at the stars Paul. It's a lovely clear night for October. It's perfect isn't it?'

'Yes darling it is. In fact I'd say it's probably the most perfect night of my life in every respect.'

There was nowhere to park when they arrived at the house. Paul dropped Alison at her door and she hurried inside to remove all Freddie's photographs from the mantelpiece to put them out of sight.

When Paul walked in he took her in his arms. 'I'd like to thank you,' he murmured. 'You have no idea how humble I feel. Never in my wildest dreams did I imagine I'd be spending the night with you. I still can't believe you're prepared to forgive me.'

He held her tight and brushed his lips against her forehead before kissing her tenderly.

Alison smiled affectionately and taking his hand she led him upstairs. 'I have four familiar words for you Paul Trantor.'

He pondered briefly. 'You'll always love me?'

'Wrong,' she giggled. 'Get your kit off.'

With a broad grin, followed by a burst of laughter he said, 'You're at it again, scarlet woman!'

'So I am. Now....er....where did I put those leather straps?' she murmured and at that, Paul's laughter reverberated throughout the house.

'God, I love you so much!'

'I know you do Paul. We were in too big a hurry the first time round for true commitment and trust.'

'I was but we're going to be fine now aren't we?' he questioned optimistically.

'After tomorrow we'll be fine.'

'Why, what happens tomorrow?'

'You'll meet Freddie and it will be an emotional time for all of us.'

'Don't you worry about that. I can handle it.'

'Whatever you say Paul,' she told him but Alison knew only too well how Paul would react when he saw his son for the first time.

She ran downstairs to answer the telephone the next morning and it was Jenny. Eagerly she questioned, 'Did he turn up last night?'

'What *are* you going on about? Did *who* turn up?' she teased.

'Stop it and tell me! Did *Paul* turn up?'

Paul arrived by Alison's side and kissed her neck.

'Yes, and everything was great. He's here now.'

'Good morning,' he shouted down the telephone.

'*I don't believe you*!' Jenny shrieked.

'Er....who told me to wear that sexy red dress?'

'Only to taunt him! I hope you know what you're doing. Did he stay the night?'

'He stayed the night,' she replied, smiling at Paul lovingly.

'Is nothing private?' he called out. 'We're getting married next month. Will you be at the wedding?'

She squealed with delight. 'Am, I invited?'

'Yes but you won't be joining us on honeymoon. You're too bloody nosey!'

'Can I talk to you later Jenny? Paul's taking me to lunch and I'm not even dressed yet.'

'Brazen hussy! So what about his fancy woman in America? Has he given her the elbow?'

'He claims Annabelle was his bodyguard.'

'It's true,' he whispered, kissing her lips tenderly. 'I'm going to get ready. Don't be too long.'

She listened for his footsteps upstairs before saying, 'We can talk now. He's gone to get ready. It's a bit awkward when he's standing right next to me.'

'So, what have you told him about Freddie?'

'Nothing at all because he still believes he's not Freddie's father. He....'

'The effrontery of that man!' Jenny interrupted.

'No, it's not like that. He's absolutely convinced he's infertile but he wants to be a father to Freddie. I'm dreading Paul's reaction when his parents bring him home this afternoon. My stomach churns at the very thought of it. It will be *so* emotional.'

'Well, good luck with that. Just call me when you can. Enjoy your lunch.'

When Paul and Alison arrived back mid-afternoon Alison appeared edgy.

'You look a bit perturbed darling. Are you feeling alright?' he asked.

'I'll feel a lot better after you've met Freddie. His

grandparents should be here around five. I'm a little nervous which is only natural I suppose.'

'Would you rather I went out until they've gone?'

'I'd rather you stayed but it won't be pleasant.'

'I've told you....I'll handle it....I promise.'

Shortly after four o'clock, Alison heard a car door close. She ran to the window and exhaled audibly. Her sudden anxiety didn't escape Paul's notice and he too felt nervous for the first time as he prepared himself for an introduction to Alison's young son.

When she answered the door, Paul heard muffled voices but couldn't recognise the speakers. Then he heard Freddie squeal excitedly, 'Mummy, Pops had a pony.'

He listened closely to the ensuing conversation.

'Did he darling? Was it a nice pony?'

'Yes, it's called Topsy.... I rided it,' he told her.

'Well, aren't you a clever boy? I like your smart new clothes. Did Nana buy you those?'

'Yes and I got presents *and* a big cake with er....'

'Candles?' Alison prompted him.

'Yes, candles.'

'Did you blow them all out?'

'No, Pops blowed some out.'

'Would you take Pops and Nana into the lounge? There's someone there I'd like you to meet.'

Paul felt a sudden rush of adrenaline as he waited with baited breath for the door to open and he was taken aback when his parents walked in.

'Mum, Dad, what are you two doing here?' Paul enquired looking shocked.

Tony looked scathingly at his son and replied, 'If

I were Alison, I wouldn't let you wipe your feet on my doormat son. I'm bloody-well ashamed of you, the way you've behaved.'

Vicky stared in silence at Paul whose colour completely drained from his face as he looked towards the doorway at the young blonde-haired child who stood before him smiling. There could be no doubt he was Paul's son.

Paul let out a shrill cry, fell to his knees and held out his arms for the child to come to him.

'Are you my daddy?' Freddie asked.

'Yes darling, I'm your daddy,' he answered with tears gushing from his eyes as he held his child for the first time and hugged him to his body. He was filled with deep emotion and love as he smelled his sweet breath and felt his small heart beating against his chest.

He opened his eyes and turned to Alison who was crying too. In a broken voice he whispered, 'I'm so sorry darling. God, I'm so sorry. I don't understand. Can you *ever* forgive me for what I've done?'

'I'm working on it,' she said tearfully, wrapping her arms around him. 'Isn't our son amazing?'

Paul couldn't reply, too tormented by thoughts of how appallingly he had treated Alison and how he had struck Mark not once but twice. He was so full of remorse he was unable to find suitable words.

'I think we'd best be on our way now,' Tony said. 'You obviously have a great deal to talk about and Paul has a lot of catching up to do with his son.'

Vicky took Alison in her arms. 'I knew it would turn out right in the end. I'm sorry it took so long,'

< honeymoon in Venice with Freddie.

seven months later, Paul hugged his we
iter Emma-Jayne and kissed her tenderly
Alison lifted her from his arms, she warn
baby, 'Never trust *anything* a man tells y
yne. Your daddy caught me out *twice*.'
ghed. 'Are you complaining Mrs. Trantor
rling, I'm the happiest person alive. She
...just like Freddie.'

g to Freddie, Alison reminded him, 'Unc
Uncle Richard will be here any minute
a-Jayne and take you to the park with yo
will you get a move on with that drink ar
ise? Great-grandma Joyce taught Mumn
ake sweetloaf. Do you like that?'
It's really yummy,' he replied, rolling h
d his head.

zed adoringly at Alison as she cradled h
. Alison had lost her innocence. No long
he shy young girl he had met at Antonia
e was now a beautiful, sophisticated youn
he mother of his two children, who looke
his eyes and he loved her with such gre

elationship had taken on a new dimensio
d conviction that would last for a lifetim
would ever come between them again.

456

and turning to Paul she continued, 'Just try to face up to your responsibilities now Paul, please.'

'Don't worry. He's here to stay now. I won't ever let him leave again,' Alison told her and gazing into Paul's eyes she smiled fondly. 'We're a family now aren't we Paul?'

'Yes darling,' he replied. 'We're a family now.'

As Alison said goodbye to Vicky and Tony, Paul returned to the lounge and lifted Freddie on his lap.

'You're my daddy and you look like me,' Freddie said with a broad grin. 'What's your name?'

Barely able to speak, he said, 'My name's Paul.'

'*My* name is Paul. Paul, Michael....er....Anthony, Trantor, Haythorne,' he uttered breathlessly.

He giggled when Paul said, 'You're a very clever boy to remember all those names.'

When Alison joined them, Paul looked at her with despair in his eyes. 'I've lost two years of my son's life. I've been such a stubborn idiot. I can't begin to imagine how difficult the last two years must have been for you but I'll make it up to you. I won't hurt either of you again, ever, I swear.'

'We survived thanks to your parents' generosity, both financially and emotionally but I hated taking handouts from them. They're two wonderful people yet you deserted them as well. How can I know for sure that you won't ever do it again?'

He regarded her with deep sincerity in his eyes. 'I can't live without you; that's why. I bought you the house Alison and it's waiting patiently for a family to fill it with love and laughter. I can't wait for the day to dawn when I take you both home with me.'

453

Once Freddie was fast asleep, they talked into the early hours. There were bridges to cross, apologies to be made and promises to keep. Alison reminded Paul that their love was strong enough to overcome anything and they must both agree to face any new challenges together. Freddie's happiness was paramount and they could move forward only when he accepted that.

Paul gave his word that the day's revelations had changed his life. He couldn't express his emotion to learn he had fathered Freddie nor could he describe how he despised himself for his former mistrust.

Cautiously he asked, 'Would you have told me I had a son had I not asked to come back?'

'No, I wouldn't. When I thought you intended to marry Annabelle, I believed it best to say nothing. I know you too well and I knew it would break your heart to learn the truth, besides which, I could never have run the risk of losing Freddie were you to find out. I've lost so many relatives Paul. I lost granddad earlier this year too. He developed Alzheimer's and deteriorated quickly. He died peacefully at home.'

He was shocked to hear the sad news. 'I'm sorry. I know how much your granddad meant to you and I liked Alfred too. Did he ever get to see Freddie?'

'Oh yes, several times. He loved Freddie and they had a special kind of affinity.'

'And how's Joyce managing on her own?'

'Exceptionally well, considering.... She's joined a local ladies' club and made a lot of new friends.'

'I'd never have taken Freddie away from you, but I do understand why you couldn't trust me.'

454

'It's water under the brid since you insist you're back

'I am. Today is a new be united family. Let's start af house tomorrow. We'll tak a time and as it's Freddie': to think of something speci

Alison would never forget house. As she walked thro breath away. It was even m brochure had depicted. It w ornamental items. The Lla and Groom that Paul bougl place on the mantelpiece i hanging imposingly in the oil painting, created by Pa photograph, taken at Puert Gainsborough style, was su

Paul was more than happ furniture, soft furnishings a enlisted the help of Maud a the perfect home, after the between Paul and their son forgotten.

The converted barn made and Freddie was already sta in art. From their first meet been inseparable.

Paul and Alison were ma civil ceremony, witnessed b relatives and afterwards the

45

two-wee
Barely
old daug
When
her new
Emma-J
He lau
'No d.
amazing
Turnir
Mark an
see Emn
daddy s(
cake ple
how to r
'Mmn
eyes rou
Paul g
new bab
was she
party. S
woman,
back int(
passion.
Their
of love a
Nothing

Sheffie

and turning to Paul she continued, 'Just try to face up to your responsibilities now Paul, please.'

'Don't worry. He's here to stay now. I won't ever let him leave again,' Alison told her and gazing into Paul's eyes she smiled fondly. 'We're a family now aren't we Paul?'

'Yes darling,' he replied. 'We're a family now.'

As Alison said goodbye to Vicky and Tony, Paul returned to the lounge and lifted Freddie on his lap.

'You're my daddy and you look like me,' Freddie said with a broad grin. 'What's your name?'

Barely able to speak, he said, 'My name's Paul.'

'*My* name is Paul. Paul, Michael....er....Anthony, Trantor, Haythorne,' he uttered breathlessly.

He giggled when Paul said, 'You're a very clever boy to remember all those names.'

When Alison joined them, Paul looked at her with despair in his eyes. 'I've lost two years of my son's life. I've been such a stubborn idiot. I can't begin to imagine how difficult the last two years must have been for you but I'll make it up to you. I won't hurt either of you again, ever, I swear.'

'We survived thanks to your parents' generosity, both financially and emotionally but I hated taking handouts from them. They're two wonderful people yet you deserted them as well. How can I know for sure that you won't ever do it again?'

He regarded her with deep sincerity in his eyes. 'I can't live without you; that's why. I bought you the house Alison and it's waiting patiently for a family to fill it with love and laughter. I can't wait for the day to dawn when I take you both home with me.'

Once Freddie was fast asleep, they talked into the early hours. There were bridges to cross, apologies to be made and promises to keep. Alison reminded Paul that their love was strong enough to overcome anything and they must both agree to face any new challenges together. Freddie's happiness was paramount and they could move forward only when he accepted that.

Paul gave his word that the day's revelations had changed his life. He couldn't express his emotion to learn he had fathered Freddie nor could he describe how he despised himself for his former mistrust.

Cautiously he asked, 'Would you have told me I had a son had I not asked to come back?'

'No, I wouldn't. When I thought you intended to marry Annabelle, I believed it best to say nothing. I know you too well and I knew it would break your heart to learn the truth, besides which, I could never have run the risk of losing Freddie were you to find out. I've lost so many relatives Paul. I lost granddad earlier this year too. He developed Alzheimer's and deteriorated quickly. He died peacefully at home.'

He was shocked to hear the sad news. 'I'm sorry. I know how much your granddad meant to you and I liked Alfred too. Did he ever get to see Freddie?'

'Oh yes, several times. He loved Freddie and they had a special kind of affinity.'

'And how's Joyce managing on her own?'

'Exceptionally well, considering.... She's joined a local ladies' club and made a lot of new friends.'

'I'd never have taken Freddie away from you, but I do understand why you couldn't trust me.'

454

'It's water under the bridge Paul and hypothetical since you insist you're back to stay now.'

'I am. Today is a new beginning of our lives as a united family. Let's start afresh and you can see the house tomorrow. We'll take things slowly, a day at a time and as it's Freddie's birthday next week, try to think of something special he'd like to do.'

Alison would never forget the first time she saw the house. As she walked through the door, it took her breath away. It was even more magnificent than the brochure had depicted. It was empty apart from two ornamental items. The Lladro figurine of the Bride and Groom that Paul bought in Mijas, held pride of place on the mantelpiece in the drawing room and hanging imposingly in the master bedroom was an oil painting, created by Paul from Dave Maxwell's photograph, taken at Puerto Banus. The portrait, in Gainsborough style, was superb.

Paul was more than happy to leave the choice of furniture, soft furnishings and décor to Alison who enlisted the help of Maud and Elizabeth in creating the perfect home, after the long-standing acrimony between Paul and their sons had been forgiven and forgotten.

The converted barn made an ideal studio for Paul and Freddie was already starting to show an interest in art. From their first meeting, the two of them had been inseparable.

Paul and Alison were married six weeks later in a civil ceremony, witnessed by their close friends and relatives and afterwards they spent an unforgettable two-week honeymoon in Venice with Freddie.

Barely seven months later, Paul hugged his week old daughter Emma-Jayne and kissed her tenderly.

When Alison lifted her from his arms, she warned her new baby, 'Never trust *anything* a man tells you Emma-Jayne. Your daddy caught me out *twice*.'

He laughed. 'Are you complaining Mrs. Trantor?'

'No darling, I'm the happiest person alive. She's amazing....just like Freddie.'

Turning to Freddie, Alison reminded him, 'Uncle Mark and Uncle Richard will be here any minute to see Emma-Jayne and take you to the park with your daddy so will you get a move on with that drink and cake please? Great-grandma Joyce taught Mummy how to make sweetloaf. Do you like that?'

'Mmm! It's really yummy,' he replied, rolling his eyes round his head.

Paul gazed adoringly at Alison as she cradled her new baby. Alison had lost her innocence. No longer was she the shy young girl he had met at Antonia's party. She was now a beautiful, sophisticated young woman, the mother of his two children, who looked back into his eyes and he loved her with such great passion.

Their relationship had taken on a new dimension of love and conviction that would last for a lifetime. Nothing would ever come between them again.